10728757

DRAGONBLOOD

DAWN OF RAGNAROK BOOK 2

BOOKS BY ALIANNE DONNELLY

BLOOD AND SHADOWS
Blood Moons
Blood Trails
Blood Debts
Blood Hunt

DAWN OF RAGNAROK
The Royal Wizard
Dragonblood
Prince of Deceit

THE BEAST
Bastien
The Beast

OTHER TITLES
Wolfen
Virtual
Function: L1VE

ALIANNE DONNELLY

THIS IS AN ALIANNE DONNELLY BOOK PUBLISHED BY ALIANNE DONNELLY
It's not bragging if it's true.

DRAGONBLOOD is a work of fiction. Names, characters, places, and incidents either are the product of the author's imagination or are used fictitiously, and any resemblance to actual persons, living or dead, business establishments, events, or locales is entirely coincidental.

Copyright © 2016 by Alianne Donnelly

All rights reserved.
No part of this book may be reproduced, scanned, or distributed in any printed or electronic form without permission. Please do not participate in or encourage piracy of copyrighted materials in violation of the author's rights. Purchase only authorized editions.

aliannedonnelly.com

ISBN: 978-1-948325-16-5

Published in the United States of America

For true strength is not contained in the breadth of a shield, or the tip of a sword. It cannot be measured by the reach of an arrow, or the precision of a strike. True strength is strength of spirit, the war cry of a soul standing its ground against the howling winds. It fears neither rain, nor cold, nor lightning—the storm is but an aspect of itself.

PROLOGUE

She was *aseti*. Outcast. She, who'd never caused harm to another, who'd shown her tribe nothing but love and given them all she had. Disowned by her family, stripped of her name, forced to live on the outskirts of their city, and all because she'd been born with something that ought never have belonged to a woman: magic.

They called her a witch, shunned her from their midst. They feared her, and they should. While the Magi relied on spells and rituals, the witch's power came from within, not from the gods. When she called on her magic, it poured out of her heart on a tide of emotions. Outcasts could not work, wed, or bear children; they could only beg and pray the tribesmen would show them kindness. A witch was a blight, a curse upon the tribe, and never allowed near the others. She couldn't even beg, and no one would look upon her for fear the curse would infect their eyes and be reborn in their children.

In all her life, only one had dared to brave such perils and secretly bring an old woman food and water: the *shansher*'s beloved youngest daughter, Mari. For her kindness, the witch had loved Mari like her own flesh and blood, and she'd cursed the *shansher* the day he'd sent Mari to the Northern king. The witch had known the girl was riding to her doom; she'd warned him not to do this, to send another in his daughter's place. He hadn't listened. No one had, because in the eyes of the Imarah tribe, the witch did not exist.

Almost a year had passed since the riders returned with Mari's ashes. Three times the rains had come and gone, while the witch waited for the *shansher* to ride north to avenge his daughter. And in all that time, no one had stood up for her. No one.

How dare they let one of their own disappear this way—a princess, no less! Forgotten, as if she'd been an outcast, herself.

Now, the witch knew they'd never right this wrong. A princess Mari may have been, but she'd still been only a woman. Consumed by hatred for every man in the tribe, the witch couldn't bear to look at any of them, lest she loose a terrible wave of magic and destroy them all where they stood. It wouldn't be a good enough end for them. For what they'd done to Mari, the witch would make them all suffer.

When the sky had turned dark and the sands had cooled, the witch stole a torch and ran into the desert. Countless stars shone above, but the moon was dark tonight, averting its face so that her deeds might go unwitnessed.

The witch looked around to make certain she hadn't been followed. She hadn't. No one cared about her. If she went missing, they'd rejoice to be rid of her. For that, too, the Imarah tribe would pay.

With her toes, she traced a large circle in the sand, deep enough to create a channel. The black powder came next, sprinkled evenly all around. When fire touched it, the powder would blaze a bright green, an irresistible lure to the *djinn*. And once she'd trapped the *djinn* in the circle, she'd make it do her bidding. It would become the vessel of her wrath.

The witch stepped out of the circle, then raised her torch high, calling on her magic. She'd seen the Magi perform their rituals, summoning the gods' good will, and she mimicked their movements from memory but spoke her own words. Three steps along the left side of the circle, four back to the right. Five to the left, six to the right. At first she whispered the words, then she spoke them, and as she rounded the circle at last, the witch shouted a command into the night, forcing her will into the air, making it congeal as black smoke. When she slammed the torch down into the black powder, green fire flared as high as she was tall, and she stumbled back from its heat.

Gasping for breath, the witch returned, squinting through the fiery veil into the circle. She saw a figure within, heard its rasping sighs on the night breeze. Harsh, foreign words hissed all around; dark groans made her shudder and trace the sign against evil over her chest.

When at last the fire died down, the witch beheld the creature she'd summoned. It was tall and thin with wide shoulders and gangly limbs, its long, black hair plaited back into a thick rope that reached the sands and coiled around its feet. Or rather, where its feet ought to have been. It wore shadows as clothes, and every time the breeze blew, the creature briefly turned to smoke, as if it would dissipate in the wind.

"I am—"

"No one," the creature said. "How dare you summon me, no one?"

"I…" She could not find her voice. The creature's red eyes glowed, following her every move, staring straight through her, into her, and the witch hugged herself for fear of having her soul ripped out of her chest.

The *djinn* laughed; a terrible sound in the night. "No one wishes to be someone. To be seen and feared."

"N-no. I wish—"

"I know what you wish. I can taste your soul, no one." It licked its lips with a long, pointed tongue, and hummed. "It is as bitter as firedust. You wish to see your mistress avenged. But where to begin? With her father who gave her away? Or her mother who gave her such a miserable life?" It floated closer, touching the blackened circle of its prison. "Would you like to see the man who took that miserable life, no one?"

The creature held out its bony hand and, with a harsh command, summoned a blaze into its palm. The flame swirled like a mad thing, twisting and stretching every which way to escape, but the *djinn*'s magic held it in place. "Look upon the face of your enemy. See how happy he is."

The witch looked, gasping at the sight.

There, the castle in the North. There, the fair-haired king sat on the bed, gazing down at a pair of swaddled babies. He looked up at the woman who'd given birth to them and smiled at her with such love, the witch felt tears slide down her wrinkled cheeks. She shook with hate. That love should have been Mari's. Those children should have been hers.

"What will we name them?" the king asked.

"My daughter's name is Liadan," the woman said. "Your son waits for you to name him."

The king peered down at the child, and at length said, "Fal. His name is Fal."

The woman smiled. "Liadan and Fal."

"They're beautiful."

Suddenly, a dark-haired man was there. "They are too much human," he said.

The king and his woman looked at each other, and a grave understanding passed between them. "They are only just born," the woman said, her eyes pleading.

"Yes," the dark-haired one said.

The witch gasped. "What demon is this?"

"He is a dragon," the *djinn* answered. "He has lived long before your gods birthed your tribe. The king is his grandson, and he is mighty with dragonblood coursing in his veins. Do you think he will be so easy to defeat?"

"Yes," the witch answered at once. "Because you will strike at him where he is most vulnerable."

"Ahh," the *djinn* breathed. "Wrath. Sweeter than a newborn's blood."

"I want you to strike them down."

"A dangerous task, and not without a price."

"I will pay it," the witch said.

"You do not wish to know what I will demand of you?"

She couldn't hear what else the Northerners said, but she did see the dark-haired one bring forth two small cups. When the king and his woman nodded, clutching each other's hand, the man gave one cup to each, and they, in turn, each fed a child from the cup.

"Now, creature—strike now!"

The *djinn* crushed the flame between his palms, and it exploded outward, knocking the witch down. From the ground, she looked up into the smoke left behind at what the *djinn* had wrought. The children screamed, one of them bursting into flames. Their parents and the dragon rushed to save them, but the witch knew it was too late.

Shaking, she touched a hand to her heart, then to her lips, and finally to her forehead. "For you, my sweet Mari. I do this for you."

"You did this for yourself." Hard hands curled around her arms, yanked her up off the ground. "And now, I take my reward."

The witch screamed, struggled in vain against the *djinn*'s hold. No, not a *djinn*; a true fire spirit would never have been able to leave its circle prison. In a rush of wind, the creature's face wavered, changed into something grotesque and terrible. Its eyes slanted crooked, its nose flattened into almost nothing, and its mouth stretched halfway around its head, opening on several rows of sharp teeth.

A *daeva*—a demon!

The witch screamed again, her own mouth forced open wide as the *daeva* forced noxious smoke down her throat. It became a living thing inside her, stretching her, pushing her aside to make room for itself. It hurt in unimaginable ways as the *daeva* cast her out.

Then the pain was gone, and she opened her eyes. She saw everything, the entire night, in every direction at once. She focused down on her body and saw it rise up from the sands. It looked back at her, its black eyes turned to red as the *daeva* smiled from her own face.

"Do not fear, no one," it said with her voice. "You may be nothing now, but a deal is a deal. I will give you the vengeance you so desired. The Imarah will pay for what they'd done, just as you wished. You simply won't be around to see it."

"What do we do?" a weeping woman whispered, turning the witch's attention back to the dissipating smoke of the *daeva*'s spell.

"I will take the girl," the dragon said.

"No!" the king cried.

"Be easy, Saeran. She cannot remain here. It is too dangerous. I will keep her safe, and you have only to think of her to be there with her. You must trust me. She is a Dragonblood, more powerful than any one of us, and until she can control it, she will need to be in a place where her fire will harm no one."

"And my son?"

A sigh. "He is a creature of water, not fire. I cannot help him."

"Then I will," the woman said fiercely.

Only when the witch heard the power in the woman's voice did she realize what she'd done. No human woman had a voice like that, one that could command the earth and heavens to move to her tune. *I have failed. I never stood a chance.* And she'd paid a terrible price for the attempt.

It was the last thought she had before the northern wind scattered her across the desert sky.

PART ONE

WILDERHEIM

 **1** 

"Shalla shansher an Imarah!" Clashing swords rang out over the screams of his dying tribesmen. "For the king and the tribe," they shouted, again and again. Seasoned warriors, workers, and even Magi, whose duty was to create, not to destroy. They fought as one to protect the women and children. Aesimar's warriors had attacked in the night, the cowards. On the one night in a moon's cycle when the *kharesh* trained away from tribe lands. They couldn't have known. Someone from his tribe must have told them. Imarah had a traitor.

"Tirasdunh!"

At Farraj's shout, Tir twisted sideways and backwards, barely avoiding an Aesimar blade. Rage simmered in his blood. He fell to the sands, rolled to his feet, but before the Aesimar dog had a chance to face him, Tir slashed across his back with his twin scimitars, the sharpest ever made. He was beset upon at once and blocked a sword and a spear in turn. Two against one were nothing for him; he was faster, stronger—he'd had to be to survive the ordeal of *kharashan.*

"To the east, Tir!"

Tir didn't question the order. He ran across the battlefield, fighting through when the path stood obstructed. At the eastern edge, he had a clear view of the entire fight. The Aesimar *shansher* sat his horse atop a dune with three of his assassin guards. He watched the fighting as one would a chess match and Tir knew that any moment now he'd turn and ride away, an unspoken order for his army to retreat. It incensed Tir, knowing that the Aesimar leader didn't want to win this battle. He only wanted to show Imarah he could strike at any time, day or night. He sowed seeds of fear and let them destroy a tribe from within. Only if the people truly believed there was no more safe haven to be found on their lands would they abandon them. Imarah was very near that point again, and Tir would eat *daeva* shit before he allowed his people to be driven completely from their homelands.

Clutching his swords, Tir ran for the dune, weaving among enemy warriors without engaging, his whole being focused on the one target he needed to take out to end this. The sand gave way beneath his feet, slowing him down, but he refused to relent. Gritting his teeth, he bore down, ran faster. Almost there. Almost at the crest. He could distinguish the markings painted in blood on the horses' bodies—symbols of Aesma Daeva, the god of violence and war, the one they worshipped and for whom their tribe was named. He knew those beasts would be sacrificed in an offering later that night in thanks for another successful raid. Their blood rites disgusted Tir. One more reason to eradicate his enemy.

He was almost close enough to hurl one of his swords, when the company turned and rode away. Tir roared and pumped his legs, but by the time he'd crested the dune, they were long gone. "No…" He spun around. In the valley below, Aesimar's fighters were running. Several *kharesh* pursued and slayed a handful before Farraj barked the order to retreat, to tend to the dead and the wounded.

Tir sliced the air with his twin swords, the need to kill someone so strong he could hardly breathe. He'd failed his people. Again. Down in the valley, Farraj met his gaze and held it, until Tir ducked his head in shame and began to make his way back. The morning sun beat upon the sands, wavering the air in mirages to break one's spirit. Not far off, where a bountiful oasis once loomed, palm trees poked up like barren poles stuck in the sand. Rocks as dry as dust marked the remains of a deep well that once had enough water to not only soothe dry throats, but also irrigate a small field and a fig orchard.

Those fig trees were gone now, years ago cut down for firewood when they stopped bearing fruit.

All of this had once been a verdant valley full of life around a burgeoning city, the tribe a thriving crowd of merchants and craftsmen, artists and singers. Now, the First Valley was dead, as his people would soon be, if he couldn't find a way to restore them.

"Anyone left alive to question?" Tir asked Farraj in passing.

"None I have seen yet."

Then there wouldn't be. Farraj missed nothing. Tir nodded and continued to the tents, where women stood outside, watching and weeping. He wanted to order them back inside, but it wouldn't do any good. They couldn't hide from this. Tir accepted a waterskin from an older worker who'd stayed to protect the women should any Aesimar dog make it through their front lines. "How is everyone?"

"The same, I'm afraid."

With a sigh, Tir nodded again and changed directions to go see to his family. His oldest sister, Halima, now a childless widow, tended to their father whenever Tir was away. She was the only one, besides himself and Farraj, allowed into his tent. None of them wanted the tribe to see their *shansher* this way. The once-mighty Dhakir the Conqueror's spirit had deserted him after Aesimar scum had taken the life of his beloved first wife. Now, he was little more than a wasted shell, sitting listless in his chair, staring off into nothing. He never spoke, rarely moved. He'd eat when Halima fed him, drink when she held a waterskin to his mouth, but he wouldn't seek them out on his own.

"Father." Tir sank to one knee before his *shansher*. "Aesimar fighters have retreated."

He didn't answer, and Tir shuddered, feeling again as though he was speaking to the dead.

"You must do something, brother," Halima said, her dark, beautiful eyes pleading. "We can't go on like this. The wells we dig run dry within a day, there's nothing to hunt, and our crops dry out or rot as soon as we plant them. We are dying, Tir."

"I know."

"Then do something!"

"What?" As the *shansher*'s last living son, it fell to him to lead and provide for the tribe. Never did a prince want his station less. It never should have been his. Dhakir had had three other sons, all of whom had met their end in battle over the years. Tir was the youngest, and the last. "Tell me, Halima! If you know something I do not, please tell me."

Halima ducked her head. "Forgive me. I meant no offense."

Tir huffed, at his wits' end. They'd tried everything. The Magi had blessed the land, beseeched the gods, called to the spirits, and even tried to summon a *djinn*. Nothing had worked, as if everything had fled this land except for the foolish Imarah, the first Aegiran tribe to be birthed by the gods and gifted this valley as their homeland. And now, apparently, the first tribe to be abandoned by their makers.

What was he supposed to do? The Imarah had lived in this valley for so long, they knew no other way to live. If they left, they'd die. If they remained, they'd die.

Farraj announced himself and stepped into the tent. "Our dead are being prepared for funeral."

"How many?"

"Twelve in all. Seventeen wounded. The Magi are tending them now. We were fortunate to return when we did, otherwise we might have lost many more."

"What of the dead raiders?"

"We will leave their bodies in the desert far from here."

"I would praise your heartlessness, Farraj, but I think that might be their way."

Farraj bowed his head. He was the oldest fighter Imarah had, still unmatched to this day. He'd served the *shansher* all his life, loved him as a brother. He was as much a father to Tir as he was a commander and a mentor.

Halima shook her head in sorrow. "All this began when Mari died."

Farraj's gaze snapped up to her. "We do not know that."

That he'd bother to answer her at all put Tir on guard. "What do you mean, Halima?"

"Nothing, *sher'nah*," Farraj said. "It is only a woman's grief speaking. You must not give the words more meaning than that."

Tir focused on his sister. "Halima?"

She would not meet his gaze. "He is right, brother. I should not have said anything."

Tir swore. "Someone tell me what is going on—*now!*"

Halima met eyes with Farraj, who shook his head.

Tir shoved to his feet and, brandishing his sword, pointed the tip at Farraj's neck. "Either speak or leave this tent."

Slowly, Farraj raised a hand and eased the blade away with a finger. "As you command, *sher'nah.*"

Tir lowered his sword but did not sheathe it. When Farraj motioned them closer, Tir and Halima sat on the ground by their father.

"Before you were born, your father led a raid on the North, hoping to win glory for our tribe with a great victory. Our warriors alone numbered in the tens of thousands then, and to the last, his men were ready to lay down their lives for their *shansher.*"

Tens of thousands. Tir couldn't imagine it. Less than two thousand of the tribe remained, half-starved and dying.

"We thought ourselves gods, trained from birth for war. The Northerners would not stand a chance, and many of them did not. We razed their towns and cities, killed any who stood in our path. But the northern kingdoms are not like ours; they are great beasts with a heart city where their kings sit, and Dhakir wanted their golden crown for himself. When we came upon the crown seat of Lyria, we found a fortress made of stone, impenetrable. They had more horses, better weapons, and knowledge of the land to use against us, and their fighters wore armor made of metal that repelled our arrows. Fortune, too, favored them. The prince of Wilderheim was there, and to keep his son safe, his king father sent countless more warriors to protect him. We were not only defeated, we were destroyed."

"Dhakir retreated, and Mari was given to the Northern prince in *ramesh feh.*" Tir knew this part, at least. A life for a life, *ramesh feh* used to be their custom for ending war through marriage. No longer. The attacking Aesimar tribe had no desire for peace, only war and death. All of the emissaries Tir had sent to offer a truce had been returned headless. The old days of honor were as gone as the water from their wells.

"Yes," Farraj said. "But she was only a babe still, and so we waited until she grew into a woman before we took her to become queen of Wilderheim."

Tir had only been a babe himself when Mari left. He couldn't even remember what she'd looked like. Still, she'd been his sister and he'd loved her. That much he knew. "So what happened?"

"We do not know," Halima said. "Not long after the wedding caravan returned, her guards and handmaidens came back as well, carrying her ashes. They said she became with child, and something went wrong. The midwife told me they did everything they could to save her, but she was too far gone. There were some who believed her Northern husband killed her to take another in her place."

Farraj swore. "Fools. They didn't know what they were saying. Their pride was thrice hurt—first with their defeat, then with Mari leaving, and the third time when King Saeran remarried. They would have fought ghosts to prove themselves, and they would have died trying."

"You think so little of your own men?" Tir challenged.

"No, *sher'nah*, but I have fought the Northerners, I've seen their magic men, and I have met their king. He is an honorable man. He would not have done harm to an innocent like Mari." He spoke with such conviction, Tir was tempted to believe him, but not convinced.

"Not long after that, our river dried up," Halima said. "With the water gone, the fig trees were the first to die, then the crops. Then the people began to sicken and then…"

"And then the *daeva* started flying through the night," Tir finished. In the absence of good and light, dark spirits had infested the valley. They came out at night, danced their wild dervishes, snatched any soul foolish enough to be wandering outside. Sometimes, they wouldn't appear for weeks; other times, they screamed and growled for nights on end. The Magi were powerless against them, their spells and rituals all for naught. Two had died trying to banish the demons to whatever hell they'd flown out of. Only light seemed to keep them at bay, so the Imarah people had taken to sleeping by lamplight.

It would not be long before that comfort, too, disappeared. With nothing left to trade, their current oil supply was all they had left. What would happen when the last drop burned away?

"Simply because one followed the other, does not mean they were related," Farraj argued. "We have dry seasons and rain seasons."

"Yes, and the rain seasons grow ever scarcer," Tir said.

"Tir, think about this."

"I am. You spoke of magic men. If you fear them so, it means they are very powerful. Perhaps even powerful enough to cast a curse on our tribe."

"Why would they do such a thing?"

"To prevent us from riding against them a second time; to keep us too weak to seek retribution for the death of one of our own." And they'd succeeded. The more he thought about it, the more sense it made. Imarah had struck out against the Northern kingdoms, and in retaliation, the Northerners had taken the life of their princess and made certain their tribe could never rise to retaliate.

Tir stood and picked up his swords.

"Tir, I know what you're thinking," Farraj said. "You cannot—"

"Oh, yes I can. You taught me that." He was *kharesh*, an assassin trained in the ways of battle and death. He couldn't raise an army against Wilderheim, but he could sneak into the kingdom to strike directly at its heart.

"No, I forbid it!"

"You forbid?" Tir snapped. "I am *sher'nah*, Farraj. You will do as you are told!"

Wide-eyed, his mentor stared a moment too long before lowering his gaze. "You would abandon your tribe, now, when they are most vulnerable?"

"I would do all in my power to rebuild what we have lost. If that means destroying the one who brought this misery upon us, then so be it. Kill the source, and the malady will lift."

"Tir—"

"Ready my horse. Halima, I will need whatever supplies we can spare. The *kharesh* are in charge until I return. You will see to the women and children."

Halima bowed.

"Tirasdunh!"

"I ride out at sunrise."

 2 

Liadan took off her shoes to tiptoe into the tunnel. She schooled herself to breathe slowly, quietly as she picked her way, avoiding loose gravel and puddles of water that could betray her presence. She knew the tunnels by heart, so navigating them in the dark was no chore. To remain undetected was the hard part.

Sneaking past the treasure chamber, she peeked in to make sure the great dragon was still asleep before she turned to go deeper into the cave system.

You're in trouble now. Her brother's voice in her mind startled her, and she barely stifled a gasp.

Hush, you! Do you want me to get caught?

"And where do you think you're going, little miss?"

Liadan cringed, freezing in her tracks.

You see? Fal said. You don't need me to get caught.

She scowled at the wet cave wall. Fal's scrying powers were still a mystery to most, but Liadan was quite certain if there was even a sheen of moisture around, her twin brother could see through it at whatever it faced. That's why rain always exhausted him. When it rained, he could literally see everything, and he couldn't always stop it from overtaking his mind.

"Where have you been, Liadan?"

"Fal tattled, didn't he?"

The dragon stretched, bringing his snout an arm's length from her. When he sniffed, the puff of his breath almost knocked her over. "I am a dragon, child. I do not need your twin brother to tell me when you are up to something. Now, would you care to tell me which tavern keeper I'll be paying off this time?"

Liadan raised her head high. "None," she said. "I didn't go to any tavern." She only ever went to those when she craved contact. She could blend in among the rowdy tavern crowds far better than at the markets, where those who saw her asked far too many questions. Unfortunately, whenever she did visit, some drunk inevitably decided to make a conquest of her, often forcing to spark a brawl to extricate herself. It wasn't her fault! Why should she be made to answer for the actions of Wilderheim's inebriates?

"Well, are you going to tell me where you did go?"

Liadan crossed her arms. "You're a dragon. Shouldn't you already know?"

He growled a little, the ground rumbling beneath her feet, and Liadan knew she was in trouble. "Pick up your sword, girl."

She looked down at her new gown, the one she'd been saving for her friend's wedding to the village elder's son. "Now?"

With a swirl of fire and smoke, the dragon transformed into his almost-human body. In this shape he stood a head and a half taller than Liadan. He had the face of her father, but hair as dark as night and a pair of smooth, shimmery horns curling out of his temples, sweeping up and back along his head. His powerful build made him the perfect sparring partner. His tail made him a cheater.

"Sword. Now." He was already stalking out of the cave and into the clearing.

Liadan stomped.

"And don't stomp your foot at me, little miss," he said from the cave mouth.

Grumbling, Liadan retrieved her scabbard from the treasure room and strapped the plain-looking thing to her waist. The blade it held was without equal. Light as a feather, yet strong enough to shatter stone. The dragon had forged it for her alone, sharpened it on diamond rock and polished it with opal sand. The handle was wrapped in the softest of leathers; the pommel was a ruby encased in a cage of steel knotwork. Spells etched into the blade made it impervious to rust and fire, though provided no magical protection to the wielder. That would be cheating.

"Draw," the dragon said.

Liadan did, and almost fell on her backside when the dragon attacked, knocking his blade against hers with enough force to drive her back against the rock face.

"You were not ready."

"You were too fast."

He leaned his weight on the blades between them. "It does not matter how fast I am. The moment your blade is free of its scabbard, you must be on your guard."

Try as she might, she could not budge him. He was too strong. Magic was her only chance, and the mere thought of it summoned fire into her eyes and hands. She smelled smoke as the sword's leather handle began charring.

But before she could use it, the dragon huffed at her, and just like that, her magic was gone. He shoved at her as he disengaged. "What is the rule, Liadan?" he demanded.

Liadan blushed. "No magic when we spar."

She'd not taken two steps away from the rock, when he came at her again. This time, she blocked and twisted away from his sweeping cut. He could say what he would about her reflexes, but even he couldn't deny her footwork was flawless. Liadan didn't fight; she danced. Light on her toes, swift and precise, but when she bore down, she had strength enough to force her opponent back.

She hadn't been able to do it with the dragon, until now. As she charged forward to launch her attack, he retreated, swiped his tail at her, but she was ready, jumping and ducking the appendage with ease. Liadan kept an eye on her opponent and where she wanted him to go, and pushed him precisely there: to the edge of the clearing, where a single row of trees hid the sharp drop-off of a dead-fall gorge. She almost smiled at how easily she was winning. The dragon was fast, but she knew his tricks now, and even when a dagger appeared in his free hand, she wasn't worried. She had her own sheathed at her back. With two blades, she put on more speed, schooled her breathing, and kept aware of her surroundings. Several times over the years, she'd tripped on a protruding root or rock and had fallen face-first into whatever the dragon had chosen to place into her path. Horse dung was his favorite.

But not today. Today, she had him on the retreat.

Almost to the edge, Liadan twirled in a complicated block-and-thrust, then moved in for the kill, shoving with her shoulder to knock the dragon off balance.

But he was no longer there, and Liadan found herself tipping forward over the cliffside. Her scream cut short when the dragon grabbed her skirts, yanked her back onto solid ground.

Though she knew he'd never let her fall, the dragon kept her at the very edge while he stared her down through eyes slitted with displeasure. "What have you learned?"

"That you cheat!" she cried, heart racing, knees wobbly.

"Liadan," he warned.

"I wasn't paying attention. I got overconfident. I thought I had you."

"Yes. It's called strategy. Brute force and fancy footwork aren't always enough to gain you a victory. Sometimes you must outwit your opponent. If you can't maneuver them to retreat to your advantage, then you must feign retreat to achieve the same. But you must be careful not to reveal your path. Make your opponent think he has you in his grasp, let him toy with you, but never lose sight of the most important thing."

"His weapons?"

"His pride."

Liadan blushed.

"An overconfident opponent makes mistakes, and you can use that against him. But be careful not to let your own pride defeat you instead."

She nodded.

"So, what have you learned?"

"Pride is a weapon I must learn to use."

"And retreat is not only a coward's way out. You must remember that. Promise me."

"I promise, Grandfather."

"Good girl." He kissed the top of her head. "Now go pack your things. You ride before sunset."

"Where am I going?"

"Home, Liadan. You are going home."

She gaped at his retreating back. *Did you hear that, Fal?*

You're coming home, he said with a distinct lack of enthusiasm. She hadn't seen the brat in years. While she was stuck here with the dragon, Fal was sequestered in Frastmir, being tutored by their mother and the water sprites. She would have thought he'd be happy to have her home.

What's the matter?

Nothing. I'll leave you to it. You have a lot to do before you ride.

Fal—

He was gone.

Something was wrong. Liadan hastened to her chambers, where she began tossing things into a bundle on her bed. She stripped off her gown in favor of her leather breeches and tunic. Her deep blue linen shirt had been fashioned for a man, and bore the crest of her father on each sleeve, embroidered in golden thread.

When trying to pack and braid her hair at the same time proved to be too much of a challenge, Liadan abandoned both to pull on her riding boots. Then she finished braiding her hair and packing her bundle. Her weapons would be strapped to her saddle, and she'd bring food in the satchel she always carried. Once she had everything packed, Liadan looked around the chamber that had been her home for the last nineteen years, and sighed.

"Grandfather?"

"Yes?" He stood in the doorway, where she knew he'd be, hiding in illusion. Now, he showed himself, still mostly human and dressed in simple, serviceable clothes. For all the treasures the dragon hoarded, he rarely parted with the pieces.

"I will miss you," she said.

He shrugged. "I am not going anywhere."

Nevertheless, she ran into his arms and hugged him with all her might. "Why do I feel like something terrible is afoot?"

"Perhaps because it is," the dragon said. He didn't sound at all concerned.

She looked up into his face. "Why do I feel like I will never see you again?"

He cupped her cheeks in his large, scaled hands. "Listen well, Liadan. There will come a day when you will have to choose between your family and everything else. It'll be a terrible choice, and either outcome will bring pain. But that day is not today."

His words held the weight of portent, and cold fear slithered around her heart at the thought of losing her family. She loved the dragon dearly. Fal was her twin, her other half, and her parents were the only people in this world or any other on whom she could always rely no matter what. How could she ever consider giving them up? What else could be so important that the prospect of losing them would be an acceptable choice?

The dragon smiled. "There now. Don't fret. Here, something to remember me by." He produced a silver torc, an almost-full circle of twisted rods with thick rings at each end, etched with intertwining knots. As he settled the weight of it around her neck, its power thrummed against her skin.

Swallowing back her tears, Liadan took a deep breath. "I have something for you, as well." Fisting her hand, she summoned fire into her palm, stoked it white-hot, then hotter still until her skin glowed bright blue. When at last she was satisfied, she let the fire cool, then opened her hand. In her palm lay a ring forged of black gold that swirled with colors when held up to the light. On the inside, the language of the ancient race spelled out an incantation in symbols far older than any her learned mother knew.

No one could restore a broken heart. The dragon's had shattered the day his beloved had died, and not even his descendants could repair it. But they could remind him that there was still happiness in the world for him to grasp; they could show him his mate would not have wanted him to mourn her for all eternity and that giving up his pain was not a betrayal, but an honor of her memory. When he wore the ring she'd forged, he'd remember the happy times he'd shared with all of them, and he'd know he was not alone, never had to be, if he didn't wish it. The ring gave him the power to summon to him any and all of his blood kin.

When he took it, Liadan didn't know whether he'd put it on or destroy it.

He did neither. The great dragon closed his fist around the ring and brought it to his heart. Then he smiled, the first smile she'd ever seen crease his handsome face. "Thank you," he said, and truly, she needed to hear nothing else.

Picking up her satchel and weapons, the dragon walked her to the stables where her mount waited, already saddled and burdened with two large bags. He didn't look happy about the unwieldy weight on his back.

Liadan frowned. "What is all this?"

"I am sending something for your brother. Perhaps he will find it useful."

While she attached her weapons and her bundle, the dragon settled a heavy fur cloak over her shoulders. "Be safe, Liadan. Be happy."

"And you, Grandfather."

When she rode out into the woods, it was to the sight of the great dragon flying through the air, breathing great plumes of fire at the gathering clouds.

 3 

With each village he passed, Tir hated the Northerners more. Such bounty, so much water he couldn't fathom it, and they wasted it in mindless play. He'd been welcomed into the inns as though he were an old friend; offered shelter, food, and a bath in a tub big enough to fit two of him. They'd filled it with water that would be tossed out the window when he was finished with it. The waste was inconceivable!

Everywhere he looked, people were well-fed, strong, and happy. They wanted for nothing, never knew a moment's worry. The sight of them only served to remind Tir his own people were dying in Aegiros. A single one of those lavish baths would have been enough water to quench the thirst of his entire tribe.

But as he neared the castle city of Frastmir, things began to change. From one village to another, Tir entered a different world. At first he thought his mind was playing tricks on him. He couldn't possibly be seeing this. Creatures he'd never seen before mingled with the villagers and townspeople, some with the ease of friendship, others with a cold distance, and still others with outright hostility.

When an old woman spoke to a little green girl with big eyes and vines for hair, Tir thought she had to be blind not to see it. But then, she took a vine into her gnarled hand, and laughed in delight when a bright pink flower bloomed in her palm.

A merchant selling earthen cups and plates looked on as a miniscule man with a giant nose and a crooked hat zipped from one item to the next, inspecting each. He licked the plates, and if he didn't like one, he made a face and shattered it on the ground. How could the merchant stand there and tolerate such abuse? Tir was about to intervene, when the little man-thing hopped onto a pedestal and shook a finger at the merchant. "You filthy cheat!" it shouted. "I gave you the best clay in all of Wilderheim to make my dishes, paid you a pouch of pure gold for your work, and this is what you give me!"

"I'm sorry, master," the man said, trembling. "I did not mean to offend."

"You did not think I would know the difference!" The little man-thing noticed Tir gaping, and growled at him.

Tir shook himself and continued on. He'd just about convinced himself not to panic, when a pure white mare with a horn growing out of her forehead trotted down the street, stopped by his mount, and nuzzled him. Tarabas tossed his head with a snort, then nuzzled her back. That was the last straw. "*Hyah!*" Tir shouted, kicking Tarabas into a gallop to get away.

At the river, he was forced to stop again. Across it lay the road to Frastmir; he could see the great, stone fortress from here. But the river was six wagons wide with a current so powerful it carried entire trees away. Along the banks were piles of broken logs that had washed downstream.

Fear gripped him. The bridge was sturdy; wagons, horses, and people crossed it with ease, not a worry on any of their faces. Still, he couldn't bring himself to nudge Tarabas forward. If it gave way, if he fell, he'd drown. No man could survive those waters, especially one who couldn't swim.

But the swell and dip of the waves unnerved him the most. For when they swelled, they rose to a person's height, and held the shape of one, too. Figures made of the purest water danced over the surface, leaping into the air, diving back. They had no faces he could discern, yet he sensed those creatures had teeth sharper than a scorpion's stinger.

Tir squeezed his eyes shut, squared his resolve, and nudged his mount forward. He kept his eyes closed, shuddering with every speck of water that hit his bare arms, imagining those creatures floating in the air next to him. They had no faces, he reminded himself. Still, he felt their eyes on him every step of the way.

Only when he heard Tarabas' hooves clop against packed dirt did he open his eyes. He didn't dare look back, only spurred the animal on faster.

If ever he had a lingering doubt that the Northerners were responsible for the slow destruction of his tribe, it was now completely eradicated. These people consorted with demons. Of course demons would be the method they'd choose to strike out against Imarah.

Frastmir was a thriving city with its fortress standing tall at the northeastern edge. The streets milled with so many people and… creatures, Tir didn't know where to look. Overwhelmed, he stabled his mount at the first inn he came across, then ducked inside. It was no less crowded in there, but at least it was quieter. Weary travelers sat together at large tables with plates of food and tankards of ale. They all spoke to one another in hushed tones and seemed a friendly enough bunch. Not a monster among them, as far as he could see.

Tir turned to the innkeeper, a beautiful, young girl with pale skin and red cheeks, and hair so light it was almost white. She smiled, and his heart lightened. "Aegiran," she said, and Tir was shocked to hear his language on her lips. "You've come a long way to us."

Dumbfounded, he nodded.

"A room, then?"

He nodded again.

The girl laughed, her voice a song to his ears. "Have you coin?"

Tir fumbled around for his pouch, pouring three copper coins onto the bar between them. It'd been enough in the other places he'd stayed.

The girl's eyes sparkled. "We barter in gold and silver here," she said, "but all manner of metal is precious to my kind." She met his gaze and swept her long tresses back behind her ear. Her long, pointed ear.

Tir almost ran, but he found courage enough to root his feet to the spot. His tribe depended on him to save them; he was meant to fight demons, not run from them.

"This will buy you supper for the night," the creature said. "But for a room, you will need to pay more."

Throat tight, Tir answered, "This is all I have."

Again that melodic laugh. "Coin is not what I want." She looked thoughtful for a moment, then said, "I will accept a kiss as my price."

"A kiss?"

She smiled. "Aye, a kiss can be a powerful thing. My kind feeds on passion. A kiss from one like you would sate me for many days to come."

At a loss for words, Tir looked around, seeking guidance, but no one paid him any heed. He was on his own.

"Do you accept the trade, son of Imarah?"

"How do you know my tribe?"

The creature pushed the copper coins around in a circle on the bar. "I know many things about you, Tirasdunh al-Dhakir."

"As a demon would," he growled.

She blinked her jewel-green eyes. "You must have never met a true demon to call me such. Know this, *sher'nah*, a demon would not barter for a kiss. He would take your soul. Demons are not welcome in Wilderheim, and especially not in Frastmir. Any known to consort with Dark creatures are executed by order of the queen."

"You expect me to believe a word you say?"

She shrugged a delicate shoulder. "Believe or not, but if you wish to stay the night, you must pay the price."

What would she do if he refused? Did he dare anger her?

No, until his mission was complete, he could not afford for someone to raise an alarm and alert his prey to his presence. Tir had one chance at this, and one alone. If he failed, all would be lost, and Imarah would be no more. He swallowed with difficulty. For his people, he had to concede.

Seeing the capitulation in his eyes, the beautiful creature leaned in with a smile. Tir met her halfway, pressing his lips to hers for the briefest of moments before pulling away again.

The creature gasped. Her cheeks flushed, her hair grew longer, her lips turned as red as blood, and when she opened her eyes again, they shone like bright green stars. Tir saw surprise in them. "You carry much pain in your heart, son of Imarah. And much darkness, as well.

You must let go of the hate you feel if you wish to save your people. Your salvation lies in the bosom of the one you call enemy. Only a strong, pure heart can burn bright enough to banish your demons, and they'll not be defeated with hate, young prince. Only with love."

Tir snatched up the key she held out to him, then escaped up the stairs to where the rooms were. Unerringly, he chose the room the key unlocked and closed himself inside, away from the madness of Frastmir and its demons. With shaky hands, he removed his swords and placed them onto the bed. A pitcher of water sat on a small wash-stand, and he poured some into a cup, gulping it down to soothe his parched throat. With each drop he felt guilty. Had Farraj been right? Should he have stayed with his tribe, instead of running away to fight an enemy he didn't know?

He thought of his father sitting in his tent, of Halima feeding him what little water they still had. Then he looked outside at a gaggle of children splashing each other in puddles on the road and remembered why he'd come.

With renewed resolve, he sat on the bed and cleaned his swords of road dust and grime. Tonight, when the sun set, he'd make his way into the fortress to put an end to this, once and for all. He was *kharesh*, a trained assassin, the prince of his people. None would see him, unless he chose to show himself. None would hear his approach, until he had a blade to their necks. The demon summoner would die by his hand, and he'd know in his final moments that he was defeated at last.

When day turned to night, Tir shed his travel clothes and dressed in his assassin's attire: a sleeveless black tunic to allow for ease of move-ment, black pants to tie into soft-soled boots, and a black hood and mask to hide his face. He tied small sheaths to his wrists with black cloth and slid throwing knives into them. His poison pouches were neatly arranged in order on a special belt. They ranged from sleeping powders to incapacitate his opponent, to snake and scorpion venoms that could paralyze or kill a man in the blink of an eye.

A *kharesh* killed silently, and never let his presence be known.

The inn's guests didn't bed down at nightfall. Instead, candles were lit and musicians summoned to entertain them. Ale and honey wine would flow in rivers down in the main room; Tir had seen it before.

He had no interest in their revelry, so long as it distracted them long enough to allow him to leave the inn, unseen. He crawled out through the window and left it open, silently jumping down into the street below. Torches lined the main road, and fires burned cheerfully in every house. Wispy, ghost-like creatures frolicked across the grass. He ignored them. Moving from shadow to shadow, Tir cut across the city to the stone fortress, where guards stood at the outer gate. The wall circled so far in either direction he'd lose precious time trying to find another way in. So Tir pulled out two of his knives and considered the stones for a moment, before he stabbed the blades into deep crevices, using them to climb up to the top.

At the edge he hung suspended, arms burning with strain as he waited for a pair of guards to pass by. Then he pulled himself up and onto the walkway. He was in luck. Not two paces from him stood a wooden staircase that led into the inner courtyard. Going down the stairs, Tir skirted the wall, keeping to the shadows as he made his way to the courtyard's gate. This one was guarded by a single armored man leaning on his spear. As he crept closer, Tir recognized the soft sounds emanating from the guard. He was fast asleep. Slipping in through the gate wasn't difficult. The hard part was finding where the king slept. Tir assessed the fortress' many levels, and the many windows in which light flickered. He could not hope to remain undetected while sneaking around inside. He had to find out which window belonged to the king's chamber and scale the wall up to it.

Then, as if by divine intervention, he noticed something odd: of all of the windows lit from within, only one was open. Though the day had been warm, the night's chill was in the air now. Tir was used to it; desert nights chilled the blood of even the hardiest men. But no one with any sense would let in the cold wind when he had a fire to warm himself. Only a king used to lavish comforts would be so wasteful.

Tir mapped out his route, shook out his arms, and started to climb. He scaled as high as the outer wall, then higher still. So far up, the cold wind snatched at him, seeking to tear him away. There were some footholds to make use of, but not enough to climb them with ease and his arms ached with strain. By the time he'd reached the window, he was out of breath, dizzy with the height, and even more determined to put an end to this.

Inside the chamber, the fire was dying down. By its fading light, he saw a massive bed with thick furs for covering. Tir circled around close to the walls, testing the floors first with his toes before putting down the weight of his entire foot. He sheathed his throwing knives and, reaching behind his back, drew out his long, curved dagger. The metal was tarnished to dull any flicker of reflected light, but the blade was sharper than anything else he owned; it could slice through flesh like butter, killing quickly and silently.

Close to the bed now, he distinguished two figures before the fire finally burned down to embers and the chamber became dark. The king and his queen slept like little lambs, tucked in each other's arms, with nary a care in the world. Tir pushed back his bilious anger and concentrated on steadying his breath and adjusting his sight to the darkness.

Imarah's salvation was his to claim. Tir would avenge his tribe, bring them back the fortune they deserved. He raised the dagger high above his head and, with all of his might, all of his grief and anger, sliced down.

The blade cut through fur, pillow, and mattress—the king and queen were gone.

"No." Impossible. He tossed aside the furs, dug beneath the coverings, and found nothing.

"You didn't think they'd make it that easy, did you?"

Tir spun, a knife already in hand. He threw it on instinct, expecting to hear this fiend die on the spot. Instead, metal clanged against stone. The dark figure moved with incredible speed, knocking his second knife from his grasp. He took a hit to his jaw, then three rapid ones to his midsection before he woke up from his stupor and struck back.

Tir caught his attacker around the throat and shoved, bending, kicking out with all his strength. The fiend grunted and fell back, coughing. Tir's satisfaction was short-lived. "You'll pay for that," the attacker whispered, and in a moment of utter lunacy, Tir thought he saw the figure glow. In the next, he was knocked backwards onto and over the bed to the hard stone floor. His training took over—he wrapped his legs around his opponent, rolled to bring himself on top, then curled his hand into a fist and punched down.

He struck the floor with enough force to crack a bone and a grunt of pain escaped him.

Hands curled into his tunic and a head butted against his nose, hard enough to make sparks of light flash before his eyes and Tir swayed, allowing his opponent to escape. No! He couldn't be allowed to live! Shoving to his feet, Tir followed.

As he lunged for the figure, fire burst into sudden life in the hearth, momentarily blinding him, but Tir saw enough of his opponent to drain all of the fight out of him. Soft, red-brown hair cascaded over graceful shoulders and framed a fierce, delicate face. A feminine mouth pulled into a vicious snarl, and beneath dark, arched brows, the woman's eyes blazed with fury, reflecting the fire's glow as though it shone out of her very soul.

Before his mind could comprehend what he was seeing, she knocked him to the ground with a well-aimed punch. His back met the hard stone surface of the floor, knocking the breath out of him and, head swimming, Tir watched the woman's blurry shape pick up his own dagger, knowing he was about to die.

Then the pommel slammed down onto his head, and darkness swallowed him whole.

 **4** 

Liadan tossed the blade away and groaned, holding her side. That bastard had broken her rib.

When Fal had called to her to ride hard, she'd not expected to find an assassin poised to kill her parents; Aegiran, by the looks of him. How in all the hells had he managed to even get inside the castle?

"Guards!" she barked.

They filed in before the echo of her voice had faded.

"Good of you to visit," she growled.

"Your Highness!" The one in charge bowed. "We didn't know you were back."

"And did you know my parents weren't here, either?"

The guards looked at one another. "Their Majesties were called away for important matters late in the afternoon," the captain said. "We were told not to expect them back until tomorrow at the earliest."

She frowned. "What important matters?"

"Other matters, your Highness."

Liadan rolled her eyes. Of course. Matters of Others took precedence over the return of their daughter. When Queen Nialei had sworn to help repair the damaged Veil between the human realm and the Otherlands, she hadn't anticipated the intricacies of Other politics;

everything required rituals and ceremonies, especially when the petitioner wanted a blood sacrifice. They only needed a drop of blood from each clan to reform the Veil anew, but with so many clans, and their blood so powerful, the Others had to be certain it would not be misused. Those who requested it had to prove themselves worthy, true, and pure of heart, a test that sometimes involved lengthy tasks and ordeals, and time in Otherlands did not often move the same way as it did here. For twenty years now, Liadan's parents had worked to restore the order of the world, and they still had a ways to go.

Liadan limped over to the bed and gingerly sat down, jerking her chin to the fallen assassin. "Take him to a cell and fetch my brother at once." They'd be questioning the intruder as soon as she could mend herself.

The guards bowed. "Yes, Highness."

After they left, Liadan sighed, staring into the fire. She could command it, speak to it, and scry its flames; that was her gift, the only true magic she possessed. She couldn't speak to the animals or the earth like her mother could. Water was for drinking, not for divining the future, and wind was nothing but chill air as far as she was concerned. Liadan was a true Dragonblood, taking after her father and her grandfather, and while she couldn't change her shape into that of a dragon, she still possessed many of their strengths and skills. She could see in the dark, create fire from nothing, and manipulate it into different forms and shapes. She could even work metals with some competence.

Her mother dabbled in many arts, but Liadan was a master of a single one. It was her gift, and sometimes her curse. As powerful as fire could be, so was it wild and difficult to tame. The dragon had spent long years teaching her how to take control of it, and she'd succeeded with only one small exception. Yet that one weakness could prove fatal at the wrong time.

All of a sudden, water poured in through the doorway, and in its wake, moss covered the walls and miniscule, yellow flowers on long, sturdy stalks grew all around. Then a vision walked in, following the stream's path directly to her, and a strange, wavering face smiled from beneath a sopping wet hood.

"Fal." Liadan smiled, opened her arms to her brother. "Up to your tricks again, I see."

Her twin scooped her up off the bed to embrace her so tightly, her broken rib screamed in protest, until it melted whole again in the way water forged down its path when an obstruction was removed. Cool comfort covered her from head to toe, healing bruises in an instant. "Sister," Fal said, his voice echoing with at least three others. "Welcome home."

"It's good to be back," she said. "But I didn't expect this kind of welcome. What's going on?"

Fal released her with a sigh. "I saw him coming from a ways off. I don't know why he's here. As far as I know, we've been at peace with Aegiros for decades."

"He was here for a very specific purpose. Why didn't you warn the guards?"

"The dragon said not to. He said you, and you alone, were to handle this, and that no one was to interfere."

Liadan tilted her head. "Is there a reason why we're still in the glen creek? I'd like to see my brother when I'm speaking to him, Fal. Can you do away with the illusions, please?"

"I… can't."

"Come on, we all know you're an unmatched illusionist, you don't need to rub it in. Let it go already."

"Liadan, I can't."

She stared. "What do you mean, you can't?"

The creek dried out, its earthen bed cracking as the flowers died and the moss turned gray. "I mean, I cannot." His visage, too, wavered into a different face. "I can't stop the illusions. Believe me, I've tried. They happen whether I want them to or not, and the more I fight them, the more violent they become."

Liadan searched his face for any feature that might mark him as the Fal she knew. Before her eyes, his nose lengthened, then widened, his chin grew a beard, and in the next instant he was as clean-shaven as a boy. Only his eyes remained the same, steady and blue. There was her brother, her twin. She cupped his cheek, the tangible truth of him underneath the illusion.

"How long has this been going on?" she asked.

He shuddered beneath her touch. "Years."

"Oh, Fal." She embraced him, her heart breaking for him. "What do the sprites say?"

"That Halflings are always flawed. But not like this. Somehow, something went wrong when Da gave me the dragon's blood. I had no dragonfire within me until then, and it didn't fit inside me as it did you."

The dragon's blood hadn't taken well to Liadan, either; like tossing oil onto a flame, it'd made her volatile, dangerous. She had to be vigilant every moment of the day and night to keep the flames contained, but they were part of her, and she could command them. It would make sense that the very fire that fed her strength kept Fal, a being of water, from mastering his own birth element. "And there's no way to undo this, is there?"

"If one exists at all, the sprites, the dragon, and our parents haven't found it yet. The rule of Wilderheim may fall to you by necessity, sister. No kingdom, even ours, will follow a king of false faces."

Liadan felt dizzy with dread. She loved Wilderheim, but she'd never wanted to be its queen. Her heart told her the path she was to walk led elsewhere. But Fal might be right. Who would follow a king who wove lies with every step he took? The people's trust had been hard-won after everything that'd happened, and there was still unrest, uneasiness with the Others who'd made their home here. The kingdom believed in King Saeran and Queen Nialei and waited for the royal pair to make good on their promise of peace and equality, but they couldn't rule forever. When it came time for them to step down, with no one but Liadan or Fal to take over, Fal's condition might push their citizens into full rebellion if she didn't step in.

But I can't! She swallowed with difficulty. "So what do we do now?"

"I don't know about you, but I would love to find out what our Aegiran guest is thinking."

Yes, so would she. "I'll talk to him."

Fal laughed. "No, I will talk to him."

"But he'll like me better."

Fal grinned, and the chamber reverted back to its former state, the mirage of illusions condensing around him, settling over him like a cloak. "I am the prince of deceit, remember?"

Liadan shook her head at the perfect replica of herself. With leathers dusty from a long journey and boots muddied from the road, only her brother's blue eyes betrayed his true identity, flashing fire from behind skeins of tangled red-brown hair. "Don't be too proud of yourself. You still don't sound like me."

Fal winked, and in her voice, more delicate and refined than she'd ever sounded in her life, said, "If anyone can get the truth out of him, I can."

"And if you can't?"

"Then I'll get something to show us the truth of his heart."

Liadan winced. "It'll be messy. I hate messy."

Fal pulled a dagger, toyed with the tip, eyes sparking with menace. "One does what one must for the good of king and kingdom."

She could hardly argue with that. "Right you are, brother. Off you go, then."

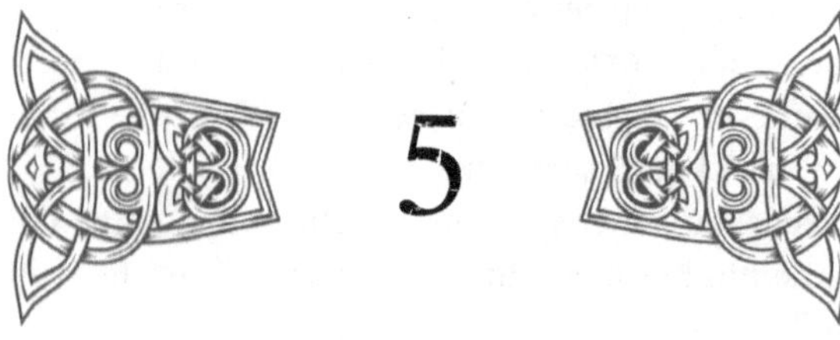

Fal left his sister to settle herself and returned to his own chambers. By the time he'd gotten there, the strain of holding such a small illusion had made him unsteady. The moment he closed the door, he shed the restraints, sighing when the chamber filled with water and fake sunlight glittered on the surface over his head.

You're making progress.

He went to the water stand to gaze into the bowl he always kept there. In its depths, Seol's face appeared, looking down at him like his own reflection. A water sprite, Seol rarely left his home in the deep underground well that fed the glen creek, but he could do what no other could: communicate through even the illusion of water. This made him a formidable ally and a master tutor, one to whom Fal owed his life.

"It was only a few moments."

A few moments longer than anything you haven't cast before. Seol didn't speak through voice, but through thoughts and images in Fal's mind. A sprite's voice was magic in and of itself, capable of killing a creature if they felt threatened, or of restoring life if they thought it necessary. They used it rarely and always with great caution.

Fal shook his head. "Why is it so difficult?"

It is your nature.

"It hasn't always been." Fal had been just fine, until he'd started making the transition from boy to man. Almost overnight, it seemed he'd cast one illusion too many, and they refused to go away. Mothers often warned their children not to make faces or they'd become stuck that way. Fal hadn't listened, playing with illusions the way a child made faces to delight his friends, and now he had his punishment: no other could look upon his true face, except through a veil of illusion.

Seol faded away, leaving the bowl empty. *See yourself,* he said. *You are still there, beneath it all.*

In the sprite's absence, the bowl reflected Fal's true face. His brows and nose were the same as Liadan's, his mouth was a more masculine version of hers, and his jaw was square with the grizzled beginnings of a beard. Fal and his twin were alike in many ways, but their differences were marked. Both had inherited the dragon's dark hair, but Liadan's fire had painted hers in its hues, and while Fal's was straight like their mother's, Liadan's curled with a life of its own. Liadan had eyes the color of charcoal, which lit with fire whenever she was around it; Fal's were as blue as the clearest lake, the only constant in his ever-changing visage.

He was a creature of water more than anyone realized, his powers so vast, they leaked out of him in illusion, and more often than not, that illusion was water. Those few who knew him were used to it, but those who were not, believed it so real, they began to drown in the waters he cast. Fal's illusions were either all around him or all over him, and the farther they spread, the easier he breathed. If he pulled them in around his body, he became a different person. If he filled the chamber, as he did now, he could be himself for a while, but not many could tolerate the strangeness long enough to truly see him.

Lamia, his tutor before Seol, had thought it was Fal's nature trying to force him home, into the waters from where he'd hailed. Fal had followed her instructions, blindly leaping into the river, which had carried him for miles, and he'd nearly drowned trying to breathe under water.

Seol's theory was that Fal's illusions made up for his humanity, which denied him water, by creating a version of it his all-too human lungs could survive.

Fal hadn't inherited enough of his water sprite ancestry to live as they did, yet he wasn't human enough to fit in on land. He felt wrong, broken. Something had damaged him, but he still believed it could be repaired. Like the Veil between the realms, something inside Fal had come undone when the illusions had overwhelmed him. If he could divine what it was, perhaps he could repair it.

One day, perhaps you will, Seol said. *But tonight, you have more pressing matters to attend to, do you not?*

"Yes." The Aegiran assassin.

Fal took a deep breath and pulled back his illusions, forcing the magic into his own skin. As the chamber slowly emptied, his form changed. His hair grew longer, his face softened, and his figure rounded to mimic Liadan. He scowled down at himself. The dragon allowed his sister far too many liberties. No proper woman went around dressed in this fashion; it was indecent.

Then he shrugged. It'd worked in a fight. He picked up the assassin's dagger and turned it this way and that in the light. A plain-looking thing, but sharp enough that he wouldn't risk touching the blade. Fal slid it carefully through his belt, then squared his shoulders and headed down to the dungeons.

It was time he had a chat with their guest.

~

Tir awoke slowly. He didn't want to. His head pounded and his right hand was a tight knot of agony, telling him he'd broken something. The instant he remembered what had happened, he shot to his feet and reached for his blade. It was gone. All of his weapons were, including his belt of poisons, his hood, and his mask.

He was in a stone cell with a thick, wooden door and a barred window hardly big enough to fit his hand through. He reached for it anyway and was pulled up short by the shackles locked around his wrists. The chains were anchored to the wall at his back, allowing him no farther than two steps away from it.

"Finally. I thought you'd sleep through the night." Fire sparked off a blade and onto a torch across the chamber, and in the meager light, he recognized the woman he'd fought.

"You," he snarled.

She arched an eyebrow. "You're angry with me? You're the one who snuck in here and tried to kill my parents. I should be the one angry with you."

"Then why aren't you?"

"Who says I am not?"

Tir yanked at his chains. "I have no time for games. If you are going to kill me, get it over with." He backed himself against the wall. The chain might be long enough to strangle her with, if he could lure her closer.

Instead of attacking, she pulled his own blade from behind her back and cleaned her nails with the tip. "Not yet. I have a few questions for you first."

"I'll tell you nothing!"

She smiled. "We will see."

"Kill me and be done with it. But know you are killing an entire tribe."

She stilled. "Do tell."

Tir bit his tongue and averted his gaze, cursing himself a fool. What had possessed him to say that? Desperation. He'd failed, and now had no way to remove Imarah's curse. He needed to go back and find another way; every moment he spent here, his tribe suffered.

"Come on, Aegiran, we both know you'll tell me eventually. Save yourself the pain."

Tir spat a curse at her in the language of the Magi.

The woman laughed at him. "Very good. If you had a drop of magic in you, I'd tremble in my boots." Then she scowled down at her boot. "Speaking of, I need a new pair."

He snorted in disgust. "A fool king to send a woman in his place. Weak. Let him come face me himself!"

"Sadly, my father is away on royal business. He's a very busy man, you know. He can't stop everything every time someone tries to murder him."

Taken aback, Tir struggled to find his voice, choking on his words.

"Your father?" This was the demon offspring of his enemy? He regarded her where she sat like a man, across from him. A beauty, true; he'd never seen her equal, not even the demoness innkeeper. Strong, too. To his shame, Tir had to admit she'd defeated him in single combat. Although, he amended, she'd had the element of surprise working in her favor. If they sparred again, he would not be so easily brought down.

She was undeniably a woman skilled in the art of combat. It showed in the set of her shoulders, in her thin but muscled arms. Her thighs encased in her leathers were powerful, well used to the saddle. She'd be a skilled rider, a fast runner, and he'd already sampled her kick to know its strength. Yet none of her mannish attributes marred her beauty; they seemed to enhance it.

If the fates had been kinder, if the coward king had been as honorable as Farraj had claimed, this woman would have been his niece.

No. No niece of his would behave in this way, dress in this way. This creature was completely shameless, and her fighting skills only proved what he'd believed all along—that the Northern king was some demon thing. He had to be, to have spawned this… this… "I will send you back to the hell you came from—"

"What is your name?" No rancor, no ire; she didn't even look at him, as if it didn't matter whether or not he answered.

Where he came from, names meant something. Tir stubbornly held his tongue.

She sighed. "What if I trade you answers? If I give you my name, will you tell me yours?"

"Demons lie," he bit out.

"And you think I am a demon?"

"It is known."

"Where? By whom?"

"In my tribe. By everyone."

She frowned. "Then your tribe has been misinformed."

Tir charged her, pulled up short by the chains. "You will not speak of them, demon!"

The woman rose. She was almost of a height with him, which unnerved him. Tir was tall among his people; few men matched his height, and he could fit most women under his arm. But this one faced him with her shoulders back and head held high, easily meeting his gaze like an equal. For a moment, Tir became mesmerized by her blue eyes. "I am Liadan," she said. "Daughter of King Saeran and Queen Nialei of Wilderheim. I am a princess of this realm and, under different circumstances, I would have welcomed you into our home as an honored guest."

"Lies."

"What reason would I have to harm you? Aside from the fact that you tried to kill my parents in their sleep. Were you too much of a coward to face them any other way?"

"Mock me at your peril, demon," he said, voice wavering with anger.

She gave him her back with a put-upon sigh. "Your name, Aegiran. I can force it from you if you make me. Don't make me."

He said nothing.

When she faced him again, her eyes were glowing. "Your name," she said, and her voice echoed.

Tir's throat locked tight; he couldn't breathe. His jaw stiffened even as his tongue moved behind his teeth, forming his name. The force of her magic stunned him. He'd never felt anything like it. His face heated, the need for air overcoming his desire to keep a secret. "Tirasdunh," he gritted out, and the force released him. Tir dropped to his knees, gasping for breath.

"Did you say Tristan? That is a Northern name. You wouldn't be lying to me, would you?"

He shook his head, opened his mouth to curse her blood, but when she held up a finger, his voice would not come.

"Truth, please."

Nothing but the honest answer to her question would come out, and the longer he remained silent, the more painful it became. He chose his words with care, revealing only what would do no harm. "Tirasdunh is my name. It is an old Aegiran name. Most call me Tir."

"Tir is our god of war. It is not a name for mortals to carry."

"Your god, not mine."

She looked him up and down. "As you say. Why do you wish my parents dead?"

Again, her demon magic slithered around his throat, commanding more words. "They killed my sister," he said, but stopped himself there.

The magic released him suddenly, and Tir hunched over, gulping in deep breaths of foul Northern air. If she wanted him dead, no better time to take his life than now, while she had him on his knees before her, head bowed, ready for a blade across the neck. If Tir had had any pride left at all, he'd stand and face her. But he couldn't. Twice felled, he'd shamed himself and his tutors. His tribe would be well rid of him. They deserved better than a weakling who couldn't even stand up to a single demon. Perhaps he was the one cursed, and with his death, his people could be free.

But what if they weren't?

"Only one Aegiran woman passed into the arms of her ancestors in Wilderheim. Your sister was Queen Mari."

Her name on the woman's lips sounded like an aberration.

She tangled her fingers into his hair, forced his head up to meet her gaze. "I know you're keeping something from me. And I know you will dance around it until all life has drained from your body before you let the honest truth pass your lips."

"Then kill me," he grated.

The woman shook her head. "Your death would serve no purpose. As your sister's served none. If you believe nothing else, then trust in this one thing: she did not die by my father's hand, or by my mother's. Her passing was a tragedy and many mourned her, my parents among them."

Tir yanked on his restraints, the pain in his broken hand a paltry nuisance compared to the agony in his heart. She was lying; she had to be. Mari's death was the reason for everything. She had to be avenged for his tribe to live.

The woman sighed and released him. "If I can't get the truth from your tongue, I will get it from your blood."

"No!"

But it was too late. With one smooth cut of his own blade, the woman opened his wrist and held it, bleeding, over a copper bowl. His struggles came to naught. "Damn you!" he screamed at her. "Damn all of you!" He called down curses upon her and her kin, invoked the dark gods whose names felt cold on his tongue and stabbed fear into his heart.

She didn't waver from her task. "Your gods," she said. "Not mine."

When she released him, Tir fought against his restraints, tried to kick the copper bowl out of her hands, but in three swift, long-legged strides, she was out of the cell and the door closed and locked behind her. He screamed himself hoarse, chafed his wrists raw, and all but wrenched his shoulders out of their sockets trying to escape.

Not until the torch had burned down to nothing and the light of day shone into his cell did Tir subside, sinking to the floor against the wall. Not until then did he realize the cut on his wrist had stopped bleeding and his broken hand felt whole.

6

Liadan was bathed, dressed, and half asleep by the time moss once again announced her brother's presence. She sat up, searching another stranger's smiling face for Fal's familiar blue eyes. "Well?"

He produced a copper bowl filled with blood, and Liadan wrinkled her nose. "What did you do, slit his throat like a suckling pig?"

"I was almost tempted to," he said.

An odd way of putting it. "Almost?"

A rosy-cheeked woman's smile ebbed. "He's Mari's brother."

Liadan gaped. "Da's Aegiran wife, Mari?"

"The very same."

"He can't be much older than we are!"

"She was only a child herself when she came here."

Liadan couldn't imagine being bartered away like cattle to some stranger in a far-off land on the feeble promise of peace. The poor girl had paid a terrible price for her sacrifice. Saeran had done the proper thing—he'd honored his oath to Aegiros by wedding Mari, despite his love for Nialei. But back then, none of them had known the truth of his ancestry, and when Mari had become pregnant with her first child, her body had been too young, too weak to sustain them both.

Only dragonblood could carry dragonblood. Mari had paid with her life for her tribe's foolish customs.

"You are certain he spoke the truth?"

"Absolutely," Fal said, and for a moment, she glimpsed his true face beneath the mask of an old man.

"Then why the blood?"

"Because he held back something important. Shall I do the honors?"

"No, I will." Liadan took the bowl and stoked the hearth fire.

"Fire is unreliable," Fal argued.

"Not for me." Scrying from fire often showed two visions: the one the petitioner sought, and the one he most desired. It took a wiser man than most to distinguish the difference and set out on the right path. But Liadan was a creature of fire; it spoke to her clearer than to anyone else, and she trusted it without question. With something as elemental as blood, she needed only to cast it into the fire to see the pure truth inside. Motioning Fal to join her, she knelt before the hearth, dipped her finger into the Aegiran's blood, and flicked a drop of it into the flames.

At once, she was cast into a vision of vast sands and scorching sun. Everywhere she looked, the air wavered as if moments from catching fire and burning the world. Liadan frowned, flicking another drop onto the flames. "His blood keeps secrets as well as he does."

Now, she saw a pile of black rocks amid dead trees, some broken in half. Nothing else. "Damn it." Another drop.

"Give it here." Fal took the bowl from her and threw all of the remaining blood onto the flames, making them hiss and spark. Liadan gasped, plunging into a vision so powerful, she was right there in the middle of it.

She stood in the heart of a great, empty desert city, among silent earthen houses with rags billowing in the windows, not a soul in sight. They'd all been driven out by interlopers, who hadn't lasted long, themselves. Nothing lasted here; not without water, which had all but disappeared on this side of the valley.

Liadan followed the ghostly trail of an exodus across a long, narrow pass that snaked like a ribbon between sand dunes—a valley cut into the landscape by a once-mighty river that was now dry, just like the well in the oasis and every other underground well that lay dug up and abandoned. Everything had dried up, even the heavens. Liadan tasted the air, and all she sensed was sand and dust. This valley had not seen rainfall in a very long time.

Not far off, movement shivered in the air like one of Fal's illusions, and she flew closer to enter a small village of tents. They huddled together like children in the night; old, worn things anchored into the sand, just enough to serve as protection against the sun and sandstorms, but no true comfort for their inhabitants.

She saw people, too. Poor people, starving, sick. Dying. Terrified people who had nowhere else to go, hounded by the horrors they'd lived though—and there were many. As the sun raced to the west and the desert turned dark and cold, Liadan looked to the south where glowing shadows flew across the sky. Black, red, gray; colors of darkness, blood, and death. Demons. They swarmed the village, snatching up one person after another, feeding on their souls and leaving behind hollow shells of flesh and blood. Empty of spirit, those bodies still moved, hungry to fill the void inside. The dead walked the night, feeding on any meat they came upon.

Liadan cried out and fled the vision, slamming back into herself in her chamber. Shaking, she struggled to her feet, trying to get as far away from it as she could. Then Fal was there. Strong arms wrapped around her, and she squeezed her eyes shut to the lie of him and let her true brother hold her, rock her, until her heart had slowed and she could breathe again. "What happened?" he asked.

In halting sentences, Liadan told him what she'd seen. Saying it aloud made the vision real to her. This had happened, and was still happening, to the Aegiran's tribe.

"You're sure?"

Liadan nodded, extricating herself from his embrace. The fire had burned out, so she laid down more kindling, along with a fresh log, and sparked a new one the human way. Once it blazed strong and steady, she stuck her hand into the flames and let them snake up her arm. It warmed her, banished the chill of the vision and brought her comfort and peace instead. "He didn't come just to kill someone, Fal. He thought if he did, it would help his tribe. He believes we caused this."

Fal swore, and the illusory lake her chamber had become began to boil around her. It looked so real, the steam made her sweat. "What do we do?"

"What can we do?"

"We should wait for Father and Mother."

Liadan shook her head. "They could be gone for months. His people don't have that long."

"You want us to help them?" The lake started to swirl in a vortex.

"Don't sound so shocked. His actions may have been the wrong ones, but his intent was honorable. He sought to help his people the only way he knew how."

"By killing. He's an assassin, Liadan!"

"An assassin who sought help from us."

Fal, now a heavily bearded, balding man sitting on her bed, frowned. "If you think I'm going to fall for that—"

"By the charter drawn up by King Saeran and Queen Nialei, none who come to Castle Frastmir seeking aid for a people, our own or Other, may be turned away without being given some form of aid."

Fal shoved to his feet and began to pace, while the water vortex grew, following his step like a shadow. "I knew you would say that!"

"It is the law, brother."

"Our law, not his! He is neither Other nor a citizen of Wilderheim. He is the enemy come to slay the king in his bed! And you would choose to reward him for it?"

"I would choose not to punish his people for his actions."

"Then let him return to them! Mari was their princess, which means, as her brother, he is their prince. Perhaps even their king."

"And you would turn away a fellow royal so easily? What if it happened here? What if it was one of us desperate to save Wilderheim, the way Mother and Father are?"

"Liadan." His tone said he was done arguing. Good. So was she.

"Very well. I suppose in Father's absence, as his heir, you are in charge. I will obey your decision. The Aegiran will be released and escorted to our borders to return to his own lands."

"Thank you."

"And I will be the one to escort him."

7

The argument that followed would go down in Frastmir's history as the worst thing to have happened since the Veil had been torn. Liadan didn't care. With her vision still occasionally making her shudder, she was in no mood to give in to her well-meaning but near-sighted and illusion-challenged brother. In the end, he could do nothing to stop her short of issuing a royal decree to keep her from riding out to Aegiros. But since her parents were nowhere to be found at the moment, a decree would not be forthcoming unless Fal forged their seal. And if he did, she'd know.

When Fal became so overcome with anger that the maids three floors below shouted about water leaking from the ceiling, Liadan put her foot down and walked out, effectively ending their sibling fight. For the moment, at least. She ran past the angry maids and the bewildered guards, straight down to the dungeons and the imprisoned assassin.

"Listen, you," she said, then stopped, temporarily robbed of speech at the sight of him. The guards had stripped the man of his weapons and his mask. Seeing his face for the first time, Liadan forgot what she'd been about to say. He was… unexpected. His hair was as dark as pitch and long enough to require a thong to restrain it, but shorter strands still escaped to frame his face.

And what a face it was. His dark skin made his pale brown eyes all but glow. He had sharp features with a proud, thin nose and a strong jaw. A true warrior, unadorned and unarmored, though his build and his scars warned her she'd be a fool to challenge him a second time. This one was used to war and pain, and there was a hardness to him, a mistrust and a stubbornness that spoke of many trials fought and won.

"Tir," she tried again, wondering if he even understood her language. "That is your name, yes? Tir?"

He said nothing, but if looks could kill, Liadan would drop dead where she stood.

She swallowed. If she couldn't make herself understood, this would turn out to be a lot more difficult. "Your petition has been heard and granted. We'll ride out tomorrow."

"What lies are you spewing now, demon?"

He had a deep voice as befitted a man of his size, and his accent gave his words a rough, mysterious quality. She could listen to him for days and never grow tired of the sound. Wait. Demon? "I am telling you that you will get the aid you came here to seek. Me."

The assassin glared for a moment, then laughed in her face. "You."

"Yes."

He laughed more, leaning forward where he sat, resting his elbows onto his updrawn knees. "You will ride to Aegiros with me?"

"Yes, that's what I said, isn't it?"

"And what can you possibly accomplish?"

Good question. Liadan had no idea what was happening to his tribe—she might never know—and going there might accomplish absolutely nothing besides getting herself killed. But instead of backing down, she produced the key to his restraints and took one of his wrists to free him. "We won't know until we get there, will we?"

He watched her face the entire time she fumbled with the shackle. Her hands shook. What was the matter with her? "Your eyes," he said. "They are different."

Liadan blushed as the first shackle fell to the floor. She took his other hand, unlocked that one, too.

The moment he was free, the assassin caught her wrist and wrapped his other hand around her throat. In the blink of an eye, he had her pressed against the wall, her feet dangling a fair distance off the floor. "You think you can play with me, demon?" he snarled.

Liadan grabbed his wrist, dug her nails into it, but he was too strong. Fire welled in her hands, glowed out of her eyes, a defense she usually pushed back in a fight like this, but these were special circumstances. Seeing her eyes change, the assassin's own grew wide, and he shouted something in his language.

Only a man, she thought. Not a dragon. A mortal. She didn't need her fire to best him. Pushing it back, she kicked the assassin right between his legs. He roared and released her, but he was in no way defeated. They moved apart to catch their breaths, and Liadan recovered just in time to duck his swing.

He was skilled in combat, but Liadan had been trained by the dragon, and fighting this man was no different. He was fast, but she matched him easily. He was strong, too—she still felt the reminder of how well he'd fought her last night. If she allowed even one of his hits to land true, she'd be done for.

Liadan fought defensively, against his erratic style, fueled by rage as much as by skill, and for a moment she was worried. If she lost, he'd kill her. He spun to put his weight behind a hit; Liadan spun the other way to dodge it. She caught his arm, wrenched it up behind his back, but instead of leaning into it, he somehow leaned forward and twisted around, bringing his arm before him while turning hers to such an awkward angle, she had to release him or risk breaking it. He grabbed her arm when she swung, and sidestepped when she would have stomped down on his feet. He now knew to avoid her knees, and when she tried to headbutt him, he flinched back, anticipating the move.

With speed to rival her dragon grandfather, he spun her around, wrapped his hands around her head and chin.

Liadan! Fal and the dragon shouted at the same time.

"Now you die," the assassin said.

Liadan had no ground to fight him unless she wanted to snap her own neck. Acknowledging her defeat with only a smidgen of regret, she closed her eyes, said good bye to her brother and her grandfather, and waited for the pain of death.

But it didn't come.

She heard the assassin behind her rasp out big breaths so she knew time hadn't stopped. Yet she was still alive, and he wasn't moving.

All at once, he shoved her away, snarling a foul-sounding foreign curse. Daring a careful sigh of relief, Liadan turned to face him.

He stared at her as if she were a monster with thirteen heads. "Why did you let me win?"

"What?"

"You have magic and you held it back. I could have killed you!"

"Why didn't you?" she asked.

His shoulders slumped, and he shook his head. "What purpose would your death have served?"

"Liadan of Frastmir, what is the matter with you!"

Liadan winced as Tir whirled around to face the robed people rushing toward them. The speaker was Councilor Braith, second oldest member of the king's royal advisory council, surpassed in age only by the ancient Kvaran, who now shuffled his feet after the rest of the company. A more outspoken advisor had never shadowed the halls of Castle Frastmir.

"Councilors," Liadan greeted. "A fine welcome you give to your king's only daughter."

"If you want to be treated as a princess," Braith quipped, "then act like one. And you"—she turned on Tir, brandishing her walking staff—"settle your feathers or I'll make you see stars."

The threat was ridiculous, considering the source. But curiously, Tir's stance relaxed, and he dipped his head in a brief nod-bow.

Liadan gaped. "How did you make him do that?"

The Aegiran snarled at her, and Councilor Braith sniffed. "Follow."

The entirety of Frastmir's council turned to follow her out as if she'd charmed them into compliance. But Liadan knew better. Braith had earned her respect with long years of loyalty and wisdom, not to mention stubborn refusal to be subdued or overlooked simply for the handicap of her sex. Decades after King Saeran had taken the throne and placed a woman wizard at his side, Braith was still the only woman on his advisory council, and only because she held on to her post with tooth and nail.

When Tir looked at her with utter confusion in his honey-brown eyes, Liadan resolutely bit back a laugh. She shrugged, then did as Councilor Braith had ordered—she followed.

~

Nialei couldn't move. The crystal encasing her was so thick, she could barely discern the shapes moving beyond it. It restrained not only her body, but also her magic; she was frozen, helpless to do anything but watch the skeletal wyvern swoop down on Saeran with a screech.

He dove to the ground to avoid its talons, then rolled as the wyvern sprayed acid from its mouth. Too close! Nialei desperately fought her prison to get to him, but she couldn't. This test was for him alone, and she was forbidden to interfere.

On the other side of the arena, the Northern Elf queen cheered the battle on with her horde of followers. Their lands were far removed from the human realm and any of its borders, sitting high in a frozen mountain range where no mortal would even think of encroaching. Thoroughly isolated, the Northern Elves saw no reason to do anything about the damaged Veil, and Nialei's petition had been met with powerful resistance in the form of apathy.

Worse, over the last few years, Others have spread the word of Saeran's agility in battle, and more often than not now, the chosen ordeal in exchange for their aid was to pit him against more and more imaginative opponents. The only way to secure the Northern Elves' aid was to give them something they rarely got to see: a spectacle—a true battle to the death between Wilderheim's greatest hero and one of this region's most vicious predators.

Wyverns were snake-like creatures with long necks and tails, covered in leathery skin. They had wings like a bat growing out of a short, barrel chest, and two clawed appendages that might have been feet. But between the length of their bodies and the awkward placement of those feet, they were physically useless. The wyvern's greatest asset was its glass-shattering screech and the acid it spewed the way dragons breathed fire.

As Nialei watched, the wyvern encircled Saeran in a wide, muscular coil of its body, then reared back to strike. Saeran had no way of retreat, and he'd lost his sword somewhere along the perimeter of the arena. Nialei tried again and again to cast her will through the crystal, to no avail. This, too, was part of the spectacle; the Elf queen wanted her to watch Saeran struggle.

She did not know Saeran.

As the wyvern paused, ready to spew a bellyful of acid, Saeran dropped to one knee and slammed his hands flat onto the hard rock surface of the arena floor. Nialei felt him reach deep inside the mountain to a lazy river of fire and draw it to the surface. The frozen rock cracked and broke at the force of the rising heat beneath his palms.

Confused, the wyvern released him and twisted in circles, watching the ground fracture. It beat its wings to escape, but the Elf queen's spell wouldn't let it; the creature battered itself against an invisible dome over the arena in a futile attempt to break free.

And all the while, Saeran drew strength from the fire, gathering it into his hands, his heart, his soul. With its added power, he rose, glowing from within like a lantern in the night, and when he held out his hand, his sword returned to him on its own, bursting into flames in his grasp.

Sensing the threat, the wyvern rounded on him and screeched. Saeran drew back, then hurled the sword, spearing the animal directly through its heart, pinning it to the dome overhead as it caught fire.

The Elven crowd fell silent.

Queen Taren rose from her seat, a warrior woman with silver hair arranged in multitudes of braids. She glared at Saeran and let the dome dissipate. The wyvern fell into a crevasse at Saeran's feet, and the queen's magic sealed it shut. With a jerk of her chin, she dissolved Nialei's crystal prison, releasing her to drop, gasping, to her hands and knees.

While Taren descended from her balcony perch, Saeran limped over to Nialei and helped her stand. "Won again," he said with a grin.

Nialei didn't share his enthusiasm; she was worried. An ordeal was meant to weigh the petitioner's heart and conscience, not the strength of his arm. And as the petitioner, Nialei ought to have been tested, not Saeran. In the past, both had been willing to submit to the will of Others for the good of all. But how long could they keep going this way?

"Are you hurt?" she asked him. Wyverns were venomous. A single scratch or bite could be fatal, even to Others.

"Nothing a hot bath and a kiss can't heal," he replied, rolling his shoulder with a wince. He looked somewhat the worse for wear, but she detected no bleeding wounds. A small blessing, but Nialei was grateful nonetheless.

The Elven crowds rumbled as they parted to allow Queen Taren passage. She was unlike any Other female they'd thus far encountered. Taren had no mate; she ruled alone with an iron fist, and it showed in her bearing. She dressed in breeches and leathers like a man, keeping her arms bare to show off the dark markings tattooed into her skin. Half of her face and the side of her neck were covered in them, making her look frighteningly fierce. She was scarred, muscled, and armed with two swords and a myriad of hidden knives.

She didn't need them. As a Northern Elf, Taren had natural control over snow and ice the same way Nialei controlled water, and as their queen, she could command every one of her kind to do her bidding with a mere thought. She lived for war, and when none could be had in her own realm, she sought it elsewhere, known to ally herself with any outnumbered, overwhelmed army, human or Other, to even the odds.

Saeran squeezed Nialei's hand. They'd long ago stopped trying to protect each other. Now, no matter what they faced, they stood side by side, working together. As Taren approached, Saeran's magic hummed against Nialei's palm, calling to her own. The queen didn't look happy; she'd bet a great deal on this battle's outcome.

"You owe me a small fortune, Halfling," she said to Nialei.

"And you owe me your blood, Majesty," Nialei replied.

Taren grunted, looking from her to Saeran, then back again. "Where is that beast of yours?"

Nialei smiled. "Behind you."

Head canted low, fur bristling, Varr stood at Taren's back, growling. He showed a mere hint of fang as a warning for the Elf queen to watch her step. No matter how many times Nialei ordered him to stay put, the wolf refused to leave her side. If she left him in the human realm, he somehow found his way through the Veil and tracked her wherever she went. If she tied him, he chewed through the binds, be they leather, cord, or metal.

Nialei wasn't quite sure what he was. He'd once died in her arms, and she'd worn his pelt about her shoulders, until the night the sorcerer, Jasper, had torn the Veil. Then, somehow, the pelt had come back to life, creating a creature who wasn't alive and so could not die, one who wasn't a true animal and so was not bound by the laws that governed them. Varr was a creature of in-between, a Halfling, just like Nialei and Saeran, both of whom he protected fiercely.

Taren snapped her fangs at Varr, and he snarled, which seemed to amuse the queen. Then she turned her back on the wolf, facing them with a terrifying smile. "I would forgive the debt in exchange for him. A fine battle hound he'd make. Fine, indeed."

"Varr is his own creature," Saeran said, not bothering to argue the debt. "He follows no one's orders, and fights no one's battles but his own."

Taren scowled. "I'd call you a liar if I didn't know better."

"The blood, your Majesty?" Nialei prodded.

"Are you in a hurry, Halfling?"

"Yes," she said, for the hundredth time. "Very much so."

Taren grinned, showing off her sharp fangs. "You ought to know better than anyone that time is irrelevant. It is a lie humans tell themselves to give structure to their lives where none exists. And by doing so, they make themselves finite." She leaned in as if to impart a secret. "That is why they die, Halfling. Not because they are human, but because they are so much *human*." With that, she sliced a sharp, crystal dagger across her palm.

Caught off guard, Nialei scrambled to produce the vial she'd brought, collecting into it several drops of Taren's blood. It was more than they needed—far more.

"I am the first," Taren said. "My blood is the purest of my kind. See that you do not waste it."

Before Nialei could utter her formal thanks, darkness engulfed her and Saeran, yanking them from the Otherland and back into Wilderheim. Nialei fought off the nausea this form of travel always induced, then looked around. They were in the east, at the edge of a long ravine that formed a natural border between Wilderheim and Ravetia, with a herd of goats grazing on lush green grass and bright yellow dandelions nearby.

"Thanks," Nialei muttered. It was past noon. Plenty of sunlight left to make their way across the fields. If they could reach the nearest village, they could procure horses and ride back to Castle Frastmir first thing tomorrow. "Was it necessary for you to show off?"

Saeran blinked. "What do you mean?"

"I mean, you could have summoned that fire at any time. You dragged that fight out deliberately."

He shrugged. "They wanted entertainment."

"And you wanted to play. Will there ever come a day when you stop risking your life in senseless displays?"

"Careful, love, you're beginning to sound like Loki."

She shoved at his shoulder. "You know what I mean!"

Saeran crossed his arms. "I seem to recall a time, not that long ago, when you were the one risking your life almost every day. Maybe it's time I put in my fair share."

She blushed, not appreciating the reminder of how much she'd changed over the years, from the young royal wizard, Nia, who'd once turned him into a toad, to Queen Nialei of Wilderheim, ambassador to the Otherlands. "It's not the same, and you know it."

It had taken years for Saeran to fully grow into his powers and learn how to control them. He'd learned from the dragon, and alongside their daughter, had slowly embraced all that his dragonblood had given him. He'd gained many of the dragon's gifts of Sight, Hearing, strength and speed, and even some mastery over fire. He could now hold his own in a physical battle as well as a magical one, but it hadn't always been so.

"You worry too much," he said. Along with his gifts, he'd also developed a sense of dragon arrogance. Nialei supposed all magic came with a price.

"I worry what this is turning us into."

"And what is that?"

Nialei rubbed her brow. "Puppets." Saeran didn't argue with that, and her shoulders slumped. He felt it, too. "This started out as a noble cause," she said, "but now it seems all we do is fight for entertainment and a few drops of blood."

Saeran pulled her close, pressed his lips to her temple. "It won't go on forever. We're almost finished. And once it's done and settled—"

"The Others will have made a laughingstock of us."

"What makes you think we were ever anything else to them? Was it not you who told me that Others live to play merry havoc with mortal lives and watch them implode?"

"It gives me such joy when my student recalls my lessons well enough to quote them back to me," she retorted, making him laugh. The sound of it rumbled from his chest, and she sighed, content to stand there for a while and simply be, without any duties or responsibilities pressing in from all sides. "We should get back home. I miss the children. And our bed."

"So do I. Especially our bed." Saeran gave an irreverent squeeze to her backside. "Well, love, we have two choices to get there: we can walk, or we can walk."

"I suppose we walk." Nialei reluctantly extricated herself from her husband's embrace and, closing her eyes, turned her face into the breeze.

Walk fast, the western wind said. *They need you.*

She looked at Saeran, who mirrored the face she made.

Saeran sheathed his sword, a muscle twitching in his jaw. "What are they up to now?" he muttered as he hopped onto a boulder and reached for her waist to help her up. He kissed her before he set her onto her feet, and Nialei sighed her aches and pains away. "Your children are a right menace, my queen."

"I wonder where they get it from, Majesty."

 8 

"…and furthermore, a princess does not battle cloaked assassins in the night on her own!"

Tir flinched, standing next to said princess being lectured by the old woman pacing before them.

"In point of fact," Princess Liadan said, "he was not wearing a cloak. Only a mask."

The old woman slammed the end of her staff on the ground. "Silence!" Then she turned on Tir. "What have you got to say for yourself?"

Tir drew back his shoulders, looking over her head at a point on the far wall. He refused to answer.

Liadan elbowed him.

He stood his ground.

She did it again, and when he glared at her, she gave him a pointed look, indicating the old woman.

Tir looked away.

"He's here to petition aid for his tribe in Aegiros," she said.

Damn her!

"Did he intend to petition it from the bleeding guts of your royal father?" the old woman retorted.

"What I intended—"

"Was to speak to my parents in private," Liadan cut in. "You can imagine that this is a delicate matter of pride. Naturally, the prince would not wish to discuss it in public court."

"Did he, or did he not attack you?"

"As you can see, I am unharmed."

The old woman narrowed her eyes. "Do not try to play me for a fool, Princess."

"You would do well to mind your place, Councilor Braith," the princess replied with steely authority. It was the first time Tir had heard her speak as one entitled to the obedience of her people. "I am still the crown princess of Wilderheim, and you will show me the proper respect."

"In the absence of your parents—"

"The rule of Wilderheim falls to the council of elders. Yes, I know. But it does not give you the authority to overrule me or Fal. When I speak, it is with the full power of the crown of Wilderheim behind my words, and you will obey my wishes. Is that understood?"

Councilor Braith compressed her mouth into a thin line, anger written in the stiff set of her old shoulders and the white-knuckled hold on her staff. Her cheeks flushed, but she answered, "Yes, Highness. As you command."

"I would advise against this," the oldest man in the company said, voice weak and raspy as if he toed the brink of death already. "We do not know the Aegiran's true intent. His tribe has already lost a member of their royal lineage here, and I have cautioned his Majesty that retaliation might be imminent. There could be armies waiting at our borders as we speak. We should prepare for war."

"If there was an army, Fal would have seen it," Liadan replied before Tir could summon enough words to use the old man's suspicion to his advantage. "The Aegiran is here alone, and the truce King Saeran had procured by marrying Queen Mari obligates us to render him aid for his tribe. Failure to do so would be a direct breach of our laws as well as of the treaty with Aegiros, and then, Councilor Kvaran, then we would truly need to prepare for war."

The elders seemed unconvinced.

"Don't you see?" she pressed. "This is our chance to mend the rift caused by Queen Mari's death. Is that not worth the risk?"

"I say no."

Tir looked over his shoulder and on instinct reached for the weapons he no longer had. Walking through the giant doorway was a creature that defied definition. It had no steady shape of its own, its features constantly changing and shifting into different faces, speaking with many different voices. Its magic was so powerful, the world around it altered in its wake. Water flooded the chamber and grass grew from the stone at its feet as clouds gathered ominously overhead. "*Daeva*," he growled.

"Oi!" the princess cried. "No fighting in the great hall."

Tir roared and charged the creature, but as soon as his feet touched the water it had brought into the chamber, he fell through it as if a deep well had opened up beneath him. Except, it wasn't beneath him. Tir was engulfed in water, yet still in the chamber, still looking at the creature. He fought to escape the prison, held his breath for as long as he could, to no avail. His lungs burned with the need for air, and he was getting nowhere.

"Not so frightening now, are you?" the creature taunted.

"Fal!"

At the princess' shout, the water dropped away from Tir, and he fell to his knees, gasping for breath, shaking, but he was completely dry. What magic was this?

Liadan went toe-to-toe with the *daeva*, arguing with it, shouting over it as Tir watched in stunned silence. The longer they bickered, the more the *daeva* began to resemble Liadan. Little things at first— the way its hands gestured, the way it stood, and then its clothing, its hair, and finally its face.

The same face he'd seen in his cell last night, with the same blue eyes that had watched him dispassionately as the creature had bled his wrist.

Liadan shoved at it, shouting, "Enough! This is *my* decision, Fal. You can go crying to Mother and Father later, but just you remember the dragon told you that *I* was to handle this and no one else was to interfere. Well, this is how I choose to handle it, so stop interfering!"

In the silence that followed, the creature's image wavered into a man very similar to Liadan. Its hands fisted at its sides and its jaw muscles twitched. While it glared at her and said not a word, Tir realized all of the water and grass had disappeared.

"You will be riding into the desert," the *daeva* said softly. "Without water, I will not be able to aid you should you encounter trouble and, make no mistake, sister, you will be riding into a kingdom full of trouble."

"I am aware," she said, subdued, staring at its face.

The creature's shoulders slumped, and water again flooded across the chamber floor, washing its face away like a mirage into something completely different. "Then so be it." The creature then turned to Tir, and crouched to put their gazes level. Tir felt dizzy watching its visage waver from old man, to young girl, to one of the elders, and even Liadan herself. "I place my sister's well-being into your care, Aegiran. Know that if any harm comes to her, I will destroy you and everything you hold dear."

When Tir had found his voice again, there was only one thing he could say: "What are you?"

"I am the Halfling son of Halfling parents. The crown prince of Wilderheim, and great-grandson of a dragon older than you can imagine. His blood is in my veins, and Liadan's. And if I can do this with water"—water once again pooled around Tir, making him gasp—"only think of what my sister can do with fire." The water receded. "Be grateful she seeks to help you. Turn on her at your own peril."

"I came to end a reign of demons, and now I am to bring one back with me?"

"Bollocks this," Liadan muttered. She pushed aside the creature to kneel before Tir, pulling a blade from her boot. He caught her wrist, but before he could stop her, she closed her hand around the blade's edge and pulled, drawing blood. "A blood oath binds all things, mortal and Other. It is this way in Aegiros, as well, is it not?"

Tir nodded, and slowly released her.

She gave him the blade, and held out her hand. "Then let's dispense with all of the nonsense and finish this. Before the gods and mortals, I vow on my blood that I will not intentionally cause harm to you or your tribe, and that I will do all in my power to help you restore your tribe to what it once was. Now, vow you will not turn against me, and will grant me protection from your tribe so I can do all of that."

Tir searched her gaze for signs of deceit. She was not like her brother. Her eyes were a deep gray with flecks of white and black, like charcoal embers, and they looked into his without wavering, waiting for him to make his choice. She held steady as her blood dripped to the floor.

"My gods have abandoned us, and yours will not listen. I cannot fight demons with armies. If you fail, we all die. When you see them, you will run, too; abandon us despite your oath."

"I have seen, Tir," she replied softly, "and I vow I will stand by you and your tribe. If you agree to our deal."

"This is very ill-advised," the creature—her brother—said.

Tir looked down at the knife he clutched, the one she'd given him without qualm, placing her trust and her life into his hands. He drew the blade across his palm, then clasped hands with her. "I vow it."

Fal buried his face in his hands. "Bloody hell."

Liadan couldn't answer him past the shiver running up her arm and down her spine. She shook herself, then stood and pulled the Aegiran to his feet, as well. Aware of their audience, she dropped his hand and wiped the blood off on her breeches.

"Have you any idea what you have done?" Braith said, breathless.

"Have the servants show our guest to his chambers," Liadan replied. "Make sure he has everything he requires. We will ride out at sunrise. Is that soon enough for you?"

Tir dipped a wordless nod.

"Good. Now, if you will excuse me, I must go prepare."

She left the great hall, taking the stairs two at a time up to the royal wing. When the door was securely closed behind her, she leaned against it, willing her heart to slow. She couldn't breathe fast enough to keep up with its beat. Lightheaded, Liadan sank to the floor and rested her head between her knees.

Someone knocked on the door.

"Not now."

"It's me," Fal said from the other side with a surprising lack of censure.

Liadan stood and let him in. Within moments, Fal had transformed her room into the waterfall clearing where they'd used to play as children. Her bed became a massive, carved tree stump that served as an altar to the gods, and sunlight filtered in through the waterfall covering her window, like a treasure waiting to be discovered. Everywhere at her feet bloomed wildflowers in all colors of the rainbow. She was slowly learning to appreciate his illusions. "Is this a peace offering?" she asked.

"You'll go west through Lyria before turning south into Aegiros," he said. "I want you to ride into Dai, not around it, and pay the proper respects to Cousin Ulrich. He'll want to see you, even if it's only for one night."

"All right," she said. It'd be good to see her cousins. They hadn't seen each other since King Halden died some three years ago. His eldest, Ulrich, now sat on the throne of Lyria, with his two younger sisters as advisors.

"I have instructed the servants to pack supplies for you. You are not to eat them unless necessary. You have coin, and you can hunt. Use that while you can. Once you run out of inns and taverns, you will have a pack full of dried meats and fruits to tide you over. Water will be scarce, so ration it, but do not be foolhardy. You must drink, understood?"

Liadan nodded. "Yes."

"Good. Now, which mount do you want to—"

"Sleipnir. He's steady and doesn't spook, and he can run for hours without cease if need be."

"He will serve you well," Fal agreed. "I would advise you to take guards with you but—"

"No one wants to ride that far south," she finished with a bitter smile. "I will be all right without them."

He reached out to embrace her, and she allowed it. "I wish to all the gods that you hadn't done this."

"I don't."

 9 

Liadan had exhausted herself making arrangements for the journey ahead, but as the sun set, as tired as she was, she couldn't bring herself to sleep. Instead, she wandered through the castle, listening to every sound and every echo. Strange, this was her home and she knew each stone like the back of her hand, but it brought her no comfort to be here.

Unaccountably lonely and anxious about what sunrise would bring, Liadan sought her brother in his chambers. They were empty. Knowing Fal could only be in one other place at a time like this, Liadan turned on her heels and headed up to his private tower library—the farthest one could get from the servants' wing without leaving the castle itself. Padding silently on bare feet chilled by the cold, stone floor, Liadan passed through the great hall and hurried up the tower stairs.

At the top, she pushed open the door to step into an underwater kingdom. Surprised, Liadan gasped, feeling water fill her lungs. She choked and coughed herself out of the room, but as soon as she'd backed across the threshold, the sensation was gone. *It's an illusion,* she realized. Bracing herself, she took care going back inside. Instinct told her to hold her breath, but Liadan fought against it, closed her eyes, and breathed in.

Not seeing herself under water helped a little, though she could still feel the soft, cushioning sand bed beneath her bare feet. It took longer than she'd thought, but eventually she convinced her body of what her mind already knew, and she calmed. When she opened her eyes again, Liadan found this world Fal had created beautiful beyond anything she'd ever seen. Light flickered and danced all around her, while brilliant flowers bloomed and swayed in a warm current that caressed her skin. A dark, mysterious cave filled the hearth, and out of it swam a school of brightly colored fish. She herself looked different. Soft webbing stretched between her toes, keeping her feet from sinking into the sand, and when she held her hand up to the light, pearlescent scales shimmered across her skin.

"Amazing," she whispered.

Fal, of course, didn't notice. Seated at the central table with his back to the door, he hadn't even heard her enter.

The dragon had sent him a trove of knowledge: animal skins branded with markings, ancient tapestries, scrolls, even stone tablets, and all of them were now spread out before him.

Liadan sidled up behind her brother to look over his shoulder, marveling at the depth of his focus as he penned a translation onto a crisp piece of parchment. Fal handled the tools of a scribe with utter reverence, considering each word carefully before he committed it to writing. The markings he translated were in the ancient dragon tongues, as mutable as dragons themselves, with no two symbols alike. It took a keener mind than most to make any sense of them, let alone divine their true meaning. "So you were paying attention during Grandfather's lessons after all," she quipped.

Startled out of his half-trance, Fal jerked his hand sideways, scratching a jagged line of ink across the page. "Liadan!"

She laughed, but held up her hands and bowed her head in contrition, while he tried in vain to contain the damage. "So this is what you do on the eve of your one and only sibling being shipped off across hostile lands to aid a deadly enemy?" His sharp look spoke more than words ever could, and his grave eyes, miraculously glaring at her from his own face, sobered her, as well. "Couldn't sleep?"

He sighed, rubbed a weary hand over his brow. "I thought this would make time move slower. I was wrong."

The school of fish paraded before him, whipping their tails left and right to seduce him with their play of colors. Fal waved a hand to shoo them away, and they scattered.

Needing something other than tomorrow to think about, Liadan looked over the dragon's offerings. "What have you discovered?"

Fal blinked down at the piece of parchment as if seeing it for the first time, and his eyes widened as he read over the translation. "Did you know this?"

"I haven't a notion of what you're looking at, so no."

He frowned at the page, consulted the skin again, compared the two, scribbled a few more things, then blew on the parchment to dry the ink before he picked it up to read. Expecting him to have forgotten she was there now that he'd found something interesting, Liadan pushed her chair back, about to leave him to it, when he spoke again. "Ancient lore tells of the coming together of six elements."

Liadan, raised an eyebrow. "Six?"

"Yes. Earth, air, fire, water, light, and darkness." He quickly counted them off on his fingers, irritated by Liadan's lack of knowledge on the subject.

She merely shrugged.

"The elements were eternal and ever-present," he continued, "and so they remained in everything born of the clash: eternal and ever-present. Where one element overwhelmed the rest, a different breed of creature emerged, stronger with the dominant element's inherent..." Fal looked at the skin for confirmation. "Attributes, I suppose. Or powers, perhaps."

Liadan waved him on, before he got too distracted by the minutiae.

"Right, yes. Stronger with the dominant element's inherent qualities, but composed of all the rest, as well, in smaller quantities. At the point of absolute balance, where no single element held dominion over the other, the equilibrium birthed a breed foretold to master all six. Yet the struggle of each element to gain dominion over the others is what strengthened them and brought life to any being born of them. In its absence, at peace, the elements settled and faded, and with them, the body did as well."

"Humans," Liadan said, sitting up to attention. "That is why they age and die so quickly."

Fal nodded. "Struggle is the driving force of life. Without it, everything dies." Again he turned his attention to the skin, and this time, Liadan was certain he wouldn't look up for a good long while. She stood to leave.

"The elements are eternal and ever-present," he read to himself. "An aspect of one is but a small part of the whole, creating a tangible connection to the eternal, and thus making the passage from one to another possible."

Liadan stopped, hand on the door handle. "What does that mean?"

Fal didn't answer.

She shrugged and left him to it, carefully closing the door behind her. No doubt by morning, her brother would have discovered some ancient magic known only to dragons and he'd be too busy experimenting with it to notice her departure. His dedication made her proud. Fal wasn't someone who'd sit and wait for a miracle. He'd done his tutors and their parents proud by working just as hard to help himself as they had to help him.

She'd miss him in Aegiros.

Strange… now that the shock of what she'd done had passed, Liadan didn't regret her decision to accompany the Aegiran to his homeland. It felt right; more so than staying here. It felt as if this was the path she was meant to walk.

As she entered the great hall, a subtle groan of wood brought her head up. She found the Aegiran on the dais, peering hard at the queen's royal seat. What in the world was he looking for?

"It's called a throne."

Startled, Tir leaped away from the chair, lowering into a defensive crouch.

"I don't suppose you have those where you come from," she said. "That particular one is spelled for protection. You can neither destroy it, nor use it to destroy whoever sits upon it."

Tir straightened, embarrassed to have been caught. "I was merely curious about the markings."

"Ah," the princess breathed, drawing closer. "Those are called runes."

As before, she was dressed in pants, but this time, her shirt hung loose to her knees, hiding her almost as well as a cape would. To Tir's shame, it frustrated him that he couldn't see what lay beneath. Only because he didn't trust her; she could be hiding weapons anywhere on her body and he wouldn't know it until she attacked. She mounted the stairs on bare feet, as silent as the night, watching him with a quizzical smile playing across her lips. "That one there, and the two next to it, mean protection against dark intents. And this one here is prosperity."

He studied the symbol she'd indicated. "These are words?"

"Not as such. They carry a broader meaning that can be interpreted differently, depending on their combinations. For example, these two together mean strength of arms, a victory in battle. But if I were to put this symbol next to that one and the one over there, it would mean strength of spirit, a blessing against corruption."

"I've seen symbols like these used before," he said, thinking of the blood marks painted onto Aesimar's horses. "They were not so benevolent."

The princess leaned against the throne's back, watching him. "Tell me about Aegiros."

"So you can destroy it more easily?" The harsh words had slipped over his tongue before he could stop them.

She had the temerity to laugh. "Yes, hateful foe, you have found me out. I dream of the day when the last Aegiran waters the sands with his blood. I have nothing else to concern myself with, except for the demise of your people."

"You mock me."

"You are astute."

"Do you not fear me at all?"

She grinned. "I do not see the purpose of it."

"You should." He stalked around the chair to her side. "In here, your warriors are but a call away. The cr… your brother has magic I would not dare incite. But when we leave, you will not have them to protect you."

She did not flee from his advance. Instead, she faced him and held her ground, her easy smile taking on a feral edge. "If I needed them to protect me, I would be worried." The princess held up her hand, then rubbed her thumb over the tips of her fingers. Her skin began to glow red, while tendrils of smoke curled up from the gentle friction. When a spark jumped, she curled her fingers into a tight fist, and when she opened her hand once more, fire nestled in the center of her palm. "Since I do not, I am not."

Tir steeled his spine against retreat. Though she'd performed the feat with frightening ease, he found himself curious about how she'd done it. He could feel the flame's heat, knew it to be real, yet her hand remained unharmed. Tir met her gaze and saw the fire's light glowing out of her eyes, as well.

The princess extinguished the flames, her eyes dimming as she did so. "Are we back to the beginning again?" she asked with the gravity of defeat behind her voice. "Is this what we will do every day until we reach Aegiros, as if a blood oath means nothing?"

Tir stepped back, then drew himself up, pride squaring his shoulders against her rebuke. "I honor my word."

"Good." She nodded. "Then I suggest you get some sleep. We leave at dawn." Giving him her back, the princess left the great hall, abandoning him in the cavernous chamber on his own.

There were no guards standing at the door, and the room they'd given him had no bars to lock him in. He could escape, leave and return to his people. But what would he bring back? Fear for them was a constant noose around his neck, choking him, pulling him back to Imarah. Tir wanted desperately to know how his tribe was faring, whether anyone was still left alive.

Prayer had never been anything but a last resort to him. Had he reached that point already, worlds removed from his homeland? Perhaps the time for it would never be more fitting than this very moment. Without an altar or any incense to guide him into meditation, he searched the wooden chair again for the symbol of strength. Placing his hand upon it felt like a betrayal, but if his own gods were too far away to listen, he had no choice but to petition the ones here.

Through a raw throat and a dry mouth, the words at last emerged. "I pray for my people. For those who cannot save themselves. I pray they be safe until I return to look after them. I pray for light to keep demons away, steel to fight off raids. I pray they know I bring back hope, and I pray it is true."

There was no sense of relief nor hint of an answer to let him know his prayers had been heard. Though he was not a religious man, he'd felt the gods working through the Magi of his tribe and he knew in his heart there ought to have been something, some unknown feeling when one was in the presence of the divine. That he felt nothing only served to prove that the gods—all the gods—had well and truly abandoned him.

Weary beyond death, Tir allowed his shoulders to slump as he made his way back to his room.

10

When morning dawned, Castle Frastmir became a beehive of frantic activity. Fal had given all of the orders himself, and it showed. Guards were posted at the gates and roaming the city to clear a path. Hostlers had readied four horses, two to ride and two drafts to carry additional supplies, bundles of which were either lashed to their backs or set aside to be added later. Cooks had prepared a hearty breakfast, none of which would be eaten, and packed heaps of dried meats and fruits, cheeses and breads for the journey.

Liadan greeted Sleipnir with an affectionate nuzzle, and an apple. "We're going on an adventure, you and I." The giant black horse bucked his head back and stomped, impatient to get going. Sleipnir was a spirited beast; he didn't like standing around unless there was a pretty mare to look at. Liadan couldn't blame him.

Across the courtyard, Tir watched the preparations, hisjaw clenching ever tighter. Liadan walked Sleipnir over to him. "This is Tir," she told the beast. "He will be coming with us." To the Aegiran she explained, "Sleipnir doesn't like strangers. He needs to get your scent, or he'll keep trying to bite you."

Tir's gaze warmed, and he held his hand up to the horse. When Sleipnir didn't nibble, Liadan nodded, satisfied with the successful introduction. "It won't be long now," she said and clucked her tongue to walk the mount around the courtyard for a bit.

Tir caught the reins, staying her as he looked into Sleipnir's eyes. "He is a fine animal," he said. High praise from someone who'd shown nothing but contempt to everything and everyone since he'd arrived.

Murmuring foreign words, he stroked an expert hand down Sleipnir's neck, made an appreciative hum as he patted the horse's deep chest. Following back across the mount's shoulder, he inspected the saddle, but it didn't hold his interest for more than a cursory glance. What he truly admired was the animal wearing it. Sleipnir was the pride of the dragon's herd. He'd been born wild, caught by the dragon, and tamed by Liadan. Standing tall, Liadan could barely see over Sleipnir's back, and he had hooves bigger and stronger than any other mount in Castle Frastmir's stables, so Liadan was shocked when the foreigner bravely bent down by Sleipnir's hindquarters to examine one of them. Even more so when the mount lifted his hind leg to show it off instead of crushing Tir like an insect.

By the time he'd finished his examination, Tir's mood had lifted a great deal. "You take good care of him," he noted.

"Sleipnir is very particular about his grooming." In fact, the mount was vain. He required frequent baths and brushing to keep his coat clean and shiny, and wouldn't let Liadan walk away after a ride until she'd brushed him down to his satisfaction.

"He is a proud animal, as well he should be."

Liadan smiled sweetly. "If it pleases you so much, I will let you groom him in my stead."

To her surprise, a smile lit up Tir's handsome face. "I accept."

Before she could quip a biting response, Fal appeared as a strapping warrior with muscled arms and scars crisscrossing his face. The courtyard overflowed with water, sending servants and hostlers scurrying for cover. Amazingly, the animals didn't even twitch. Could they see through the illusion?

As Fal approached, Tir tensed beside her, reaching for his dagger, but Liadan slapped his hand away, so he curled his fingers around Sleipnir's reins instead. Sensing his tension, the mount snorted, shifting his girth to shield Tir and bump Fal farther away.

Liadan glared at the horse. "I see where your loyalties lie."

"All is ready?" Fal asked as Sleipnir pushed against his side, making him trip sideways a step farther. Fal ignored it.

"As ready as it can be, I suppose," Liadan answered. "Thank you for all this. For everything."

"I only wish—" Another bump from Sleipnir. "I wish—" The mount chomped at his bit, glaring at her brother with one shiny, dark eye. "I wish I could—" Bump. "Stop it this instant," Fal snapped, changing into a wrinkled, old woman, "or I will put thistle in your mane."

Sleipnir tossed his head and shifted away from Fal, turning so he could slap him with his tail.

"Mane and tail," Fal growled, face rippling into a mask of menace.

Sleipnir whinnied and cowered against Tir.

Having settled that, Fal, now a lanky youth with gangly limbs, adjusted his robes and gave a nod of satisfaction.

Liadan bit back a grin.

"I brought this for you." He searched his pockets and pouches, finally withdrawing a plump, glass vial of crystal-clean water, small enough to be worn around her neck, holding no more than a swallow or two of liquid.

"What is this for?"

"I don't know yet," Fal said. "Last night I fell asleep in the library and dreamed of a great river sprouting from the desert sands. But all that water came out of a bottle no bigger than this." He shrugged, as if he couldn't understand it himself. Portents and visions divined from water were never clear in their instructions. "The dream doesn't matter. If nothing else, this will allow me to see you and speak with you if your drinking water runs out. Don't lose it."

"I won't."

Fal huffed and, pulling her into his arms, embraced her so tightly, her feet almost left the ground. He held her for a long while, not speaking, but Liadan didn't need any words.

"I will see you again soon," she promised.

"Be careful."

She nodded, then wriggled, asking to be released. Her brother stepped back, gave a farewell nod of his own, and retreated into the castle. Neither of them had had much practice with good byes.

"Mount up," she said to Tir, pulling herself into Sleipnir's saddle.

When the hostler, Micah, brought out Tir's horse and handed him the reins, he was forced to release Liadan's. After inspecting the new animal the same way he had Sleipnir, Tir looped the reins around his hand and walked the mare back to the stables.

"What are you doing?"

"I have a horse," the Aegiran replied. "My Tarabas is stabled at the inn past the green."

Liadan gaped at his back as he walked the mare all the way to her stall to remove every bit of man-made gear she wore. He then took more time to brush her down and speak what looked like a prayer against her forehead. And all the while, the hostlers stared at him as if he'd lost his mind. Liadan couldn't be certain he hadn't.

Sleipnir was getting restless, fidgeting and stomping left and right, shaking his head in irritation. His ear-splitting whinny finally summoned the Aegiran back out. He nodded to Liadan and her mount, then walked beside them when she nudged Sleipnir forward. The draft horses were tied to a lead, so well-trained, they didn't need a human touch to tell them where to go. Nevertheless, as they made their way through Frastmir, Tir fell back to visit with them, as well.

It irritated Liadan beyond words, but she didn't know why.

"Horses are precious to my tribe," he told her. "We used to have herds of them. Others would come from the farthest reaches of Aegiros and beyond for the privilege of acquiring one from us. We never parted with a mount without looking into the eyes of the one who would ride him."

"What happened?"

"What do you think?" He replied. "You should know; you said you have seen it."

"I've seen only what your tribe is now, not what it used to be before."

"You can only take the sights I possess. I have few memories of that time. They say our herds were scattered across the sands of Aegiros; our people chased them away to fend for themselves when we could no longer feed them. Some ran. Others stayed and starved with us."

Liadan was tempted to inquire whether they'd killed the horses for food, but the way he leaned against the draft mare while she nuzzled him told her it wouldn't be wise.

"Tarabas and another, a mare, are the last of their herd. Their sire died a good death in battle five moons ago. Tarabas and Zara will not leave, and my people do not have the heart to slay them."

"How do you feed them if you have no food of your own?"

"However we can," he replied grimly. Liadan didn't ask more.

Past the weaver's cottage, the road widened out into the market square, where merchants had opened their shops, preparing their wares for the day's crowds. In a little while, the square would be thick with people going about their daily tasks, but for now, it was still navigable on horseback.

To the left, the path forked down toward the rowan grove, and to the right, a vast expanse of the city green stretched on as far as the Hallowed Mountain. The meadow was tended by the clerics whose sanctuary sat atop that mountain peak. It was quite a distance away, across the green, through the woods, and up a long, treacherous staircase carved into the bedrock. Initiates entering the order's sanctuary for the first time walked the path on their knees to prove their humility and devotion.

"Over there." Tir pointed to the Wanderer's Tavern Inn.

A slow, wicked grin spread across Liadan's face. "This is where you bedded down?"

Tir glared, but Liadan ignored him and dismounted, headed for the tavern and for the innkeeper she'd known since childhood. *Won't she be happy to see me,* she thought with a wicked chuckle.

As the princess dashed into the inn, Tir gritted his teeth, taking hold of Sleipnir's reins to secure them to a post. Casting a wary glance all around, he saw many faces, none of which looked his way. Strange how the city's people treated the princess as if she were nothing more than another traveler. Did they even recognize who she was? What sort of ruler was unknown to her own people?

Loath though he was to leave the horses by themselves, Tir had no choice; gods only knew what manner of mischief the madwoman was up to now. He patted Sleipnir's neck. "Scream if there is trouble."

The dark horse nodded as if he'd understood.

Keeping an eye out for angry little man-things and creatures made of plants, Tir ducked into the inn after Liadan.

"Welcome back, *sher'nah*," the fair-haired innkeeper greeted, though her coy smile was wary now that the princess stood before her. She was still as beautiful as the first time he'd seen her, yet she paled like a ghost next to the princess with her vibrant eyes and wild, red-brown hair, her skin as smooth as cream and cheeks flushed from the sun. "Have you found what you sought?"

Why had he not noticed before how lush the princess' lips were, or the way her jerkin molded to her body? "I do not know," he answered with a frown.

The fair-haired creature smirked. "Then all is as it should be."

"We are here for his belongings and his horse," Liadan said, a hint of warning in her tone.

"Are you now?" the female said sharply. "And whatever would he need the horse for? He has you, does he not?"

What did that mean? And why had the princess' face flushed, eyes heating with the fire that seemed to be her true nature? In her anger, she looked even more arresting, and Tir found himself drawing closer.

The innkeeper glared at her, a challenge no one in Imarah would have dared against the *shansher* or any of his kin. It incensed him on Liadan's behalf. He prepared to intervene, but as quickly as the princess' temper had flared, it subsided, and she smiled beatifically, leaving him stunned. "Where is my head today?" she said. "I apologize. It's been so long, I've forgotten all things are bought and sold in your fine establishment. Of course, you will want your due, yes?"

The innkeeper gasped a protest as the princess caught her by the back of the neck and kissed her on the mouth. The creature's cheeks flushed the same way they had when she'd bargained a kiss from Tir, but now her skin darkened, her hair curled, and her entire being glowed like a star. When Liadan released her, the innkeeper fell back and, clutching her chest, wheezing out, "Gods damn you, Liadan." A moan fought its way past her lips, and her fingers curled, sharp claws suddenly digging into her flesh.

"I would tell you to duck," Liadan said to Tir, "but I don't think it'll do any good now."

Tir couldn't tear his gaze away from the innkeeper. Her glow intensified, and then, as if she could no longer contain it, she screamed, and a burst of blinding light flooded the inn.

Tir reached for Liadan and pulled her down. Arms around each other, they held on while the world disappeared around them and the unearthly scream carried on.

In the next instant, the inn fell dark and silent. Liadan's head lifted, her nose bumped into his, and then Tir was kissing her, desperate for a taste of her lips. It was more pressing than the need to draw air into his lungs or to feel the ground beneath his feet. His fingers tangled into her hair while hers clutched at his belt, and Tir heard nothing but the slight catch of her breath, saw nothing but a flash of fiery eyes and red-brown hair. And he wouldn't have felt a blade pierce his heart past the delight of her body pressing against his.

Slowly, sounds began to intrude and the haze of blindness cleared. A man stumbled out the door. Another fell to his knees and retched. Somewhere near the back, yet another man wailed with such terrible grief, it wrenched Tir and Liadan apart. Her eyes were shocked and confused when they looked into his.

The innkeeper sagged against the bar with a heavy thud and spat venomous noises their way. Tir and Liadan ignored her, still staring at each other, holding their breaths, waiting.

When the man wailed again, Tir sucked in a sharp breath, recognizing the sound of a soul dying. It shuddered through him, making his fingers curl harder into Liadan's waist, fearing she'd be ripped away from him at any moment.

The princess squeezed her eyes shut, prying free of his viselike hold to push to unsteady feet. Nothing took her away from him; she left on her own, and the moment their connection broke, the desperate need to possess her ebbed in such a rush, it left Tir feeling drunk and confused, angry to have been played a fool.

Having summarily dismissed him, Liadan sought the weeping man's form in the shadows, then looked to the innkeeper once more. "Kala?"

The fair-haired creature begrudged a nod.

"No," Liadan whispered, rushing over to the grieving man. She caught his face in her hands, urging him to look at her, but he couldn't lift his gaze, sobbing his heart out on the tavern floor. Liadan spoke to him in words too strange and too quick for Tir to understand, but he heard the sentiment behind them. When nothing else worked, Liadan pulled the man into her arms and rocked him, wept with him.

Despite the sting of whatever trick she'd played on him, Tir sensed her heartfelt compassion, and his chest ached to see tears well up in her eyes. He couldn't stand the sight of it. With a hard look at the innkeeper still struggling to compose herself, he pushed to his feet, then ran upstairs to retrieve his belongings. On his way back, he bypassed the tavern altogether and headed for the stables instead. Tarabas was where Tir had left him, a docile mount with few cares in the world, aside from his next meal. Ever since they'd entered fertile lands, Tarabas had eaten his fill, and his ribs no longer showed through his brown coat. Tir greeted him, inspecting the animal from head to toe to make certain no harm had come to him since they'd parted.

Once he was satisfied his mount was hale and well-fed, Tir saddled him, then led him outside to join the other three, letting the horses sniff and nose each other until Liadan emerged, wiping her wet face on her sleeve.

Tir pretended to occupy himself with the supply packs, but he needn't have bothered. Liadan swung into Sleipnir's saddle and, without pause or a single word, steered him onward and away from the inn, the drafts obediently following.

Tir mounted Tarabas and nudged him to catch up, but even when he pulled alongside Liadan, she wouldn't look at him, staring straight ahead. With so many questions burning in his mind, he didn't notice they'd come up to the bridge until cold water sprayed his bare arm. Tir made the mistake of looking sideways and found a water creature hovering above the river's current, its head canted sideways as it watched them.

Tir nudged Tarabas on faster, but the mount refused to pull ahead of the larger Sleipnir. Crossing the bridge was the most terrifying experience of his life, but once they were all safely on the other side, Tir remembered his questions and he turned in his saddle to face Liadan.

"You needn't look at me that way," she said, avoiding his gaze. "It wasn't real. Galen is a succubus; they feed on passion and return it in kind. If they take in too much, their bodies can't hold on to it and it must be released. Those too close can't help becoming overwhelmed by the excess that gets absorbed into them. Succubi call it a purge."

Tir committed this to memory. "That man, who was he?"

Liadan's chin wobbled, and she pressed her lips together tightly. "His name is Geir. When the Veil thinned and Others began to walk among us in plain sight, he was a soldier in my father's army, charged with keeping order and peace. He was also the first human to be openly mated to an Other, a wood sprite who gave up everything to be with him. Kala's clan was against the union and shunned her. But wood sprites feed off the connection amongst each other, and without her clan, Kala began to change and weaken. Geir begged and pleaded with them to help her. He was willing to give his life to save her, but they refused. They told him she was beyond their help, too human already to receive nourishment the way she used to.

"Last I heard, Geir had petitioned my parents for help, but there was little they could do. Kala's body had become human, mortal, but her soul was still that of a wood sprite, and though she could ingest food the way we do, her soul starved."

"She died?"

"Yes. She held on for twenty years. Galen said she asked to be taken to the rowan grove two moons ago. She took her last breath in Geir's arms and turned into a sapling. When Galen purged, she brought his most powerful emotion to the surface, amplified it a hundredfold. Gods, I can still feel it. If I'd known, I never would have…"

"What did you tell him?"

"I told him…" Liadan sniffed and rubbed her eyes. "I told him to be strong for her, that an Other's mate-bond was as eternal as their souls. It bound them beyond strife, beyond death. I told him he would be with her again."

"Is that true?"

"I don't know," she said quietly.

Tir shuddered. "Gods save me from such a wretched fate."

"You don't need gods for that," she retorted. "Just keep to your own and don't fall in love with an Other."

11

They rode almost without cease for the rest of the day, stopping only once in the town of Crossroads to take their midday meal. By the time the sun had dipped low, they were almost to the Western Ridge, a mountain range that formed the border between Wilderheim and Lyria. Though the pass was well-tended, it was treacherous to navigate at night, so they bedded down at the Royal Inn.

It was as good as its name suggested and was a convenient rest stop between the capital cities of Dai and Frastmir. Since the monarchs of the two kingdoms were related by blood, they visited often and were all well known to the old innkeeper, Jonah.

As soon as Liadan was recognized, Jonah summoned hostlers to care for the mounts. Liadan was too weary to object when one took Sleipnir's reins to lead him to the stables. She shuffled indoors, then collapsed into a plush seat by the hearth, already half asleep.

Magda, Jonah's wife, pressed a bowl of hot stew into her hands and set a bottle of mead beside her. Liadan managed a polite, "Thank you," but she couldn't eat more than a few spoonfuls. Setting it aside, she stared into the fire and let it soothe away her aches and sorrows. Next thing she knew, movement jarred her awake as someone scooped her up out of the seat and, startled, Liadan blinked to focus on Tir's dark face. "What are you doing?" she asked.

"Taking you to bed."

"You think highly of yourself."

"To *your* bed, Princess."

"Oh." He climbed the stairs slowly, carrying her as if she were a child. "I can walk."

"I know."

"Then put me down."

"I will." And he did. Once he'd reached the room they'd prepared for her, he laid her down onto the bed, then knelt at her feet to take off her boots. After setting them neatly to the side, he came back to cover her with a thick blanket. "Sleep well," he said.

"And you," she remembered to reply before he left, closing the door behind him.

With the light of the hallway shut out, Liadan couldn't fight her exhaustion any longer, and sleep claimed her as she was—fully dressed and dusty from the road.

In the morning, roosters announced the rising sun, crowing one over the other to impress the hens. Liadan hoped one of them would get cooked for lunch. She climbed out of bed and stretched, working the aches out of her sore muscles. By the hearth, her bath stood ready, gone cold from the night before. She stripped and stepped into the tub, calling up just enough fire to make it boiling hot. She washed quickly, redressed, and pulled her boots back on. No time to dry her wet hair. Tir would be anxious to move on, and she couldn't blame him. They'd tarried too long yesterday and had lost more time than they could afford.

Tying her wet tresses at her nape, Liadan hurried out the door and almost ran into Tir. For a moment, they stared at each other, at a loss for words. "Good morning," she finally said.

"And to you," he replied.

Silence.

Tir cleared his throat. "They have prepared the first meal down below."

"Oh, good."

He nodded. "Yes."

More silence.

"Are the horses ready to ride out?" she asked.

"Not yet. I will see to them." Happy to have something to talk about, he waved her to walk with him as he explained, "I took care of them last night and put our supplies away so I would know where to find them. It won't take long to get on our way again. Did you sleep well?"

"I don't remember," she said wryly. "I suppose that means yes. And you?"

"I slept." A mysterious answer from one who already said little. Unless horses were the topic of conversation, apparently.

"The innkeeper said there are merchants setting out for Lyria."

"Then we should hurry. We need to get ahead of them before they enter the pass, or their wagons will block the road and it'll take us twice as long to cross the range behind them. I'll settle our bill with Jonah, you start saddling up. I'll meet you in the stables in a moment."

He murmured in agreement and hurried ahead to see to his duties. Liadan, meanwhile, sought out Magda. "It's been a while since we've seen one of his kind this far north," the innkeeper's wife said, something brittle in her tone.

Liadan had no time to examine it. "I wish to thank you most kindly for your hospitality. We will need food to take with us, and then I can settle with you for the two rooms and your services."

"One room," Magda corrected.

"I beg your pardon?"

"One room, Highness. The Aegiran slept in the stables."

"Why?" Surely his love of horses didn't extend that far.

"I suggested he would be more comfortable there." Despite a flicker of unease in her eyes and a nervous folding of her wrinkled hands, the innkeeper's wife continued to speak her piece, nose in the air. "My husband fought alongside your father's men in the war. He knows what manner of people they are, and neither of us felt it appropriate for him to sleep under the same roof as one of the royal heirs. We thought your Highness would have requested it yourself, had you not been so worn out from your journey."

Fire burned through Liadan's veins, and she had to step away, take a deep breath to rein it back in. "You made him sleep in the stables?"

Realizing she'd misjudged, Magda sputtered. "W-we run an honest business here, and extend every courtesy to our royal guests. Why, we'd give the clothes off our back to one in need!"

"And you will," Liadan said thoughtfully. Reaching out to Fal in her mind, she made certain her brother was awake and listening. She wanted him to hear what she said next. "Listen well, Magda Westborn. You will pack your best food and wine for me and my Aegiran companion. We'll also require soaps and cloths, and spare clothing, if you have any."

"And you will, of course, pay for it all?"

"Oh, yes. A contingent of royal guards will be arriving from Frastmir before the day is done to give you what you deserve."

Magda paled. "Your Highness, please forgive us if we overstepped, but—"

"You've done far worse than that. You have insulted and mistreated the prince of Wilderheim's long-time ally. In your place, I would pray he is more forgiving than I."

What manner of punishment do you think will be fair? Fal asked.

The lofty bitch made him sleep in the stables. What would you do?

Leave it to me, he replied, and Liadan knew the next time she came riding into the Royal Inn, Magda and her husband would not be there. "Why are you still standing here?" she demanded of the woman. "I gave you an order. Move!"

Are you all right? Fal asked.

The nerve of them!

Yes, what nerve to be suspicious of a strange man travelling with the king's only daughter.

The stables, Fal!

I heard you the first time. Do you honestly think it'll be any different in Lyria?

She hadn't considered that. The war with Aegiros had been a terrible thing, but for decades, there had been nothing but peace between the northern kingdoms and the south.

Magda and two of her servants came rushing back in no time, carrying cloth bundles. They set everything before Liadan with bows so low, they almost touched the ground. Muttering pleas and apologies,

Magda kissed Liadan's hand.

Liadan pulled away. "Leave me." *Why did you make us ride through Dai, if you knew this would happen?* she asked Fal.

I wanted you to see how he'd be treated—the mistrust, animosity, and hatred, perhaps even violence. He will have no friends there.

He will have me, she insisted.

As if she hadn't spoken at all, Fal added, *You need to see it and prepare yourself, because everything he'll encounter, you will feel twice over, once you step foot in Aegiros.*

And there was the crux of it. Lyria had won the war with Aegiros. Though it had sustained much damage, they'd had victory on their side, and a chance to reclaim their kingdom. Tir's tribe had been not only defeated, they'd been humiliated, and then hurt yet again when Mari had died in Wilderheim. They had more reason to stone Liadan to death than to trust she'd do anything to help them. A life for a life was meant to end a war. What if they demanded her life in exchange for Mari's to settle the debt?

Liadan snatched up the bundles and went in search of Tir. When she found him, he'd already burdened the drafts with their supplies and was saddling his own mount. "I would like you to change before we ride out," she said, handing him a bundle of clothes from Jonah. They wouldn't fit him well, but they'd make him look less threatening than his Aegiran attire.

"Why?"

"Please," she said.

Tir must have read something in her eyes. He accepted the bundle, but made no move to disrobe. "I do not care what they do or say. I do not fear Northmen."

"I know. But I do."

He stalled for a moment longer before he left to do as she'd asked. While he was gone, Liadan finished saddling Sleipnir, then checked to make sure nothing was overlooked. The innkeeper and his staff didn't come near either of them again, though several stuck their heads around corners to watch from a distance.

As the merchants started on the road headed west, Liadan led the horses outside. At last, Tir emerged. Jonah's pants were too short and too wide on him, but at least the shirt was serviceable. He'd tied back his long, black hair, but even though he was now dressed in the proper way, nothing could hide the dark shade of his skin or the proud set of his shoulders. His eyes dared anyone to cross him, and the swords strapped to his saddle made him look all the more menacing when he mounted Tarabas.

"Does this please you?" he asked, without looking at her.

"No," she said honestly. "Once we cross the pass, we will get you clothes that fit."

"I do not want more costumes!" Tir snarled. The clothes she'd made him wear felt ridiculous; nothing fit as he was used to, making him feel a fool for giving in to her request. When he sat on Tarabas, the pant legs pulled out of his boots, exposing the skin of his calves, and he was drowning in a huge shirt with sleeves so wide, he could have made two more shirts out of them. Everything hindered his movements, and it did nothing to disguise what he was.

"Then the next time a peasant tells you to sleep in the stables, you tell them who you are," the princess returned, matching his ire. "Tell them who you ride with." There was a challenge in her eyes as they locked onto his. Last night, when he'd taken over the care of their horses, he'd thought they assumed him to be a servant. He'd been given a pallet and a cold meal, but after he'd carried Liadan to her room, the proprietors had become outright hostile, all but chasing him back out to the stables.

Tir could have demanded better simply by telling them who he was. He hadn't, because he'd already known it would only make matters worse. He'd chosen instead to hide in the stables, where the animals showed him more courtesy than these Northmen.

Liadan wasn't trying to humiliate him; she was giving him a choice: Either try to fit in as best as he could and hide among these people for the time being, or show them who he truly was and hold his head up high when they threw their rocks.

Tir looked around at the merchants who'd stopped to stare at him. They took in his face and his clothes, then looked to his companion and sneered. Liadan noticed, too. But rather than abandon him and set herself apart, she stayed by his side, enduring their judgment while he made his choice.

"How hard can we push the drafts?" he asked. Tarabas might have looked half-starved, but he was strong and fast by necessity. Compared to what he'd been through to get there, the journey back would be a pleasure ride. Sleipnir had energy to spare, if the way he pranced restlessly was anything to go by. But the draft mares were so burdened, he didn't want to risk injuring them.

In answer, Liadan clucked her tongue, and Sleipnir took off, setting the pace at an easy trot. Tir hadn't come this way riding north, hadn't even looked toward Lyria, but had instead ridden straight to Wilderheim and its royal city. To see the mountains open up before them as if the rock had cracked under immense pressure was a marvel to him.

Inside the pass, the path wasn't straight, and it wasn't as easy as he'd hoped. The rocky walls stretched so high on either side, he couldn't see their tops, and the path's curves tricked the mind. If he held a hand just below his eyes to cover the dirt road, the walls looked like seamless rock, and when the path was too narrow for the burdened mares to walk side by side, Tir found it difficult to breathe. He kept his gaze skyward to remind himself he was not entombed, and to look for telltale signs that they were about to be buried beneath an avalanche of spine-crushing boulders.

It didn't help when Liadan said, "The path isn't usually this narrow. There must have been a rock slide recently."

"Are you frightened?" He was.

The princess grinned. "No. These mountains are the toughest rock anywhere in the world; there's little that will harm them. When the masons quarry it for stone to build up castle walls, they blunt their instruments a thousand times to remove a single block. The rock slide must have been triggered by lightning. And look up, prince. The skies are clear."

"Fortune favors us, then."

Liadan's whoop bounced off the stone in an endless echo.

Despite her confidence, Tir did not take a full breath until they'd emerged on the other side. From there, the road was clear across the countryside. Herds of cattle grazed here and there, and dark patches of forest dotted the landscape as if drawn on a map. More wagons and merchants came toward them, and Tir looked back into the chasm. How did they think to pass through, when those from the other side hadn't yet emerged?

"There's an order to the pass," Liadan explained. "Travelers must make their way from Wilderheim first, and all must be safely across before the sun is at its zenith. Those going the other way aren't allowed to enter until then, and if anyone is caught in the pass at the wrong time, those going opposite are entitled to force them to return."

Tir was only too happy to be through it.

The ride eased somewhat after that; the road was well-traveled and plenty wide. To spare the horses, they slowed down to a walk, and Liadan adjusted her seat in Sleipnir's saddle to lie back on top of him. A blade of grass held between her lips, she watched the clouds and hummed a tune, completely at ease and trusting her mount to know his way and take care of his rider.

"How can you do that?" he asked.

"It's easier than sitting on my arse for days at a time. Try it."

"I'd rather not."

Liadan laughed.

Tir's lips twitched in answer, but he schooled himself not to smile. "When we stop to rest, I am going to burn these clothes."

"Do you want to change now? I promise not to look."

He scowled. How easily her mood had improved from this morning. "Why are you so happy?"

She shrugged. "I am comfortable. The day is warm, the sun is high, birds are singing. My disgruntled companion has stopped growling at me, and I look forward to seeing my cousins. There is much to be happy about. Why are you so *un*happy?"

"My tribe is dying."

She squinted at him, shading her eyes from the sun. "Tell me about them. Do you have brothers and sisters?"

"Yes," he replied shortly, thinking again of Halima. Was his father still alive? What if another raid had happened in his absence?

There, at least, he did not worry. Farraj and his *kharesh* would fight to the death to defend them. What worried him more were the demons, and the thirst and hunger.

"Are you wed?"

"No."

"Is there a sweetheart waiting for you?"

"A what?"

"Someone you care for. Someone you might wish to court or wed one day."

Tir flushed when her teasing tone brought to mind the day before. He blamed the innkeeper's purge, as Liadan had called it, for making him lose his head, but regardless of what the magic had made him do, he couldn't deny a kernel of what it'd made him feel had remained afterwards.

Before, he'd viewed the princess as a strange and powerful creature, a skilled fighter with magic beyond imagining, whose beauty only made her that much more dangerous. Though he was still wary of her abilities, what he saw now was her spirit. Liadan embraced life, and everything it brought her, as a gift. Her joy made him forget his worries, and her smile, so easily given, coaxed one from him in turn, and although it made him feel like a traitor for wanting to embrace such happiness, Tir found the temptation of temporarily shucking off that immense burden almost too hard to resist.

Liadan made him want to be happy when he had no right to be, and that made her more dangerous than the fire she wielded with such ease.

When he failed to answer her, Liadan sat up in her saddle. "Anyone you fancy?" she prodded. He didn't say a word, and she frowned. "I am not sure what to make of that."

"Good."

She scowled, muttering something under her breath.

Satisfied to have won this small victory at least, Tir shifted in his saddle to ease some stiffness out of his legs. He'd almost forgotten the princess was there, when she said, "Teach me your language."

With a put-upon sigh, he said, "*Naras tograth fa toran di taprath.*"

She repeated the phrase smoothly, and Tir suspected that was all it took for her to memorize it. He'd have to be careful what he said in her presence. "What does it mean?" she asked.

"It is an old proverb. It means: a wise man knows to hold his tongue."

12

Liadan continued to talk on her own, undeterred by Tir's lack of communication. If she'd prattled for hours on end, he would have been tempted to cut off his own ears.

A wise man, however, would have learned by now that Liadan was unlike any female he'd ever met. She talked, yes, but everything she said had some use to him. She spoke of the northern weather patterns—how the sun sometimes mercilessly beat down for weeks on end, but when the heat wave broke, a massive storm cooled the air within hours. They were passing through just such a heat wave now, and knowing the signs of an approaching storm would help them seek shelter before it broke.

She talked of snow in the winters, when the air got so cold, water in the clouds froze and fell to the earth in white flakes, covering everything from valleys to mountaintops.

She spoke of Lyria as a kingdom of learning, open to all who sought knowledge of art, music, and philosophy, and eventually her story led into the war his father had waged. Hearing about it from the lips of a Northerner grated on his conscience; he wanted to call her a liar every time she described the Aegiran armies as brutal savages who destroyed everything in their path, raped and killed everyone in sight, women and children, alike.

When she told him about the villages burned to the ground and wiped off the face of the world, he couldn't listen any longer. "Enough! Cease your lies. My father is an honorable warrior and leader of our tribe. He would never have ordered such atrocities."

Though momentarily silenced by his outburst, Liadan was in no way cowed. "It's easy to believe the best of our people and the worst of our enemies, when neither of us was alive to see them at war," she said, not unkindly. "You don't need to believe my word. The villages I speak of are south of Dai on the way to your tribe. We will follow the path your father took, and you will see for yourself."

Several villages lay along their path to Dai, but Liadan took them around whenever she could, or rode straight through when there was no avoiding it. The provisions procured from the inn would last them through their midday meal, but once night fell, they'd have to stop somewhere. Late in the afternoon, they passed through yet another village, and this time Liadan stopped long enough to purchase roasted meats and fresh bread before they moved on. Even in that short pause, Tir got a good look at the disdainful faces all around them. No one dared show disrespect to Liadan, but plenty averted their faces from Tir, closed their shops, even herded their children away at the sight of him.

At the edge of the village, only fields and a road stretched as far as he could see. They wouldn't reach another settlement before night fell. "Dai is about a day's ride that way," Liadan said.

"Do you mean for us to ride through the night?"

"No, but we can't stay here."

Tir agreed.

"We will make camp over there by the willows." She pointed to a small group of trees with long branches of leaves like a woman's tresses. They had to leave the road to get to it and only then did Tir admit, if only to himself, that Liadan had a fine head for strategy.

Amid the trees, they were sheltered from the elements and hidden from easy view, but if he climbed one, he could see as far as the last village they'd passed before this one. Anyone searching for them in the night would be carrying torches, and he'd see them long before they saw him. The creek provided water, and the grass was softer than most beds. Tir much preferred it to the stables.

While he tended to the horses, Liadan gathered wood and prepared their evening meal. Nothing lavish, but even a scrap of meat was luxury to a man who went hungry most days. With some sunlight still left after they'd finished eating, and with nothing better to do, Tir got up to stretch and put his body through its paces.

He'd never say so aloud, but the ride was taking its toll on him, too. His back and legs ached from long hours in the saddle. Exercise helped to loosen the sore knots in his muscles, and so he concentrated first on stretches, then on push-ups and sit-ups, and finally on his combat routines. Tir became so absorbed in the movements he knew by heart, he didn't notice when full night fell.

By the time he'd finished, his body was still sore, but more limber. He returned to the fire and spread his pallet beneath the willow tree.

"You do that well," the princess said.

"Make camp?"

"No, what you were doing before. Can everyone in your tribe do that?"

"Yes," he lied.

"Even the women?"

Tir glared, and Liadan smiled with a hint of gentle mockery, but no censure.

When she said no more on the subject, curiosity compelled him to ask, "Who taught you to fight the way you do?"

"My grandfather. He's really my great-grandfather."

Tir frowned. "How old is he?"

She laughed. "I don't think even he knows anymore. He was a king before humans knew such a word existed. Or so he says. I've never met another dragon to confirm his claim, and they are such solitary creatures to begin with, I doubt they would ever come together long enough to form a nation for a king to rule over."

"You're speaking nonsense."

She opened her mouth to reply, but then, seeming to think better of it, thrust her hand into the fire instead, rearranging the logs and making the flames dance to her tune. They contorted under the force of her magic, creating shapes like ethereal puppets. A great, winged lizard flew across the embers, and, by comparison, a miniscule woman looked up at it.

"Once, a very long time ago, there lived a great and mighty dragon. He was as ancient as the sky, wiser than the most learned mystics, and lonelier than an orphaned child. One day, a young maiden got lost in the woods and wandered into the dragon's lair. She was stunned by the riches she encountered. Her village was starving, their crops destroyed by famine. She looked through the treasures, and her heart swelled. A single piece of it would feed her village for a month or more. Surely no one would miss one shining jewel from a mountain of them."

The flames enacted her story, enchanting Tir with their display. His gaze followed the maiden through a dark tunnel, and as she reached out to pick up a piece of treasure, his heart beat faster, anticipating what was to come.

"The maiden picked up a heart-shaped ruby and slipped it into her pocket. But as she stepped from the cave, a terrible roar shook the ground beneath her feet and a great, lumbering beast chased her out into the clearing. She fell to her knees to beg forgiveness. She wept for her people, pleaded with the dragon to take her if he must, but to spare her village—save them."

In the fire, the dragon rose up onto his hind legs, beating his powerful wings in a show of dominance as the maiden cowered. But then the dragon stilled and settled, bringing his massive head down to look into the maiden's weeping face.

"The dragon took one look at the maiden and fell in love. He gave her a wagon of riches to make her village wealthy, then showed her the way home. Overcome with gratitude, the maiden took the treasure to her village elders, but although they rejoiced at her return, offered her anything she desired, the maiden's heart pulled her back to the dragon, in whose eyes she'd seen her very soul. She returned to his lair, and for her, the dragon made himself human and took the maiden as his mate."

Tir saw the beast transform and take the maiden's hands ever so gently into his. She fell into his arms, and the couple embraced, a passionate kiss sealing their joined fate.

"But their happiness was short-lived. As much as the maiden loved her dragon, she was still human. The child she conceived took her life as it came into this world, for only dragonblood can birth dragonblood. The child was a girl, and she became the dragon's whole world. She grew up learning from her father, sheltered from the sorrows and the treachery of human hearts. But when she grew into a woman, it was time for her to leave her father's lair and make her own way in the world. Not long after she left, she fell in love with a human king and wed him, never speaking a word of her heritage."

The scene split into two. In one, the maiden danced with her human husband while the whole kingdom rejoiced. In the other, the lone dragon paced his cave of treasures, roaring at the walls, breathing helpless plumes of fire, desperately worried for his child.

"When the queen conceived, she worried history would repeat itself, but she was half dragon and had faith in the power of her blood, and so she never shared her fears with her husband. Alas, faith alone was not enough. When the child was born—a boy to succeed his father on the throne—the woman died just as her mother had, for no one can live with only half of their being."

As the great dragon roared his grief, the human king fell to his knees at his wife's deathbed. He picked up his child, embraced him, but from the way his head turned toward his dead wife, Tir knew the king had loved her too much, and that no one would ever take her place.

And so it was. "The king never remarried," Liadan said. "But the child his wife had given him grew hale and strong, beloved by his people. Strengthened by war, yet tempered by his goodness and the love he would find, he became a far greater man and a better king than his father could have ever hoped."

The old king faded, and his son took his place. Above his head swirled a circle with the shadow of a dragon in flight caught inside. The disc shrank and settled onto the king's chest like an amulet.

"That man is my father," Liadan finished. She released the fire, and Tir remembered to breathe again. Liadan's voice saddened as she told the rest of her tale. "He'd already fallen in love with my mother when Mari arrived in Frastmir to honor their pact. For the peace they had forged, my father wed her against his heart. My mother couldn't stand to see it, and so she left, traveling north, until she came upon the dragon the same way my great-grandmother had. That was when she learned of my father's bloodline. But by the time she returned, Mari was already with child, too weak to sustain herself and the babe. They both died."

"Yet you live," Tir said bitterly. "Your mother survived, while my sister died."

"Tir, my mother isn't human. I am a Halfling daughter of Halfling parents. There has never been a creature like me, or Fal, and not even the dragon knows the limits of what we can do. Our magics are too dangerous for us to test them."

"I do not wish to speak of this anymore," he said, lying down on the pallet and throwing an arm over his eyes.

Liadan sighed, but said nothing. Instead, she fed the fire to keep them warm through the night, then lay down to sleep.

Long after her breathing had slowed, Tir lay awake, hearing Liadan's tale again in her own voice. He couldn't rid himself of the words; they'd become seared into his mind. If her story was to be believed, then Mari's death was nothing more than the unfortunate result of a series of tragedies. An accident borne of ignorance.

If her story was to be believed, then the Northern king and his mate had nothing to do with the maladies plaguing his tribe.

The possibility offered him no comfort. Without the origin he'd been so certain to have found, Tir had no way of knowing what might lift their curse. If there was anything at all.

13

While quaint, picturesque little towns and villages abounded in Lyria, the castle city of Dai was very different by comparison—almost a kingdom in its own right. Even from a distance it dominated the landscape like a bright jewel sitting majestically among polished rocks. Purple and gold flags jutted out from each tower, indicating the royal family was in residence. Two massive banners hung down the walls on either side of the main gate: one for the royal house of Dai, the other for Frastmir. Fal must have sent word ahead. This was a not-so-subtle hint that Ulrich knew she was coming, and expected her to make an appearance in his home. Blast her brother's meddlesome ways. How much had he told Ulrich about her quest?

Liadan announced herself to the armored knight guarding the gate, then watched Tir's face transform as they followed a dispatched messenger into the city. Her father had told her much had changed in Dai since the war. Before, it'd been open, with no defenses to speak of aside from a poorly trained city guard. Now, a great wall surrounded the city, but its architects had created it in the same way they did everything else: as a work of art.

Past the gates, the city opened like a breath of air. Spires rose to the sky where temples and sanctuaries dotted the streets. Houses rose upward rather than out to the sides, creating wide, sunny passageways lined with trees and fountains. The castle road had been paved with colored bricks laid out in magnificent patterns, the houses painted in bright hues and hung with banners to identify the families or merchants who owned them.

In the city square, entertainers gathered to display their craft. Liadan and Tir passed jugglers and painters, but stopped to admire the dancers performing to match the singers and their musicians. They used instruments from all corners of the world, their unearthly music filling the square.

A small group of merchants had taken up a patch in the middle, facing every direction to display their wares: delicate glass beads, seashells from Synealee, ceramics from Ravetia, jewels made by Wilderheim's craftsmen, and cloths spun in Aegiros.

But while they all smiled at Liadan, eager to make a sale, the moment their gazes touched on Tir, their faces shuttered, eyes growing fearful. Tir had reclaimed his own clothing, dressed now in the way of his people; not the fearsome assassin draped in black, but certainly not like any Northerner. He held his head high and met each unfriendly gaze without flinching. Liadan admired his courage, but worried his pride might incite the citizens of Dai into a frenzy.

Tir dismounted to examine the tiles at his feet, and she noticed the inlaid metal plaque not two steps from him. She hopped down from Sleipnir and crouched next to Tir. "Amazing, isn't it?"

"This must have taken years to create."

"Yes," she said. "This square is a monument to honor those who've fallen in the war. Where you're standing is where they lit the first pyre to burn their dead. It blazed so high, citizens of the neighboring Synealee saw it and mourned with the city."

"I have seen the city wall. My father would not have been able to breach it if they closed the gates."

"The wall was not erected until after the war. When your tribe came riding in, they got as far as that pillar over there." She pointed to an old, half-destroyed pillar of gray stone, so damaged, so out of place in its modern surroundings, many believed it was a jest. "It used to be one of many encircling a bell tower that called the clerics to their meals."

A nearby soldier nodded his agreement. "It used to be connected to a sanctuary filled with scrolls and tomes," he said. "The pride of Dai's philosophers. It was the first thing the Aegirans burned to the ground. But not before they barred the doors to lock the clerics inside."

The fast-paced song ended, and in the quiet pause, Liadan watched consternation form on Tir's face. He didn't want to believe them; even with the truth staring him straight in the face, he didn't want to think his father had been such a monster. Liadan couldn't blame him.

A flute aired a haunting song; the first strains of a sorrowful melody. A female singer joined in, voicing the words of an ancient ballad, while the dancers tightened their circle, moving 'round and 'round, weaving together, hands joined, like a living knot. In seamless transition, they separated, scattering like a swarm of butterflies, moving through the square to every person present. They kissed the guards on their cheeks and touched hands with the merchants, who bowed to them in return. A pair drifted over to Liadan and Tir, and as one dancer with beautiful brown eyes lined with kohl caressed Liadan's cheek in welcome, the other, dressed in green-and-blue silks, took a flower from her hair and pressed it into Tir's hand.

At a loss, Tir stared at it for a moment, then caught the dancer's hand as she turned to leave him, and he touched his forehead to the back of her wrist in reverence.

"Our city welcomes all who enter it in peace," the soldier said. "Wherever they might have come from."

Face drawn, Tir rose and, without a word, took Tarabas' reins to walk him the rest of the way to the castle.

The grand structure was encircled by an open green to welcome everyone, its road leading directly to the courtyard, where the king and his family already waited to greet them. Ulrich's children, ten-year-old Esmee and eight-year-old Marco, squealed and ran to Liadan, throwing themselves at her. She laughed as she hugged them.

Ulrich, his queen, and his sisters were slower to approach, smiles cordial but restrained. "Cousin, welcome," Ulrich said.

Liadan embraced him. "It is good to see you. You look well." He'd inherited his father's kind eyes and warm disposition, but unlike the former king, Ulrich was shrewd when it came to the kingdom's defense.

"And you," he replied.

Stepping back, Liadan pulled Tir to her side. "Allow me to introduce Prince Tirasdunh of Imarah. I am escorting him to Aegiros to aid his tribe. Tir, this is my cousin, King Ulrich of Lyria, and his wife, Queen Aria; his sisters, Sidda and Penelope, and his children, Princess Esmee and Prince Marco."

Tir bowed to each in turn, showing a great deal more respect to even the little children than he had to her and Fal. Liadan didn't begrudge it.

"Any friend of Liadan's is a friend of ours," Aria said in welcome. While Sidda and Penelope shared a marked family resemblance with their brother, Aria stood out among them like a rare jewel, with her bright red hair and brilliant green eyes. She was a foreigner in Lyria. Her father had been a sailor whose ships supplied Lyria along their north-south coastal trade routes, and Aria had often accompanied him on his visits to Dai, and had played with Ulrich and his sisters while the king and the sailor negotiated prices.

She'd charmed them all from the first, eventually taking her father's place at the negotiating table, and it had surprised no one but Ulrich when he'd finally asked her to be his queen during a heated argument over the exorbitant price of sea urchins. All these years later, she still won every argument—and, from what Liadan had heard, her cousin was only too happy to let her. "Please, come in. You must be weary from your travels."

Esmee tugged on Liadan's sleeve. "Lia! Lia! Will you dance for us?"

"Yes! Please, Lia, dance for us!" Marco mirrored his sister, tugging her other sleeve.

"Children, let your cousin rest awhile," Ulrich said sternly.

"*Pleeeeaaaase*, Lia." Esmee pouted. "After dinner?"

Liadan laughed. "After dinner," she promised.

Squealing in delight, the children abandoned her and turned on Tir next. While Esmee stared at him, wide-eyed, Marco touched the curved blade sheathed at his side.

"Are you a demon?" Esmee whispered in awe.

"Can you kill a man with a finger?" Marco questioned suspiciously.

"Why is your skin so dark?"

"Why is your blade crooked?"

"Children!" Ulrich snapped.

They released Tir, running to hide behind their mother's skirts.

"My apologies, Prince," the king said, flushing. "They have never met one of your people in person."

Tir bowed a quiet nod in response.

To fill the awkward silence, Aria said, "My handmaiden will show you to your room, Liadan. We've prepared one for the Prince, also. Your Highness, if you would follow my steward, he will lead the way."

Tir was about to tell them he must see to the horses first, but they'd already been led away and he'd been too preoccupied watching Liadan with her family to notice where they'd been taken.

Liadan nodded in encouragement, which left him no choice. He followed the expressionless young man into a lavish chamber with a massive bed and a terrace overlooking a beautiful green garden. The satchel containing his few belongings had been set neatly on a chair by the bed.

"If it pleases you," the steward said, "the bathing room is just over here." The man showed him to an adjoining chamber with a square hole dug into the floor. He pulled a lever, and water pumped in. "If you require anything, the bell pull will summon a servant to see to your needs. The royal family shares dinner in the dining hall at sunset. I will see to it someone accompanies you to join them when you are ready."

Tir had no words. When the steward left, he didn't have the energy to wonder at the magic of pumping water from stone. Instead, he swirled his hand in the pool, shocked to find it warm. For a long time he sat there, mind and soul in turmoil, until the sky began to darken and the echo of children's voices brought him to his feet and out onto the terrace. A trio of servants lit lanterns and torches around the garden, while the royal children danced about, chasing fireflies.

He'd already been overwhelmed at the grandeur of Frastmir, with its massive castle and strange creatures. But Dai was far beyond even that. Tir had never seen anything like it, and he doubted he ever would again. All of the world's wonders seemed to have been gathered into this jewel box of a city, and he'd never seen a more beautiful sight.

To think his people had tried to destroy it made him want to howl in denial. The princess' word, he could have dismissed. Seeing it with his own eyes made all of his beliefs crumble around him. He'd thought the Northerners were savage brutes, hiding in their cavelike castles, massacring the scantily armored Imarah warriors.

But these people were more like children than fearsome fighters. They sang and danced, and opened their arms in welcome. There was no glory in destroying a place like this. That it seemed his father hadn't cared, so long as he'd gained his golden crown, troubled him immensely.

What was he to do? What would he say to his people when he returned and they asked him about the monstrous North?

The eve had darkened into night while he'd stood there and stared. Tir washed quickly and, dressed in his cleaner clothes, laced up his boots just as a servant knocked to escort him to dinner. He followed the woman, who kept her head down, perhaps to avoid the sight of him, meeting Liadan and her own escort in the entry hall. She wore a silken blouse that exposed her shoulders and billowing pants that narrowed at her ankles. He'd glimpsed similar attire once in front of a wealthy sheikh's harem, but those women hadn't worn embroidered jerkins to cinch their bodies.

Liadan blushed at his regard. "My cousin stands on ceremony. He insists his family wear their finest to dinner."

Tir looked down at himself. The clothes he wore were the finest he owned, but after weeks on the road, they were rumpled and dusty despite his best attempts to set them to rights. "Am I presentable?" he asked, not wanting to offend his hosts.

"You look fine," she told him with a smile, then threaded her arm through his with an ease of familiarity he didn't expect. "Come, they're waiting."

Expecting a grand feast and a hive of servants, Tir was surprised when they entered a rather small chamber with a single table for the diners and several more lined along the walls with food laid out on platters. King Ulrich rose to welcome them, and Tir bowed to him and his family.

"Family is important to Ulrich," Liadan said quietly. He had to lean his head closer to her to hear her whispers. "No servants are allowed in during dinner unless one is summoned. The king and his wife will fill their plates first. Then the guests, then the sisters, and finally the children last."

Tir nodded and took his seat by her side. The queen asked Liadan about her family, and they conversed easily while the king perused the food tables. When he took his seat, the queen followed his example, but Tir noted the king did not touch his food.

"We wait until everyone has had their turn before we eat," Liadan explained.

After the queen returned to her seat, Liadan nudged Tir to stand. He took his plate and followed her around the room as she pointed out what the different dishes contained. Tir wasn't particular about his meals; if it was edible, he'd eat it. But this bounty overwhelmed him. He stayed away from exotic dishes and instead served himself what he knew, taking only what he intended to eat.

Once the sisters and the children had had their turns, the king raised his chalice in a toast. "We welcome our honored guests. We share our food and wine, and offer shelter for as long as need be. Let us drink to their health."

Everyone echoed the blessing, and drank. At last, the king picked up a knife and the feast began. Among Tir's people, men and women took their meals separately, and children weren't allowed to sit with adults. Here, not only was the family all together, but they also conversed throughout the meal, speaking easily to each other, even the children. Esmee and Marco were much better behaved now than when he'd first met them; they sat quietly and ate the same as all of the adults, spoke up only when they had something to say, and caused no trouble at all.

"Prince, Liadan tells me your tribe has fallen on difficult times."

"Yes," he said. "Our valley has become barren and we are beset by maladies."

Ulrich frowned. "Forgive me, we don't often hear news of Aegiros. As I understand, there are many tribes, yes? Why not seek aid from one of them?"

"Our politics make such a petition unwise. The resources of Aegiros are scarce; most tribes struggle to keep their people alive. Imarah's valley may have lost its water, but it holds symbolic value as the First

Valley, the origin of all Aegiran tribes, and many seek to overtake it. Another tribe would demand the land in exchange for any sort of aid, and if we gave it up, there would be nothing left for my people. We would die."

The king looked at Liadan, some silent message in his eyes, but she did not answer.

"Liadan," the queen said, "how is your brother faring?"

"As well as can be expected. I've brought him a small mountain of forgotten lore. I expect he will be too busy sorting through it all to notice my absence."

The queen nodded. "That is good. When we learned of his condition, we had our clerics search through the archives, but I'm afraid our knowledge of magics and Otherkind is very limited."

"He knows you would help if you were able," Liadan said. "The sweets you send are most comforting in his trying times."

The queen laughed. "I will be sure to send more."

At last, their plates were empty, and everyone sat back to relax.

Everyone, except for the little children, who quivered in their seats, staring at Liadan. She pretended to ignore them as they squeaked, trying and failing to be quiet, but their anticipation was palpable. Though the king glared at them, the women couldn't help the smiles they hid behind politely raised hands.

"*Liiiiaaaadaaaan*," little Marco whispered.

Liadan rolled her eyes. "Gods help me, all right."

Her capitulation was met with ear-piercing squeals of delight as the children jumped up and raced out the door.

Shaking her head, Liadan pushed to her feet. "Thank you for dinner," she said. "The food was wonderful."

"Yes," Tir added, standing to bow. "I am most thankful, as well."

"Now I beg forgiveness, as I am about to be set on fire."

Ulrich chuckled. "Don't keep them waiting too long, or they truly will take a torch to you."

Liadan gave him a crooked grin, then followed after the children.

Curiosity compelled Tir to go after her, but he wasn't familiar with the etiquette of leaving the room while the king remained seated.

Queen Aria saved him from making an awkward mistake. "Why

don't we all go? It's been so long since I've seen Liadan dance."

King Ulrich indulged her and rose from the table. The women stood as well, but waited for the king to lead the way. "Come," he said to Tir, clapping him amicably on the shoulder. "I would wager a horse you have not seen her dance yet."

"You would not lose."

They went into the garden, where the servants had moved stone benches from the central area onto the grass. While the little heirs danced around Liadan, chanting in delight, she laughed and scolded them playfully, then chased them off. They ran to perch on the very edge of a bench, their bottoms touching it just enough to satisfy their cousin, but Tir could see by how tense they were that they might leap to their feet again at any moment.

The sisters seated themselves by the children to keep them in their place, while the king and queen took the opposite bench. Tir cast a questioning look at Liadan, but she only smiled a mysterious little smile, nodding for him to sit by the king. He did, waiting to see what she would do.

"Now, we all know the rules, yes?"

"Fire burns," the children chorused. "We do not touch it."

"That is right." Liadan nodded and, crouching down, rubbed her hands together as though chilled. When she breathed on them, a cloud of sparks blew out from between her palms.

The children cheered.

She did it again, this time pushing to her feet and spinning around, spreading that cloud of bright yellow sparks all around herself. Before it dissipated, she spun again, holding out one hand as if to throw something, and a plume of fire followed her movements.

And then she danced. Her toes traced fiery trails along the ground, her hands drew lines and circles of fire through the air; her entire body glowed from within, her hair transforming into flaming ribbons that whipped around her as she moved. The sight left Tir breathless. She was stunning, graceful, an accomplished dancer, to be sure, and the spectacles she created with her flames drew even the most timid servants and maids out to watch.

Her body swayed and rocked, twisted and spun to a rhythm only she seemed to hear. But Tir felt it; with every beat of his heart, he felt it. Liadan circled, seeking out each face to make certain her spectators were all paying attention, and when she returned to the center, her dance quickened, her movements so fast, Tir lost sight of her behind the streams of fire blurring together into an almost solid sphere around her.

Then the sphere exploded up and out, and the flames contorted into the shape of a giant dragon that rose high into the sky before it finally disappeared.

Applause and cheers drew Tir's attention back to the garden and to the winded dancer who grinned and bowed, laughing when the children mobbed her, demanding she show them again.

Next to him, the king laughed and slapped his back. "Breathe, my boy!"

Tir shook himself, then clapped in belated praise.

When Liadan managed to extricate herself from the young ones to come to him, Tir pushed to his feet, taking her hands in his to examine them.

"What are you looking for?" she asked.

"Fire burns," he quoted her, searching for any sign the flames she'd played with might have harmed her.

"Yes," she said coyly, "I do."

Startled by the jest, he met her gaze. She looked so happy; her spirit shone through her eyes, as if no moment in time was more beautiful and joyful to her than this.

King Ulrich cleared his throat, and Tir released Liadan's hands as if she'd scalded him. She might as well have. "It is late. You both must be wearied by your travels. Prince, are your chambers to your satisfaction?"

"Very much so," he replied, unable to tear his gaze from Liadan.

"Good, good. Then if there is nothing else you need, I think we should all retire for the night. Please excuse me, my royal decree will be required to corral the children back into their beds after all of this excitement."

Servants again escorted them back to their respective rooms. The same steward from before informed Tir the first meal would be served whenever he was ready, then left him alone with his thoughts. As exhausting as the day had been, as troubling as he found all he'd learned, Tir lay awake, staring at the ceiling, unable to think of anything other than Liadan and her flames.

When he closed his eyes, he saw her perform again, this time for him alone, and his heart raced at the artful mastery with which she controlled her element. He fell asleep imagining what it would be like if he could do the same, dance with her amid the flames.

In his dreams, the world around him burned, yet he was unharmed. He passed through the fires as if through gossamer veils, and in their center, found the princess Liadan. She danced, but not for pleasure. Her face drawn in concentration, her brow pinched in anger, she wielded her flames like a weapon that no creature could withstand. Shadows swooped down toward her, demons whose shapes he knew all too well. They clawed at her, screamed at her. Tir knew she felt the sting of their claws, but she never stopped. Her wrath burned them to cinders as they fled, and when at last the final demon fell, Liadan's hands dropped to her sides, her knees buckled, and she collapsed in a faint.

Crying out, Tir rushed to her side, but found no heartbeat in her chest, no breath on her still lips. The fires died around him, leaving the world as black as pitch, and in his arms, Liadan's body turned to ash.

"*She did what!*" King Saeran boomed, and even the queen flinched.

Fal drew breath to repeat himself, but was instantly silenced.

"Don't speak a word. Gods damn it, boy, I thought at least one of my children would have the sense to think before they act!"

"Majesty—"

"And where in all the hells were you?" he demanded of the elders.

Braith hunched her shoulders. "We tried, your Majesty, but she was too fast. What was an old woman like me to do?"

Fal rolled his eyes, mirroring his father. Neither of them believed her to be helpless for even an instant. Old she might have been, but not *that* old.

"Your Majesty," Kvaran tried again. When no one interrupted, he seemed surprised, but regained his composure and continued. "Her Highness may have acted rashly, but her thinking was sound."

"How sound could it possibly have been if she swore a blood oath to an Aegiran?"

"She did worse than that," Fal murmured, bracing for an explosion of temper rarely seen from the royal pair.

"Woden have mercy," King Saeran prayed. Then, as if he could hardly speak the words, he asked, "How much worse?"

Fal looked to his mother for support, but she was too busy scrying the air for Liadan. "You won't find her," he said. "I already tried." The moment Tir and Liadan had entered the Western Pass, Fal had lost contact with his twin, unable to feel her in his mind. It was as if a Veil had descended between them, and he couldn't help suspecting it'd been deliberate. As closely as Liadan's disappearance coincided with his parents' return to Castle Frastmir.

Queen Nialei gave up with a frustrated sigh. "How much worse, Fal?"

"She swore a blood oath *with* him."

Silence fell upon the great hall, punctuated only by the clicking of Varr's claws on the stone floor as he paced nervously around the king and queen. The wolf pawed at Nialei's robes, whined softly to get her attention, but she didn't move, didn't even breathe, and neither did Saeran.

"I had no idea he would do it," Fal said. "I thought he would simply accept her oath and be done with it. But before I could blink, the bastard cut his hand and took Liadan's—"

"Everybody out," the king ordered on a harsh whisper, his face deathly pale.

The elders hurried through the door, and Fal wondered if any of them had the slightest notion about what he'd said.

"What words did she speak?" Nialei asked, her eyes gleaming with a fragile hope that the situation wasn't as dire as they thought.

Fal gathered water into a ball and summoned the past into its depths. The great hall appeared inside it, empty of all but the royal siblings and the elders. The Aegiran knelt on the floor, and Liadan pushed Fal out of the way to crouch face-to-face with him. She sliced her hand with the assassin's blade and said, "Before the gods and mortals, I vow on my blood that I will not intentionally cause harm to you or your tribe, and that I will do all in my power to help you restore your tribe to what it once was. Now, vow you will not turn against me, and will grant me protection from your tribe so I can do all of that."

The Aegiran hesitated. "My gods have abandoned us, and yours will not listen. I cannot fight demons with armies. If you fail, we all die. When you see them, you will run, too; abandon us despite your oath."

"I have seen, Tir," his sister replied, "and I vow I will stand by you and your tribe. If you agree to our deal."

Nialei pressed a hand over her mouth to contain a whimper. Her knees buckled, and she sank to the floor. Saeran wrapped her in his arms, but both king and queen were shaken.

In the watery vision, the other Fal said, "This is very ill-advised."

The Aegiran looked down at the knife he clutched, then drew the blade across his palm and clasped hands with Liadan. "I vow it."

Nialei sobbed, turning her face into her mate's shoulder.

"Have our horses saddled," Saeran ordered, voice quivering. "If they rode through Lyria, we can intercept them in the south before they reach Imarah."

"You can't," Fal said. "Mother's oath to restore the Veil prohibits her from leaving Wilderheim except to go to an Otherland."

"I swore no such oath," Saeran growled.

"But you are bound to Mother."

"He's right," Nialei said. "You can't go after her any more than I."

"I will not let my only daughter be tricked into this! Send the guards, round up a gods damned army, summon the dragon—just bring her back!"

As though he'd been waiting at the door, the dragon entered the great hall in his human form. Though he stood taller than Saeran and had darker hair, the two were mirror images of each other. And neither of them had aged a day since reaching adulthood. "You fret for nothing," he said. "Liadan is precisely where she needs to be."

His words shivered across Fal's mind with the same resonance he encountered whenever he tried to reach out to Liadan. "It was you," he realized. "It's your magic keeping us from Liadan."

Nialei gasped. "How could you?"

The dragon's distant gaze turned on the queen. "No one can undo a blood bond; not humans, nor Others, or gods. The girl chose her path and forged her own destiny. I would not keep her from it any more than I would have kept Saeran from taking you as his mate. Interfering now will only make matters more difficult for her."

"I trusted you with my daughter's safekeeping!" Saeran snarled.

"And she is safe, for the moment," the dragon replied.

Incensed, the king advanced on the dragon, but Nialei intervened.

"Can you still bring her back?"

The dragon sighed. "I will not, and neither will you. There is a shroud of Darkness over the First Valley. I cannot see through it, but I sense its origins were the day the twins were born. Liadan might be the only one who can discover if there is a connection."

Nialei gaped. "What?"

"What are you saying?" Fal demanded.

Saeran rounded on the dragon. "You sent my daughter into Demon lands?" With each step he took, his ire rose until flames licked out of his palms and engulfed his arms like gloves. "You dare step foot into my home and tell me you sent my daughter to her death!"

"Saeran!"

Nialei's warning went unheeded. Saeran caught the dragon by his throat, eyes blazing with blue flames. Fal had never seen his father this way and prayed to all the gods he never did again.

"Saeran, stop!" Nialei broke his hold and stepped between them.

The dragon was unaffected by Saeran's attack, which incensed the king even more. "I did not send her anywhere. I merely afforded her the opportunity to choose on her own."

"She is my daughter!" Saeran fought Nialei's hold on him, but it was a halfhearted attempt. As powerful as she was, Saeran's love for his queen kept his own strength in check.

"Yes," the dragon said, "and the time has come to let her live her life, as I have done with my own."

The reminder of his mother, and of her death, ripped an anguished howl from Saeran.

"Da…" Fal tried, but words failed him.

"They have not yet left Lyria," Nialei said. "If you fly, you can stop them before they do. You can bring her back to us."

The dragon sighed.

"Please," the queen begged, another thing Fal hoped to never see again. Nialei, one of the most powerful wizards who'd ever lived, a Halfling daughter of a water sprite and some unknown woodland Other, had never had the need to beg anyone for anything.

"I cannot," the dragon said. "The path Liadan chose to walk cannot be altered except by her own choice. If she wanted to return, she could have done so a thousand times."

Fal couldn't breathe. He escaped from the great hall and the sight of his parents breaking down into helpless tears, slammed the doors to his chambers and rushed to the bowl of water. He slapped the surface to summon Seol.

His mentor appeared instantly. *Fal, is something the matter?*

"Can you bring her back?"

Seol blinked his overlarge eyes. *No,* he answered simply, without a hint of remorse. *Blood binds all things. The moment your sister joined hers with the Aegiran, her fate was sealed to his.* He cocked his head. *Did you not hear the dragon?*

"I heard every word."

Then you did not listen closely enough. If the Darkness plaguing the prince's tribe is tied to your births, then perhaps the answer to your control over the illusions you weave is hidden there. Liadan could mend you. If she survives.

The thought had briefly crossed his mind, but the feeble hope had quickly been extinguished by his fear for his sister's life. He would not sacrifice her to make his own existence easier. "If she dies—"

Then she dies, Seol retorted in a tone he always used when Fal tried his patience. *You will live. Damaged as you are now, but you will live. I will live. Your parents will live. The world will not mourn a Halfling's end, not even one as powerful as Liadan.*

With a roar, Fal hurled the bowl against the wall with enough force to break its copper shell in half. This was his fault; he'd listened to the dragon's instructions, when he should have listened to his own heart. If he had intervened as he'd wanted to, Liadan would never have handfasted the human; she would have fumed and blustered, and blamed him for all manner of petty grievances, yes, but she would have been home, she would have been safe.

What's done is done and cannot be undone. The chorus repeated in his mind until he thought he'd go mad with it. He had to do something.

Fal ran out of his chambers, headed for his tower. In all the gods damned lore, countless secrets forgotten by time, there had to be an answer. Fal would find a way to fix this, if it was the last thing he did.

In the morning, the king's guard requested Liadan's presence. The captain, a long-time friend and companion to Ulrich, was familiar with the dragon's teaching methods and had offered to spar with her whenever she was in Dai. It was good exercise to keep her muscles loose, but it didn't offer much of a challenge. She half-hoped Tir would be there. Having fought him before, she itched to match her blade to his again.

Liadan was tempted to ask him but, although he'd stopped snarling at her and giving her dirty looks, he still kept his distance. She wondered at that, since he'd had no trouble carrying her to bed during their last night in Wilderheim, or taking her hands after her dance as if worried she might have hurt herself.

The Aegiran prince-turned-assassin confused her more every day. One moment, they were almost friends; the next, he retreated inward where she couldn't reach him. She wanted to understand him, if only to interpret his brooding silences as something other than contempt for her and everything she stood for. Liadan was used to all sorts of different reactions, but somehow, Tir's mattered more than anyone else's. That couldn't bode well.

She shook her head to rid herself of a frown, then picked up her sword and met the captain in the training ring. The dragon had taught her better than to let her mind wander during a fight.

Vale's preferred weapon was a spear longer than she was tall, with a metal point the size of her forearm and a weight that could tip Vale's page sideways if the youth wasn't careful. It gave him a farther reach than Liadan's sword; she'd need to be faster and more cunning to get at his weak spots.

With little more than a cursory bow, their bout began. Right away, Liadan felt the toll of having spent too much time in the saddle. She should have done as Tir had, practiced on her own when they'd stopped for the night. Now, the careless oversight was costing her.

"You've slackened in your training," Vale taunted as his men-at-arms gathered around.

Liadan grinned, refusing to show weakness. "I thought I would be kind this first time. You present a much larger target than I anticipated." She skirted his spear, then elbowed him in the gut.

Vale groaned, sweeping the spear to trip her. When her back hit the dirt, he leaned on his weapon like an old man on his walking stick, and jeered. "And you've slowed down."

Liadan pushed to her feet. "I'd like to see you after a week in the saddle." Their weapons clanged together, and the men-at-arms cheered.

"Delicate princess bruised her backside, did she?" Vale slapped said backside, to the wild hoots and shouts of his men.

"Oi!" she cried. "Did your mum not teach you it's rude to grope a highborn lady?"

Vale grinned. "She tried, but I liked my Da's lesson better." He spun his spear in the air, exposing his belly, a trick she wouldn't fall for again. Vale was wicked fast when he wanted to be; one cracked skull last time they'd sparred was all Liadan needed to learn that lesson. "He said there's no difference between highborn and lowborn when their skirts come up."

Liadan scowled, showing off her pants and lack of a skirt. Vale took the invitation, openly ogling her legs, which distracted him enough to lower his spear, and allowed Liadan to knock him back on his arse.

"Foul!" one of his men cried.

"What foul?" she demanded, singling him out.

The youth, a trainee by the looks of him, flushed and tugged at his messy hair. "Unlawful use of feminine charms?"

Liadan thrust an imperious finger at Vale. "He is swinging what amounts to an enormous wooden cock at my head, what is that?"

"Your lucky day," Vale answered, kicking her feet out from under her.

Liadan fell forward, but caught herself before her face hit the dirt. The guards whooped as Vale snatched her up by the ankle, and pulled her across his lap. Liadan gasped when his meaty hand delivered a stinging slap to her backside. Bracing herself, she curled her head down, then pushed off with her toes. The flying somersault hooked the crook of her knee around his neck and brought him down. Taking advantage of the new position, Liadan locked her ankles together to get a good choke hold on him. "What do you say?"

Vale grabbed for her thighs. "Thank you, gods?"

She smacked his head, and squeezed tighter. "Try again."

"Yield!" he choked.

"Better." Liadan released him and rolled to her feet.

As he sat on the ground, Vale rubbed at his neck, grinning while he caught his breath. "Must say, I've never had a sweeter defeat. Do you end all of your fights like that?"

"My father would skewer you if he heard you talk to me that way," she said, but she, too, was smiling.

"Then I say I must be lucky twice. First, to get my head between those lovely thighs; and second, to escape your father's wrath. The gods are generous today."

Liadan laughed, shaking her head at his banter, until she caught sight of Tir watching them from the shadow of a column. She saw little more than his outline but felt the weight of his stare, and a shiver of awareness ran up her spine.

"Liadan, a word?"

She'd only glanced away for a moment to acknowledge Ulrich's summons, but when she looked back, Tir was gone. Had she imagined him there? "On my way, cousin."

Vale pushed to his feet, then swept a cordial bow, though his eyes never left her face. His smile was wicked when he said, "Until next time, Highness."

Liadan winked at him before following Ulrich into his private study. He wasn't happy with her, she could tell, but he'd seen her spar with Vale before. The captain's mouth was perhaps bigger than was wise, but he was an honorable man. Ulrich wouldn't have appointed him to his post otherwise.

The king of Lyria seated himself in a smaller version of his lavish throne. "Do you know what you're doing?" he asked without preamble.

"I missed the first meal," she realized. "I apologize. It was bad of me to leave my companion unattended in your care."

"Gods damn it, I don't care about the meal, Liadan. I care about you prancing off to Aegiros on your own. Does your father know about this?"

Surprised by his outburst, Liadan answered carefully. "I imagine he will soon, if he doesn't already. I didn't wait to ask for his blessing."

"Because you knew full well that neither he, nor your mother, would have allowed this insanity if you had. And now you've put me in the position of having to make the decision in their stead."

"Nobody asked you to intervene, cousin. I don't need—"

"You do!" Ulrich insisted, then snapped his mouth shut and shoved to his feet to pace while he regained his composure. "I cannot pretend to know what all of this is about. I've not a drop of magic in me, thank all the gods, and I am well aware the rules are much different in Wilderheim than they are here, especially for one of your unique lineage."

"But...?"

"But you are so young—"

"I am a woman grown."

"Barely," he shot back. "Not a fortnight ago, you were living in seclusion in the dragon's cave, and the last time I spoke to your parents, they called you their 'little hatchling.' And now you expect me to let you go riding off alone with *him*? Do you have any idea what your people will say? What mine are saying already?"

"Do you think I care?" she challenged quietly. "You're right, Ulrich. You don't understand what's happening. If you did, you wouldn't be wasting my time on this discussion."

"I want you to take a contingent—"

"They'll slow us down. We can ride faster on our own. As it is, we've already lost time because of the drafts. We may have to leave them here and go on with Sleipnir and Tarabas alone."

"You've lost your bloody mind."

Liadan shrugged. "As my grandfather likes to say: you can't lose something you never had."

Ulrich shook his head. "No, I won't allow it. I can't let you leave."

She laughed. "What will you do? Lock me in the cellars?"

"If necessary."

"Ulrich, be reasonable. You can't keep me here any more than you can stop the tides from turning, you know this. I swore an oath to help Tir and his tribe."

"And you did so without a notion as to what would be required of you. Tell me something, cousin, when is your next cycle?"

Liadan felt the blood drain from her face.

Ulrich spat out a foul curse. "Foolish girl! What do you expect me to do now? Wish you well and pray?"

Liadan couldn't bring herself to say another word. Turning on the balls of her feet, she kept her pace just short of breaking into a run as she headed for the door.

"You'll kill him, Liadan," Ulrich called after her, "without ever meaning to."

She slammed the portal shut behind her.

"Princess—"

Startled, she spun around, swinging.

Tir caught her fist before it connected, but he showed no ire at being attacked without provocation. "Are you well?" he asked, voice too low, face too close to hers.

"Fine." She stepped back. He didn't release her hand. "I only need a moment to gather my gear, then we can be on our way."

Tir stared as though waiting for her to say more. When she didn't, he nodded and released her. "I will saddle Sleipnir and Tarabas with our most pressing supplies."

So he had listened to her fight with Ulrich.

Liadan hugged herself against the feeling that he'd somehow uncovered one of her secrets. When she returned to her chambers to pack, her hands were shaking. She tossed her sword onto the bed and paced awhile, rubbing the torc around her neck for comfort. She'd tried to reach out to Fal to let him know she'd arrived safely in Dai, but only silence had answered her call. She'd met with the same when she'd sought the dragon in her mind. His magic was fleeting in the torc's twisted rods, but even that soothed her. And it steadied her hands long enough to finish packing.

Ulrich didn't see her off. In his absence, Aria acted as ambassador wishing them both a safe journey, offering blessings for Tir and his tribe.

Liadan embraced her, grateful her cousin had found such a wonderful woman to rule by his side. "Be safe, cousin," Aria told her. "I will pray for you both."

"And you, Majesty. I will see you again soon."

They set off through the city, their mounts burdened with enough supplies to last them a week if they rationed properly, but they only had two waterskins between them. Refilling them in village wells along the way was no hardship, but Liadan worried what they'd do once there was nothing but dry dirt and sand beneath Sleipnir's hooves.

"I did not ride this way coming north," Tir said. "How long until we reach Aegiros?"

Liadan calculated the time from what she'd seen of Ulrich's maps. "Three days, if we rest the horses. Two, if we ride hard."

"Then let us ride." He spurred Tarabas on with a savage shout, taking off without a backwards glance.

Sleipnir reared and whinnied as if Tir had insulted him by starting a race without notice, and ran headlong after him, eager to prove himself better.

They didn't stop or speak again until late afternoon, when the skies darkened with a great thunderstorm that forced them to seek shelter.

They were in luck to find an abandoned stone cottage, half destroyed, but with three walls still standing and a roof that hardly leaked at all. Liadan built a fire where it was shielded from the worst of the rain. There was enough room for both of them and the horses, and once Sleipnir had herded Tarabas into one corner so he wouldn't stomp them to death in his panic, everyone settled.

They ate in amicable silence, Tir keeping a watchful eye on the storm, Liadan lost in her thoughts. She could tell the thunder made him nervous, but as a proud warrior, he didn't show fear beyond the occasional jaw twitch.

Liadan studied him across the flames while he was too preoccupied to notice. All her life her family had told stories about the Southerners, about how fierce they were, nigh unstoppable in battle. Fal used to say if an Aegiran ever met a true berserker, it'd be a battle people would sing about until the end of time. They'd admired them for it, seduced by the mystery of a people they'd never encountered.

Yet so many feared and despised them. In Lyria, even the mention of Aegiros was met with contempt, memories still too fresh, even decades after the war. Only now, having met Tir and spent time with him both on the roads and in Lyria, watching how the other North-erners looked at him, listening to what they said about him, could Liadan see the great pains her Da had taken to make sure neither of his children would ever know such hate.

Tir was his own man, strong and proud, but his pride didn't blind him to other possibilities. Liadan knew it was custom in Aegiros for women to be overlooked, but while among the Northerners, Tir had shown her and her family the same respect he would have afforded another man; he listened to her, even when he didn't want to hear what she had to say, and she wanted to believe he trusted her, as well. Not because he had to, but because he deemed her worthy of his trust.

That might change once they entered his homeland, where she'd likely be expected to adhere to his customs the way he'd honored hers, and Liadan wasn't certain what that would do to them. She'd never bowed to anyone in her life, nor had any reason to follow anyone's orders without question. In Aegiros, she might offend simply by meeting a man's gaze, and everyone would look to Tir for guidance where she was concerned.

One man's disdain she could handle, but she couldn't stand in opposition to an entire kingdom. Could she trust Tir not to betray her in favor of his pride? His blood oath bound him to keep her safe from those in his tribe who meant to do her harm, but there were many ways to do that, including locking her away in a cell somewhere until the end of time.

Tir met her gaze across the flames, and Liadan flushed to have been caught staring, but she didn't look away. Trust was such a fragile thing—so difficult to forge, so easy to shatter. Her heart told her this was right. The man sitting before her had already proven he'd do whatever it took to help those he loved, and Liadan admired him for that. She could only hope that, in time, he'd come to regard her as someone worthy of even a fraction of that devotion. Because without him, her life was forfeit in the desert.

Tir was the first to look away, turning his attention back to his meager meal. When he'd finished it, he gazed into the fire, his bright eyes heavy-lidded. *What does he see in the flames?* she wondered, when lightning struck outside, making him flinch. He tensed, staring at the rain as if it would come in and drown him in his sleep. Floods were common in this region, which was why they'd taken shelter on a hill, far from any danger. Tir was well aware of this, yet every time lightning struck, his body went so rigid, she could see his neck muscles go taut. Still, when the bright light had faded, he mastered his fear and relaxed a little.

"Thank you," she said to distract him.

His gaze swung back to her, and he frowned. "For what?"

Liadan blushed. "For not asking questions." If he'd heard her tell Ulrich they'd be leaving the drafts behind, he must have also heard Ulrich call his dire omen after her.

"Would you have answered if I did?"

She shrugged, ducking her head.

"I thought as much." She could tell he wasn't happy about it, but he didn't say anything more.

Liadan yawned. After another long day in the saddle, her back ached. She stretched up and to the sides, twisting left then right to work out the stiffness along her spine, wincing each time something popped. Then she set out her pallet and hunkered down for the night. Despite the storm's din, Liadan was so tired she fell asleep the moment she closed her eyes, without another care in the world.

Thunder woke her some time later as the worst of the storm passed overhead. What had started out as a downpour with an occasional distant lightning flash had quickly turned into a deluge mixed with ice as bolts struck the hill almost without cease. They lit up the night, shook the ground with deafening booms, terrifying Tarabas and making even Sleipnir nervous.

Liadan got up to soothe them, not even giving her riding companion a second thought, until she heard him roar outside. By the light of the storm, she found him in the middle of a clearing that used to be the village square. He was shirtless, soaked through, brandishing his daggers, and shouting at the heavens as though he dared them to strike him down.

He stomped amid the lightning storm, waved his blades, screamed at nothing, while fires sprouted left and right, extinguished almost immediately by the endless torrent.

Terrified he would get himself killed, Liadan shouted, "Are you mad? Get back here!"

But the storm was too loud for her voice to carry, and as the lightning intensified, the crazed Aegiran began to dance.

"Tir, get back here!" She waved her arms to get his attention to no avail. Her choices were reduced to throwing a fireball at him or going out there herself. He wouldn't have appreciated the first, and she wasn't mad enough to attempt the second. What in all the hells had set him off like this?

As he turned in a circle, she screamed at the top of her lungs, "*Tirasdunh!*"

Finally, *finally* he looked her way. His feet stilled, and his bare chest rose and fell with harsh breaths. Even from so far away, Liadan could see him shivering. She waved for him to come back inside, praying she wouldn't have to ride into Aegiros with his dead body slung over Tarabas' back.

Tir tilted his face up, catching the icy rain a moment longer to defy her. When he stalked back into the cottage, he flung his daggers to the floor and backed her against the wall.

Liadan felt the chill radiating off his skin. He had to be freezing. For his sake, she flicked her hand toward the fire to stoke it hotter. Without a log to keep it burning, it wouldn't last long, but at least the small burst of heat would help him recover faster.

Instead of gratitude, his face contorted into a snarl. "I do not fear cold," he spat. "I do not fear rain, or ice, or your thunderstorms."

"I never thought you did—"

"And I do not fear you." It was as much a challenge as a declaration.

Startled, Liadan looked into his honey-brown eyes. All she saw there was defiance and pride, and something else she had no name for, something that hadn't been there before tonight. She didn't know where it'd come from, but it burned as hot as her flames and dared her to provoke it.

Her hand reached up of its own accord to the side of his face, but she stopped herself just short of contact, and hovered there in indecision. Tir swayed closer, bracing his hands to either side of her against the wall. Though his skin was chilled, his breath blew hot on her face, while his heart beat loud enough for her to hear it over the din of the storm.

The memory of Galen's purge came back to her in a rush, making her own heart flutter in her chest. She could still feel the press of Tir's lips, the strength of his arms as he'd pulled her close, the passionate shudder that had racked his body, eliciting a pleasured moan from her in turn. Galen didn't create something out of nothing; her power could only seek out a seed of emotion and burst it to life. For her purge to have affected them both in such a way, a kernel of attraction must have already existed.

It was still there. Even knowing how ill-advised it was, Liadan wanted Tir to kiss her as he had then, she wanted to feel his arms around her, to lean on his strength, to share her fire in kind, and it frightened her.

Tir's gaze lowered to her lips, and he leaned in closer still. Liadan's breath hitched in anticipation, but prudence held her back and, cheeks flushing, she pressed her hand to the center of Tir's chest to stay him.

"Are *you* afraid?" he challenged quietly.

Liadan stuck out her chin. "I fear nothing."

"I think you do." He leaned into her, and her heart gave a hard thump from the sheer intensity emanating from him. "You stand firm against armed foes, look with contempt upon those who scorn you, true. But you do hold fear in your heart, and it is one that cannot be convinced away."

She scoffed.

Undeterred, Tir merely smiled. "You fear what happened in the succubus' inn was not her doing at all. You fear that if I kiss you again, you will respond the same way you did then." His tone dared her to prove him wrong, but his eyes weren't as certain; they gazed into hers and questioned, as if by guessing at her fear, he had revealed his own.

No, he was wrong. She felt nothing more than a remnant of Galen's purge, and she'd prove it to both of them.

They were of a height, and standing so close, their noses almost touched. Liadan had to only tilt her chin forward ever so slightly to press her lips to his. Tir sucked in a surprised breath and stiffened almost to the point of retreat, but then stopped himself and pressed into her instead. The chill of his rain-soaked flesh shouldn't have affected her, yet Liadan shivered. And just like in Galen's inn, she couldn't keep herself in check. Her arms wrapped around to lock at his back as his cold, trembling hand cupped her cheek, while the other slipped into her hair at her nape. And just like back there, Tir's lips moved restlessly over hers, harder, hungrier, until she opened to him, and he groaned, deepening their kiss.

For long moments, they strained together, as if nothing else mattered. The storm faded into silence, time ceased to exist, breath became secondary. Tir's arm came around her, squeezing hard. His hand fisted in her hair, snapping strands to bring her closer, to prevent her retreat. Fire lit her blood until her skin began to glow and heat, until the water trickling down Tir's chest evaporated with a hiss. Only then did he pull back enough to look at her.

And as she watched his lust-hazed mind comprehend what he was doing, Liadan recalled Ulrich's parting words. Her fire cooled in a hurry; her skin's golden glow faded, and her arms dropped away. She extricated herself from Tir's embrace, then looked away from his baffled expression. "You should come sit by the fire," she said softly. "You'll catch your death."

Face flushed, he stepped back and did as she bade. He'd stopped shivering, but water still ran from him in rivulets, a dangerous state to be in; a wet body succumbed to the cold much faster than a dry one. They'd been fortunate enough to have found shelter so quickly before, but with only their small fire for light and warmth now, it'd take too long for Tir to dry off on his own.

"Do you trust me?" she asked, lips still throbbing from the passion of his kiss.

"I do not fear you," he repeated sullenly.

"Yes, you said that, but do you trust me?"

Tir studied her while he made up his mind. His gaze held hers, then moved lower to her lips; he rubbed his mouth and chin with the flat of his palm in a move rife with frustration, then gave a curt nod.

Liadan stacked more wood on the fire, then knelt beside Tir. He turned to face her, wary but curious, and allowed her to take his hands into hers. "Don't move." She closed her eyes and called up her flames. They poured through her veins and into her hands, bursting out of her skin for just a blink before she tempered them with her iron will into a soft glow. Tir gasped, but she didn't let him pull away. Slowly, with careful manipulation, she sent the flames licking along his skin, close enough to warm, but not to burn. His breathing grew harsh as her fire covered his arms, his chest, and then the rest of his body, but he held as still as he could. Within moments, his hands had warmed, and when Liadan opened her eyes, she found his own squeezed shut. But his hair was dry, as were his pants, and his skin was flushed rather than chilled.

"Open your eyes," she invited.

He did, and through the shroud of fire, she saw his fear melt away into wonder as he looked down at himself. "How is this possible?"

Liadan smiled and called her flames back. "Fire doesn't have to burn."

PART TWO

AEGIROS

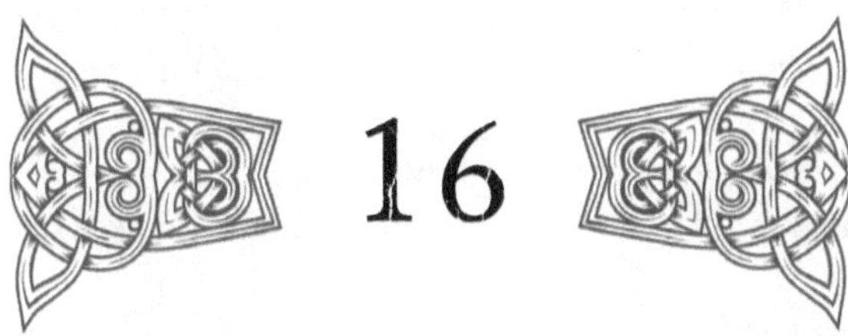

16

After a day and a half more, the border between Lyria and Aegiros loomed on the horizon. It was delineated by a change sharp enough to make out from a distance. Forests gave way to grasslands, with little more than a lone tree or two to dot the landscape; shrubberies were dry and bare, the ground hard beneath their feet.

They'd dismounted to walk the horses across the divide. On their way through villages ravaged by war, all Liadan had managed to procure in the way of provisions was a small bundle of dried fruits and two additional waterskins, which might suffice her and Tir, but the horses would suffer. From here on out, she'd have to rely on Tir and his knowledge of Aegiros to keep them all alive until they reached the First Valley.

According to him, the valley lay at the heart of Aegiros, equidistant from the north and the south. While many oases of varying sizes lay scattered across the lands, the First Valley used to be the largest, carved out of the desert by a mighty river that had long since run dry. If his estimations were correct, they'd reach his tribe in three days. More, if they encountered trouble. With no roads to follow, they'd need to rely on the sun and the stars alone. Aegirans might have been master navigators and cartographers, but without a map or recognizable landmarks, Liadan felt utterly lost in their world.

Tir, on the other hand, seemed to gain confidence along the way. "We will ride through Sadirak," he said, pointing at nothing to the southeast. "You will need proper attire before we leave the grasslands."

She frowned. "Is this your idea of revenge for the innkeeper's clothes?"

His lips twitched. "You would think so."

The answer did nothing to placate her. "I have no need of different attire."

He shrugged. "As you wish. But I would advise otherwise. The desert sun can be merciless, even to one well-acquainted with fire, and the winds can strip tears from your eyes and make them as dry as dust in a blink." He looked her over from head to toe, reached out to brush a skein of hair away from her flushed face. A brief smile, almost wistful, disappeared all too soon as he pulled back and shifted in the saddle, nudging Tarabas a step farther away from her Sleipnir. "Your fair skin will suffer the worst, I think. Better to cover it, than have it blister and peel."

Since the storm, they'd both adopted a distant, formal air when conversing, as if that could somehow undo what had been done. It didn't work. The memory of their kiss, the burning quiescence it'd brought with it, and the sleepless night that had followed were all too insistent to be ignored. It all came back to her during unguarded moments, when conversation stalled yet again, and the landscape failed to provide sufficient distraction. Too often Liadan snuck glances at him, and too often she felt him watching her when he thought she wouldn't notice.

It'd been a mistake; she shouldn't have let it happen.

Determined not to endure another awkward silence, Liadan asked, "Is that why your people wear so many layers of robes? I thought it was to enforce modesty."

He nodded. "That, too."

The unapologetic way he'd said it made her laugh.

Her humor was short-lived. The farther south they ventured, the hotter the sun beat down. Liadan's legs chafed in her leather pants and her jerkin was cinched too tight, making breathing more difficult, until she began wishing for the comfort of skirts. Tir was right. She could not go on much longer dressed the way she was.

When tents and buildings came into view on the horizon, she spurred Sleipnir on faster, desperate for the relief of a little shade. Mercifully, Tir didn't mock her for it. He even haggled with a merchant on her behalf for some new attire. Liadan would have paid every last coin in her purse for something made of cloth instead of leather, but Tir knew better how to negotiate. Within moments the merchant handed him a bundle of clothes, gesturing to something farther away.

Tir bowed and paid the man a gold coin. "Here." He gave the bundle to her. "He said the market well is dry, but there is a fountain not far off. I will take the horses." The poor things were frothing at the mouth, they were so thirsty. "When you are ready, follow this path and turn right at the red tent. I will meet you there."

"Thank you."

He grunted. "Do not take too long. We should not tarry here."

His caution put Liadan on guard. She undressed in the privacy of the merchant's small tent, never so grateful to be out of her leathers. For a moment, she stood where a small breeze cooled her bare skin before she bound her chest and put on the clothes Tir had procured for her. She'd feared the long, cumbersome robes she'd seen the women wear. Much to her surprise, the bundle contained clothes meant for a man.

Liadan picked out dark blue pants to make riding astride easier, and a wide and roomy white shirt that was so thin it was almost sheer. It came with an embroidered tunic to match the pants, and some sort of headscarf she couldn't figure out how to knot. Liadan didn't care. When she finally stepped out of the tent, she took her first deep breath without choking on the hot air.

She could finally think, and the sights around her piqued her curiosity. Sadirak was more of a thriving marketplace than a city. Everywhere she looked, merchants displayed their wares as people and caravans milled about. There were tents that contained clothing, weapons, and earthenware, while in other places, meat cooked over an open fire and drink was sold in earthen jugs. Men and women alike were dressed from head to toe in robes and scarves with only their eyes and hands showing.

Liadan regarded the long piece of cloth in her hand. How had they managed to fold and twist it so neatly? The process eluded her. She approached the merchant showing off his clothing to another passerby and bowed to him the way she'd seen Tir do. "Thank you," she said.

The merchant spat a few strange words at her, then turned his back.

Liadan frowned. Had she offended him somehow?

Since he refused to face her again, she decided to search for Tir.

As soon as she'd stepped away from the tent, however, the sea of travelers swept her along in its wake, and before she knew it, she was lost. Strangers glared, merchants shooed her away, men with scimitars shoved her aside as they passed, and it took all Liadan had to hold on to her temper.

She walked the passageways, trying to find her way back, but amid so much chaos of cloth and color, Liadan became hopelessly lost. Around one corner, a man paraded emaciated people in chains on a stage for an audience to see—slaves for purchase. Around another, cages lined a long wall made of sun-dried bricks. Inside them, wild beasts paced, snarled, lashed out when someone came too close, forcing their handler to crack a long whip to make them settle. He was missing an eye and his bare arms were riddled with claw marks, but his fingers were weighed down with thick, golden rings, and he walked like a king among beggars in gold-embroidered shoes.

In a covered alcove, a man dragged a woman to one corner and shoved her to her knees while she wept, her hands clasped together as she implored him. But the man showed her no mercy, striking her again and again. Liadan set out to stop him, but several other women rushed in, shoving her out of the way as they crowded into the alcove and hid the pair from sight.

Her hasty retreat brought her into a tent, where an old woman sat embroidering a length of silk. An oddly scented haze of smoke filled the space, turning everything as soft as a dream. A gossamer partition separated the front section from the back, and Liadan saw several other women sitting there together, drinking from golden chalices. They were draped in the most beautiful gowns, their hair fastened with golden chains and beads, their veils serving to accentuate their features rather than hide them.

Soft music drifted in from somewhere unseen; a dreamy melody she wanted to sway to. It was much calmer here than in the marketplace outside, a much needed respite that beckoned her deeper.

The old woman rose from her seat to bow to her, and Liadan smiled, returning the gesture. She beckoned Liadan closer and poured something into a chalice, offering it to Liadan on a polished silver platter. One sip of the syrupy-sweet wine made her waver on her feet, but did nothing to quench her thirst. Liadan wanted more.

When she stumbled, the old woman caught her by the elbow, steadying her, guiding her along. Already she was pulling Liadan toward the others, but something didn't feel right. Liadan frowned and shook her head, peering over her shoulder at the market street that suddenly seemed miles and miles away, bathed in a harsh light that wavered everything, split it in two.

The shadows were cool, the pillows looked so soft.

Liadan couldn't think. "No I must get back. My… Tir. He'll be waiting for me."

The old woman stroked her arm, kept pulling her along.

Perhaps she should stay awhile. Tir was probably looking for her even now. If she kept moving, they'd never find each other. Yes, better to stay here. Another step, and another pair of hands caught her elbow. She smiled at the younger woman to her right. A third approached, stroked her cheek, while a fourth at her back brushed her hair. Liadan's eyes closed, but she forced them open again. She was so very tired.

One by one, the women disappeared, and the world tilted, lurched. Instead of the sun-bathed chamber with the beautiful women, she was in the old woman's dark tent, with Tir staring into her eyes. "… leave you for one blink and you… *masiranah*…"

Liadan smiled, giggled. Tir cupped her face, and in the next moment, he was shouting at someone behind her. Then he was so close, prying her eyes open. She frowned and pushed at him, but her arms wouldn't work properly.

"Liadan… hear me?"

"'course I hear you," she groused.

More shouting and odd noises assaulted her. When he leaned her into him, her forehead fell against his shoulder, hiding away the world.

Tir pushed her back, and her head lolled. How was she still standing? Again, he forced her eyes open, irritating her, but a dreamy sigh made her smile. "So pretty." She grabbed his shirt with her clumsy hands and swayed close, bumping her nose against his in an attempt to kiss him. But kiss him she did, and for a moment sweeter than the wine had been, Tir drew her close and kissed her back.

But then he pulled away and dragged her into the harsh light that forced her eyes to roll back in her head. Her knees buckled, and he slung her over his shoulder, bouncing her with every step. Blood rushed into her face until it throbbed, but the fresh air cleared away some of the cobwebs from her eyes.

When he set her down onto her feet again, she heard water nearby, and felt Sleipnir bump her with his nose. "What's… happening?" she asked, words slurring.

"Hush," Tir said, his voice strained even to his own ears. He steadied her by her shoulders until he'd ascertained her balance—precarious, but she was standing on her own. Rage simmered in his chest as he tied her hair back, then deftly knotted the scarf around her head, tucking in the veil to cover her face. "How do you feel?" he asked. The old hag had given her opium; he could still taste it from her lips.

Liadan nodded listlessly.

Tir curled her fingers around Sleipnir's saddle. "Do not let her fall," he ordered the horse. Tarabas stepped up on her other side, helping to keep Liadan upright between them, hiding her from sight, and Tir cursed himself again for the thoughtless mistake that could have cost the princess her life.

Only after he'd walked the horses to the fountain had Tir realized he never should have left her alone. *Masar*, drivers who specialized in acquiring pleasure slaves, were prowling the alleys in groups for new merchandise. Tir had spotted them right away; their distinctive scarves were unmistakable in the crowds. Their sheer numbers should have put him on guard, but he'd thought Liadan would be safe until she met him at the fountain. She should have been no more than a few steps behind.

When she'd failed to meet him, Tir had torn through the market-place looking for her, abandoning the horses to their own devices. It was a miracle no one had thought to steal them.

Taking their waterskins, Tir now returned to the fountain to refill them. His hands shook, and he kept looking over his shoulder for any sign the *masar* were trailing them. Once their harem keeper had a person in her clutches, *masar* didn't take kindly to someone relieving them of their prize. Liadan had been two steps and one golden lock on her collar away from becoming part of the *masiranah*. Her fair northern skin would have made her an exotic treat worth several fortunes, and the *masar* would come for her if Tir didn't get them out of Sadirak before the harem keeper told her men what she'd lost.

Tir hurried to retie the bulging skins to their saddles, then hoisted Liadan astride Sleipnir. Though she held on, she slumped, head lolling, and Tir didn't know whether she could keep her seat for the ride. Not willing to take the chance, he mounted behind her and tied Tarabas' reins to Sleipnir's.

Liadan leaned back into him, head against his shoulder. If she wasn't asleep yet, she would be soon. "Hold on, Princess," he murmured into her ear, kicking Sleipnir into a punishing sprint out of Sadirak.

He didn't slow until the marketplace was a dark smear behind them and the grasslands had begun to thin. They weren't being followed yet. A small blessing, but he'd take it gladly.

Liadan stirred with a tired moan. "Where are we?"

"Safe," he answered. For the moment, at least.

"What happened?"

"You walked into a slaver's den."

"Slaves. Saw them. Bad."

"Yes, very bad." Tir didn't want to think what might have happened had he not gotten to her in time. Imarah had had a run-in with the *masar* before. Years ago, an old woman who'd made for an innocent enough lure had passed through the First Valley with what she'd called her daughters. She'd managed to lure several of their maidens into her caravan before her *masar* had arrived and revealed her for what she was. Dhakir's *kharesh* had slaughtered the lot of them and retrieved the girls before they'd made it to the borders of Imarah. But other tribes, Tir knew, didn't always fare so well.

Liadan touched her hand to the arm he'd wrapped around her.

She was steadier in her seat now. He ought to release her, but try as he might, he couldn't make himself move. "Saved me?" she asked.

Two little words, but so much fear and hesitation behind them. Tir flinched and clutched her tighter. "Yes."

She sighed, and her hand dropped away. She was asleep.

When night fell, the day's heat dissipated so quickly it left Tir chilled. In her sleep, Liadan had her ways of keeping warm—the fire that lit her blood gave her skin a gentle glow while it warmed her body to stave off the night's chill. The waxing moon gave plenty of light to ride by, but it was foolish to push the horses. Tir stopped at an outcropping and dismounted, then carefully lowered Liadan from the saddle to the ground. He rummaged through all of their supplies, pulling out every piece of clothing, every blanket, and every rag they had.

He rolled out the pallets, one next to the other, covering them with a blanket for more warmth. Without a fire, it would be a miserable night, but better than waking up to *masar* swords at their throats. The horses came next. Tir saw to each of them in turn, whispering words of reassurance and thanks. Had it not been for them, they might not have escaped Sadirak in time. A little water wasn't sufficient to show his gratitude, and neither was the care he took in brushing them down, but at least after two of their waterskins were emptied and the horses had settled, Tir himself was calm enough to face Liadan again without panic clawing at his chest.

She lay asleep on one side of the wider pallet. Tir knelt beside her, checking that her breathing was steady, that her heart was still beating strong. Opium was a dangerous drug; it could dull pain and induce sleep, but if used incorrectly, sometimes those who ingested it never woke up. But Liadan would recover. If nothing else, the heat of her skin assured him she was alive and well. In fact, she burned so hot, it warmed him, too. They might not need a fire after all.

Tir removed her headscarf to keep it from tangling around her neck while she slept, settled down next to her, closed his eyes, and willed himself not to dream, but the same vision that had plagued him since the night Liadan had danced pulled him into flames once again, unwilling to release him for even a single night. He knew where he was; despite the darkness, he knew the shape of each flame, found his way along the selfsame path to Liadan, the way he always did. He watched her battle dance yet again, watched her fight the demon swarm as he did every night, until the last one burned to cinders. And when it fell, when she looked at him and smiled, Tir's chest constricted until his own heartbeat caused him pain. He knew what was coming; dreaded it to the depths of his very soul. And he could do nothing to stop it. "We won," Liadan said, and before the last word had slipped from her lips, she collapsed in his arms and turned to ash.

Tir started awake as the first blush of morning lightened the eastern sky, to find himself entangled with the princess. She was pressed back against his chest, huddled as close as she could get. Tir didn't know when his arm had come around her, or when his face had found a cushion in the crook of her neck and shoulder, but he'd never before slept so well on the cold, hard ground.

Troubled, and far more comfortable than he had any right to be, Tir extricated himself, careful not to wake her. When he sat up and turned away to stand, Sleipnir was there, glaring one shiny, black eye at him. The stallion snorted, then adjusted his front hoof in an almost-stomp.

Tir held a finger to his lips to silence him. In answer, Sleipnir tossed his head, stepping back just enough to allow Tir to stand. Once they were eye to eye, Sleipnir shifted sideways, then bumped him away a step, and then another, and another, until he'd herded Tir away from Liadan. Having removed him from his mistress, Sleipnir took a stand at her back to guard her sleep.

Tir marveled at the mount's intelligence and loyalty. "Guard her well," he said and, entrusting him with Liadan's safekeeping, walked off a fair distance to perform his morning rituals.

17

Frastmir was holding its breath. Word had reached the castle that Liadan and her companion had passed through Dai and crossed into Aegiros. Aided by the queen, King Saeran spoke to his cousin, Ulrich, and confirmed that both riders had been in good health, unharmed, and eager to continue their journey when he'd seen them last. Now that they'd left Ulrich's demesne, no one was left to aid the king and queen in bringing back their daughter, and the city waited tensely to see what they would do.

Fal had no time to dwell on any of it. The shroud hiding Liadan from his mind was thinning day by day, and he feared when it disappeared completely, she'd be beyond his help. He'd spent every waking moment in his tower library, poring over everything the dragon had sent him, praying there'd be something in all of those texts to fix this. He'd found the first bit of hope early on: the blood oath Liadan and the Aegiran had sworn was binding, but not permanent. As long as no feelings stirred between them, once Liadan had completed her task, she should be free to return home.

Queen Nialei had wept with relief when Fal had told her so. But the danger still remained. Liadan was clever, but rash. If she did something more to upset the balance, the bond would tie not only her fate, but also her soul to the Aegiran, and not even death would part them.

Fal had spent days since his discovery searching for ways to help Liadan fulfill her obligation; the sooner she was done, the better. But he hadn't unearthed anything on the subject of demons or curses. Instead, the dragon's lore was filled with tedious extrapolations of the elemental world, the laws of nature and Otherkind, politics and basic magics, but little on the interactions between all of them.

The more knowledge Fal uncovered, the less he felt he knew. There was so much humans had either forgotten or had never known about, things that could mean the difference between life and death. They walked a fine line every day, now that the Veil was disintegrating. Without its protection, stepping into the wrong Otherland could kill a human with a single breath. Some Others had magic so potent it shone out of them, and one look could turn a human into stone.

Fal's translations took time. Finding some sort of order to them took time. Figuring out whether it was immediately useful took time—time Liadan did not have.

Frustrated, Fal shoved to his feet to pace. His legs had gone numb from all the sitting, and his knees almost buckled beneath him. He braced himself on the table, and beneath his thumb he spotted the first translation he'd penned. The jagged line of ink across the page marked where Liadan had distracted him. Half smiling, he picked up the page and read what he'd written.

Frowning, he read it again. No. Impossible.

Eyes widening with every word seen anew, Fal read through the text a third time, and his heartbeat quickened when he realized what it could mean. He swiped clean an area of the table, then dug through the pile of materials for the branded skin the translation corresponded with. His eyes skimmed the markings, comparing the symbols to the words he'd written. No mistake, at least none that he could find. "Gods, this could be..."

He dropped everything and ran out of the library, tripping over his feet on the way down. In the great hall, he ran into his father, almost knocking them both to the ground. "Sorry," he said, pulling away. He didn't have time to hear what Saeran called after him, let alone to answer.

The waterfall he favored as his own secret hideaway was close enough to not require a horse. Even so, it took him a half-day to get there on foot when he wasn't rushing. At a full run, it was less time, but more frustration. The path wasn't clear through the woods; he had to fight his way through bushes and shrubberies, tearing his cloak along the way. He didn't care.

The woods opened onto a meadow, with the waterfall just on the other side. It wasn't very big, but it flowed into a basin large enough to form a small lake before it emptied into the creek. He'd used to bathe here in the summers, before his illusions had forced him into seclusion in the castle. It was the perfect size for what Fal needed to do now. After so much time at his studies, the run had wearied him; his legs wobbled as he stalked across the meadow to the lake, where he took off his shoes, shrugged out of his cloak, and waded into the waist-high water. Its chill embraced him, and he let the gentle waves revive him, clear his mind. He waited patiently for his strength to be restored, because what he was about to do would require a great deal of concentration and tenacity. As far as he knew, no one had ever attempted anything like this before.

Fal was about to make history, and he couldn't suppress an eager smile or the way his heart thundered and his limbs itched to move. And then he began, and all awareness of the outside world slipped away.

~

Tir spent the day teaching Liadan his language. He also kept a careful eye on her, as though he expected her to fall asleep again at any moment. Liadan didn't remember much from the day before, but it must have been worse than Tir let on; all he'd tell her was that she'd stumbled into a slaver's den and he'd had to retrieve her. When she'd asked him why he still fretted, now that all was well again, he'd tensed and refused to answer.

As closely as he watched her, Tir also kept an eye on the endless stretch of cracked and barren earth behind them. Did he worry they were being followed? Liadan suspected her lessons were meant more to distract him than to teach her, but she didn't mind. With nothing else to do, it was as good a pastime as any.

It hadn't escaped her that Tir hadn't just saved her life; he'd saved her from a lifetime of pain. Liadan had seen slaves being sold, buyers fighting and bartering over them. Her own fate would have been much worse. Back in the marketplace, the old woman had drugged her to make her docile, but not unconscious, which could have only meant one thing: they'd wanted her pliant but awake for their use, and they would have continued drugging her to keep her that way. In time, her Other constitution would have helped her adapt—her body would have learned to resist the drug's effect. But if Tir hadn't found her, she might not have regained enough sense to defend herself from their abuse.

No meager thanks or gesture of gratitude would ever be enough. Liadan owed Tir her life. And instead of lording it over her, Tir seemed determined to forget it'd ever happened. It relieved her of the need to address his kindness, but made her wonder whether the real reason he didn't want to acknowledge it was that he'd rather have left her there.

When the sun approached its zenith, Tir pitched a makeshift shelter to shield them from the worst of its heat so they could eat a small meal and rest the horses. Now that they'd left the marketplace behind, he was keeping their pace slow, and for good reason. Everywhere Liadan looked she saw nothing but dry, cracked earth. Her eyes hurt from the sun's glare, and her feet ached from walking on the hard ground in the shoes Tir had bought with her gold. She was hot and tired, and missing her home and her family.

Even the horses were miserable. Sleipnir didn't do well with his black coat. In fact, he was so desperate to escape the sun's heat, he didn't even twitch when Tir dusted him with sand to dull and lighten his coloring. A small relief, but she could tell it made a big difference.

All too soon, Tir took the shelter apart, and they set out once more. Liadan's feet dragged, and she leaned on Sleipnir more than she wanted to as they walked the mounts to spare them the weight. They'd started the day with two of their waterskins already empty, and the other two wouldn't last much longer.

Time and again, Liadan imagined seeing a distant greenery, but it was all a trick of the unrelenting blast of sun. As a creature of fire, the heat shouldn't have bothered her as much as it did. It might have been a simple matter of getting used to it—a reasonable assumption, since she'd never had trouble acclimating to winter's snow and ice—but even during the worst, most miserable northern blizzard, she'd never lacked for water.

Amazing how easily one could take such a small thing for granted when it was in abundance.

"How do you say I would like some water?"

Tir spoke the words in his tongue.

Liadan repeated them, but she was starting to slur.

Tir laughed. "You asked me whether there is water in the goat."

"There probably is," she muttered.

Still chuckling, Tir handed her his waterskin.

She pushed it away.

"Drink," he insisted.

"I have my own."

"And you haven't touched it. Did I not tell you not to ignore thirst?"

"Yes, you did. You did, Fal did, almost everyone I've told about this journey, did. It doesn't change the fact that this water is all we have for gods only know how long. I am not about to drink it all the first day." Her next step dragged, and she tripped over her own feet, managing to right herself before she fell outright.

Tir caught her elbow, made her stop. "You would rather die of thirst?"

"Give me that." She grabbed the waterskin and took a swig. It was warm, but that didn't matter. As soon as it touched her tongue, Liadan wanted to drink all of it down as fast as possible. She was so parched, she wanted to weep, but she was still right—they had to ration what they had left. Unfortunately, the little mouthful did nothing to quench her thirst, only reminded her of what she was missing, and the longer she held the skin, the more it tempted her to drink her fill. Tired of fighting, Liadan took one more sip, then forced herself to give back the skin. "Happy now?"

"Yes, I am." He had to be as thirsty as she was, though she couldn't tell by looking at him. She hated him a little for the ease with which he moved, when her legs felt weighed down with lead.

What she wouldn't give for a tree. Just one. A great, big oak, with a heavy crown of leaves and a soft cushion of grass at its base.

When green on the horizon once again teased her tired eyes, Liadan couldn't help letting out a small squeak of misery.

Tir followed her gaze, then looked back with a dazzling smile. "Mount up," he said, following his own orders, and before she was even settled into her saddle, he took off toward that spot, leaving Liadan to catch up.

The green patch she'd thought to be an illusion grew before her eyes. "It's not going away," she said, breathless. An oasis in the middle of the desert, with several tall palm trees at the foot of a small pile of rocks that fairly passed for a mountain. Large-leafed plants grew there as high as her waist, and water glittered in the middle of it all. "It's real!" she cried, and spurred Sleipnir on faster.

Tir laughed when she pulled ahead. She didn't need to tell Sleipnir what to do; he was as thirsty as the rest of them. With a gleeful whinny, he charged right into the creek and all but threw her off to get a drink.

Liadan dismounted, slipped and fell onto her backside in the creek. Laughing, she lay back, never so happy to swim fully dressed.

But it wasn't enough. Tilting her head up and back, she saw water pouring out of rock to pool at the base of the mountain. She just knew it would be deep enough to submerge herself. Desperate to wash off all of the dust and the sand, Liadan got up and pulled the scarf from her head. Her tunic came next, and by the time she'd wrestled off her shoes, Tir was staring at her with what looked like trepidation.

"What are you doing?" he demanded.

She couldn't draw enough breath to answer him beyond one word: "Water."

Finally free of the shoes, she got to work on her shirt, which stuck to her back. She almost suffocated trying to pull it off over her head. When at last she did, she grinned triumphantly at Tir who flushed and turned his back. Modesty was the last thing on her mind. She shed her chest binds and pants, and waded naked into the water up to her chest. The chill of it took her breath away, but she ducked underneath and screamed in pure joy to be there.

Liadan would have stayed there forever, but the need for air forced her to resurface. She gasped, taking her first full breath since the day's heat had become almost unbearable. "Gods, I needed that." Treading water, she watched the trees sway above her, until it suddenly struck her she hadn't heard a word from Tir. Lifting her head, she found him exactly where he'd been a moment ago, still with his back to her, staring off into the distance.

"What are you doing?" she asked.

"Praying for patience," he retorted.

Liadan laughed. "Is the fearsome assassin shy?"

He muttered something she couldn't hear.

"Stop being stubborn. Who knows how long it'll be before we find anything like this again? You shouldn't waste it."

He didn't move.

"I promise I won't look."

His shoulders tensed, but beyond a backwards glare no doubt meant to shut her up, he did nothing.

He left her with no choice. Forced to resort to dirty tactics, she called, "Tir you smell. We both do. I am not going any farther until we bathe."

Tir shook his head and started unloading the horses. As soon as Sleipnir and Tarabas were free of their burdens, they waded into the water and soaked themselves, stubbornly turning their noses up at Tir's commands to come out. Letting them speak for her, she lay back and floated, ignoring Tir. She was beginning to doze off when Tir's curses brought her head back up to watch him wrestle his boots off his feet. Biting back a smile, she turned toward the waterfall to give him some privacy.

"You won't regret it."

"I already do."

It was truly beautiful here, reminding her of the glen her brother favored—the same waterfall, the same pool and creek, the only difference being the color of the rock and the foliage. That, and the fact that twenty or thirty paces in any direction lay a vast expanse of burning desert. If she looked past the waterfall, she could even see a little cavern, just like the one back home.

A soft splash and hiss heralded Tir's approach. Liadan was tempted to turn around, but the water was too clear to disguise their nudity.

Tir didn't seem to mind; his gaze burned a hole between her shoulder blades. It would be only fair to see him in turn, would it not?

She swiveled, sinking lower, so the water rose up to her neck.

Tir must have had the same thought; she was left with a view of his back. A fine back he had, with lean muscle moving beneath his skin as he waved his hands back and forth in the water.

"It's deeper over here," she said.

"I know," he replied.

"No need to get testy. I only meant there's plenty of room. You needn't cower all the way over there." Oh, Da would have flayed her hide for this, but she couldn't help teasing a little. "I don't bite."

"But I might." He'd said it so softly she almost missed his words, but she shivered at the feeling behind them.

Liadan worried her lower lip between her teeth. From him, she might not mind the bite, but it wouldn't do for him to know that. "I should thank you," she said instead. "You rescued me from what might have been a very unpleasant situation in Sadirak."

"You would not have been in such a situation if not for me. You owe me nothing."

"Nevertheless, I am grateful." Without thinking, she reached out to touch him.

Tir flinched away. "Don't. I never thought you to be cruel; I don't want to start now."

"I only wanted to—"

He swore and moved away, wading to the edge of the basin. "This was a mistake."

"Wait! I offended you, and I'm sorry. I promise I won't touch you again. Look, I'll even turn my back." She did just that, facing the waterfall. "See? All is well. Please don't go."

Tir's movements stilled, and that sensation of his gaze caressing her returned. She heard him come back into the water and risked a sideways glance to see where he was.

"No looking!"

"Sorry!" Liadan faced forward, but she didn't need her eyes; the water displaced at her back as he came closer, and she sensed the heat of him on her skin the same way she felt the sun. Staring straight ahead, she started when her brother's image wavered in the mist. "Fal?" But it was gone as quickly as it came, and Liadan shook her head, wondering whether the heat had finally driven her mad.

"Liadan? Are you all right?" In an instant, Tir was so close, one step would bring him near enough to touch. Out of the corner of her eye, she saw his hand hover by her shoulder.

Before it could settle on her, someone reached out from behind the stream and grasped onto her, pulling her over to the other side. She sputtered, fought to free herself, but it was Fal's voice that cried her name, his arms that pulled her into a tight embrace. She wiped water from her eyes, heart thudding, to see where she was. "Wha… What is this?"

Trees towered all around under an overcast sky, and the water was a damn sight colder than it had been a moment ago.

"An aspect of one element is but a small part of the whole, creating a tangible connection to the eternal, and thus making the passage from one to another possible!" Fal cried. "I did it, Liadan! I figured it out."

Stunned beyond words, all she could do was stare. "What did you do?"

Fal pushed away from her with a gasp and slapped his hands over his eyes. "You're naked!"

"What did you do, Fal!"

"Why are you naked!"

Behind her, Tir's voice echoed, distorted by the water's flow. "Liadan? Liadan!" He was in the pool where she'd stood a moment ago, staring through the waterfall. Could he see her?

"Tir!"

He stepped away, searching the pool's surface. "Liadan!"

She slapped Fal's shoulder. "What did you do?"

"I'm sorry! I had to do something. Mother and Da are at their wit's end, we couldn't reach you, the dragon wouldn't help, and then you crossed into Aegiros and Da was this close to raising an army to go after you—"

"Stop!" Dear gods, how was she supposed to follow a word of that? "Will you put your hands down?"

"You're naked!"

"I was bathing, you dolt! The first bath I've had since leaving Dai."

"Then why is *he* in the water?" Fal demanded.

Her temper flared, warming the water around them. "Send me back. Now."

"I can't. Da will wring my neck if he finds out I had you and didn't keep you here."

"Fal!"

"You can't go back to him!"

"I have to! Or have you forgotten my oath? You were there when I swore it."

Fal dropped his hands to meet her gaze, eyes furious as he grated out, "I was there when you bloody handfasted yourself to the Aegiran assassin!"

Her jaw slackened. "What?"

Fal's features settled into his own face and, drawing in a deep breath for patience, he raised a hand to block her nudity, voice strained as he explained, "The words you spoke bound you to him, and his blood bound him to you in return. You are handfasted until your oath is fulfilled. The bond will fade, but only if you don't…" He gestured with his free hand. "You know."

"What?"

"You *know*."

Liadan shook her head. "What are you talking about?"

"Consummate!"

"Fal!" She slapped him on the head this time.

"Stop hitting me and listen. This is important. If you mate with him, it'll bind your soul to his. Not just until death, but forever. Do you understand? If he's slain in battle, you could die. If he grows old and passes on, he could take you with him."

Liadan struggled to understand. "I made myself mortal?"

Fal said nothing.

"But we exchanged blood. If his had this effect on me, what did mine do to him? He could just as easily have been made immortal." Or at the very least, longer-lived.

"It'll do you no good trying to understand it. None of us know what the exchange has wrought in both of you. All we know is that as long as you're with him, you're in danger. I can't let you go back."

Liadan shook her head. None of that mattered now. "You have to. The oath will compel me, no matter what you do, until I have finished my task, and Tir's tribe doesn't have time to waste."

Fal appeared to debate his choices.

"*Liadan!*" Tir called again, more frantic this time.

"Fal, please, you have to send me back."

His shoulders sagged in a sigh. "Remember what I told you, and don't lose that vial. Now, more than ever, water's my only window to you should you need help."

"Yes, yes. I understand."

"Gods keep you, sister." And he shoved her back through the waterfall, right into Tir's arms. The impact knocked him backwards, and they fumbled to untangle themselves. Liadan had no trouble finding the surface, but Tir struggled, and she had to reach down to help him. He couldn't swim, she realized.

"Are you all right?" Liadan asked, trying to look into his face.

He pushed her away, coughing up the water he'd inhaled. When he could breathe again, he turned on her with a fury she hadn't seen since that day in the dungeons of Castle Frastmir. "What tricks are you playing at?" he demanded.

Liadan backed off from his advance, cornering herself against the waterfall.

He grabbed her by the shoulders and, spinning her around, shoved her away from it. "I thought the *masar* had caught up to us! I saw someone pull you across the water, and then you were gone! Where did you go?"

"I didn't mean to, I—"

"Cease lying!"

Fire flared through her, and she struck without thinking, curling her fingers around his throat. She squeezed just enough to keep him still, but the heat of her fire sizzled against his skin, and Tir gasped, falling silent. "I've made allowances for you, Aegiran, time and again, and I am grateful for your help in Sadirak. But by the gods, if you call me a liar one more time, I will burn you to ash where you stand, blood oath or no. Do you understand?"

He gave a curt nod, as much as her hold would allow, and she released him with a shove. Tir wisely stepped out of reach and touched his throat, where the red mark of her palm print faded even as she watched. He'd feel no lasting effects.

She sighed. "I did not lie. Water is my brother's element, not mine. He found me and pulled me through, back to Frastmir to tell me—" She cut her sentence short.

"Tell you what?"

It would serve no purpose to tell him what Fal had imparted; neither of them could change what had been done, and telling him would only put more strain on their already difficult situation. "That my parents have returned and are angry with me for leaving. He tried to keep me home, but I made him send me back. To you and this godsforsaken dead land. Because I honor my word."

"Your brother can travel through water?"

"It would seem so. But he will not take me back a second time."

"You are right in that," he replied, his words a dire warning. "If I must leash you to me to keep you here, I will." Then his face flushed, and he quickly turned his back. She was still naked and, standing straight, the water wasn't deep enough to hide her. Before, the thought of being seen this way wouldn't have bothered her, but what Fal had told her changed everything.

There would be no more teasing the prince, no more breathless kisses, and no more bathing naked together. If mate-bonding with him wasn't the worst that could happen, then it came very, very close. She couldn't risk either of them living the same misery Geir felt every day, not even if the smallest chance existed they might be happy together for however long they had to live.

18

The horses refused to hold still long enough for Tir to saddle them; every time he came near, they shook off his touch and crossed to the other side of the oasis. Nevertheless, he tried three times, and on the third, got pushed into the water, fully dressed, for his efforts.

"Leave them," Liadan called. "They deserve the rest. We can shelter here for the night."

Though the day was long from over, if the horses wouldn't leave, neither could they. Giving up, Tir waded out of the pool and squeezed as much water out of his clothes as he could without taking them off. Never again would he disrobe in front of the princess. Nor would he ask her to do whatever she'd done that night of the storm. He'd rather freeze to death.

Instead, he built a small fire and sat as far from Liadan as he could. If she noticed, she wouldn't meet his gaze long enough to mock him for it.

He shouldn't have looked. To see her suddenly disappear had scared years off his life—a depth of fear matched only by his anger at having her returned from her brother. Never would he have thought it'd be so easy for others to take her—right from under his nose!

Never would he have thought the idea of losing Liadan would bring him such—

Tir shook his head hard. No. He thought nothing. He felt nothing. Gods, he shouldn't have looked.

But he had, and now the sight had been seared into his mind for all eternity. Liadan was exquisite. Her skin was as pale as milk, her body strong with muscle, yet graced with feminine curves. Tir rubbed at his eyes, wishing he could scrub away the image of her from the inside of his eyelids. If the princess noticed anything amiss, she said nothing. Risking a glance across the fire, he found her staring into its depths, lost in thought as she played with the glass vial from her brother.

Just as well.

After a silence long enough to make his tense shoulders relax, the princess opened her mouth. "Do people wed in Imarah the way we do in the North?"

Tir flinched, reaching a hand up to his throat. This was not a discussion he wanted to have today. Perhaps not ever. But to refuse to answer would mean admitting a weakness, and that was something a *kharesh* would never do. "Why do you ask?"

She shrugged. "Father told me Mari was chosen to wed him. But they wed in the Northern way, and he never spoke of Aegiran customs of courtship. Either he didn't know, or there aren't any."

"We wed," he said carefully. "Each tribe has its own customs, but the punishment for breaking them is the same everywhere."

She looked up, a question in her eyes.

Tir quickly focused on the flames. "Women who dishonor their husbands are stoned to death."

He could hear a disgruntled frown in her voice when she said, "I thought men were allowed to take many wives in Aegiros."

"They are. A man may have as many wives as he can feed and clothe."

"Then are women not allowed to have many husbands?"

"No."

"Why not?"

"It is the way it has always been."

Her silence carried a heavy weight of disapproval.

"This bothers you," he observed.

"Of course it bothers me!"

"Northerners allow only one wife for each man?"

"Yes. And we mate for life."

He'd already known this, but the way she'd said it gave him pause to consider the full implications of such an arrangement. "What happens when the woman dies?"

"Her husband mourns her," she retorted. "What happens to an Aegiran's wives when he dies?"

"If he has male kin, the wives go to them. If not, some tribes allow the women to be burned on his pyre."

Liadan looked horrified by the thought, and in truth, the practice had never sat well with Tir either. Imarah hadn't burned a wife in many centuries, but the mercy created complications of its own. Without a husband to care for them, women were forced to fend for themselves, to sell their crafts or their bodies to anyone willing to pay. Rare was the man who'd take into his household a widow not of his family, so the choice of starving on her own or dying with her husband was one each widow had to make. In some tribes, they fell willingly upon the pyre.

"You needn't worry. You are not human, remember?" He did, but the reminder changed nothing. What was seen, could not be unseen; did not want to be unseen. "You cannot be harmed by fire." Nothing good could come of this preoccupation he'd developed, but the more time he spent with Liadan, the easier he forgot that. She was becoming a flame he kept circling like a moth and he feared one day it would burn the flesh from his bones.

Her eyes sparked with fire as her face took on a faint glow. "Know this, *mortal*"—she spat the word as an insult, but through her bluster of anger, Tir saw a chink of hurt and instantly regretted his words. "When I choose to mate, it'll be with a male who is my equal in all things; who will love and cherish me as I do him. And I will no more abide him taking another than he would me cuckolding him for sport. When I breathe my last, it'll be with his arms around me, and I'll know I have loved with all my heart and soul, and have been loved the same."

When I breathe my last…

We won.

In his mind's eye, the vision of Liadan's naked form went up in flames, turning to ash as she died. "I begin to understand why North-men only take one wife. If they are anything like you, one would be more than enough to keep a man busy for the rest of his life." He'd meant it as a good-hearted jest, but it only seemed to make matters worse.

"You mock me."

"No," he said in earnest, searching for the right words to explain. "To share such passion with another, to look into her eyes and see a helpmate rather than a helpless female in constant need of protection, I cannot imagine such a blessing."

Liadan's temper calmed, her eyes dimming to charcoal. "Your people depend on you a great deal."

"Yes."

"Your wives will as well."

Tir nodded. If his tribe survived long enough, he'd be expected to take a wife, perhaps more. With so many of their men dying of starvation or in battle, only a handful were left to care for the women. Of those, half were too young to wed and the other half already had two or three wives, and their children to look after.

"That must be a terrible burden to bear."

It was.

"But it is one of your own making. Aegiran men, I mean."

Ire heated his blood at her words, but he couldn't argue. She was right.

Liadan sighed and pushed to her feet. "I shouldn't have broached the subject." She put the vial into her saddlebag, retrieved her sword, and removed herself to the other side of the oasis to train on her own.

For a while, Tir watched her, absently noting the elegant mastery with which she wielded the blade. Aegiran steel was nothing like the Northern blades; their scimitars were thinner, sharper, and curved, meant to slice through flesh, not break apart metal armor. It afforded them more speed and less weight to carry in their scabbards.

He'd seen men in the North struggle just to walk in their armor, let alone draw their blades. Many had had massive swords strapped to their backs, the pommels sticking out over their shoulders and the tips all but dragging on the ground. Tir couldn't conceive of any use for such a thing.

He'd hefted Liadan's sword—a work of art if he'd ever seen one—and he'd found it wasn't as heavy as he'd have expected, but it was still more cumbersome than his scimitar. She must have grown used to it, however, because when she moved, the sword was not its own thing; it was an extension of her arm, and moved with her every which way, down to the smallest twitch of her wrist.

She practiced with her right hand, then switched the hold to her left. Finally, she drew a long dagger and repeated each routine with two blades instead of one. Each time she altered her weapons, she moved slowly at first, measuring each strike with precision borne of relentless training by a master. By the time she'd put on a burst of speed to repeat the whole thing, her movements were so ingrained in her limbs, he'd have been surprised if there was even a finger's width variation in them.

In practice, Liadan was a gifted swordswoman. But could she fight, too, or was this simply another form of dance to her? Tir pushed to his feet, intending to find out. If she was to fight with his *kharesh*, he needed to know she could hold her own. He couldn't have inexperience costing them lives.

But before he could make it across the oasis, Liadan suddenly dropped her blades and clutched at her stomach.

"Did you pull a muscle?" he teased.

Liadan cried out and dropped to her knees, hunching over.

"Liadan?" His steps quickened.

She looked up, face pinched with pain. With obvious difficulty, she struggled to her feet. "Sleipnir!"

The black mount answered her summons, reaching her a moment before Tir.

"What's the matter?" Tir asked.

"It's time again, my friend." She held her shaking hand up to Sleipnir, who sniffed at her fingers and tossed his head with an agitated snort, stomping his hooves.

Tir caught her hand to get her attention. "What are you doing?" Her skin was too hot; unnaturally so. "What's the matter with you?"

"Three days," she said, her voice unsteady. "I will meet you back here in three days."

"What?"

Sleipnir lipped her shoulder, and she pulled away from Tir to stroke the mount's forehead. "I'm sorry. It's not safe for me to stay here."

"You are not leaving!"

Her face contorted, knees buckling a second time, but when Tir reached out for her, Sleipnir shouldered him aside to support his mistress himself. He lowered to his knees so Liadan could mount. She barely kept astride, clutching Sleipnir's mane with a white-knuckled grip. "Please, Tir, I don't want to hurt you. This is something I cannot control. Stay here. I will be back in three days' time, I swear it."

"No," he growled and whistled for Tarabas.

Liadan moaned, leaning over Sleipnir's neck. All it took was one touch to spur the mount on, and he galloped off so fast, Tir was stunned. He couldn't waste time gathering their supplies. Refusing to let that female out of his sight again, he followed after her. But as fast as he knew Tarabas to be, Sleipnir was faster, and within moments, they'd left the oasis far behind.

She would not get away so easily. Tir kicked Tarabas into a hard sprint to catch up. When he did, Liadan was slumped over Sleipnir's back, moments away from slipping off, and the horse wasn't slowing down. Cursing himself a fool, he reached across to drag her onto Tarabas, but Sleipnir veered off, taking his mistress out of reach.

Tir tried again, but Sleipnir refused to let him take her. Risking his own life as well as hers, Tir squared his balance, pulled his feet up, and crouched on Tarabas' back, clutching his mane. The next time the mounts came close, he jumped, landing astride Sleipnir behind Liadan.

The instant he did, Sleipnir reared, throwing them both off. Tir took the brunt of the impact, landing on his back, Liadan on top of him, and she grunted, rolling off him, but she lacked the strength to stand. Breath knocked out of him, Tir sat up and reached for her, only to recoil when Sleipnir charged at him.

Sensing a threat, Tarabas intervened, and both horses reared, fighting each other. Sleipnir was bigger, stronger, and unrelenting, and he pushed Tarabas back as far as he deemed necessary, then turned on Tir with an angry snort.

Fearing for Liadan more than himself, Tir turned to shield her, but she was already crawling away from him, and what little distance she'd gained was enough for Sleipnir to get between them. Stomping his hooves ever closer, he herded Tir away. Tir pushed to his feet, trying to see around the mount, but he only caught a glimpse. "Liadan!"

His voice brought her head up, and Tir shuddered when she looked at him. Her eyes were pure fire, her face veined with bright red-gold cracks like the earth beneath his feet. Smoke curled up from her skin, and her hair billowed over it, turning to flame, one strand at a time. "Stay back!" she warned, and her shout turned into an agonized scream.

Tir shoved at Sleipnir to let him through, but with a sharp whinny, the mount half-reared again, kicking out with his front hooves to push him back even farther. Fear had widened his eyes, and his tail twitched with agitation. Tir realized the horse wouldn't let him through, because Sleipnir himself didn't want to be there.

A flare of heat struck him, pulling his skin tight and dry across his face. Sleipnir kicked out with his hind legs, tossing his head, desperate to escape. With no other choice, Tir relented, and went a distance farther until Sleipnir calmed somewhat and let him see Liadan.

Tir's heart stuttered. It had to be the distance making her seem so small. Yet even from such a distance, the waves of heat exuded by her huddled form overpowered the sun. He'd seen her engulfed in flames before, but this was different. On her hands and knees, Liadan curled her fingers down to claw at the earth, and where they touched, fire erupted. But it wasn't the bright glow he'd become familiar with; these flames were darker, a sickening shade of blood, with little of the bright yellow. And they weren't just licking over her; they were burning her, bursting out of the cracks in her skin until her entire body was aflame, and then became the flame.

Liadan disappeared in that inferno, and Tir could scarcely make out the outline of her body. The flames flared out, then pulled in tightly, then burst out again—a cycle that repeated endlessly, growing bigger and hotter and so loud he heard nothing else.

Tir gasped for breath after he'd held it too long. He was rooted to the spot, unable to move or look away as Liadan burned. This was his nightmare brought to life. Worse, because he couldn't even go to her.

Beside him, Sleipnir stood and watched, waited for the gods knew what, his tail twitching every so often while his agitated snorts punctuated the ebb and flow of Liadan's fire. But he didn't move, standing loyal watch over his mistress, watching her die.

At the worst of it, the desert wind whipped a flare into a vortex that pulled the flames into the sky, and for a moment, Tir could almost make out Liadan's form. The next flare was smaller. The one after that, smaller still.

As the heat slowly died down, Tir and Sleipnir dared to approach, step by step. Tir followed the animal's instincts, trusting them more than his own, and didn't go closer unless Sleipnir matched him. The fire shrank, lightened, and then cooled, until it was once again the shade he'd come to associate with Liadan.

When it'd died down enough to reveal her, Tir stopped in his tracks. Her clothing had burned away in the maelstrom, the torc around her neck glowed bright, and her skin, still veined in blood red, flickered like a burning ember. She lay on the ground, unmoving, and he couldn't tell whether or not she was breathing; couldn't get close enough to see for himself.

Little by little, Tir inched his way forward, hoping and praying he didn't get to the princess only to have her turn to ash in his arms.

When at last he'd reached her, the red cracks had sealed into unbroken, luminescent skin, and the desert had become dark. Night had fallen while Liadan had burned, and now her faint glow was all the light they had. Tir reached out, tentatively touched her arm. She was hot, but no longer burning. He found her heartbeat, strong and steady in the side of her neck, then held his hand beneath her nose and felt her breath, soft, but sure.

Tir cupped her face, angling it up so he could check her eyes. The movement did nothing to rouse her. "Liadan, wake up. Can you hear me? Open your eyes."

She didn't stir.

Sleipnir nosed at her hair, then sneezed at the sharp scent of ash and soot, but didn't recoil. Instead he kneeled, jerking his head at Tir.

Tir shrugged off his shirt and threaded Liadan's arms through it to clothe her. He picked her up, but instead of slinging her over Sleipnir's back, he mounted with her in his lap. Sleipnir pushed to a stand, then began walking in what Tir hoped was the direction of the oasis. Eventually, Tarabas fell into step with them, eyes still big, wary of the larger mount and the glowing woman Tir held close to his chest.

When he saw the shadow of their oasis, Tir slumped with relief. They'd made it. The fire he'd built had gone out, but at least the plants provided some shelter from the freezing night. For the second time in as many days, Tir rolled out their pallets and settled Liadan on one side. He left her only long enough to gather more dried palm fronds for a small fire and several dry gourds he'd earlier seen scattered around, then sat nearby to begin his watch.

The flames swayed toward Liadan to mirror her breathing. It unnerved him enough to move her sleeping form farther away. Then he resumed his seat, pulled out his blade, and got to work on the gourds.

If he slept, all he'd dream about was fire. Better to stay awake and wait for Liadan to open her eyes.

If she ever did.

19

Liadan woke to shivers racking her body. It happened every time she literally burned herself out; her fire needed time to rebuild, and while it did, she was left chilled to her very soul. Opening one bleary eye, she found Tir's face a hair's breadth from her nose. She gasped, and he glowered.

"You're alive."

"You sound disappointed." Her voice was hoarse. She was parched and starving, and her arms quivered with strain when she pushed up onto her elbows. Oh, how she hated this.

Tir caught her arms and unceremoniously dragged her to lean back against one of their packs. Then he shoved a cup at her face, giving her no choice but to let him pour water down her throat. She would have fought him, but the water tasted so cold and crisp, she was too busy gulping it down. "More," she demanded when the cup was empty.

"Not yet. Eat." He curled her fingers around a piece of bread and dried meat as if she were an invalid.

"Your bedside manner is atrocious." Liadan took the nourishment and made herself chew before she swallowed each small bite.

"Are you ill?"

"No," she said around a mouthful.

"Are you hurt?"

She shook her head.

"Then you'll forgive me for being slightly irritated at having to watch you sleep for *three bloody days!*"

Liadan flinched. "I told you to stay here," she reminded him.

His face darkened with fury. Clearly, that had been the wrong thing to say.

"I'm sorry?" she ventured.

"You will explain." She could hear his teeth grinding. This was not good.

With a sigh, she stuffed the last bit of bread into her mouth, chewing slowly while she considered how much to tell him.

"You will explain in detail," he said, as if he'd read her thoughts. "And then you will explain this." Before she could react, he stuck his hand into the fire and pulled out a burning coal. Liadan's jaw slackened as she stared at his hand, black with soot but unharmed, proffering the ember as a silent accusation.

The last swallow of her dry meal stuck in her throat. "When...?"

"Sometime while you slept. A log cracked and rolled away from the fire. I reached for it and tossed it back on the fire without thinking."

"It doesn't hurt?"

He winced, more an expression of agitation than pain. "I feel the heat. It burns *into* me, but it doesn't hurt."

Liadan took the coal to inspect his hand. Just as when she'd branded him, the skin of his palm was red, but already fading. She looked at the coal in her free hand, turned it this way and that. The live ember, hot enough to sear any man, was no more than a warm, glowing gem in her own hand, but *she* was fireproof. Tir should not have been. Unless... "It must be my blood. Somehow it's protecting you."

"It didn't when you burned."

"You didn't touch me then." She remembered that much; Sleipnir had kept him away.

"What happened to you?"

Liadan flushed, threw the coal back into the fire. Tir deserved an answer, no matter how much he might come to regret asking. "It's my moon cycle," she said.

He frowned.

Squirming beneath his relentless stare, she explained, "When mortal girls become women, their fertility is cyclical. A woman can't conceive a child until she's blooded, and when she is, once every month, her womb bleeds."

Tir paled, and two patches of bright red stained his cheeks. "I know this."

"Yes, well, Otherkind have cycles, too, except ours are different. Mine revolves around fire, my core element. Instead of bleeding, I burn. The pangs signal a firestorm, then the flames consume me. It exhausts me, and I sleep for three days afterward so my body can restore itself. My mother would call it a wizard's sleep. But I am Dragonblood, not a wizard."

She waited for him absorb that. For a long time, Tir didn't speak and had trouble meeting her gaze. To disguise his unease, he stoked the fire with his bare hand, then shook his head at the lack of damage and poured more water for her from a strange-looking bottle. "I should not have asked."

"You should not have followed. It's dangerous, for me and everyone else. I can't control the firestorm when it overtakes me. You could have died."

"I should have left you alone and naked in the desert for three days instead?"

Liadan grimaced. She hadn't thought of that when she'd mounted Sleipnir. Her only thought had been to get far enough away so she wouldn't hurt him. "I suppose not."

"This happens every month?"

She nodded.

"It looked… painful."

Liadan chuckled at the understatement. "Fantastically painful."

"How do you… How can you…?"

"Bear it? I've no other choice, do I? I can't change what I am. I wouldn't want to, if I could. All magic comes with a price. This is simply mine."

Sleipnir came to her, head low, and nuzzled her neck.

She smiled and patted his forehead. "You did well. Thank you."

The mount chuffed and lipped her shoulder.

"Why did you not tell me before?"

Liadan drank some more, then ate another bite of dried meat before she answered. "I don't usually make it a habit to reveal my greatest weakness to strangers. The firestorm may be deadly to others, but it doesn't last long; half a day, perhaps. And afterward, when I sleep, I am left completely defenseless. A tricky fellow might think to sever my head from my shoulders while I wasn't aware of it, and I couldn't do anything to stop him."

"You think I would do such a thing?"

"No, I suppose not."

Tir pushed to his feet, and Liadan suddenly realized he was shirtless. "You trusted your horse over me!"

She gaped. "Not long ago you told me I should fear you, and now you want my trust?"

"That was before—" He cut himself off, frowning into the distance.

"Before what?"

He gestured with his hand.

"Oh, what is that supposed to mean?"

Tir scowled, and reached for her arm. "It means get up." He pulled her to her feet, then turned her north. "Do you see that?"

Liadan squinted into the distance. The day was hot, the air wavered, and she could hardly tell where the ground ended and the sky began, but as her sight adjusted, faint, dark smudges appeared on the horizon. "Are those riders?"

"We should go."

"Why?" she asked, but ran for her pack anyway to rummage through it for her spare set of clothes. No chest binds; she tore up her scarf to repurpose it, then retied her vial around her neck. It'd been a stroke of luck that she'd taken it off before riding out. The fragile glass wouldn't have survived the heat.

"We don't have time for this," Tir called while he saddled Tarabas.

In answer, she yanked off his shirt and tossed it at the back of his head. "Then stop dawdling and get dressed." It took her mere moments to bind herself and dress. She saddled Sleipnir while Tir secured their supplies, and only when she'd settled astride her mount did she remember she had no shoes. She'd left her riding boots behind in Sadirak, and the ones Tir had gotten for her had burned in the firestorm.

"Can you ride?"

How was she supposed to walk without shoes?

"Liadan!"

She met his gaze. "No shoes."

Cursing, he dismounted and ran for a low plant by the palms, cut off several leaves and shoved them into her arms before he mounted again.

"How are these helpful?" she demanded, balancing an armful of thick, green blades with hard, spiked edges.

"Ride!" he ordered, and took off.

Swearing as only a girl who'd grown up frequenting Wilderheim's taverns could, she stuffed the plants into her saddlebag, and spurred Sleipnir after him.

They put countless miles of sun-baked earth between them and the oasis, rode so hard and so long, Liadan lost all sense of time and direction. Nothing marred the barren landscape to tell her where she was, or which way they were going, and it terrified her. The sheer emptiness felt as if it would swallow her whole; she could disappear here, and no one would ever find her.

"Do you know where we're going?"

"South," Tir answered. How could he be so certain?

Liadan scanned for insects scurrying across the ground, but found none. No birds circled, and no fragments of bone showed any hint that a living creature of any kind had ever passed through here.

Tir had stopped talking altogether. His jaw was tense all the time and he kept looking over his shoulder. She hoped it was because he wanted to see whether or not they were being followed, and not because he was lost. They'd left no tracks, which meant they could have been riding in giant circles and never known it because they'd have never crossed their own trail.

Sleipnir was slick with sweat. The horses couldn't take much more of this. "Tir, stop!"

"A little farther, we're almost there!"

Tarabas jerked sideways with a scream, but Tir pulled him back in line.

"We're killing them!"

Tir leaned low over Tarabas' neck, spoke into his ear. Liadan couldn't hear what he said, but the animal seemed to gain some strength from the words and ran on, forcing her to keep up on Sleipnir if they didn't want to be left behind.

Ahead, the desert changed. At first, she thought the mounds were mountains, but the closer they got, the better she could see. Not mountains—massive sand dunes. Beneath them, hoofbeats softened, and Liadan stared out to the left and right, marveling at the change. Sand blew across the hard-packed ground in small flurries, lapping at the cracked earth like an eternally frozen sea and those dunes might as well have been waves.

Tir led them up the crest of one dune. Liadan worried they'd sink into the stuff, but although it was slower going for the mounts, they still managed, scaling the next one, and the next, until Tir finally deemed them far enough to stop. He dismounted and pressed his forehead to Tarabas', speaking soft words to calm him.

Sleipnir wasn't so easily soothed; he chewed at his bit, shaking his head as if the feel of his bridle irritated him. Liadan retrieved her waterskin and a hollowed-out bowl she'd found strapped to her supplies. She poured out as much water as the bowl could hold without spilling, then fed it to Sleipnir. When he'd drained it, she refilled the bowl again, and then one more time until the skin ran dry. Liadan stroked him a couple of times, as much in thanks as in apology, then she retied the skin and the bowl to his saddle before rounding on Tir.

"What is the matter with you? You could have killed us all!"

"I did not," he said shortly. Tarabas quivered beneath his hand. He'd given the stallion as much water as he dared, but despite the additional water he'd collected into the gourds, it wouldn't be enough to sustain them. They'd have to ration as much as possible until they reached Imarah.

"Who were those riders?" she demanded.

"I don't know."

"Then why did you run? They could have had supplies!"

"And you think they would have shared? Look around, Princess. This is not your world; it is mine. And in it, you eat and drink what you can steal. I counted at least seven in their company, maybe more. With luck, they would have taken the horses and every last bit of useful provisions we had and left us for dead. More likely, they would not have bothered fighting. They would have slit our throats and taken over the oasis." Worse yet, those riders could have been *masar*—the ones from Sadirak or elsewhere, it would have made no difference—they never traveled in groups fewer than a dozen.

"They wouldn't have dared. And if they did, they most certainly would not have won. I could have—"

"What, Princess? Killed them all?" He couldn't tell whether her cheeks were red from the sun or the heat of her blush. As powerful as Liadan was, he had no doubt she could have dealt with the riders handily, even weakened from her firestorm. But that had been the farthest thing from his mind when he'd rushed them away from the oasis. With Sadirak still too close for his liking, and the *masar* no doubt on their trail, he could only think of getting Liadan as far away as possible. How incredibly foolish of him; trying to protect the immortal fire warrior he was bringing back to save his tribe. He couldn't even think it without feeling embarrassed. "That would make you no better than them," he told her. Better she believed he'd done it to spare her conscience, than to suspect him of being motivated by useless sentiment.

"Can one afford to be merciful in a fight to the death?" she challenged softly. "Tell me, *sher'nah*, I am certain you would know better than I." Before he could answer, she turned her back on him and mounted Sleipnir. "What now?"

Tir was only too happy to let the matter rest. "These dunes run north to south. If we follow them south, they will lead us to the First Valley." They were still too far west. They'd emerge in the First City, or just east of it. He hoped it was the latter.

He let Liadan set the pace. Now that she had at least some sense of direction, she didn't need him to lead, and she seemed to be calmer when she had control over where they were going.

Despite their mad race to reach the sands, Tir wasn't satisfied they hadn't been followed; the sensation of being watched prickled at the back of his neck, but no matter how many times he sought the source, he found none. The dunes hid their presence better than the open desert, but by the same token, they also hid whoever was on their trail. Not wanting to distress Liadan, he kept his suspicions to himself and his hand on the pommel of his sword.

They rode through the night in weary silence, which gave him too much time to think. He wanted to rail at Liadan again for keeping her firestorm a secret; she could have gotten them both killed!

But what worried him more was his newfound ability to touch fire without being burned by it. He'd never considered what mingling his blood with an Other might do, what it might turn him into. Was he still human? Was the relentless pull he felt toward Liadan, the maddening protectiveness and curiosity, a product of the blood oath, or of his own treacherous feelings? The closer they rode to Imarah, the more he questioned the wisdom of bringing her along, and each repeated nightmare strengthened the dread that he was taking her to her death.

Tir told himself his fear was unfounded; that she'd come along of her own volition—had forced his hand to take her with him—and that her death, should it come to that, would mean little to him, even less to his tribe. But he didn't believe his own lie. Even knowing it was ill-advised, Tir cared whether Liadan lived or died. He cared whether she trusted him, whether she was tired, or hurting, or worried.

He feared examining those feelings too closely, lest he discover they ran deeper than was wise. They'd reach Imarah soon enough, and when they did, Tir would remember his duty, and Liadan would once again be nothing more than a tool he'd use to fulfill it. He would not do something as idiotic as fall in love with an Other.

But even with the waxing moon and millions of stars twinkling in the sky above him, he found no reassurance in the night's cool darkness; no comfort in its beauty, when all he saw was Liadan's gently glowing form swaying in Sleipnir's saddle. She turned to him, smiling wearily, and Tir was dismayed by his sudden hope that maybe none of his worries were as bad as they seemed. So what if Liadan's blood had changed him? Maybe its magic would make him strong enough to save his people, make him into the king they deserved. Maybe it had bound him to the princess in some elemental way, and she felt the same inexplicable pull toward him in return.

Maybe, just maybe, he wouldn't turn out like Geir at all.

By morning, the parallel sand dunes had shrunk into the hard, arid ground of the First Valley, and red clay houses appeared on the horizon. Tir's heart sank. The First City.

Liadan gave him a beatific smile. "We made it." With a triumphant whoop, she stood up on Sleipnir's back, spread her arms wide, and shouted strange words at the sky.

Tir swallowed, shifted uneasily in his saddle. He didn't share her enthusiasm.

How could he?

There was a reason Imarah had left the First City all those years ago.

20

They entered the city as the last of the night's coolness evaporated and the sun reclaimed the earth. It was exactly as Liadan had seen it in her vision: empty, abandoned; a ghost town with invisible eyes, watching them from every dark window and open doorway. Eerie winds howled through the passageways, and small items blew across them, mimicking the sound of running feet.

At first, they stopped in every house, searching for any usable items. Shoes were Liadan's highest priority. But aside from broken shards of pottery and torn rags, they found nothing but dead air. Worse, it was death on the air. She wouldn't ask—didn't want her suspicions confirmed—but Liadan knew many had died here. Hundreds, perhaps thousands. There were no markers to be seen, but this whole city was a burial ground, and each step felt like she was dancing on her own grave.

The city sprawled along the sides of the wide river basin Tir had mentioned. Only dry clay remained of the once mighty river, darker than the surrounding earth and the obvious source of building material.

"How long ago did the river run dry?" she asked, keeping her voice barely above a whisper.

Tir's jaw muscle twitched. "Almost twenty years. They say it happened too quickly. One day, children played on its banks; the next morning, the basin was half empty, and dead fish were floating on the surface. The day after that, those fish were baking on the dry clay of the riverbed. The Magi said it was an omen, that the gods were testing our faith. They sacrificed three goats, three mules, and three horses to appease them. Instead of water, the gods sent us a swarm of locusts and a plague."

They turned onto a much wider street that led to a set of large buildings. Unlike the clay houses, these were made of stone and marble, with tall pillars supporting bright white roofs. One stood on each side of the street, and beyond them, straight ahead, loomed a massive palace with gilded ornaments and golden statues. "The First City must have been very rich."

"Yes. These used to be the stables. The troughs were filled by canals leading from the river, so the horses always had fresh water. And the palace was built by Khalil al-Raseph, the greatest of our kings. He built it to house his twenty wives and seventy-five children. Their orchards were so fertile, not even all of his kin could consume all of the figs. The fruits were left to rot on the ground to fertilize the next season's harvest."

"All this precious metal… Why is it still here? The city must have been raided countless times since then."

"What good is gold to a man dying of thirst, if there is no water to buy with it? The raiders took our wines, fruits, our animals, and sometimes our women. The gold and jewels would have been nothing but a burden."

Most of the palace windows had been broken out, but the remaining ones were filled with a mesh-like cage. The main doors must have been massive to fill the hole in the wall they'd left behind. Small pieces still hung off the hinges, and Liadan leaned close to examine one no bigger than her hand, but with a carving of a woman's face and hair easily recognizable. Such beautiful detail in so small a piece.

Tir joined her there. "The portals were covered with carvings like this. They said *shansher* Khalil wanted to immortalize the likeness of each of his wives and children. His first wife and his oldest son were carved into ebony statues for the palace orchard. When the raiders came nineteen years ago, my father set his eldest sons to guard the orchard and those statues." Tir shifted, and his voice became grave. "He should have had them guard the women and children instead. The first battle took three of his wives and seven of his smallest children. They threw the babes from the balconies. Those who survived were trampled by their war horses."

Tears choked Liadan. She didn't know what to say. He must have been old enough to remember it, and those children had been his brothers and sisters. She reached for his clenched hand to offer what little comfort she could, but he shoved to his feet away from her. "There used to be a well in the orchard, dug quite deep. With any luck, there will be a little water left in there. Do not stray too far. There is evil soaking every tile and every pillar here. We must stay together."

Horses in tow, they walked through the empty palace with its cavernous chambers, where the only thing supporting the floor above was a series of pillars. Beyond the main building, the orchard Tir had mentioned was a wasteland; what few trees remained were barren sticks in the ground, many of them no more than blackened stumps. Dried grass and weeds crunched beneath her bare feet, and Liadan winced each time she stepped on a thorn.

The well was housed in a wide circle of twelve pillars that used to support a roof. In the center, marble benches once provided a respite for tired feet. Now, all but one were shattered to pieces, their bright white shards littering the ground. The well itself was as wide as Liadan was tall, with a set of pulleys for lowering a water bucket into its depths. The mechanism was destroyed, but that didn't seem to matter to Tir.

He took the length of rope, tested its strength and, tying one end to a tree stump, tossed the other end into the well. "You can't mean to go down there!"

"How else do you think we will get the water?"

"If there even is any. Tir, that rope is twenty years old. What if it breaks?"

"Then I will use my blades to climb back out. Stop fussing, woman, and find me a bucket instead."

Growling, Liadan searched for anything that might be useful. She found three buckets, all broken. "I see nothing," she complained, but Tir was already halfway down the well.

"Then look inside," he called back. "There might be more in the stables. But don't take too long."

Liadan ran, not keen on wandering alone if she could help it. The stables were as grand as the palace. She might have admired them, except their sheer size made her search more difficult. Liadan checked each stall, every nook and cranny, but found nothing.

Until she looked up toward a loft not much larger than a shelf. There, stacked in a row and untouched by the violence that had destroyed this place, were at least two dozen wooden buckets. But there was no ladder. "Bollocks."

Her nape prickled, and she spun around, sword in hand. No one there. Nothing moved, no whisper of sound betrayed another's presence. But Liadan felt it. Wary, she kept her sword unsheathed as she looked through the stalls again. She found a frayed piece of rope and an old, warped horseshoe.

It would have to do. Tying the rope around the metal, she returned to the loft. Her first throw missed by a hair's breadth. Her second, however, caught in one of the bucket stacks, and the eerie feeling of being watched intensified. One sharp tug, and the buckets toppled from the loft. Two broke apart on impact, but the innermost one survived. She did it again with three more stacks until the rope snapped, but by then, she had four solid buckets in her grasp. Though it made her twitchy, Liadan sheathed her sword so she could carry them all at once, and raced back to the orchard.

The sight of Sleipnir and Tarabas grazing on dry grass eased her a little, but not enough. She needed Tir out of that well. "Are you still alive down there?" she called.

Tir cursed, and a large piece of marble flew out of the well. "Too much debris to see anything. I need to clear it out to get to the earth."

"Here." She pulled the rope up, tied a bucket to it, and lowered it down into the well.

Tir filled it with marble and rocks, and Liadan hauled it out. Empty bucket into the well, heavy bucket out of the well, over and over until her arms quivered with strain and her shirt was soaked with sweat.

On her next pass, she sent him a waterskin, along with some bread and hard cheese.

"Thanks," he called up.

She sat with her back against the well while they ate and rested. "We should have taken Fal with us. He can find water anywhere."

"That might have been good to know before we left."

Liadan chuckled.

"Tell me about your dragon. Is he truly as fearsome as your fire story?"

Liadan smiled, missing her grandfather. "Oh, yes. He's as tall as a mountain, and when he stretches out his wings, they cover entire fields. One of his fangs is as large as I am tall." At least that's how she'd always thought of him.

"Does he have wings like a bat?"

"No. He… It's difficult to explain. He's scaled like a lizard, but the scales on his wings are softer, more flexible than the shield scales on his chest. They're almost soft enough to be cloth, but you'd break your sword if you tried to cut them from his wings."

"Sounds like magic."

She grinned. "It is. When he changes shape, he burns the old body and reforms the ashes into the new. But he can do it so fast, you'd miss it if you blinked."

"Can you do the same?"

"No. Perhaps if I'd been born in Otherlands, where magic saturates the very air, I might have learned to harness the ability. Here, the taint of my human blood prevents it."

They fell into a companionable silence while they ate. Liadan imagined he mirrored her pose, sitting against the wall of the well, and if he weren't so far below, they'd have been back to back. It was pleasant outside, the kind of midday when the grass beckoned the weary to rest their heads upon it. The grass here was too dry for that, but if she strung up a blanket between those trees, it would do just as well. With the promise of shelter nearby, Liadan could even appreciate the sun shining down on her. How beautiful this place must have been before the drought—bright green grass all around, with pathways of marble stones here and there. She'd never seen a fig tree, but she could imagine them, weighed down with fruits. Children would play nearby, and beautifully attired wives would stroll through the orchard, arm in arm.

It's not so different from Dai.

Liadan didn't realize she'd spoken aloud until Tir answered. "No, it was not. Different people, perhaps, but the First City was as much a place of beauty as your Dai and Frastmir. The river was sacred to my people, blessed by the goddess Inaras. It could heal the sick, restore the weary. Travelers would come from all corners of Aegiros to fill even one bottle with it."

"And I am sure they paid well for the privilege."

"No. It is a great sin to sell what is given by the gods. Many left tokens of gratitude in our temples, but those offerings were for Inaras, not the Imarah." He sighed. "We should finish this."

They'd already cleared most of the debris. When he began to dig, he filled the bucket with earth and rubble, and Liadan lost count of how many times she'd hauled that bucket up. But as the day wore on, the dirt inside became darker and damper, and she redoubled her efforts, hope giving her strength when she didn't think she had any left.

Then Tir whooped in triumph, and she grinned. He'd struck water. "Bucket! Quick!"

Liadan lowered it down, and after a long moment, he tugged on the rope to signal it was full. She carefully pulled it up, then squealed in delight to see the murky liquid inside. She poured it into a waiting bucket and sent the old one back down. While Tir filled it, Liadan gave the first to Sleipnir and Tarabas, letting them drink.

She returned to the well, pulled up the second load, and poured it into a new bucket. "How much is there?" she asked. The horses could use at least two or three more turns each, but so could she and Tir.

"Keep pulling it up."

She did, and they kept at it until the horses were sated, wandering away to graze. Liadan filled every container she could find: the waterskins, the strange bottles and bowls, even some serviceable clay dishes she'd found inside the palace. With all of that and four full buckets, they ran out of containers, while water continued to trickle up through the dirt in the well. Giddy with excitement, she helped

Tir up and out as the sun began to set. He was covered with mud, but his smile was as brilliant as hers felt, and as soon as he was safely out of the hole, she threw her arms around him.

He laughed as they embraced. "There is more down there if we can find something to get it out with."

"Isn't it enough to know it's there?"

"No. Tomorrow it might not be."

His waning good mood said he spoke from experience, and it sobered her, as well. They had plenty for a couple of days, at least, and it should be enough until they set out for his tribe, but who knew what they might find there, if anything?

They took the containers inside the palace and lined them up along one wall. Tir found an old oil lamp, Liadan lit the wick and, keeping close together, they searched through the building. In one chamber, furniture lay in broken piles, so they gathered the wood for a fire. In another, chests of silks and gowns lay scattered and forgotten, dirty with dust and soot. Liadan searched through them until she found a scarf to replace hers and spare clothes that would fit them both. Tir managed to dig out several pairs of shoes that would fit her.

The palace had no kitchens, only a cool, underground pantry, which was in somewhat better shape than the rest of the place. Tir found two more buckets and several bottles that looked sturdy enough to survive on horseback. They took them all, and returned to the great hall by the orchard.

Though Liadan didn't want him to, Tir crawled back inside the well to fill the new containers, still worried the water would disappear as quickly as he'd found it. It'd happened often enough to his tribe, and he refused to let it go to waste. When he came back out, he took one of the buckets to wash and changed out of his muddy clothes.

The garments he donned were familiar to him—they'd used to belong to his eldest brother, Zeke. At five years old, Tir had thought his brother a giant. Zeke had used to laugh, picking Tir up one-armed to show off how big and strong he was; had carried him on his shoulders and pretended to forget Tir was there. He'd died a year after their tribe had fled the city, his soul devoured by a demon. Now, Tir couldn't reconcile the memory of his brother with the clothes he'd put on. They were too small to have belonged to him, surely, but the ornate letter Z embroidered into the collar didn't lie.

By the time he'd returned to the palace hall, Liadan had started a fire, and set out their pallets and a small meal. She wasn't eating. Instead, she scanned the shadows for unseen threats.

"Keep the fire going and we will be safe," he said. "Demons fear light. They will not come near us while we're inside it."

Liadan scowled. "You could have said so." She got up and, sparking fire in both hands, went back into the orchard to call the horses. Once they'd clattered inside, she set fire to the ground along the entryway. "There, that'll keep them out."

"For a while." From that side, at least. The look she gave him made Tir laugh. "Eat. We are as safe here as anywhere." And while she ate, he retrieved the aloe leaves he'd gathered and cut a silk scarf into strips.

"What are those, anyway?"

He came to her side of the fire, pulled out his eating knife and, with a few careful slices of the blade, exposed the leaf's soft, juicy center, squeezing the excess juice into a small container he'd brought from the pantry. "Give me your feet."

"No, I need them."

Tir scowled.

Liadan rolled her eyes, proffered one foot, and he winced at the amount of damage it'd sustained in just one day. She'd not complained a single time, and he knew she'd been running over thorns and shards in the orchard, not to mention the hard, scorching city ground.

"There's no need for this, you know. They'll be healed by morning."

"Perhaps," he allowed. "But what if we need to run before then?"

Liadan made a face, but didn't protest when he dipped a cloth into the closest bowl of water to wash the wounds of dirt and dried blood. The skin was tender and cut up, redder than he would have liked.

"Urine helps," Liadan said, and when he looked at her, horrified, she shrugged. "That's what we use at home to stave off infection."

He shuddered. "Animals." Liadan laughed, coaxing a smile from him in return. "My people use honey." Since he didn't have any, though, he instead applied the aloe—it'd soothe the cuts and help them heal, but she'd have to be careful. Using clean silks, he tied strips of the leaf core to her soles and helped her put shoes on. "Try not to walk on them tonight, if you can help it."

"Don't worry, I won't run away into the night to battle demons on my own."

How easily she jested about things she didn't understand. "See that you don't."

The night was eerily quiet. Even without people, there ought to have been some noise—the hiss of insects, the squeak of bats, even the unearthly howl of wild dogs would have been preferable to this silence.

Tir hadn't slept a full night since before Sadirak, and his head dipped lower and lower until he dozed off where he sat, weary to his very soul.

Danna Tir...

Tir jerked awake.

Liadan blinked at him, bleary-eyed. "Sleep. I can tend the fire."

It must have been a dream; his mind was playing tricks on him. Settling a blanket about his shoulders, he lay down and closed his eyes.

Danna... danna Tir...

Half-asleep already, Tir tilted his head back toward the source of the childish voice.

In the middle of the gaping entryway stood a small girl dressed in dirty rags, long, matted hair covering half of her face. He sat up so quickly, his head spun, and Liadan started. "What is it?"

"Meagara bahran a mi, danna Tir." Please help me, uncle Tir.

"Tir? What's the matter?"

At Liadan's voice, the girl gasped and ran.

"No, wait!" Tir stumbled to his feet after her.

"Tir!"

He followed the girl out of the palace and into the streets, heedless of the dark night closing in on him. One of his kin needed help; Tir didn't stop to think how a child so small had found her way here alone. She was fast. He almost lost her as she weaved between buildings, but he kept going. "Wait," he called after her. "Please, I won't hurt you!"

Her sobbing cry broke his heart. He ran faster to catch up to her, and found her around the next corner, huddled with her back to him against a wall at the end of the pass. Her little shoulders rose and fell with harsh breaths. He stopped so as not to startle her. Then, moving ever so slowly, he approached the weeping child. "What is your name?" he asked in their tongue. "Where is your mother?"

"Dead," she wailed.

His step faltered.

Liadan slammed into him, almost knocking him over. "What—"

"*Shh!*" He righted her, never taking his eyes off the girl who'd now turned toward them. He still couldn't see her face. "What is your name, little one?"

"Tir..." Liadan warned.

He waved her away. "Go on, you can tell me."

"I have none," the girl said.

Liadan tugged at his shirt. "Tir, we should go back."

He brushed her off. "Don't tell me you're afraid of a child," he said, then turned back to the girl. "How can that be, dear one? Everyone has a name."

"Help me." She reached both bone-thin arms out to him. "Please help me, uncle Tir."

He opened his arms to her in return, but Liadan knocked them down and grabbed his wrist, her nails digging into his skin. "Children have feet!" she snarled.

Tir looked down to where he was certain he'd seen the child's toes curl into the dirt. There was nothing. She stood there, yet she didn't; the ragged bottom edge of her overlarge shirt hovered above the ground like a spectre.

"Please help me, uncle Tir. I am so hungry." The girl moved forward, her body swaying as if she'd taken a step, but as the wind billowed her shirt, it revealed no legs to carry her meager weight.

A fireball flew from Liadan's hand and struck the child, who stumbled back a step, head bowed to look down at her charred shirt.

"Run," Liadan said.

Tir backed up a step as the child tipped her head sideways, then snapped it up, her face contorting into a monstrous demon as her jaw unhinged, the better to bare rows upon rows of needle-sharp fangs. And she screeched so loud, Tir almost fell to his knees.

"*Run!*" Liadan screamed, pulling him along when he tripped over his own feet.

They raced back toward the palace as more of those unearthly screams echoed throughout the city. Tir felt them gathering, closing in on them, like a swift frost creeping along the ground. Liadan started glowing, all but the hand she had on his arm turning bright hot to illuminate the passageways. She veered left and, with a blast of heat, set fire to an old barrel. Back right and an old sack of wood chips exploded in a burst of light.

One more turn, and they were on the main path to the palace. Shadows with gray, skeletal faces and glowing red eyes swarmed between them and the safety of those walls, their fury palpable, their claws and fangs glinting in the night. Tir had seen them before, knew well what they could do, and that knowledge made him falter.

Liadan squeezed his arm, nails digging harder into his flesh, forcing his gaze away from the ravenous swarm to focus on her. He twisted free and clasped hands with her instead, fingers entwined so tightly, they wouldn't be separated unless a blade sliced them apart. "We need fire!"

Flames burst from her in a bright flare. "Don't let go, and don't stop!"

The flames licked across her arm over to him, covering him like second skin, and Tir gasped to feel their heat—heat, but not pain. The protection of Liadan's blood held steady, keeping him safe within her fire, and she stoked it as bright as their mad dash would allow, building a shield in the front, with long tendrils trailing around to cover their backs.

Demons screeched and scattered as Tir and Liadan ran headlong through the swarm. All around, Dark shadows swooped down time and again, trying to sink their claws through the flames. Scraps of darkness caught aflame, forcing them back, incensing them further, but Liadan's protection held.

They ran up the palace stairs, and Liadan barred the entrance with a wall of fire so high, the flames licked at the ceiling. Before Tir had even caught his breath, she did the same with the orchard doorway, and then the hallways at either end. Only when she was certain they were safe did she extinguish their living shield and release him.

He was about to thank her, when her hand cracked across his cheek. Anger blazed in her eyes, hotter than her flames.

Demons howled outside, battering themselves against the fiery curtain, while Liadan stared him down without a word, daring him to break the silence. "Never—again," she grated after a while. "Do you hear me? We move together. We fight together. You do not run out on your own—"

"The way you did?" he shot back.

She struck out again, but this time, Tir caught her hand. Liadan broke his hold and shoved at his chest, hard enough to make him step back. "My risk was a calculated one and posed danger to no one but me! Yours could have killed us both, you thoughtless, arrogant—*argh!*" She left him to pace back and forth between one flaming doorway and the other. The demons' cries intensified whenever she neared one of them.

Liadan fisted her hands in her hair. "How long will they keep screaming like that?"

"Until the sun forces them back into hiding," he begrudged.

Her hands lowered uneasily, and she eyed the barrier she'd erected. "My fire didn't kill it," she said softly.

"No, it did not."

With those words, the fragile hope he'd nurtured to be bringing salvation back to his tribe, died.

21

Neither of them slept a wink that night. Beyond Liadan's fear that the fires would go out if she closed her eyes, the demons were too loud to allow for rest. So many of them floated through the air; shadows and scraps blacker than the night, colder than ice, but at the same time, burning with a darkness Liadan had never encountered before.

And all she could think was: *My fire didn't kill them.* Hadn't even harmed the one masquerading as a child. Her entire strategy to defeat the demons had been to burn them. But if blades couldn't defeat them and fire couldn't harm them, what else could she do? And if fire couldn't kill them, why did it keep them out? Were the demons toying with them? She could believe it. Sometimes, when the fires parted just a little, she could see those soulless eyes staring at her, picking her out.

Though the demons were nigh indistinguishable through the fiery curtain, the longer they raged, the more familiar their voices became. She recognized the child by the way it wailed at the very edge of her flames, coming closer than any of the others; a steady, black shadow staring at her without cease, promising revenge.

She could pick out the ones who'd tried to score her back with their claws—they cawed in challenge with voices so powerful, they lured Tir to the fiery wall. He didn't cross, but when he retreated to her in the center of the room, he looked shaken, haunted. Worried he'd step through if she dozed off, Liadan coaxed him to sit beside her, linked her arm through his and sang bawdy drinking songs to drown out the demonic howls.

She knew the demons who'd eventually destroy her. They were the ones who, instead of ramming the fiery barricades, flew around the palace, searching for another way in. Several had already darkened the hallways, their screams echoing inside the palace. She felt the icy chill of those above them, heard them claw at the floor to dig their way through.

The worst of it came before dawn, when the demons' screeches began to sound human. Liadan flinched to hear three men scream in terror, then shivered with dread when, for a moment afterwards, the night fell deathly silent.

By the time the sun had chased them all back into hiding, Liadan was cramped from head to toe, and never so happy to see daylight. Tir stood first, wordlessly offering his hand to help her up, and she took it, wincing at the pins and needles in her legs. Tir steadied her, held her fast, when she would have pulled away. Startled, she met his gaze in silent question. Without a word, without looking away, he lifted her hand to his lips, then pressed it to his chest over his heart.

Humbled by the show of gratitude, she nodded a half-bow. "One life debt repaid. Only one left to go."

"There is no debt between us, *shai'iss*. But if there was, it would be mine. And I could never repay it, if I were to live a thousand years."

"*Shai'iss*? What does that mean?" Though Liadan was a quick study, she still had a way to go to fully comprehend the intricacies of the Aegiran language. One thing she'd come to understand, however: words beginning with that particular sound were usually associated with honor and respect. *Shansher*—king. *Sher'nah*—prince.

The brief smile Tir allowed never reached his eyes. "One day, perhaps I will tell you."

It was too dangerous for them to stay in the palace another night. After a quick, small meal, they gathered their supplies, studiously avoiding each other.

Tir checked the well and found it dry again. Deeper into the orchard, however, he found a two-wheeled cart in good shape. "From here on, we follow the riverbed. It is as good as a road, and will lead us to Imarah."

Liadan helped him load the cart with their supplies. All of their water was contained in three buckets, six earthen bottles, and whatever they'd brought with them to the First City. Five more canisters of oil were just enough to fill the cart's empty spaces, and a pile of clothes and blankets stuffed in between steadied the load.

Sleipnir and Tarabas had spooked badly the night before and now shivered, stepping out of the palace. Liadan spoke to her mount, touched him often for reassurance, but kept close watch on the shadows. She wanted to believe the demons were gone but couldn't convince herself of that when she kept seeing their eyes in every dark window and doorway.

Tir caught her hand when it began to smoke. "Save your strength. You will need it for the night."

"How much farther to Imarah?"

"Two days, perhaps two and a half with the cart." He eyed the rickety thing, which was serviceable enough, but jarred the load with each turn of the wheels. To preserve as much water as possible, Tir had covered the buckets with large platters and weighed them down with rocks, but it still seeped out through chips and chinks along the rim.

"Is it wise to be bringing it with us?" They could ride faster without it. Liadan didn't like the thought of getting caught out in the desert night again.

"It is never wise to leave water behind in the desert."

Liadan sighed. She knew that, of course, but last night's demon swarm had left her rattled and she couldn't help the urgency thrumming in her limbs, commanding her to move faster, to run away. Tir had warned her it would happen, and she flushed anew to remember how cavalierly she'd dismissed his words back in Wilderheim, thinking herself invincible.

Perhaps she was, but so, it seemed, were the demons.

Worry about them later, she told herself. *For now, focus on reaching Imarah.*

Tir wasn't the only one who'd ever had the idea of using the river as a road. At almost equidistant intervals, someone had built ramps down into the basin. Many were weathered and broken, but several still looked sturdy enough to be useful. With the cart between them, Tarabas and Sleipnir had to step carefully to avoid breaking a leg, but they managed, and Liadan breathed a sigh of relief when both horses and cart were firmly on the hard, clay bottom.

Dolls and wooden toys lay broken and trampled along the river-bed. Chests of treasures had been tossed aside as too useless to carry. Shattered cart wheels lay everywhere, but also weapons and saddles. "My people used the river to flee the city," Tir explained.

Liadan imagined the tribe making their way east, children crying for their homes, women hunched under the burden of their earthly belongings; she could almost see dead horses on the north bank, men stumbling around, driven mad by thirst.

Eyes and ears sharp for threats, they walked quickly out of the First City. Solid buildings became sparse and the farther they went, the less debris they found, until all evidence of humans having come this way disappeared. What once used to be a fertile valley was now dried to dust; nothing smaller than a tree remained, and those had long ago fallen over, having lost all moisture until they littered the valley floor like bones.

Soon, they lost sight of the city, and Liadan's apprehension of the setting sun redoubled. She wanted to move faster, to get as far as they could before night fell, but it would do no good. Darkness begot darkness. The demons they'd seen last night could just as easily come crawling out of the cart's shadows, if they didn't fear the light.

"You are quiet," Tir said.

"What is there to say?"

"You need not worry. You are protected by the brave Tirasdunh al-Dhakir, remember? No harm will come to you here."

His attempt to cheer her up didn't have the intended effect. "One thing we never discussed, *sher'nah*, is what will happen if neither of us is able to fulfill our oath."

"That will not happen."

"But it might—"

"It will not," he snapped, and stopped the horses to face her. "I swore

I would keep you safe, and I do not intend to fail."

"And what about me?"

Tir brushed back a stubborn lock of her hair, his thumb caressing her cheek. "You said you would do all in your power to aid us."

"My power is fire, and we both saw how weak a weapon it turned out to be."

"Did you not also tell me you have never tested its limits? You said it was too dangerous to try." He gestured all around them. "Nobody here to harm. No homes to destroy."

Had it been an order, Liadan would have fought him. But Tir had offered the possibility as an invitation and she was more than tempted to take him up on it. In Wilderheim, too many trees posed a hazard, and too many people and animals were in danger of being hurt. Here, as Tir had said, there was nothing.

Liadan looked to Sleipnir. "What do you think?"

Sleipnir snorted and nosed her sideways, all but shooing her away.

Tir took the reins from her. "Keep in sight of us, if you can. We will not stray from the riverbed. And if there is trouble, I expect you to scream."

"Likewise," she said.

With a bracing breath and watchful of anything out of the ordinary, Liadan crossed to the north bank and climbed out of the basin onto the hard desert ground. She kept step with Tir below, but let him take over the watch as she turned her sight inward.

Never before had Liadan questioned where her fire came from. Her soul felt like a tangible entity—a molten, fiery core swirling in endless eddies, flaring and condensing to mirror her moods. It fed her blood, and licked along the inside of her skin. She closed her eyes, imagining that core growing larger and hotter, and in her mind's eye, it slowly changed colors from red to gold, from gold to blue. The heat of it filled her chest, spread out into her limbs. The sun's rays were nothing compared to the inferno she stoked within her.

It frightened Liadan, made her stumble. There'd be no controlling such a fire if she let it loose. Worse than the firestorm of her moon cycle, which consumed only her, this blaze would explode outward as far as her soul could reach, and absolutely nothing living would escape it. If she lost control, Liadan could burn this world to ash.

Hands shaking, she pulled the fire back. It fought her control, refusing to be banked and imprisoned, now that it'd tasted the freedom of fresh air, the power it could hold, and the battle with herself left her breathless. Too much too quickly, and she tripped over her own feet, falling to her knees, gasping. But her fire was contained.

Down in the riverbed, Tir sent her an encouraging nod.

To stop would mean disappointing him.

Liadan pushed to her feet, closed her eyes again. When she reached for her soul's flames a second time, she drew out only a little, and in her hand, it swelled into a ball as large as her head. Bit by bit, she grew and shrank it, testing the ease with which the flame could be manipulated.

Red fire was the easiest; it was the coolest, and warmed rather than burned. Yellow fire was more willful; like the sun in the sky, it warmed from a distance, but too much or too close, and it began to burn. This was the fire she'd hurled at the demon last night and it'd done little more than tickle the thing.

Liadan shrank the orb. The smaller it was, the hotter it burned, until a bright blue marble circled around in her palm, jumped up and down, and then, of its own accord, levitated out of her grasp and shot into the sky. She'd lost it. "Bollocks!"

"What do you need?" Tir called.

"Something to hold the flame," she returned.

In answer, Tir tossed her sword up to the bank.

Liadan stared at the blade by her feet, while Tir moved on with the horses and the cart. Between one breath and another, she lit on an idea. The dragon had spelled the blade to be fireproof. She picked it up, called a small flame into her free hand, and polished the blade with it as she would with oil. As the steel heated, it caught the flame and held.

Liadan raised the sword aloft, swung it left to right, concentrating on the fire, and grinned from ear to ear when it didn't extinguish. She tried a combination or two; slowly at first, then at her fastest. The blade and the fire held.

With a few running steps, she caught up to Tir and kept pace with him as she gradually fed the blade more heat. Red flames turned yellow, then to blue, and still they held. She dragged the tip along the ground, charring a thin, black line alongside her path.

With the blade upside down, the flames licked up to her hand, coating it, and she eased them up to her elbow, but no farther. When her sleeve began to smolder, she was forced to extinguish her experiment. Liadan was fireproof, but her clothing was not, and she couldn't afford to lose another pair of shoes.

After wiping soot from her blade, she returned to the basin and accepted the waterskin Tir handed her. "Well?"

"I suppose we'll find out when the sun goes down."

22

When the shadows turned long, it became too dangerous to continue. Their pace had brought them to a fork in the riverbed, a natural rest stop, where remnants of old fires still marked the red clay with black soot. Tir remembered this place only too well; it was one of his earliest memories from childhood.

The night his tribe had stopped here, there'd been no music, only the sound of a people mourning—women had wailed, children had screamed, men had argued. Fights had broken out over which way the tribe should go come morning. Many had believed there'd be water and hope where the river branched out into creeks, and they'd hoped to find another flood plain like the one that had sprouted the river at the foot of the Silver Mountain to the west.

But Dhakir al-Bashir, Dhakir the Conqueror, hadn't wanted to stray from their eastward path, convinced their salvation lay where the sun was born each morning. Surely the source of light and life would succor them and restore their strength. He'd described visions sent to him by the gods each night, of black caves deep underground, caverns where crystalline lakes glistened and diamonds glittered in the walls.

Those who'd heard him had been scandalized—they were desert people, not cave dwellers!—and fights had become brawls, which had grown into a small revolt. In their fear and desperation, the once-proud people had turned on each other like savage beasts, tearing into one another worse than any demon could. By dawn, the tribe had split into two, each half going its own separate way.

To this day, Tir didn't know what had become of those who'd gone south, following the lead of Khiron, Dhakir's last remaining brother.

"Do you think they'll follow us?" Liadan asked as they dragged a dead tree down into the basin for firewood.

"I do not know."

When they dropped the wood onto a charred patch of red clay, Liadan worriedly wiped her hands on her pants. "There won't be enough."

The firewood would last through the night, but Tir knew she wasn't talking about that. Fire only burned with something to hold the flame. In the absence of wood or oil, Liadan could sustain a blaze, but for how long? Already she'd tired herself out practicing throughout the day, and neither of them had slept the night before. Tir was exhausted, and could only imagine the weariness Liadan must have felt.

She wiped the sweat from her brow with one shaky hand. With the other, she clutched the vial her brother had given her, and Tir didn't need to hear her thoughts to know what they were. "You are afraid."

"I'm tired," she lied. "That's not the same thing."

Tarabas fidgeted, tossing his head, prancing left and right. Tir went to soothe him, and glimpsed a familiar sight to the north. "Liadan!" He raced back and began to unload the cart.

"What are you doing?"

He grinned at her. "Help me turn the cart over."

"What?" She tossed pouches and bundles to the ground, and carefully arranged bottles to one side.

"No, over here. We need to cover them with the cart."

"Have you lost your mind?"

Tir only laughed.

For all its age, the cart was damned heavy, and when they tipped it over, they had to carefully manipulate it to keep it from buckling under its own weight. With their belongings safely stowed, Tir unsaddled the horses. "Find my tent and put your veil on."

"Why do I have a very bad feeling about this?"

"Because you are a smart woman. There's a dust storm coming."

"And you want to outrun it?"

Taking the tent from her, Tir herded Liadan toward the north bank. "That would be a waste of a perfectly good storm," he said. "Keep close to me."

"What about the horses?"

"We have to leave them behind." Horses had better instincts when it came to natural phenomena. They'd be better off on their own than where Tir planned to take Liadan: straight into the heart of the storm.

She saw the billowing wall of sand rushing to meet them, and gasped, stopping in her tracks. They needed to reach the dunes before the storm washed over them. Tir grabbed her hand and dragged her along, running as fast as his feet could carry him. They reached soft sand with mere moments to spare, and Tir quickly pitched the small tent. Not enough to cover more than their upper bodies if they stretched out, but that's all they needed. The storm was almost upon them with a roar so loud he couldn't make himself heard, and winds so powerful they snatched at his clothes and hair.

Liadan fought him, refusing to go into the tent, but Tir wrestled her down into the shelter just as its sides bowed inward with the force of the storm. Her eyes widened, and she gasped for breath. She snatched off her veil, clawed at the tent wall. "W-we're getting buried!"

"Shh," he soothed, catching her flailing hands against his chest so she could feel his steady heartbeat. "We're getting hidden."

Liadan shook her head, struggling to free herself. "No! We'll die!"

"Liadan—"

"And Sleipnir—the demons—"

"Liadan, stop!"

"—they'll kill him!"

Tir silenced her frantic tirade with a kiss, and Liadan stilled against him so completely, she stopped breathing. Her heart raced, pulse throbbing in her lips against his. Tir had only needed her to calm down before she fainted, but once he'd had a taste of her, he wanted more. Shifting closer, he tangled his hand in her wild hair, pulling her tight against his body, relishing the way her hands curled into his shirt.

Little by little, she softened, and he rubbed soothing circles over her back until the fear had ebbed out of her. Until she kissed him back.

But all too soon she pushed away. Tir allowed her enough room to break their kiss, but not enough to pull out of his embrace. "Have you changed your mind about taking an Other as your mate?" she asked.

Tir's mind was slow to catch up to her words.

She took his silence for an answer and shifted farther away, as far as the small tent would allow. "Then you shouldn't do that again."

~

At its strongest, the sandstorm tore at their meager shelter, winds howling worse than the demons had the night before. Still, the worst of it came when all sounds dulled to almost nothing. Liadan's legs had become buried in the sand, its weight pinning her in place. In the tomb-like darkness, she desperately pushed against the tent wall, marking the depth of the sand by the amount of resistance she met. Tir had set the tent with one corner against the coming storm to carve a wedge into its force. Had he built it with the flat side facing north, the cloth would have torn apart in moments.

As it was, Liadan schooled herself not to panic. From the floor of the tent, she traced the cloth up to the height of her shoulder. Nothing but a solid wall on the other side. A few hand widths farther up, still more sand. Liadan paused, glancing to where the tent's ceiling marked her final hope in two meager hand widths. With a shuddering breath, she licked her dry lips, then eased her hand higher. At the very top, barely two finger widths of cloth depressed into a softer layer. Still not emptiness, but enough to tell her the surface was within reach.

The bastard Aegiran had buried them! A small sound escaped her, and she held her breath to contain more of them. But her fire betrayed her weakness. As her fear rose, Liadan began to glow, illuminating the cramped space. Had it somehow gotten smaller?

She pushed at that small patch of tent, testing its give to reassure herself that there was still a way out.

Tir curled his fingers around hers to stop the frantic movement. "Be at ease," he said. "Sleep."

"Will that make dying easier?" She couldn't take a deep enough breath to satisfy her lungs; they screamed for air, but with each gasp, there was less of it, and the tent walls were pressing closer with the weight of the entire desert.

"We will not die," he insisted, pulling her hand down and to her front. With his chest against her back, he embraced her, speaking quietly into her ear. "Every storm passes eventually. Every fear can be overcome. Close your eyes, and see yourself standing on the surface."

Struggling for breath, Liadan closed her eyes, firming her chin against a quiver.

"Can you see it?"

She imagined the hard, cracked ground they'd crossed to get to the sand dunes, and pretended her feet now pushed against its sturdy surface.

"Feel the sun on your face. Breathe in the hot air." Tir's voice was so steady, its timbre reassuring enough to calm her mind.

Liadan inhaled, and by some miracle, her throat opened, allowing for a full breath. She let it out slowly, then tried again, picturing herself soaring on the dragon's back. She grasped on to the vision, with the whole of the sky open to her, every which way she looked, and Tir at her back, flying with her. For a moment, lost in thought, her body felt lighter, cushioned by feathery clouds; her quick heartbeat echoed her exhilaration, not her fear, and Tir's arms were a welcome embrace. She reformed her courage from his strength, found comfort in his voice, and slowly released her fear, placing her trust wholly in him. And for just a moment, Liadan felt at peace. Despite the near-suffocation inside the tent, Tir's words lulled her, and she began drifting off to sleep.

And then the first demonic scream reverberated through the night sky.

Liadan gasped, tensing against Tir.

"Be still," he said, pulling her closer. "They will not find us here. Not before the morning sun forces them back into hiding."

"B-but they're out there," she replied.

"Yes."

"That means the storm has passed." Which meant they could get out! How the bloody hell did he intend to get them out? And why wasn't he doing it?

His stubbled cheek rasped against hers in a smile. "Yes. Now we need only wait for morning light."

What? No! "I can protect us," she said quickly, clawing at the tent to get free. "If we dig our way out, I can make another shroud like before. The demons won't touch us—"

"You would choke us on smoke before we managed to dig ourselves clear. You must be patient." He pulled her hands down a second time, and a third when she fought free of him.

"I can't breathe!"

He caught her hands one more time, pressing them to her chest with his arms around her, binding them in place so she couldn't move. "Then how can you speak?"

Liadan shut her mouth. Her struggles eased, but her mind still raced with the possibility of getting out, breathing real air.

"Try to sleep," Tir said. "In the morning, this will all have been a dream."

"How can you be so calm?"

He smiled. "What should I be instead? Sometimes in battle, all you can do is wait. During the ordeal of *kharashan*—"

"The ordeal of what?"

"Our tribe used to train some of the fiercest warriors in Aegiros. They were legion, back in the day. When we were driven out of the First City, most of the *kharesh* took the path south with my uncle and his family. He was the one who'd trained them all. He thought my father was mad for continuing east, downstream of a dead river. Only Farraj and a few others chose to stay with the *shansher*. They had sworn their lives to him, and refused to break their oath. My father knew strife would follow us, and so he ordered Farraj to continue training the men in the same way they had always been trained. He does so to this day."

Liadan absorbed all of this in silence.

Tir waited for her to offer an opinion, and when she didn't, he continued. Speaking of his people was a balm to his restless soul. While they were still in his mind, they were still alive. "When men train with the *kharesh*, they are not called as such. They are still only men. To become true *kharesh*, they must pass the ordeal of *kharashan*.

We hold these rites sacred, and each man must face the ordeal on his own. Some succeed and become *kharesh*. Some fail, and return to their family homes in shame. A few, too foolish or proud to admit defeat, fight to the death in hopes of making it through."

"You are one of them now, yes?"

He grunted in answer.

"You must have found it easy, being the prince of your tribe."

Tir tempered his laugh into a chuckle. "Hardly. The *kharesh* make no exceptions for anyone, regardless of station. When I faced my ordeal, I still had two older brothers who would have led the tribe after my father's death. I was no better than any other in training, and I was treated no differently."

"I see."

"Do you?" he replied, greatly amused. "Would it surprise you to hear I almost died during the ordeal?" In truth, he should have died. He'd been too young, forced into the *kharashan* too soon, because Imarah had needed every man they could spare. But that was no excuse. A true *kharesh* was always prepared, no matter what the circumstances. His ordeal had lasted three days, and by the end of it, he'd been reduced to crawling back to his tent, too weak and too sick to walk upright. But he'd made it back. Five of the others had not, their bodies forever lost to the desert sands.

Liadan replied with a thoughtful hum.

In the ensuing silence, demons swooped down toward the sands, screaming their rage. Liadan gasped, tensing in his arms.

"What does that mean, *hmm*?" he asked to distract her.

Her breathing ragged, she said, "I-I was only thinking of my grandfather, and what he would have made of the *kharesh*."

"Was the dragon's training any easier for you, being his granddaughter?"

"Ha! I think not. And if he ever says otherwise, he is a gods damned liar."

The demons quieted for a moment.

"He thinks I'm cursed, you know," she continued, and from the way she said it, Tir couldn't be certain of her meaning. There was a definite note of mockery in her voice, but also unease, as if she herself couldn't decide whether or not to give it credence. "Halflings are always complicated. When Fal and I were born, the dragon thought to spare us a lifetime of anguish. He fed us a drop of his blood to settle our magic and make it easier to control. It had the opposite effect. More so in Fal than me, but you've already seen proof of that. To this day, the dragon swears on the soul of his mate that some outside force must have interfered, else it never would have turned out the way it had."

"Why is your brother so different?"

She sighed. "Perhaps because of our elements. Fire is volatile, but also short-lived. It needs to be nurtured into a blaze, and when its fuel is removed, it burns out. Water is eternal. It flows infinite and holds no shape of its own. It is life itself."

"Water can extinguish fire," Tir said.

"Yes," Liadan replied. "If there's enough of it, even the fiercest blaze will die in its path."

"This does not worry you?"

"Why should it?"

"Your brother's power is unpredictable; he could kill yours without meaning to."

"Never. We are Dragonblood at heart. We are not only twins in body, but in soul, as well. To kill me, he would kill part of himself." Liadan rolled her shoulders, shrugging off his hold. "I'm all right now. You can let go."

"What if I do not want to?"

"You should," she said gravely.

"I would not have expected a woman as brave as you to be shy of a man's touch."

"Perhaps I simply don't like yours."

Her sharp retort hit its mark only too well, and Tir released her, shifting to the other side of the tent to put as much space between them as their shelter would allow. "So fire does burn after all."

Liadan said nothing. She curled in on herself, away from him, and as she did, her glow dimmed, leaving them in darkness once again.

23

They judged the time of night by the demons above the sands. Whenever their dervish died down, it heartened Liadan that they could start digging their way out, but then the noise picked up once more and with such force, she felt as though they were right on top of the tent.

They screamed for so long, she feared the sun would never rise again. But eventually it did, forcing the demons back into hiding. After a sufficient amount of time had passed, Tir declared it safe to reemerge. "Move over," he said, and Liadan shifted as close as she could to the tent wall.

Tir grunted, moved around, elbowing her a few times as he carefully extricated his legs from the sand. Crouching free, he tore into the tent's top on his side, and light flooded in. Liadan cried out, looking over her shoulder. The sands were nowhere near as high there as they were on her side, and Tir crawled out easily, then reached back in for her. Grasping her forearms, he pulled her out, a task much more difficult than it had been for himself, but once she stood in the sun, Liadan wanted to weep with joy. She turned in circles, clutching the vial of water in one fist, thanking the gods for allowing her to see the sky again.

"We made it!" She whooped and laughed.

When Tir didn't reply, Liadan turned around. He was already walking away from her, the torn remnants of their tent tucked under his arm. He gave a shrill whistle to summon Tarabas, but kept heading toward the riverbed, leaving Liadan to her own devices.

"Are you angry with me?" she called after him, rushing to catch up.

"No." He whistled again.

"You are! Why are you angry?"

"I am not angry with you," he said.

Liadan shook her head. "You might as well tell me. I won't stop asking until you do."

Tir rounded on her. "I am angry with myself!" he snapped. "For allowing myself to be distracted from my goal. For wasting my thoughts on you, when I should be thinking about how to save my people." His face darkened with the force of his words. "What do you want from me, Princess?"

"Nothing!"

"So you say. Yet you've done nothing but try to seduce me ever since we have ridden out of Frastmir. You lure me closer, then you push me away and turn your back. I'm sick of it!"

Taken aback, Liadan gaped. "*I* try to seduce *you*?"

"Bah!" Tir threw his hands up in the air and walked away from her.

"Wait!" Running to catch up a second time, she grabbed his arm, but he shook her off.

"Tarabas!" There was no sign of either horse.

"Tir, stop!" Liadan pulled ahead of him to bar his way, to force him to meet her gaze, but he slipped sideways around her. "What do *you* want?" she called out, tired of chasing him through the desert.

Tir halted in his tracks.

"I know my sole purpose here is supposed to be to save your people, but is that all you really want from me—you, not your tribe? Is that why you kiss me for every time I kiss you? Why you looked at me just now as if I broke your heart?"

His hands fisted at his sides, shoulders rising and falling with deep breaths. He wouldn't face her, staring off into the distance while he composed himself.

"Play the innocent victim of my heathen wiles if you want, *sher'nah,* but let's have it all out now and settle things between us before we move on." This time, when she stepped closer, he didn't move away. "Tell me I offended you with my forwardness. Tell me being so close to me is unacceptable. Tell me a prince of Aegiros would never stoop to desiring a Northerner who so readily accepts a man's touch. And then tell me why you so readily give it anyway."

A few more steps brought her up to his right, and his gaze flickered sideways before it skittered away again. His jaw was set, his arms taut at his sides.

"I don't say this to challenge or offend you," she said, voice lowered. "I say it, because when we reach Imarah, none of it will matter anymore."

Tir turned to her, his mouth, not long ago so soft and warm, now set in a thin, angry line. And still she saw how hard he fought himself to hold on to that anger, even as his gaze warmed, if only a little. It saddened her, and softened her voice further still, almost down to a whisper. "Out here, only the sky and sand can see us, and one man and one woman mean little enough to them. Among your tribe, you will no longer be just a man; you will be their prince. I will be a stranger at best, an enemy at worst, and you will need to convince them otherwise. Can you look them in the eye and make them believe I can be trusted, when in your heart, you resent me?"

The tension in his shoulders dissolved. "Resentment, Princess, is the farthest thing from my mind."

Hers, as well. But Liadan couldn't tell him so, lest she kindle a hope that would destroy them both. "Remember Geir?" she said instead.

"Remember the ember?" he returned.

With an ear-piercing whinny, Sleipnir bounded toward them from the south with Tarabas on his heels. Liadan was immensely relieved both horses had weathered the storm. Sleipnir almost knocked her off her feet with his nuzzle, and Liadan embraced him around the neck, then ran her hands down his back and sides, checking for injuries. Aside from being covered in a thick layer of dust, the mount was perfectly all right. "Hello, handsome," she crooned. "I've missed you."

Sleipnir snorted and tossed his head, throwing off a cloud of dust.

They walked the horses back to the river basin and to their cart of supplies which, to Liadan's surprise, was still there, exactly as they'd left it. When they turned the cart onto its wheels once more, the buckets and canisters underneath were still whole. Parched, Liadan snatched up one of the waterskins and drank her fill, throwing caution to the wind as Tir and the horses did the same.

"We lost about half of our water to the desert," Tir said after a while. They'd likely lose even more along the way.

"Do we have enough left to reach Imarah?"

"Difficult to say," he hedged. "We have another day's ride to find them; plenty of water left for that."

"But no telling what we'll find when we get there," she finished for him, "if anything."

Or anyone, Tir thought, rubbing his chest to soothe away the pain of it. Anything could have happened to his tribe while he'd been away, and the dust storm would have been the least of it.

"But that's not all that worries you, is it?" Liadan said gravely.

Tell her, his mind urged. *Tell her everything.* Yet his heart refused. How could he tell her what he feared? That the dreams that troubled him nightly were a portent of the future. That he might be bringing her to his tribe, only to watch her die. That she truly might save them all from the demon plague, but at the cost of her life.

Every night before sleep, Tir prayed for guidance from the gods, and every night they sent him visions of fire. He'd sworn an oath to keep the princess safe. He'd also sworn one to bring salvation to his tribe. Tir was coming to understand he would have to break one of these oaths before long, something he'd never done in all of his life.

Instead of answering her, he said, "From here on, we will be riding through battleground. The Aesimar tribe has been riding on Imarah every chance they get. They have claimed territory between the First City and the eastern edge of the valley where my tribe now sits, and they patrol it tirelessly."

"I thought you said Imarah still claimed the First Valley as their home."

"Yes," he replied, "by virtue of our birthright. But we do not have the men to protect it. Most tribes have already heard of our curse, and fear of demons keeps them from the valley and our abandoned city. But Aesimar worships the dark god, Aesma Daeva, for whom demons are kindred spirits. They fear neither darkness, nor pain, nor death. They live for war and murder, and each of their kills is an offering to their god. And so, to honor Aesma, they keep attacking to crush our spirits, rather than to kill us all outright. They will continue to do so, until the last *kharesh* falls, and we become chattel. Until that time, we are still an enemy, worthy of sacrifice."

"Demons bent on devouring my soul, tribesmen out for my blood, is there anything else I should be wary of, that you have not yet mentioned?"

Tir scowled at her irreverence, but her unconcerned smile put him at ease. "Scorpions," he replied.

"Well, come on, then. It seems we have our work cut out for us." Liadan set about repositioning what was left of their supplies on the cart. Tir watched her try to wrestle an unwilling Sleipnir to pull the cart, but the stubborn horse rooted his hooves. She pulled his head close and spoke to him softly until he finally huffed and relented. And all the while, she showed not a morsel of unease; she hummed, for all the gods' sake! The same way she had on the ride into Dai, lying across Sleipnir's back as if everything was right with the world.

"Why are you so at ease?"

Liadan shrugged. "The wait is the worst. We're close enough now that I need not anticipate; I can plan. I like that much better."

Tir shook his head in disbelief. "Only a fool feels no fear when confronted with death."

Liadan grinned. "Death is easy," she replied, securing the cart's harness to Sleipnir. "It only concerns those who are left behind. Try living for endless ages after everyone you've ever cared about has passed on. My mother used to say she'd rather die a thousand deaths with my father, than live a thousand years without him." Her hands stilled on the pack she'd been about to tie to Sleipnir's saddle. Her shoulders tensed and she turned her face away.

"What is it?"

Liadan shook her head, but couldn't meet his gaze. "Nothing. We should head out. The farther we can get before noon, the better."

"As you wish," he replied. Checking to make certain they'd left nothing behind, he set an easy pace east along the riverbed. Liadan had strapped her sword and her dagger to her waist and draped a veil over her head, loosely looping it around her neck to keep it in place. She bore the heat as well as a Northerner could, and Tir had to admit he was glad to have brought her back with him.

But long after they'd left the last remnants of human settlements behind, Liadan was still tense and quiet, and wouldn't tell him what was bothering her. With one hand holding on to Sleipnir's reins and the other loose by her side, it wasn't battle readiness that affected her so. Her mind was far away, her gaze lost in some distance Tir couldn't breach; she might as well have been back in Frastmir.

At noon, when the heat had become unbearable, Tir pitched the remains of their tent and handed her a waterskin. But when she would have taken it from him, he held on. "Tell me your greatest fear," he said.

Liadan raised her chin a notch higher in challenge. "Tell me yours."

"I fear that, in the end, nothing I do will make a difference. I fear the gods have forsaken my tribe and will turn on anyone who tries to save it. And I fear that one day soon, I will stand alone on the crest of a dune, the last of my tribe, and watch the valley burn at the hands of Aesimar."

Liadan acknowledged this with a nod. "I fear losing the ones I love." With a wry smile, she added, "And I'm not very fond of being buried alive in sandstorms, either. Have I earned my drink now?"

Tir inclined his head, relinquishing the waterskin. When she handed it back, it was still heavy with water, and Tir drank as much as he dared, hoping his tribe had found another water source in his absence, though the odds were against it. "I should mention," he told Liadan, "Aegirans are very superstitious people."

"Superstitious? No!"

He grinned, welcoming the return of her good humor. "Yes, indeed. I know, it comes as a great surprise."

"You want me to hide my fire," she guessed.

"Yes. For your safety, as well as theirs. Save your flames for the demons. Please."

Liadan tilted her head. "What would they do to me if they knew what I can do?"

It didn't bear thinking. "The Imarah would kill you."

"They might *try*."

"Aesimar would seek to possess you. Their magic men are very powerful; they can summon *djinn*, even *daeva*, and keep them prisoner in chains that are inscribed with dark spells. Only the one who spelled them locked can unlock them again."

"And, being immortal, if I were to be taken, I might be enslaved for all time."

"Yes." He coughed to clear the coarseness from his throat.

She nodded and pushed to her feet. "Thank you. Forewarned is forearmed. We should get going."

"Even this does not frighten you?" he asked, baffled.

Liadan slowly turned to face him. "A few days before I left the dragon's cave, I had a strange dream. It frightened me at first, but the more I think about it, the more accepting I am of what I saw in it."

Tir's breath locked in his chest; his hands on the burning sands were suddenly cold with dread. "What did you see?" he made himself ask. It couldn't have been the same dream he'd been having each night.

"I think… I think I saw my true form, the way I would have looked had I been born in Otherlands, rather than in the human realm. This body is mine, but it's only one incarnation of my being. The other is a reflection of my true soul—the Halfling daughter of Halfling parents, a Dragonblood with human blood in her veins." She smiled, but her eyes were sad. "Believe me when I say, demons or raiders, dark gods or magic men, I am not the one who should be afraid."

24

Where the river had cut its path through the valley, once-lush grounds were now as hard as rock, sun-baked by the incessant heat. To a certain distance on either side, the world was a flat and empty wasteland of otherworldly wrath. Beyond that, golden sands rose in great dunes, lapping ever closer as the desert reclaimed the river's former demesne.

And all was deathly quiet.

They passed the dead oasis where Imarah had camped. Not a scrap of their presence remained, save for mounds of fire ash. Tir hadn't expected to find them there; their water would have run out, as it always did, and forced them farther. He'd discussed it with Farraj before leaving for Wilderheim, and both had agreed the only choice was to keep heading eastward toward Temple Mountain. If any water remained in the valley's underground streams, with Inaras' blessing, they'd find it there. The mountain range was another day's ride away as the cart rattled, and as anxious as he was, Tir had to force himself to keep a steady pace.

The farther they went, the shallower the dry riverbed became, widening until he could no longer tell where it ended and desert began, and then the hard earth once again disappeared beneath a sand dune. It didn't burn their feet any less. Nor did the breeze offer any comfort from the day's heat.

"Say something," Liadan said. "I can't stand this silence."

"What should I say?" he returned.

"Anything. Sing, for all I care."

Tir chuckled and checked the sun's progress in the sky. Night would come quickly. He hoped they reached his tribe before then. His nape prickled with the unease of one being watched from a distance, and Tir swept his gaze across the dunes to the north and south, searching for any hint of people. He found none, but his mind's disquiet didn't ease.

"Well?" Liadan prodded, clutching Sleipnir's reins so hard, the mount tossed his head in agitation. Could she sense the same?

"Perhaps you should talk," he said. "You are much better at it than I."

Silence.

He frowned. "Princess?"

On the other side of the cart, Liadan squinted into the distance ahead. "Do you see that?"

Tir blinked hard, then looked where she pointed. On the horizon, with heat mirages obscuring the view, shimmered a dark spot—there one moment, gone the next, and then back again. "I do," he replied, but he wouldn't trust his eyes until they'd gotten much closer. He clucked his tongue, urging Tarabas on a little faster, and Sleipnir matched him.

"Is it your tribe?"

The shape solidified for a long enough moment for Tir to recognize the western mountain range. "It should be."

"That's good, isn't it? We made it."

Tir shook his head. "Something is wrong." The tumult of shadows writhed halfway in between, too far from Temple Mountain's oasis. He mounted Tarabas. "Keep going with the cart. I will ride ahead."

"Oh, no. You are not rushing out on your own again." Faster than he would have thought possible, Liadan unhitched Sleipnir from the cart and mounted. "We can come back for all of this later."

Rather than argue, he urged Tarabas into a gallop. With each mile they passed, the feeling of dread grew until they'd gotten close enough for Tir to see figures milling about. He sucked in a sharp breath. "Ride!" he shouted, digging his heels into Tarabas' sides. With a sharp whinny, the mount reared, giving Tir just enough time to draw his blade, and then he took off straight toward the embattled *kharesh*.

Behind him, Liadan whooped, a signal that propelled Sleipnir forward so fast he overtook Tarabas in moments.

Tir swore. "Wait!" He raced to catch up, but the princess wouldn't be stopped. She plunged into the fight with no care for consequences and without knowing which side to fight for. But as Sleipnir reared, his massive hooves striking out with enough force to instantly kill a man, Tir saw he needn't have worried. The Aesimar raiders had decked themselves out in full armor, all the better to intimidate, and wielded two blades each, both polished to a shine. In comparison, the starving Imarah wore nothing but their linens, their swords dirty and worn from long years of constant fighting. They were also vastly outnumbered. This was no raid. Had the Aesimar *shansher* finally lost his patience? If so, then this could be the end of Imarah.

Tir roared his battle cry and dove straight into the fight, keeping his seat on Tarabas' back for a better view and cutting through the enemy with cold efficiency. He evaded attackers unless he had a clear opening to kill, methodically working his way deeper into the throng, while Liadan cut outward and split the forces into two. Tir had no choice but to leave her to it. Aesimar wouldn't have attacked like this unless they'd sensed a mortal weakness, which could only mean one thing.

Dhakir the Conqueror was dead.

No, he wouldn't believe that until he saw it for himself. Tir shut his ears to the sounds of his people dying, refused to look at the half-pitched tents, torn and bloodied, with bodies lying dead inside. Aesimar must have caught them unawares as they were setting up camp for the night. Bloody cowards! Giving his back to an enemy he'd fought against his entire life, Tir rode straight for the camp's center, to the one tent that stood taller, larger than the rest. Dismounting at full gallop, he cut through five Aesimar dogs to rush inside.

The walls billowed in the breeze. The carpets were covered in sand, and pillows were scattered around everywhere; large water jugs lay overturned and empty, and Dhakir's ebony seat was fallen over onto its side.

The tent was empty.

None of his father's possessions were there. Halima was gone, her veils and loom removed, probably to the women's tent, where she'd huddle in fear with the children and unwed women of the tribe.

Tir staggered back, but no matter how far he retreated, he couldn't escape the sight.

"To the south, Tir!" Farraj's voice broke through his shock, and Tir whirled around, expecting a blade to descend.

It didn't.

Instead, he watched the battle shift away from the camp and back in the direction of the Aesimar leader, who once again observed the fray from his high perch atop the crest of a sand dune. He was draped in pure white, his armor fashioned of polished gold, and from such a distance, he shone like the sun in stark contrast to the black mount beneath him. He looked like the Dark god himself, come to reap Tir's tribe from the face of Aegiros.

Then Sleipnir screamed, and Tir's gaze shifted lower, picking him out in the fight. He was riderless, striking out at those closest to him as if he'd been bred for battle, hooves crushing bones and bodies, massive girth shoving people aside, forcing them to retreat or die.

Where was Liadan?

"Stop gawking, boy, and move!" Farraj snapped, running forward to contain the damage. He limped, his clothes were stained with blood, and his left arm was bandaged. How many raids had the tribe endured in Tir's absence? How many of his tribesmen were still alive?

Tir clutched his sword tighter, drew his second and followed.

Liadan rolled to her feet and charged the bastard who'd pulled her off her horse, running him through and turning on the next. These were trained fighters—fearless, methodical, and without mercy. Their blades were sharp, their strikes swift, and they moved so easily across the sand that always pulled Liadan into its depths. Nevertheless, the dragon hadn't wasted years training her for her to fall in her first skirmish. Drawing her dagger, Liadan faced the enemy, with her back to Sleipnir, trusting him to protect it. Forward press, clear some room; pull back and draw them in. Right into her blades. Aegiran scimitars

were curved, shorter than her own, which gave her a longer-reach advantage. But theirs were lighter and sharper, which meant they moved
faster, sliced easier. Her strategy became to strike fast and kill, rather
than wound. The longer the fighting continued, the more she'd tire.

An armored fighter rushed her with a shout, and she twisted out of
the way, then followed through to slice his back open from shoulder
to hip. The next landed on her dagger, straight to the hilt. Two more
came at her at the same time. Liadan whistled, then clashed with one,
listening for the bone-crushing thud of Sleipnir having taken out the
other. Through the fray, Liadan looked for Tir but saw no sign of him.
His people, however, were everywhere.

She could tell at a glance which ones were Tir's *kharesh* and which
were not. Though all looked thin and haggard, slowly dying of thirst
and hunger, the *kharesh* stood out by the force of their relentless attack.
They fought like madmen, throwing themselves at the enemy, driving
them back in sheer recklessness. They opened themselves up to being
wounded in order to deliver a killing blow, and while Liadan admired
their devotion to their tribe, their fighting technique frightened her.
They didn't fight to win; they fought to take down as many as they
could, then die a heroic death. Tir's arrival had gone unnoticed, and
until they saw him, they'd think their cause was hopeless.

Liadan kicked out, shoving an Aesimar fighter back. "Sleipnir,"
she barked, and the mount pivoted toward her, striking down more
of them with his hind legs. After sheathing her dagger, she caught
the edge of Sleipnir's saddle and swung up. "Steady does it," she told
him before she stood on his back to make herself as tall as possible.
She only had moments, so she raised her sword high and shouted as
loudly as she could, "*Imarah! Sher'nah bahrai sephri! Kharesh gavoran!*"

Sleipnir screamed and reared, throwing her off. Liadan landed
hard, breath knocked from her lungs and her sword from her hand.
As she stared at the bright sky, her vision darkened, the surrounding
warriors nothing but shadows blending together. She shook her head
hard, wiped sand from her face, then gasped, rolling aside just as a
curved blade sliced down. Her attacker followed, separating her from
Sleipnir and the sword lying behind him. Liadan scrambled backwards,
hands and feet burying in the sands. *Too slow!*

When he roared and cut down again, she fell back and, kicking her legs up and over her head, rolled smoothly until she had her feet under her again. The curved blade slid deep into the sands, and Liadan pushed forward, drawing her dagger. But her feet slipped, and instead of stabbing him through the heart, the blade buried into the flesh just above his hip. Liadan lost her balance, the weight of her descent sliced him open, and when he shouted and reeled back, arching away from her, his innards spilled out before him.

A hoarse cry rose up from one of the Imarah, followed by another, and then the whole tribe seemed to be screaming into the dying light. "*Shalla shansher an Imarah!*" they shouted, rallying for one final push against Aesimar. The raiders hesitated, eyes flashing with uncertainty for just a moment before they, too, rallied, and the fighting intensified.

Liadan grabbed the dead man's blade and shoved to her feet, heart racing with the heat of battle, blood boiling in her veins, the fire of her soul licking across the underside of her skin. It wanted to burst out, to roar in answer to Imarah. But she ruthlessly pushed it deep down and fought her way back to her own sword. With its comforting weight in her grasp, she shouted into the sky, echoing Tir's tribe. "*Shalla shansher an Imarah!*"

From some distance off, Sleipnir whinnied and galloped full tilt toward her, swinging his head back and forth to clear the path. As he ran by, she caught onto the saddle, swung easily into her seat, and renewed her press south, toward the group of Aesimar generals overseeing the battle from the crest of a dune.

One of them blew a horn, its deep sound reverberating across the valley, and down to the last, the Aesimar raiders fled after their departing leaders. Liadan followed, cutting down as many as she could, but eventually, Sleipnir stopped in his tracks, refusing to go any farther, letting the survivors escape. Only then did she notice him shuddering with each massive breath he took. Liadan dismounted and came around to his front. "Oh, no…"

Sleipnir's chest was cut open from shoulder to shoulder, dripping blood onto the burning sands. His great head drooped and he rested his forehead against her shoulder.

"Easy, handsome," she crooned, even as her heart fluttered with fear for him. "It's only a scratch, nothing more. You'll be stalking pretty mares again in no time."

The *kharesh* headed toward them. Now that the enemy had retreated, they were in no hurry to reach as far as Sleipnir had taken her. Liadan couldn't see Tir among them. Where was he?

Sleipnir huffed. He was losing too much blood, and if she didn't do something, he'd die before they could get him back to the camp. Licking her dry lips, Liadan made a decision. With the tribesmen still a ways off, she turned Sleipnir around so his hind quarters faced them, then called up her fire. "I am sorry, my friend, this will hurt terribly, but please, please trust me." Pulling together the edges of the wound with one hand, she dragged a glowing finger across the seam as quickly as she could, searing it shut.

Sleipnir screamed, lifting his head, eyes wide with fright, but he held still for the gruesome procedure, trusting her with his well-being.

The *kharesh* ran forward, spurred by Sleipnir's obvious distress.

"Easy," she soothed, and she tugged off her scarf, draped it around his front like a necklace to hide the raw wound before the warriors descended on her in a flurry of angry shouts and pointing fingers. Liadan understood not a word, but she did comprehend what they wanted when someone tried to tear Sleipnir's reins from her hands. She knocked the man sideways and drew her dagger.

In an instant, she was surrounded by a group of very angry men all armed with swords pilfered from corpses. Liadan's fire flared inside her, this time refusing to settle so easily. They wouldn't harm Sleipnir, that much she knew. But none of them would hesitate to slit her throat from ear to ear, if it came to that.

Liadan steadied her gaze on the man she'd shoved. He looked furious, his eye twitching, no doubt unaccustomed to a woman staring him down. She refused to look away. The moment she did, these men would lose all respect for her, and she couldn't have that. For their sakes, they had to acknowledge her as a person, not as a woman; not one of them, not a member of their caste to be pushed aside and ignored. As her mother had done before her, Liadan needed to establish herself as separate from the hierarchy, neither superior nor subject to anyone.

"*Revroha thran,*" the man said. She recognized *thran* to mean north, or northern. *Revroha*, whatever it was, didn't sound very respectful.

Where in all the hells was Tir?

"*Haromi preh thum rekar, revroha thran.*" Long journey and dying. If Liadan guessed correctly, he'd just told her she'd come a long way to die.

"*Rheo, kharesh,*" she replied in greeting, introducing herself the way she'd seen people do in Sadirak. "*Baikal Liadan al-Saeran, shansher thranai fasgaoi ben.*"

They fell silent at hearing a Northerner speak their language.

Then, as one, they all burst into laughter.

It wasn't quite the reaction she'd expected. Flushing furiously, she clutched the dagger tighter, eager to beat them down a peg, when she noticed riders approaching from the camp. Tir on Tarabas led the charge, with another behind him on what had to be the last remaining horse of the Imarah tribe. Bloody finally! Though they were too far away to hear properly, their shouts turned the men's attention away from Liadan.

She shifted around Sleipnir to get to the sword still strapped to her saddle, but another *kharesh* barred her way, placing a blade to her neck. Liadan stilled, inclining her head just a little to let him know she understood, and wouldn't move again.

Tir shouted in his native tongue, and the *kharesh* exchanged looks amongst them. He rode full tilt toward the man who held Liadan at swordpoint, forcing him to back away or be trampled. Free of him, Liadan unsheathed her sword, preparing for another battle, if necessary.

As the second rider approached, Tir wheeled Tarabas around and dismounted, shoving Liadan behind him and her sword down to her side. More angry, foreign words followed, too fast for her to catch their meaning; he was arguing with the *kharesh*, while the second rider, still mounted, gazed steadily at Liadan.

He was older than the *kharesh* on the ground, hair streaked with white and weighed down with golden adornments. She drew herself up and met his gaze, waiting for another outburst.

To her surprise, he touched a hand to his heart, then his mouth, then to his forehead, and he bowed as deeply as the saddle would allow. "I offer greetings to the daughter of the North," he said with more respect than she'd encountered in a long time. "I am Farraj al-Talib, faithful servant of the *shansher* and *shensari*."

At his words, the *kharesh* quieted. They stared at Farraj first, then at Liadan, while Tir openly gaped.

"Well met, Farraj al-Talib. I am Liadan of Frastmir, daughter of King Saeran and Queen Nialei of Frastmir, crown princess of the realm of Wilderheim."

He bowed again. "Well met, and welcome." He dismounted and handed the reins to a *kharesh*. "We are in your debt, Princess. Without your timely arrival, our tribe would be no more. Please accept my humble thanks."

She bowed respectfully. "How many dead?" she asked.

Farraj glanced at Tir, then replied, "Too many. Eight *kharesh* have met an honorable death in battle. At least fifty brave men died defending our weak and wounded. The rest were women."

"And how did they die?"

"By the grace of the gods, swiftly. They died fighting for their children."

"A death as honorable as any warrior would receive in battle."

Farraj inclined his head. "As you say."

"The sun is setting," Tir said. "We should get back before darkness falls."

Farraj barked an order, and the *kharesh* moved out, back to camp, leaving Liadan in the company of Tir and Farraj.

25

"What do you think you are doing?" Tir demanded the moment the others were out of earshot.

Farraj dismounted and, ignoring the outburst, approached Liadan and her mount. "My lady, will you permit?" he asked, indicating Sleipnir.

"Farraj!"

"The Aegiran fascination with horses is well known to me by now," she replied, glancing warily between Tir and Farraj. "But might it wait until after we return to camp? Sleipnir needs seeing to."

Farraj inclined his head. "Of course." Rather than ride, he walked his own horse to keep pace with Liadan, giving Tir his back, an insult he'd never have dared with Dhakir.

Tir grabbed for Farraj's arm. "I asked you a question," he snapped.

With a swift move belying his obvious injuries, the *kharesh* leader sent Tir sprawling into the sand in front of Liadan's feet. "While you catch your breath down there," Farraj said in their native tongue, "consider carefully your actions today. And *think* before you speak. It is not my place to mentor the *shansher*, nor, by the gods, do I wish it to be. But mark me, boy, too many have laid their lives on the sands today, believing you had abandoned them. Too many more survived, thinking they'd be better off if you had never returned. You have lost more here than you can imagine in your absence, and you will lose more still if you act the hothead you were before you left."

Stunned, Tir said nothing.

Farraj offered his hand to help him to his feet and, speaking in Liadan's language, he added, "We have much to discuss, I am sure. But this is not the place, or the time."

The sun always set quickly; already it'd lost its warmth. It would be dark soon, and they were quite a distance from the safety of the tribe. Flushing, Tir allowed Farraj to help him to his feet, but not before noticing the glistening trail of blood that matted Sleipnir's coat. Before Liadan could protest, he pulled away the scarf she'd tied around the horse's neck, then sucked in a sharp breath.

The princess drew herself up, raised her chin. "As I said, my horse needs seeing to."

Farraj pushed Tir aside to take a closer look and, with a gentle hand, caressed Sleipnir's quivering chest above then below the wound. The animal was visibly shaken and in pain, something no one of Tir's tribe would ever ignore. Farraj scrutinized Liadan, no doubt searching for whatever she'd used to cauterize the wound. Finding nothing, he said, "Your father is King Saeran of Frastmir. I knew him when he was a boy. I was there when he offered himself in *ramesh feh* in the war, and later, when he wed our Mari. Is he well?"

"As well as can be expected, I suppose," Liadan replied uneasily.

"And your honored mother? I have not stood in her presence, but I heard she is an extraordinary woman."

"Yes, many do say so."

"We should hurry back," Tir said before Farraj could ask more. For Liadan's sake, he tempered himself, biting his tongue against more angry words. If he was to gain the tribe's favor for her, and regain it for himself, he'd require the older man's aid.

"As my *shansher* commands," Farraj replied, not taking his eyes off Liadan.

They walked the horses back swiftly, racing against the setting sun. "You fought well today," Tir offered, earning a confused look from Liadan.

"Are you truly so surprised?"

Her voice betrayed neither remorse nor grief—that did surprise him. "You do not weep for the lives you have taken?"

Farraj turned his head to better hear her answer without seeming too curious.

Liadan held Tir's stare, seeming to give the question serious thought before she replied, "No. I respect and honor life, and I will fight to protect it. But I will also show no mercy to those who try to destroy it. Those men I killed today would have killed many others, had I not stopped them. No, I do not regret taking their lives."

"Women are meant to give life, not take it," Tir said.

"Then perhaps you should not think of me as a woman, but as a weapon," she returned immediately, then clicked her tongue to urge Sleipnir on faster. Had he offended her? Tir looked to Farraj for guidance, but found no help in the general's responding shrug.

Numerous fires began to flare ahead, lighting the way home. As they neared, Tir saw Imarah had become much more resourceful in his absence. The tribesmen had gathered up the dead Aesimar, stripped them of their weapons and armor, then arranged the corpses around the camp. Although they gave off a noxious reek, they burned steadily, and would do so for a long time.

The tribe had already gathered, desperate faces eager to see if the news spoke true about Tir's return. Many had tears in their eyes; more still glared angrily as the three of them passed, with the young *shansher* in the lead. No one stopped the company and no one offered any greeting. Instead, the tribe waited for Tir to explain himself or to offer hope.

Tir's throat felt tight, his jaw stuck, unable to form words. Shamed by his actions and Farraj's reprimand, he could only look straight ahead as they passed through the tribe's midst.

At the *shansher*'s tent, Farraj called to one of the men who'd followed them. "This is Matek," he told Liadan. "He will take good care of Sleipnir for you, and he can be trusted."

Liadan nuzzled the mount, while Matek led away Tarabas and Farraj's Zara. They all waited with the princess until he'd returned for Sleipnir. When Liadan relinquished his reins, the mount snorted and rooted his hooves, refusing to be budged. But Matek spoke to him, lavishing praise in a soothing tone until Sleipnir relented and allowed himself to be led away.

Tir entered the tent first, followed by Liadan, and Farraj last. He righted Dhakir's seat, but couldn't bring himself to sit in it. Instead, he carried the heavy chair to the edge of the tent, then sat on the pillows and motioned for the others to do the same.

A short, veiled woman hurried inside, carrying a silver tray of libations. The repast consisted of three small flatbreads, a little cheese, and a bottle of wine. Tir glanced at Liadan to measure her reaction.

The princess nodded her thanks to the woman, and said, "There is a cart of supplies to the west. We left it behind when we saw the fighting. Someone ought to retrieve it."

"At first light," Farraj said, as the woman hurried out of the tent. "It is not safe to venture outside the camp during the night."

Though clearly displeased by that answer, Liadan nodded in acceptance. Had Sleipnir not been injured, Tir would wager she'd have ridden out on her own for that cart, consequences be damned. And Farraj had called *him* a hothead.

"Where is Halima?" Tir asked, breaking a flatbread into halves and handing one to Liadan. When she shook her head to decline, he firmed his mouth and forced the bread into her hand. He had no stomach for food, either, but to refuse an offering when the tribe already had so little would have been an insult.

Rather than reply, Farraj leaned back and regarded Tir. "You rode out of Imarah, determined to slay the bringer of this demon curse. Without a word to anyone, you left your tribe to seek the blood of the Northern king and his wife. And now, you come riding back with a woman at your side. A warrior, no less, who not only slayed three score Aesimar fighters, but also seems to have an unknown ability to cauterize wounds without fire, and introduces herself as a crown princess of Wilderheim, daughter of the very man you wanted to kill. You will explain."

Tir drew himself up. "You forget your place, Farraj."

"I forget nothing! Do not sneer at me and call yourself my better, whelp. Dhakir earned my loyalty by caring for his tribe to his last. He heard the raiders coming, when he had not heard a single word in many years. He saw them drag Halima from the tent, and he roused himself to defend her. He may have languished as one brokenhearted for too long, but he died a warrior, defending his daughter, when his only remaining son had fled and abandoned them!"

Tir blanched, hands growing cold. *I never thought... Never imagined...*

Into the silence, Liadan quietly asked what he couldn't. "Did Halima survive?"

Farraj didn't answer right away. When he did, he lowered his head. "Forgive me. It is not my place to speak of these things in front of outsiders. These are private matters of family; I should not have said what I did."

Tir was bursting to know the answer and, by Farraj's covert glare, the old man knew it. He was deliberately withholding it to prolong Tir's torment. "For a faithful servant of the *shansher* and *shensari*," Tir grated, repeating his earlier words, "you show neither faith nor servitude."

"What was your plan, Tirasdunh?" Farraj returned, then indicated Liadan with a polite wave of his hand. "You have brought whom most of the tribe consider a blood enemy into our midst, not in chains, but armed with blades. How would you have explained to us?"

"I most certainly would not have introduced her as my wife!"

Liadan's back shot ramrod straight. "What?"

"You are a fool, boy. A damned, naïve fool. They would have stoned her before you could think up a proper excuse."

"What is this about a wife?" Liadan demanded.

For the first time since they'd sat down, Farraj hesitated, seeming at a loss for words.

Tir couldn't resist an opportunity to put him in his place. "When he introduced himself to you before the *kharesh*, he called himself a servant of the *shansher* and *shensari*—the king and queen. As he said, Dhakir the Conqueror is dead, which makes me the *shansher* of Imarah."

"It was safer for them to think Tirasdunh has returned with a queen by his side," Farraj told Liadan, glaring at Tir. "As *shensari*, you are under his protection, and no one may lay hand on you. I did it to spare you their wrath."

Liadan shot to her feet. "Well, undo it!"

A queen! Had they been anywhere but in Aegiros, Liadan would have admired Farraj's quick thinking. Even a fake queen had immense power to dictate her will unto her people. She could have ordered the entire tribe to break camp and trek across the desert back to the First City, and farther west in search of more fertile ground, and they would have obeyed instantly. They might have quietly questioned her actions, but they would not have dared to oppose her. She'd have had no reason to fear displaying her fire; indeed, it would only have solidified her authority over them.

But where, except in Aegiros, did the title of queen hold so little meaning? Among the desert tribesmen, women were regarded as little better than chattel—they were bartered with, bought and sold, kept under lock and key, disallowed to keep company among the men or even to speak their minds. A queen's station in Aegiros meant nothing other than she belonged to the king.

Farraj pushed to his feet to face her. "You are too young to understand the ways of our world. We have not the time for me to explain, but you must believe me when I say, you would not have survived the night had I not said what I did."

He spoke the truth Liadan already knew. That didn't make hearing it any easier. Earlier, she'd taken a calculated risk in joining the fight. What better way to earn the tribe's trust in her fighting skills than by showing them she could hold her own? Liadan and Sleipnir had saved lives today, of that she had no doubt. She'd been well on her way to establishing a unique position among the Imarah, and before she could have solidified it, Farraj had undone it all.

"You wanted to be accepted," Tir retorted.

Liadan shook her head. "This cannot be the only solution." If for no other reason than her blood oath, the closer she and Tir got, the more dangerous it would become for both of them.

"It is," Farraj said.

"No, you don't understand," she insisted. "What I came here to do, I cannot do while shackled to Tir's side like a shadow."

"Would it truly be so bad, pretending to be my wife?"

A handful of words, and Liadan was pulled back to the riverbed that morning. The same sadness now darkened his golden gaze, the same pride drew back his shoulders, and the same subtle challenge lowered his head. Once again, he put himself on the line, and once again left it to Liadan to be the rational one. Gods, but she was weary of fighting this same battle for both of them. "Think, Tir. You know what I am, and you know I won't be able to hide it. What will happen when your tribe discovers you not only brought a creature like me among them, but also bound yourself to her in marriage?"

Tir knew the answer, and if Farraj's flush was any indication, he did, as well. The Imarah wouldn't abide another betrayal from their king, especially not one so grave. They'd rise against him, banish them both at best, murder them at worst.

She'd come here expecting to change the world, not realizing the world was much too big to be changed by one woman, even a Halfling.

Without another word, she shook her head and stalked out of the tent. Tir called after her, rising to follow, but she quickened her step, and Farraj's voice stopped him in his tracks, giving her time to get away. She didn't slow until she was certain neither of them would come looking for her.

Full night had fallen while they'd talked, and while the sand beneath her feet was still warm, the air had grown cold. But it was the scene before her, not the night air, that chilled her to the bone. Hugging herself about the middle, Liadan strode through an unfinished camp devoid of people. Many tents had been erected, creating pathways and alleys, but at least half of them were dark, empty, gaping tombs and markers for those who should have lived there, and the closer she got to the edge, the more such tents she passed. Not a soul stirred out in the open. Those still alive huddled around small fires, safely hidden by billowing cloth, and their whispered prayers hissed on the wind. Liadan didn't need to understand the meaning; she felt the fear behind those words.

At its very edge, the camp's boundary was stark enough to give her pause. Behind her stood a multitude of tents. Before her lay a line of burning corpses, and beyond that was nothing but sand. She gazed up at the stars, recognizing few. They twinkled, so far away, they seemed unreachable, yet at the same time so heavy, Liadan felt as though they'd crush her.

What am I to do?

She looked around. Not a human in sight, no signs of any demons. After two nights of their howling screams, Liadan had expected them to swoop down the moment the sun set safely behind the horizon. But now, alone in the night, she sat on the sand with her back to a tent and, drawing the water vial from around her neck, held it up to the firelight. "Fal," she said softly. "Can you hear me?"

No answer.

Liadan sighed. "I suppose it was too much to hope for at least that little comfort of your voice. Well, I found them. I traversed the desert and found the Imarah tribe, and brother, it's even worse than we thought." She rubbed her brow, hating the lack of response. "I wish you could see it. There are endless stretches of sand everywhere you look. The sky is so blue, there's no word to describe it, and the sun's so bright, at its zenith, it feels as though fire's eating you alive. But at twilight and gloaming… Oh Fal, it's so beautiful, it takes your breath away." She imagined what the First City must have looked like back in its day—streets filled with people, groves of fig trees, marble fountains spraying glistening drops of water toward the sky. She could almost smell the spices perfuming the air.

All gone now. Nothing but an exotic dream, faded into ruin.

"*Beela thran.*"

Liadan jumped to her feet, tucking the vial into her belt at her back.

An old woman melted out of the darkness between tents. She was short, stooped, her step uneven with a heavy limp. Her clothes were rags, a tattered scarf slipping off her grizzled white hair, her bare feet sinking into the sand as she walked. "*Rah, beela, beela thran. Tosma beela, rah. Abu rekar semerekara a tibokar.*"

"I'm sorry, I don't understand what you're saying."

The woman smiled, further creasing her wrinkled face to expose a mouth with only two stumpy teeth. She nodded, reaching out to Liadan. "*Rah, beela thran, nomarehraba dath. Mea idrah shensari preh thum aiii.*" She shook her head, on the verge of tears. "*Bahran a mi. Meagara, bahran!"*

"*Ves!*" Farraj suddenly shouted, rushing to intercept the woman, pushing Liadan behind him.

"What are you doing?"

He ignored her, pointing furiously in the direction the woman had come from. He crowded Liadan away, but never took his eyes off his target. "*Aseti, ves begos!*"

The old woman hissed, eyes sparking angrily. "*En emeil baseeri, kharesh!*" She spat on the sand. "*Hamme daeva deogobor feh. Kalikarai a ti an ebeo Dhakir!*"

Breathing hard, Farraj drew his shoulders back, and his blade sang out of its scabbard. He gripped the hilt so tightly, his knuckles stood out stark white.

"Stop!" Liadan cried, grabbing for his arm. "What is the matter with you? She's just an old woman!"

Farraj shook her off. "Do not interfere," he ordered.

The woman laughed, pointing at Farraj. "*Daeva emeil baseeri. Baseeri an el tiath Imarah.*" She spat again, then turned her back on Farraj, shuffling away into the shadows whence she'd come.

After she'd disappeared from sight, Farraj turned on Liadan. Sword still in hand, he grabbed her arm and dragged her off in the other direction, closer to where the flames were at their highest. "You will not go near that woman again," he said.

"I will do as I bloody well please! Release me, Farraj, this instant."

After turning her to face him, he did. "Do you have eyes, Princess? Yes, I see that you do. Do you know how to use them? Then look around. Do you see anyone walking the night here? Not a one! Everyone who values their soul is too afraid of the darkness to leave the safety of their lights. Yet there, a feeble old woman, brave enough to wander the very edges of our camp, all on her own. Did you not wonder why that is?"

"Perhaps she has more courage than you," Liadan retorted. "And she was not the only one walking around in the night. I was there, as well."

"You were there, because you do not know any better. *She* had other reasons."

"And what were they?"

"She is *aseti*. An outcast—a witch. Damned by the gods to wield evil powers."

"I have powers," Liadan told him, head high. "Will you cast me out, as well? Your *shensari*, as you called me? Do it! I'd rather keep company with that old woman than with any man who regards my very nature as a scourge!"

Farraj seethed, sword arm quivering with tension. "She is different," he insisted. "*En emeil baseeri, kharesh.* Do you know what that means? My curse upon you, *kharesh*. *Hamme daeva deogobor feh.* May the demons drag you into hell. *Kalikarai a ti, an ebeo Dhakir.* You will suffer my eternal wrath—"

"Along with Dhakir," Liadan finished, her anger cooling slightly. She'd understood that part, at least. No wonder the *kharesh* had reacted so badly. Superstitious, Tir had called his tribe. The word was too trite to describe the true depth of their fear of magic. "She cursed you."

"Me, and all of Imarah."

"And still you let her live."

"It is said a witch cannot be killed by an ordinary weapon. If a man slays a witch by human means, her soul will be reborn from his wife, devour his children, and drive him to madness."

"If it eases your mind, Farraj, she may have spoken the words, but there was no power behind them. I would have felt it. You are safe from the old woman's curse."

"Perhaps," he allowed. "Perhaps her words were nothing more than that. But make no mistake, *shensari*, we are all already cursed. The *shansher* is even now pacing in his tent, mourning his family, thinking grave thoughts of his tribe, no doubt. And he has cause."

Yes, that much, Liadan believed. No natural thing could so quickly bring a thriving civilization to this. Mighty rivers didn't just dry out overnight, and demons didn't leave their hellish worlds unless someone broke through the Veil and summoned them. But something else worried her. Liadan hesitated before asking, "Did Halima survive?"

Farraj heaved a great sigh. "She did," he replied. "Gravely injured, dishonored, she lived to see the next sunrise, to watch her father's pyre be built. In her delirium, she called for her brother, and when he did not appear, she joined her father in the flames."

Liadan's stomach clenched, eyes stinging with tears. "Why would she do that?"

"She believed, as we all did, that Tirasdunh would never return. You can plainly see the state of our people. There isn't one among us who can afford to take on another hungry mouth, when the ones he already has are starving. Halima would have been *aseti*, an outcast left to fend for herself. She would not have lasted long. She knew this and chose to die to spare herself long days of suffering."

The thought was incomprehensible to Liadan. She'd been born blessed with so many gifts she used to take for granted: a loving family; a kingdom rich in magic, food, and water aplenty—all gifts she'd known not many shared. But never in her life could she have imagined this much suffering. How much pain and grief must Halima have endured; how defeated and helpless must she have felt to have done what she had?

"I am deeply sorry. For everything you and your tribe have endured."

"As am I."

Silence stretched between them, heavy with meaning, and broken up by the roar of fire all around them.

Back home in Wilderheim, a night like this would be filled with music and song. In towns and villages, the kingdom's people took great joy in coming together at the end of each day to share a meal and to entertain each other. On the outskirts, in the wilds, Others roamed relentlessly, their ethereal voices lilting on the breeze; they could be heard in the hiss of wind through the trees, and in the gentle gurgle of creeks and rivers. Liadan hadn't realized until now how much she missed those sounds.

After a while, Farraj sheathed his sword. "I have given you some thought, *shensari*."

She winced. "You call me queen, but I'm not one of you. I'm not Tir's wife, and I never will be. A union between us would be disastrous."

He regarded her with unabashed curiosity, and Liadan felt as if he could see through her, as if she'd somehow revealed far more than she'd intended. "I think you do him a disservice. Yourself, as well. But that is not my place to ponder. Of course, you both have your reasons for it, and I am not one to pry. I am but a humble warrior who can only see what I see in your eyes." He smiled, kindly, mysteriously, then just as quickly, turned and indicated she should walk with him. "My point was that perhaps there may be a solution to the dilemma of your presence more suitable to your character. A title better suited to a weapon than a woman."

With no solutions of her own forthcoming, Liadan inclined her head and joined him. "Speak it then, my good man. I am all ears."

26

"You may speak."

Itamar al-Jiri, right hand to the Aesimar *shansher*, and the High Magus of the tribe, licked his dry lips with a sticky tongue. The *shansher* had removed his armor, and now sat behind his writing desk, glancing over reports neatly written on papyrus sheets. He didn't raise his head to acknowledge Itamar, and nothing in his tone of voice or demeanor betrayed any hint of his displeasure at the disappointing outcome of their earlier push against Imarah.

And that was precisely what worried Itamar so gravely. The *shansher* was at his most dangerous when he seemed the calmest. *He is only a man,* Itamar reminded himself. But a man was never only a man when he used demons to do his bidding.

"We have suffered losses," he reported, his own voice so tremulous, it brought the *shansher*'s head up. Tensing his hands by his sides to hide their quiver, Itamar pulled his shoulders back and continued in a stronger voice, "Six score dead; one hundred wounded."

The roving remnants of the once-powerful Imarah tribe had been slowly dying for a long time. Itamar didn't understand why the *shansher* had allowed them to continue. But last night, on word that their prince still hadn't returned, he'd ordered an end to it. Their warriors had gathered in the hundreds, armed in full regalia, and set out at daybreak to claim a glorious victory for Aesimar—and they'd nearly had it in their grasp; so close, Itamar had almost tasted it.

They hadn't lost the battle; they'd ceded it. "We had not expected Imarah to rally as they did," Itamar added with a note of apology, though he had nothing to regret. His preparations had been flawless; his plans executed to perfection. It was the *shansher* himself who'd ordered the retreat.

"No, indeed." The *shansher* set aside his reports, and for a long moment, he quietly stared into the shadows behind Itamar with such intensity, it made the High Magus want to look over his shoulder. But one didn't turn his back on the *shansher*, unless he wished it marked with a whip. "Tell me, Itamar, what did you see through your longlooker, down in that valley today?"

Itamar blanched. "I... I—"

"When the rallying cry went up, and Imarah caught its second wind, you saw something through that tube that made you doubt your eyes. I saw it in your face. What did you see?"

Itamar couldn't find the words. How was he to describe to the *shansher* what he could scarcely believe himself?

"It must have been that young warrior," the *shansher* pushed. "The one who rode in on the black hellbeast. Magnificent animal, was it not? At least a score of my men fell beneath its hooves, and it protected its rider as I've never seen a horse do before." He smiled as though imagining such an animal in his possession, and Itamar breathed a small sigh of relief at the change in subject.

The *shansher* adored horses, and in years past, one such mount would have proven invaluable. The newly formed Aesimar tribe had warred and conquered constantly, absorbing smaller, weaker tribes and training them to act and think in accordance with their laws. Back then, the *shansher* had always been the first to ride into battle, and the last to leave it.

But those days were gone. Having acquired enough men that even today's losses didn't weaken their forces, the *shansher* no longer partook in the battles, but instead watched from a high perch as he would a performance put on for his enjoyment.

Why did you sound retreat? Itamar thought, struggling to understand. *They were ours! The last dregs of Imarah, kneeling at our mercy! Why did you not finish it?*

Coming back from his internal musings, the *shansher* once again looked Itamar in the eye, silently demanding an answer. "Did you recognize him? It was not Tirasdunh; the prince kept to the edges of the tribe to protect his people. The stranger pushed outward into our line of offense. Who was he?"

"Your Highness," Itamar said, using the lofty Northern title he knew the *shansher* preferred. "He was… He was a *she*."

Never before had the High Magus thought he would feel such fear from so small an action. For no more than two blinks of an eye, the Aesimar *shansher* stilled so completely, the entire tent seemed to grow cold. "A woman?" he asked quietly.

Itamar shuddered, and coughed into his fist, embarrassed by his weakness. "Yes, your Highness. A Northerner, by the looks of her. As pale as the sands."

The *shansher* leaned back and stroked his long beard. "I will know everything there is to know about her."

Itamar bowed low. "I will consult our seer—"

"No. I will have it from Kaliban."

"Your Highness…"

"A woman roused the dying *kharesh* to rally and fight like devils against my army. Six score of my men are dead, and all of them her fault. This is no ordinary woman, Itamar. I will know her. Make me ask again, and I will send you to her to ask in person."

Itamar schooled himself not to whimper. "As my *shansher* commands."

Bowing out of the tent, he hurried across the camp to the western edge, where the Magi had settled. There, he summoned Rafi, Pirro, and Dar, the three who, along with him, were the keepers of Kaliban. The four of them together hefted the heavy, metal chest, carrying it back across the camp to the *shansher*'s tent. Despite the heat of the day, whether placed in the sun or in the shade, the chest's metal was always cold. Itamar's hands had cramped by the time they'd set the chest down before the *shansher*.

Chanting their spells, the Magi circled it four times, then each knelt on one side to unlock the clasps that held the lid. After removing it, they reached inside to pull out another box, this one smaller, made of ebony, and carved with intricate protection spells. Placing this chest onto the carpet next to the metal one, they once again chanted prayers before repeating the procedure of removing the lid. Inside the ebony chest lay an even smaller one made of ivory and white crystal; a chest small enough that one man should have been able to lift it out himself, yet it took all four of them to remove it.

One last ritual of spells, and Itamar unlocked the tiny white chest with a shaking hand. From it, he removed a golden oil lamp, shined to a polish, its surface dulled by patterns of black frost. The lamp chilled Itamar's hands so much, he couldn't hold it for longer than a moment and, turning quickly, he placed the lamp down onto the *shansher*'s desk, then stepped far back to kneel by the others, and joined them in droning a quiet prayer.

The *shansher* pulled his sleeve down to cover his hand, then rubbed the oil lamp, disrupting the frost pattern. At once, a plume of noxious black smoke streamed out. Unlike smoke from a fire, which rose into the sky, this one was so thick and so heavy, it poured like water across the surface of the desk, congealing until it formed the figure of a man-shaped creature, solid yet as insubstantial as mist. Itamar wrinkled his nose at the stench of rot and death that always accompanied Kaliban's appearance, and lingered for days afterwards.

"My master summons me," Kaliban said, his voice a hissing rattle reminiscent of a venomous snake. It struck fear into the soul of any unlucky enough to hear it, and the *daeva* relished that fear, savored it like a treat. "What is your wish?"

"A woman of the North thwarted my victory over Imarah today," the *shansher* lied, holding his hand over his nose and mouth. "My wish is to know who she is."

Kaliban raised his hands high above his head, the chains that bound him rattling loudly. Power, ancient and cold, gathered along the tent's ceiling, swirling to create a vortex to another world. In it, terrifying and incomprehensible shapes began to form, Only Kaliban could decipher them and convey their meaning to the *shansher*. Itamar had warned the *shansher* many times that creatures of Darkness, even imprisoned ones, often mixed truth with lies; he wouldn't have believed the *daeva* had he told them the sky was blue and the sun set in the west. But the High Magus was merely a tool of the *shansher's* ambition, just like everyone else.

An ugly, scornful laugh rattled around the *daeva*, and his form shivered as if he would dissolve into mist. "Your first wish gave you a tribe," he jeered, "and your second brings its demise!"

Itamar shuddered, faltering in his prayers as the *daeva* spun his evil spell. The vortex above the *shansher's* head stretched down, spinning with visions and demons reaching out to claw the unwary. "You wish to know the woman of the North? She is Vengeance. She Who Walks Through Fire will not be stopped by magic, or by sword. She will cut darkness with a blade of fire, and tear hearts out of the bodies of her enemies. She will claim yours, Khiron al-Bashir, deserter of Imarah, and you will see it burning in her hand before your soul has left your body." The *daeva* laughed cruelly, jangling his chains with such vigor, Itamar feared he would break out and destroy them all. For the first time since they'd bound Kaliban, Itamar feared those chains were nothing but a cruel trick, worn willingly to give them all a false sense of security while the *daeva* bided his time and schemed.

"*Enough!*" Khiron slammed his fist down onto the desk, overturning the oil lamp. "Begone, fiend! Back into your prison!"

Still laughing, Kaliban's form dissolved into smoke, taking his vortex with him. Little by little, he streamed back inside the lamp, his final words rattling softer, as if for Khiron alone: "You will call again, *shansher*, and your third wish will cost you dearly. You will call. You will. And I shall answer… for the price of your soul."

The *daeva* was gone.

Dar rushed to return the lamp to its resting place. His flesh sizzled when he touched it, rousing the others from their stupor to come to his aid. The lamp steamed when they placed it into the white chest; the ebony sealed in its warmth; and by the time they'd locked the metal, the entire chest was cold once again.

They rushed the whole thing back to its resting place in the Magis' tent, but when Itamar returned to the *shansher*, Khiron was as pale as a sheet, wide-eyed gaze fixed on the table where the lamp had scorched it.

"What does my *shansher* command?" Itamar asked timidly.

"Bury the chest," Khiron rasped, breathing hard, "deep in the desert, where no one will ever find it."

"And what of the woman?"

Khiron al-Bashir, deserter of Imarah and *shansher* of Aesimar, stroked his beard with a shaky hand. "She is merely a woman," he mused, "and as you like to remind me, *daeva* lie. I will not give its words credence."

"Indeed." Itamar bowed low. It wouldn't do to point out the sweat on Khiron's brow, or the quiver in his voice. Only a fool would throw his *shansher*'s weakness back in his face, and a fool Itamar was not.

For all that he claimed to have the Dark god's favor, the leader of Aesimar feared him as much as any mortal man, and for all that he pretended to use Aesma's creatures as his minions, as any other mortal man, Khiron was nothing but their puppet.

The *shansher* had bought three wishes from a *daeva* for the price of his soul. It wouldn't matter where Itamar buried that chest, Kaliban would not be cheated of his prize; he'd come from the ends of the world to collect on his debt, with interest, and Itamar intended to be very far away when that happened. Better to be caught and executed as a traitor; better to slowly waste away of thirst in the desert and pass into the arms of his ancestors, than to relinquish his soul to a *daeva*'s eternal hunger.

Win or lose, Khiron would never see the First City again.

Perhaps that was for the best.

27

Sleep eluded Tir all through the night. He paced the tent like a tiger denied his prey, reeling from the news Farraj had so callously delivered. Dhakir the Conqueror was dead, his only remaining daughter burned on his pyre, and Tir was the last of his family left alive, a prince who'd never wanted to be king.

He'd failed to break the curse, his tribe was doomed to slowly die on the scorching desert sands, and Tir was helpless to stop it.

Passing by the ebony seat again, he felt a chill run up his spine, as if his father's ghost still sat there, watching him and demanding his due. Imarah was now Tir's responsibility, and with all of their lives resting on his shoulders, Tir couldn't breathe.

He wanted to scream, to curse the Northern king again, to lay the blame at Liadan's feet. Her fire storm had cost them three days; if they'd ridden straight to the First City, straight through to Imarah, he might have saved them, and his sister might still be alive.

But his anger found no easy victim. Liadan didn't return to the tent the entire night. He waited for her with angry words lodged in his chest, ready to let loose—and he desperately needed to let them loose, the ache too great to keep contained. But she didn't appear.

When light caressed the tent wall, Tir held his breath, waiting for

Liadan to enter; she'd shone that brightly many times before. To his disappointment, it wasn't Liadan, but the morning sun illuminating the world outside that thin sheet of cloth. Day had quietly dawned while he'd walked countless miles in circles throughout the night.

Weary, he rubbed the sleep from his eyes and stepped out into the open, preparing to face the impossible task of bringing his people solace.

"*Imarah, awaken!*" Farraj bellowed somewhere nearby, and dozens of little bells rattled in unison. "*Imarah! I summon thee!*" The bell staff thumped in rhythm to his words. Like the rest of his tribe, Tir followed the noise, curious.

In the small gathering space among the blood-stained tents, Farraj stood tall, slamming the bell staff down and shouting, "*I challenge the brave and the strong! I challenge Imarah! Who will answer? Who will submit to the ordeal of kharashan?*"

"Farraj! Have you gone mad?"

The man ignored him. "*Who will answer?*" he repeated, casting his gaze over the gathering of men and women who looked at each other, frightened, confused. They hadn't seen a *kharashan* for many years, not since Dhakir had lost his will to live and their people had begun to die off like flies. Courage had deserted them long ago, their strength sapped more and more every day.

Imarah didn't need a trial of strength now; they needed help. "Leave off, Farraj," Tir said, tired of pretending to be strong. "Do not make a mockery of us."

"*I challenge the brave and the strong!*" Farraj shouted again, voice booming as very few could. "*Who will submit to the ordeal of kharashan?*"

A hum of confusion swept through the crowd as a man stepped forth, joined by another, and then a third. As they each came forward, the tribe hailed them with cries of honor, quietly at first, afraid of making too much noise, but by the fifth, they cheered as loudly as they could, and Tir was left speechless.

"*I challenge the brave and the strong! Who will answer?*"

Two more stepped up, and Tir's people raised their fists in the air, chanting for their braves. From the other side of the gathering, a boy of no more than thirteen crawled out and ran to join the petitioners. People laughed when his mother dragged him back by his ear. Even Tir allowed himself a chuckle, his dark mood lifting as he beheld his tribe's spirit and realized the wisdom of what Farraj had done. Even in their darkest time, he gave them cause to feel strong, to act brave, to face a challenge they could overcome.

He felt Liadan approach before he saw her; the familiar heat of her fire, the scent of smoke and woman ever present around her. He turned to her with a smile, but she paid him no attention, her determined gaze focused on Farraj.

Someone had given her a change of clothes. Billowing pants tucked at her ankles into soft leather shoes, the same kind the *kharesh* wore into battle. Instead of a shirt, she wore a laced vest to cover her torso, leaving her arms bare, painted like a heathen warrior with swirls and symbols that also marked her uncovered face. Her hair, plaited tightly back, shone with red streaks in the sun, and the twisted torc at her neck gleamed. She looked like the Othercreature she was, and Tir realized at once what was about to happen.

"Do not—"

"Will you do something for me?" Her charcoal eyes flickered red-gold with her fire as she pressed something into his hand, curling his fingers around it. "Keep this safe," she said.

Tir gazed down at the small glass vial of water from her brother. What was this? By the time he looked back up, she'd stepped out to join the petitioners. "Liadan!"

She ignored him, standing tall next to the ninth man to make an even ten, and the crowd fell silent. With all eyes trained on her, Liadan didn't flinch; she kept her chin up, her back straight, her gaze forward.

Farraj stopped shouting for the brave, and as people hummed with displeasure, *kharesh* entered the circle, no doubt to remove Liadan, to beat her for showing such brazen disrespect to their men. Tir stepped forward to intervene, but Farraj once again thumped the bell staff onto the flat stone, hard enough to crack the shaft. He did it again, and again, in a slow, steady rhythm that demanded their silence and attention. He looked at each of them in turn until the *kharesh* retreated one by one beneath the authority of his stare and everyone else quieted in deference to it. Farraj lingered longest on Tir, sending a silent message: *Do not interfere. Do not let her be undermined again.*

Tir curled his fingers into fists at his sides, mindful of the fragile vial Liadan had entrusted into his keeping. His feet cramped, aching to move, to drag Liadan away from the center and into safety behind tent walls. The ordeal of *kharashan* was no laughing matter; men had died during its challenges, some had disappeared, never to be seen again, claimed by the desert forever. He knew what she was thinking—to prove herself a warrior among them, strong enough to lead and defend them. A fool's errand, and one that would get her killed.

And Tir knew Farraj had helped her orchestrate it. The man wouldn't have called a *kharashan* for any other reason now, of all times, when they grieved their *shansher* and so many others who'd fallen. The two of them had schemed behind his back to do this. He'd wring both of their necks when all this was over. Starting with Liadan's.

If she made it through.

Gods, please let her make it through.

28

They wanted to stone her. Every last one of them, beginning with the *kharesh*, who'd see her participation as the ultimate insult, wanted to see her broken and humbled on the ground at their feet. Well aware of the turmoil she'd caused just by stepping into the circle, Liadan steeled herself to stand tall. This was only the beginning.

She felt the tribe's animosity like countless sharp needles pricking her skin, but didn't dare show her unease. She was strong; she could and would complete the ordeal. To think any less meant allowing weakness into her heart, and Liadan couldn't allow that when so much was at stake.

Tir bristled twenty paces away. He was furious with her, of that she had no doubt, but he was allowing her to do this without interference, and that humbled her. He'd told her how difficult the ordeal of *kharashan* was, as had Farraj, and now both of them showed incredible trust by letting her prove what she could do.

Liadan didn't intend to fail them. A polished scimitar waited for her at the end of the ordeal and, by the gods, she'd make it far enough to claim it.

The man standing next to her huffed his anger; the tribesmen sneered, shaking their heads. And through it all, Farraj continued to beat a steady rhythm, demanding respect and obedience to the ordeal. He did so for a long time, until the tribe joined in, clapping to the rhythm he set. The beats came faster, and faster, until the tribe shouted and cheered once more, and then Farraj roared to the heavens and shouted a summons.

One by one, the petitioners followed him through the crowd to the first challenge. Each was touched by the people he passed, receiving a blessing for success from the men and women of Imarah. They showed no such deference to Liadan, who brought up the rear; instead, they withdrew, some turning their backs. One man spat at her feet, but was quickly yanked back and admonished. Liadan didn't catch the angry words, but she heard "*shensari*" among them.

When she felt a hand on her shoulder, she braced for a blow, but it was Tir who'd suddenly appeared beside her, walking tall and daring anyone to question whom the *shansher* chose to favor. "Thank you," she said softly, knowing what it cost him to do this.

"By the gods, do not thank me for walking you to the gallows," he grated in response.

"Would you miss me if I were to perish?" she asked, fighting back a smile.

"As a horse would miss a swarm of gnats. All the same, I will keep your trinket safe, if you do something for me in return."

"What is it?"

The line stopped in front of a black tent strewn with animal skins, and Farraj placed himself at the entrance to stand guard. After a ritual of hopping and huffing to give himself courage, the first petitioner stepped inside.

Tir grasped Liadan's chin, gently turning her face to meet his gaze. "Come back alive, *shai'iss*." His golden eyes burned with so many words he couldn't say before he pressed a chaste kiss to her forehead. Then he stepped back into the crowd.

Stunned by the gesture, Liadan searched for him, wanting to reassure him somehow, but she couldn't see him anywhere. *I'll make it through,* she vowed. *You'll see. I'll prove you haven't made a mistake in bringing me here. I will fulfill my oath.*

The petitioners entered the black tent one at a time, summoned by a strike of Farraj's staff. Liadan watched them each prepare in their own way before they stepped inside, and while she waited her turn, she recalled everything Farraj had told her last night.

The ordeal of *kharashan* consisted of three trials through which the petitioners proved both their worth and their strength. First, a trial of the spirit. Inside the black tent sat the last remaining Magus of the Imarah tribe. He was ancient, his face covered by a black veil so he couldn't be recognized. Upon stepping inside, the petitioner drank a potion known only to the Magi, one forbidden to anyone else, as it induced visions and hallucinations, lowered one's guard and forced them to speak only the truth.

Once the potion took effect, the petitioner was asked three questions, each with only one acceptable answer, and the petitioner had to speak it truthfully.

Who are you?

I am a blade of Imarah.

What do you want?

To serve the shansher and my tribe.

What will you sacrifice?

My all, and all of myself.

If the wrong answer was spoken, or spoken dishonestly, the petitioner was expelled from the ordeal and shamed by the tribe, never to attempt it again.

I am a blade of Imarah, Liadan repeated to herself as the seventh, and then the eighth man entered the tent. None had yet emerged; they'd all continued on to the next trial. *I wish to serve the shansher and my tribe. I will sacrifice my all, and all of myself for the good of the tribe.*

The ninth man entered, leaving Liadan alone in the circle of people who'd grown as quiet as death. She schooled herself not to fidget. *I am a blade of Imarah.* A blade did not waver.

The sun rose higher. Liadan's mouth felt dry; already she'd been standing there for a long time. But no one offered a drink of water, and she wouldn't ask for it. Every pain and discomfort, Farraj had warned, was part of the ordeal. And so she waited, keeping her eye on the tent's entrance and on the staff in Farraj's hand. Any moment now it'd strike to announce her turn, and she'd step into the tent to face the Magi.

Suddenly, the tent flap billowed, and the ninth petitioner crawled out. A collective gasp sent the tribe a step backwards from the weeping man whose limbs shook as he dragged them forward. Though he had no injuries that Liadan could see, his eyes were haunted, terrified, and he wailed, cried out words she didn't understand as he crawled toward those closest to him. They stepped away, spat on the sand. Abandoned, the man collapsed onto his side, curled in on himself like a child, and wept. No one came to help him.

Farraj struck his bell staff against stone, summoning the last petitioner.

Tearing her gaze away from the crying man, Liadan licked her dry lips and stepped forth, faltering only the slightest bit as she stepped from the searing light of the desert sun into the tent's total darkness.

The scent of smoke and incense hung thick in the air. Carpets had been laid one over the other to cushion her feet from the sand. The Magus struck a wooden stick against a brass bowl, in a soft gong to direct her toward him.

With her dragonsight, Liadan had no trouble seeing in the dark; yet even so, she saw little more than shadowy shapes. Everything inside the tent was black: black walls, black carpets, black veils draping over the Magi, black bowls and chalices. Only the polished brass gong gleamed bright. She approached and knelt before the Magi, bowing so low her forehead touched the carpet before she sat back on her heels and waited.

Who are you? What do you want? What will you sacrifice?

I am a blade of Imarah. I wish to serve the shansher and my tribe. I will sacrifice my all, and all of myself for the good of both.

Without a word, the Magus pressed a black cup into her hand.

Liadan brought it to her mouth, and the sharp, herbal scent stung her nose. Whatever was in that cup would be more potent than any spirits she'd sampled in the past. After taking a deep breath, she drank down the bitter brew underlaid with an unfamiliar sweetness that lingered on her tongue.

At once, the ground swayed, and the cup tumbled from her numb fingers as she tried to hand it back. Her heart raced; sweat broke out on her brow and upper lip. She braced herself forward on her hands as her stomach clenched, trying to cast out what she'd drunk. But Liadan gritted her teeth and swallowed it back.

Head swimming, she tried to focus her gaze on the brass bowl, waiting for the questions to be asked.

Who are you? What do you want? What will you sacrifice?

The bowl began to glow so brightly, she had to squint against its glare, and she felt herself falling forward, felt immense power pierce the darkness and reach out for her.

It didn't ask her identity.

It called her by name.

Liadan shuddered at the whispery voice that screamed inside her mind with such strength, her skull threatened to explode. She bit back a cry of pain and squeezed her eyes shut, pressing the heels of her hands into them to keep them from popping out. Without support, Liadan slumped forward, her forehead falling to the carpet once more.

Who are you? What do you want? What will you sacrifice?

The questions didn't come. Instead, in the thick darkness of her own drugged mind, pale shadows formed into blurry shapes. White smoke thickened to form the ghostly face of a beautiful woman with eyes shining like stars. In an instant, it dissolved, replaced by a pair of graceful hands dancing through the air in intricate patterns, shaping a wordless spell. Once again, the darkness broke the vision apart, thickening, fighting to keep the apparition away.

It was a Veil. Although she'd never seen one, Liadan nevertheless recognized that the darkness was some sort of barrier holding the apparition back. It seemed to have a mind of its own, moving, swirling, repairing itself every time the pale woman of light managed to break through even a little.

She called to Liadan, summoned her by name, and Liadan was helpless to disobey, pulled into the suffocating black sea that blanketed the entire valley.

"You risk much, young Dragonblood, by undertaking the ordeal," the woman whispered, and Liadan fell to her knees, covering her ears. The woman spoke in Aegiran, but somehow, Liadan understood her perfectly. "Do you seek Imarah's approval? They will not give it.

Not for this."

"I… I am a blade of Imarah," Liadan said, choking on the darkness that poured down her throat every time she opened her mouth to speak. If only she could get the words out, speak the answers, the first trial would be over. "My wish is to… serve the *shansher* and my tribe."

The apparition formed long enough to laugh in Liadan's face before the darkness banished it back again. "You are not of Imarah, young Dragonblood, and you serve no one but yourself."

A terrible wind knocked Liadan sideways, swirling the darkness so thin, she could almost see through it. Lights flashed in the immeasurable distance, a different face inside of each; they called out to her—some in anger, some with hope in their eyes—and their voices touched her mind, imparted knowledge she'd never had before. Their language became hers; their names as familiar as her own family's; their history became etched in her mind like a memory of her own.

They were gods. Once worshipped by Imarah, they'd been banished beyond this black Veil that none but the mighty wind god, Vayu, could penetrate.

"Do you know what you have done?" demanded Inaras, the great Mother of Life, as the black Veil once again reformed to hide the others.

Liadan could no longer tell which direction she'd come from. She couldn't breathe, until that great wind once again swirled around her, diluting the black sea enough for her to take a breath and find her voice, and desperate to escape this in-between, she quickly said, "I will sacrifice my all, and all of myself for the good of my tribe." As soon as she'd finished, the Veil once again reformed. It leaked into her eyes until she feared she'd go blind, and in her fear, magic pooled beneath her skin, glowing out of her like a living flame.

The darkness squealed, but instead of retreating, it forced its way deeper into her.

"Yes, that is true enough, at least," Inaras replied, her terrible voice thoughtful. Liadan felt the goddess' gaze on her.

"Am I… finished?" Liadan gagged. All around her, the Veil screamed soundlessly, imposing its terrible will on her soul, and the more Liadan fought it, raising her fire to glow brighter, the harder the darkness struck her. If it couldn't expel Liadan, it would rend her apart from the inside. She wouldn't last much longer here, but Inaras held her fast by the force of her will alone.

"No, young one, your trial has only just begun."

The wind returned on its third pass, fanning her flame and providing a small respite. *She weakens, Inaras,* hissed the great god, Vayu.

Taking heed, the goddess spoke quickly. "Listen, and listen well, Dragonblood, for many lives depend on you. Lives of *my* people. Are you worthy of them?"

The darkness had filled her limbs, turning them as cold as ice, and Liadan shivered. "N-no," she answered, humbling herself before the great Mother of Life. "Your people are great, and incredibly strong. I am… not worthy of them. I have… not proven myself to be as strong. I… don't know if… I am."

Ghostly hands caressed her face, forcing her to look up into a pair of shining eyes. "You must be," Inaras said. "It was one of my own who summoned the demon for her revenge. No outsider could have banished me from my own people; only one of the Imarah could have done so, and the curse will keep me from them until the Veil's maker is dead, or I am.

"I weaken in exile, young Dragonblood. Without my people's prayers, soon, even I will not have enough power to restore the First Tribe. You *must* triumph! You must draw out the demon and slay him; destroy the shroud of Darkness over the First Valley. You will never be a blade of Imarah, young Dragonblood; you will be my Vessel, the flame with which I'll burn my way back to my people. And you will burn so bright, it'll reduce you to ashes. That is the oath you swore to my prince, and that is the price your oath will exact. Do you understand now what you have done? Are you willing to sacrifice yourself so they might live?"

The goddess' face dissolved and her hands faded away. Liadan was forcefully shoved out of the Veil, slamming back into herself, her physical body convulsing to expel the residual darkness. Sporadic bursts of light flared from her, reflecting off the brass bowl into dozens of sharp beams.

The Magus' voice trembled with fear as he asked, "Who are you?"

At last, the question she'd been waiting for. But Liadan could no longer answer as she'd been instructed. Shaking, disoriented, she rose to her hands and knees and answered the only way she could: "I am the flame of Inaras." She spoke the words in Aegiran, the sounds effortlessly flowing over her tongue as if she'd spoken them all her life. Her skin's glow settled, burning away the chill of the Dark Veil and feeding her strength.

The torc at her neck, the dragon's gift to her, vibrated against her skin, reminding Liadan of her heritage. *I am a Dragonblood, the Halfling daughter of Halfling parents, a crown princess of my people, and an Other with powers none have yet seen, not even I.* And now, with the goddess' hand on her shoulder, those powers would be greater still. They'd consume her in the end.

Perhaps that had always been her fate.

The moment she thought it, her inner light intensified enough to illuminate the Magus' face behind his veil.

Eyes wide, mouth slack, he gasped softly, leaning back. But despite his fear, he asked, as ritual dictated, "What do you want?"

Dizziness assailed Liadan as she pushed herself up to sit back on her heels. Although the Veil's darkness had burned away, the potion's effects still ravaged her body and her mind, and Liadan couldn't focus on any of the six shadowy Magi now floating before her. When she reached up to wipe her brow, her hand passed over her hair instead, and she dared not shake her head, lest she topple over and never get up again. "I wish to fulfill my oath, to break the curse and restore Imarah to what it once was."

"W-what will you sacrifice?"

Silence followed. Liadan stared at the brass bowl, and in its depths saw the reflection of her own eyes, glowing as brightly as the goddess' had done. The final answer would seal her fate. In Wilderheim, she hadn't known what she was doing when she'd foolishly spoken her oath. Now it was too late to undo it. She had no choice but to keep going forward. Her life, her very soul was bound to the Imarah tribe by that oath, and the only way to free herself was to free them.

Her light dimmed, plunging the tent into darkness once more.

"My all, and all of myself," she finally answered the Magi.

The first trial was over.

29

Farraj stepped away from the tent to indicate the final petitioner had passed the first trial, and Tir's shoulders slumped in relief. She'd made it through.

Then he saw his shadow, barely peeking out past the tips of his toes. Midday. The ordeal of *kharashan* had no time limit; whether a petitioner took a day or seven to return to the tribe, it only mattered that they return at all. But there was a reason why they'd stopped calling for it. When the threat of demons loomed over everyone the moment night fell, the risk was too great for any one man to venture out into the desert on his own.

Today's first petitioner would already be well on his way to the final trial. Liadan, the last, had lost a half-day waiting; she'd have even less time to finish the ordeal and return to the relative safety of the camp before nightfall.

She will make it through, Tir told himself. Her oath would compel her to return, would give her the strength to meet each challenge quickly and without delay.

And if the demons came…

Fear for her and for his tribe suddenly lodged in his throat. He looked at the glass vial he still clutched, raised the looped thong to hang it from his neck, then reconsidered and took the vial to his tent instead. He wrapped the delicate bottle in cloth, then in leather, and finally in sheepskin, then placed it into the ebony chest where Dhakir had kept all of his most treasured possessions. It was empty now, those treasures burned with him on his pyre. Swallowing back his grief, Tir forced himself to his feet. There was work to be done.

Emerging from the tent once more, he caught Farraj just passing by.

The older man sighed. "Leave her to it, Tirasdunh. She must complete the ordeal if she is to be one of our tribe on her terms. It is the only way."

"I know," he replied, causing Farraj to raise his eyebrows in surprise. "That is not what I want to say to you." Liadan had been right; she couldn't have remained *shensari* for even a day. If she had, the tribe might have come to accept her, but only as an extension of him. For Liadan, that would have been a slow, withering death.

"Then what is it?"

How to explain? "I know you don't believe I am worthy of leading Imarah. No, do not interrupt. You are right to doubt me, but I ask you to trust me now. Something bad is heading toward us; I feel evil coming on the wind, and I need your help."

"Anything," Farraj answered at once.

Tir nodded. "Gather the *kharesh*. Liadan and I left a cart of supplies in the east. Water, oil, clothes, shoes; anything we could take with us from the First City."

Farraj blanched. "You rode through the First City?"

He ignored the question. "I will need two riders to come with me to fetch the cart. I fear we will need every last scrap of those supplies before the night is through."

"Yes." Farraj nodded. "It will be done at once."

~

Liadan stumbled out of the tent, falling to her hands and knees a few paces from it. The sand burned her palms, the sun seared her back, but the air was clean, and she breathed in deeply, hoping it would ease the potion's effects.

When she felt strong enough to look up, she saw no one around except one veiled woman sitting before her. The black tent was far behind her. She'd walked farther into the desert than she'd thought.

Sitting back on her heels, she wiped the sweat from her brow and faced the veiled woman—the second trial. Seven bottles sat in the sand in front of her, all identical, all neatly aligned. This was the trial of the mind. Last night, Farraj had told her that each *kharesh* was not only a warrior, but also a trained assassin; they learned to kill by any means, with weapons, trickery, or poison, and to that end, each wore a belt lined with these same venoms and poisons in varying degrees of potency. The weakest would make Liadan fall asleep for days and, by the rules of *kharashan*, she'd be left to her own devices until she awakened—*if* she awakened. The strongest would kill her instantly.

The poisons would be unmarked, but always arranged the same way on a belt. Not by potency, but using a code each *kharesh* learned before taking the ordeal. They learned it early on, and repeated the lesson often, so that, should the need arise, a *kharesh* wouldn't need to think about which bottle to reach for; he'd know it instinctively, wasting no time when it mattered most.

The veiled woman waved her hand over the row of bottles, then brought it to her mouth, tipping her head back. Liadan was to choose one bottle and take a drink. What was the order Farraj had taught her? Her memory was excellent on most occasions, but with the potion still muddling her mind, Liadan couldn't recall his words. There had been a rhyme to it… Venom, poison sleeping draft. *Wasting time! Gods, what was the order?*

The veiled woman pointed at the sky, then eastward to the mountain range. Liadan was far from finished; she had to make haste.

She reached for a bottle, then hesitated. Thirst made her tongue stick to the roof of her mouth; she'd give her sword arm for a sip of water. Liadan glanced to the east, where the mountain range loomed dark red above the sands, marking the location of her third trial. She couldn't head toward it until she'd passed the second.

No more time to waste; the longer she stayed there, the worse the heat would become. And what would it matter, anyway? Liadan was Other; she didn't react to poisons the same way humans did. Whatever was in those bottles wouldn't kill her—it couldn't. At worst, she'd fall asleep for a few days, but she'd recover eventually.

Liadan snatched up the third bottle on the right, downed its contents in one swallow. Warm liquid slid down her throat, and hope surged that she'd made the right choice. Liadan's questioning look to the woman was met with a bow of her head and a motion of her hand to indicate she should continue.

She stood, ready to move on—

—and her knees gave out under her. She dropped to the sand, stomach twisting painfully. Her entire torso clenched in a merciless cramp as the poison she'd just imbibed contorted her insides. She embarrassed herself by vomiting in front of the veiled woman, but she was still alive.

Struggling to her feet again, Liadan took a shaky step and, by the grace of the goddess, she didn't fall. One more step, and the cramps subsided a little, but ten steps farther, they returned with a vengeance, sending her sprawling once more. Liadan writhed on the hot sands, tears of pain stinging her eyes. This was worse than the pain heralding her firestorm. The poison exacted its price for her foolishness by making her crawl when she ought to have been running.

But Liadan refused to give up. She crawled ever eastward, gaze locked on that mountainside as her guiding beacon. When she could, she got up and walked; when the pain knocked her to her knees, she crawled. Step by step, Liadan approached the mountain, and when she got there, the pain had become too much and she blacked out.

By the time she woke, the sun was already kissing the edge of the horizon. *I'm alive,* she thought. Potions, poisons, trekking through the desert—none of that had stopped her, and Liadan was so close to her goal, she could almost see it. There, halfway up the mountain, something glittered in the saddle. Her prize beckoned—a shining scimitar to mark her a *kharesh,* worthy of looking the tribe in the eye instead of staring at their feet in submission. *I am a blade of Imarah.*

You will be the flame with which I'll burn my way back to my people.

Liadan smiled recklessly, reaching up for a small outcropping above her. "Wait until Mother hears about this."

30

The sun was halfway behind the horizon when the eighth petitioner, now a *kharesh*, returned to camp with a gleaming scimitar in hand. Farraj stood on the ceremony of clasping forearms with him to welcome him back, but Tir refused to waste any more precious time. They'd already distributed the clothes and shoes to those most in need of them, and what little water had remained, they'd given to the returning *kharesh*, but Tir had kept two bottles back for Liadan.

No one had glimpsed any sign of her yet.

"It's taking too long," he muttered, hands clenching at his sides.

"She is strong," Farraj replied. "She will come back."

"Before the sun sets?"

Farraj said nothing. If she wasn't already on her way back—and someone would have seen her if she were—the only way Liadan would return from that mountain before nightfall was if she truly sprouted dragon wings and flew.

"What does the woman say of her second trial?"

"She says nothing," Farraj answered, "as it should be. The trials are Liadan's to overcome, not ours. If any of the stories about her parents are true, if anything you told me about Liadan is true, then you need not worry about her. Worry instead for your people."

Tir forced his gaze away from the setting sun to look around. The *kharesh*, old and new alike, stood ready with their scimitars at their sides. Their celebration cut short, each had been given a bowl of oil and a cloth with which to varnish the blade, and each had been instructed to light those blades on fire at the first sight of a demon. The rest of his tribe knew nothing of it, but they must have sensed the same thing Tir had: as bright and as hot as the day felt, a chill seeped up from the sand and the air felt heavy with dark magic. Not a single breeze swept by to lighten the oppressive weight of portent. Tir had felt this way before, while riding through Lyria with Liadan, just before the storm had broken right over their heads.

Not knowing what else to do, Imarah had gathered in the center of the camp, forming a circle with the women and children in the middle, and the men standing guard around them. Everyone watched the eastern mountain, though whether they watched for Liadan or for a demon swarm, Tir didn't know.

The sun dipped lower; his shadow grew a little longer. To the north, the horses whinnied, and Tir ran to them at once. He passed the Magus' tent with a cursory glance at the old man drawing giant concentric circles in the sand.

When he'd left Imarah, only two horses had remained: Tarabas and Zara. Now, the shelter held six horses in all, some still wearing the symbolic markings of Aesma Daeva that couldn't be washed off except with water.

At the very back of the shelter, Sleipnir tossed his head, kicking at the post his reins had been tied to. Sensing his fear, Tarabas, too, tried to rear away from his tether, and their distress riled the others into a panic.

"Easy," Tir soothed, approaching with his hands raised. "Calm yourselves. Calm…"

Sleipnir reared, tearing the post from the sands. It swung wildly, still attached to his reins, and Tir ducked to avoid a blow. He took two running steps, vaulted astride the black stallion, and hung on for dear life with his legs as he struggled to free Sleipnir from the straps. The horse reared again, then dropped forward and kicked out, jumped and twisted, doing his worst to shake Tir off his back.

Tarabas and the other horses squealed, drawing others of the tribe to try to calm them. They were dividing the group. Tir almost had the strap undone, when Sleipnir reared again, this time so far back, he lost his balance and toppled over. Tir couldn't move away fast enough; his foot caught beneath the horse's girth, and something popped painfully in his ankle. The stallion scrambled back to his hooves, leaving Tir in the sands, but with the straps now loosened, Sleipnir shook out of them and galloped off toward the mountains in the east.

Tir was glad. "Run quickly," he said, wincing as he probed his ankle. Nothing broken; the pain would ease in moments. "Run to her, and keep her safe." He got up, keeping his weight on his good foot, and shouted, "Everyone fall back! Free the horses; they can take care of themselves! Set them loose and fall back!"

~

The final challenge, a trial of the body, was the longest, and the most grueling. Farraj had warned Liadan it wouldn't be what it appeared; the trial didn't begin until the petitioner had reached the point of total exhaustion. The trek through the desert to the mountain range had been a pleasurable respite compared to the wretched climb to the saddle. Liadan steadied her foot on a hold, then reached up with her opposite hand. The red rock was searing hot, something that wouldn't normally have bothered Liadan, but it was also sharp and brittle, with blade-like edges that cut into her palms and broke off in her skin. Every time she let go, she had to wipe her palm to remove the debris, wasting precious time and energy.

Her mouth was parched; her lips were cracked and peeling. She squinted against every breeze, but dared not completely close her eyes, even with sand constantly blowing into them. She had no tears left to wash it out. What was worse, every so often, her stomach clenched with painful cramps, remnants of that accursed poison she'd drunk. Weak and shaky, she had to test the security of each hand- and foothold twice before trusting her whole weight to it. Wasting even more precious time.

At an outcropping large enough to hold both of her feet, Liadan stopped to catch her breath, squinting against the sunset. In the distance, she saw the Imarah camp huddling small on the vast expanse of glistening sands, its people like miniscule dots moving rapidly among the tents. The other petitioners had no doubt made it back to camp already. There would be celebration and much honor bestowed on all of them. Would anyone notice she hadn't yet returned? Would they care? Like as not, they'd be happier for her to disappear altogether.

Not about to give them that satisfaction, Liadan gritted her teeth and looked up. The saddle wasn't far; already she'd made it two-thirds of the way. *One final push,* she told herself. *I can make it there. I will stand with the kharesh as one of them.*

So determined, Liadan launched up and caught a protruding lump of round rock. It gave, detaching with a soft crack, and she cried out, swinging from her one secure handhold. Blood on her fingers made her weakened grip slick and as she dangled hundreds of feet in the air, her hand began to slip.

In a desperate bid to save herself, she swung for another hold, and the tips of her fingers brushed it without gaining purchase. She swung again, stretching farther… *There!*

A sharp point speared into her palm, but at least the natural hook anchored her, even if it did hurt like hell. She braced her feet and pushed up.

The sun dipped lower, two-thirds down behind the horizon by the time she'd reached the saddle. By then, Liadan couldn't keep her feet under her. She sat down hard, head lolling back, and allowed herself a moment's rest to catch her breath. When the sun set, she'd have to summon her fire to climb back down, and wasn't sure of the wisdom of that.

Her eyes began to close.

Can't fall asleep… Liadan forced herself back to her feet to look for her blade.

Breath left her at the sight before her. Fifty paces ahead rose four majestic columns with intricate symbols and patterns carved directly into the rock face where the saddle met the higher mountain. Behind them, a small flame flickered deep inside a black tunnel. Its light drew her forward, and she cautiously entered the abyss, tracing the ground with her toes before shifting her weight forward. Her feet dragged, her knees were weak, her hands throbbed with a bone-deep ache that overpowered even the sharp pain of her many bleeding cuts. The flame danced somewhere just out of reach, singing to her of a beautiful, gleaming sword set on an ornate pedestal. She kept going, steadying herself against the tunnel wall, unconcerned about the bloody streaks she left across the faded paintings.

Not far ahead, Liadan rounded a bend in the tunnel, and all at once, there it was—on a small stone altar in the center of a cavernous chamber, a shallow bowl of oil had been set aflame to illuminate the polished scimitar set on a carved ebony frame. The blade shone, its metallic melody sharper than any sword she'd ever wielded, aside from her own. The guard was darker, an intricate construction of brass and gold that sang to Liadan in the purest of tones. The handle was wrapped in leather dyed a deep red, ending in a pommel shaped like an onion with a bright red tassel dangling from its tip. Beneath the stand lay a leather scabbard, a whetstone, a cloth, and a small vial of oil. A more magnificent prize, Liadan had never seen.

Mesmerized by the beauty of such an offering, she approached the altar.

The fire suddenly flared a warning.

Liadan gasped, pulling back a blink before a scimitar sparked against the altar's edge.

"You did not think it would be that easy, did you?"

Liadan leaped aside as the warrior launched his attack. She spun a clumsy pirouette to the left and ducked another swing of his blade, retreated from his merciless forward press until she found herself with her heel past the edge of the chamber. He'd almost expelled her back into the dark tunnel and, having done so, he backed up to the altar to guard her prize.

"Save yourself the pain of death, Northern scum," he said in scornful Aegiran, every word of which Liadan now understood. "Go back to your demon homelands and leave us in peace!"

Undeterred, Liadan started forward again. The warrior brought up his blade, slashed in an arc, driving her back a step farther into the tunnel. The gleam in his eyes told her that was precisely what he'd wanted. The tunnel was dark and narrow, a much more difficult place to maneuver around a swinging blade. If she let him, he'd force her all the way out and off the cliff.

Liadan needed to stay in the chamber; it was her only chance of getting that sword. She tried again to get past him, and again he drove her backwards. Feigning left, she dove beneath the swing of his blade to the right and rolled along the floor, back inside the chamber. He roared as he came after her, his sword sparking off the stone walls. Liadan kept low, kept moving, but her strength sapped quickly, thighs burning with strain as she rolled and crawled around the chamber in a pathetic display. The dragon would have been ashamed.

The fire called to her, singing enticingly; it was just there, a tool to be used, and a weapon much easier to wield than a sword. Fire was light; it moved on its own, an extension of her. But to use her power over it against the *kharesh* would forever deny her the respect she needed. No, to win this trial, she had to do it on his terms—as a warrior, not a Magi.

Of course, that didn't mean she couldn't make use of it the mortal way. Shoving to her feet, she stepped into the warrior's next swing, drove her fist into his stomach, kicked his feet out from under him. He recovered in an instant, now enraged and out for blood, and when he came at her next, he held the scimitar in one hand and a dagger in the other. Liadan turned and ran at the wall, launched off of it, twisted in a graceful somersault over his head to land behind him. Her balance was off; she stumbled and fell onto her backside, striking her elbows on the hard stone floor as the warrior crashed into the wall and howled with rage.

An opponent quick to anger is one easily defeated, the dragon had always said. As the *kharesh* spun around, hurling his dagger at her, Liadan ducked it, using her momentum to get back to her feet and grab for the bowl of fire. Its metal was searing hot, the oil inside it sloshing as she swiped it off the altar and flung it at the *kharesh*. A speck landed on her arm, and fire flared eagerly along the back of it up to her shoulder, igniting her hair.

The warrior didn't escape it, either; he screamed as burning oil coated his left side, boiling his skin off, and the smell of charred flesh filled the chamber instantly.

Liadan shook out her hair, extinguishing her own flames with a thought, before she rushed to put him out. The ground was on fire where the oil had spilled; she kept them safely away from it despite its seductive call.

Tears of pain ran down his face, but he made not a sound. The warrior would be in a great deal of pain for a long time; his left arm would be scarred, disfigured for the rest of his life, but he'd survive and would retain the use of his limb.

Liadan stepped away to let him catch his breath. His eyes were bloodshot, his breaths rattled, lungs filled with smoke. He coughed, swayed on his feet, then leaned back against the chamber wall, shaking the entire time. From there, he stared at Liadan for a long time, fighting a silent internal battle, then finally allowed himself a small nod of thanks.

Liadan inclined her head in reply. "Do you need help down the mountain?" she asked in fluent Aegiran.

In answer, the *kharesh* pushed away from the wall with a groan and raised his sword. He could barely keep his feet under him, but the blade, even quivering in the space between them, didn't lower, the tip pointed squarely at her chest.

"I just saved your life!"

"A *kharesh* fights to the death!"

"Eight others must have come through here before me. Did you kill them all? You must have, since you're still alive."

"A *kharesh* fights!" he repeated. "A *kharesh* is not *kharesh* until he crosses blades with the enemy." His gaze flickered to the scimitar still resting on the altar.

Understanding dawned. Liadan slowly reached for the sword, keeping a wary eye on her opponent.

Her hand met the warm softness of leather; her fingers curled around the handle. The warrior didn't move, save to shift his feet farther apart for balance. He wouldn't last much longer. She eased the weapon off the stand, then brought it forward, touching the flat of her blade against his.

The warrior nodded. "Hail *kharesh*," he said. "Liadan of the North, *shensari* of Imarah. I am Muhammad al-Hassan, and I claim you as a sister, in battle and in… blood—"

Liadan caught him before he hit the ground.

All at once, the fire went out, plunging the chamber into darkness, and a great wind swept past Liadan. "*Riiiide…*" commanded the whispering voice of Inaras. Then again, louder, "*Riiiide!*"

Liadan lay the fallen *kharesh* on the ground, then ran out of the cave. The last rays of sunlight had winked out, its dying glow still painting the western sky in hues of purple and pink, but in the distant south along the foot of the mountain range, a pitch-black cloud obscured the stars. That blackness raced across the desert toward the Imarah camp, and even from so far away, Liadan heard the demon screams piercing through the night.

She froze. Not a single flame burned in the camp. "They'll be massacred…"

A sharp whinny echoed far below her. Sleipnir stomped at the base of the mountain, tossing his head, kicking out at the rock with enough force to make it crumble. He could feel them coming.

Liadan glanced back at the tunnel behind her. This was a temple to Inaras; it had stood for countless centuries, and though the chiseled inscriptions had faded, the goddess' power was palpable in the very stone it'd been carved into. She had to believe Muhammad would be safe inside.

"*Riiiide!*" the wind commanded again.

Liadan moaned, drawing on the dragonfire in her soul. Her skin began to glow, flickering like a living flame caught inside her. Its heat banished the growing chill, made stone hiss when she touched it with her bare hands. With her scimitar sheathed at her waist, Liadan scrabbled down the mountain toward Sleipnir. His whinnies became louder—more screams of fear than cries of alarm—and he pranced back and forth. As soon as she'd mounted his bare back, clutching his mane, he bolted off so fast, it stole her breath away. They flew like the wind over the desert sands, and still couldn't hope to outpace the demon swarm. *We'll never make it,* she thought, watching darkness descend upon the camp.

31

Faster than a sandstorm, more powerful than a northern gale, the demon swarm swept through the camp, razing everything to the ground. Tents blew away beneath its force; stands and stalls splintered. Knocked off their feet, the people of Imarah screamed in terror. They saw nothing, felt nothing but the icy wind that stole breath from their lungs and drew tears from their eyes.

"Hold!" Tir shouted, though he could barely hear his own voice.

The *kharesh* scrambled to their feet, sparking flints to light oil, but the wind was too strong for it to catch.

"Hold!" Tir repeated. "It's only wind!"

No one heard him, and with sand kicking up and no light, they couldn't see him waving for their attention.

Tir grasped the arm of the closest *kharesh* and shouted by his ear, "Get everyone close together and hold steady!" If they could shield the center from the wind, fire would catch more easily.

The *kharesh* nodded, passing the message on to the next, and little by little, the tribe drew together, with the warriors surrounding the women and children.

Someone screamed, a sound Tir knew all too well. He couldn't see who'd fallen to demons, but when the scream cut short, he knew a warrior had dealt him a mercy blow.

Then, all at once, the wind stopped. Shouts faded into silence, and the tribe raised their heads, casting frightened gazes all around.

Tir let out a cautious sigh, and his breath misted. "Is everyone all right?" He shivered, chilled to the bone, and looked down to see white frost creeping across his skin.

"Hiru is dead," came the answer.

"Nai'mah needs a bandage!"

Farraj joined Tir, gaze roaming for the threat that seemed to have disappeared. "What happened?" he asked. With the tents gone, they could see for miles to the west and to the south. All was empty, the night perfectly still and quiet, but neither of them believed the demons had truly gone.

"I don't know," Tir answered, uneasy in the dead silence. Demons didn't leave when they had their prey surrounded and helpless. Why would they take only one and then give up? "*Kharesh*," he called softly, "light the oils."

Flints sparked and oil ignited, illuminating the night. Someone set the fallen Hiru on fire as a precaution. He'd be given the proper honors another time—if anyone survived to speak the words. For now, they needed light and assurance that he wouldn't rise as Forsaken.

"Too quiet," Farraj murmured.

Tir hummed in agreement.

"Where did they go?" asked someone else.

Tir circled the group, looking out in every direction, his gaze lingering on the eastern mountain range. No movement, no light, no telltale flash of fire among the dunes. He didn't allow himself to contemplate what that might mean.

She's not dead. Their blood bond would have told him if she were. As long as his tribe was in danger, Liadan's oath would compel her to aid them. "Where are you?" he whispered.

"Uncle Tir," a small voice suddenly said, freezing him in his tracks. He turned his head to the west and again beheld the bedraggled little girl-child from the First City, standing alone and a fair distance off, with her dark, matted hair falling over her eyes and her small, dirty hands loose and defeated by her sides.

Tir wasn't the only one who saw her.

"Zia?" one of the women cried. "Zia! It's you!" Three *kharesh* held her back as she desperately tried to run to the child, screaming for her daughter.

"Where is she, Uncle Tir?" the demon-child asked in a soft, quivering voice, ignoring the woman and the commotion she'd caused.

"Tir," Farraj warned quietly, "she has no feet."

"Where did she go?" the demon asked again, more urgently this time. "I can't find her."

"Everyone stay together," Tir ordered, not daring to look away from the demon. "Keep to the lights." They needed more fire. It had taken a wall of it to keep the Dark creatures out of the palace when they'd attacked in the First City. But what else could they burn here? The demon storm had swept everything away.

"Where did you hide the daughter of fire?" the Dark child demanded, body quivering, hands fisting. Her voice changed as it grew louder, and Tir shuddered at the terrible sound.

Farraj grabbed Tir's arm. "They want Liadan?"

"They want her *first*." He pushed Farraj off to draw the sword he'd strapped to his side, and the heavy Northern blade sang out of its scabbard, briefly reflecting firelight. The demon hissed furiously.

"We want the daughter of fire!" The child grew bigger, rising higher off the sand. A gust of icy wind swept past Tir. "She belongs to us!" Inside a whirlwind of its own making, its dark hair turned into misty shadows, revealing a horribly deformed face. "*Where did you hide the Northern bitch!*" It rushed Tir with a scream, knocking him to the ground, giving him no chance to shout a warning as the floodgates opened and demons descended from above. Someone shouted for fire; someone else screamed.

On his back, with claws of ice digging into his chest, squeezing his heart, Tir couldn't breathe. The demon's eye sockets glowed red with bloodlust, and a hideous grin mocked him as it sank its incorporeal fingers into his core. A pained groan escaped Tir as the demon latched onto his soul and slowly, so very slowly, began to pull it out. Viscous saliva dripped onto his exposed flesh, burning like acid, and all the while the demon watched, enjoying Tir's torment. Tir's hands and feet went numb; his lips turned cold. *This is the end*, he thought. The last of his tribe would not only die, their souls would be devoured, never to rejoin their ancestors in the afterlife. In one fell swoop, Imarah would cease to exist.

The demon gave a hard tug, and Tir's back arched, head tilting backwards. Blurred flashes of fire danced across his vision—Imarah's vain attempt to fight back, to survive just one more night. Their desperate voices blended with the unearthly demon screams; bodies flew up, never to fall back down. Tir fought the demon's pull, dug his fingers into the sand, commanded his heart to keep beating. But no matter what he did, he couldn't break free. The demon shrieked louder—a dark cackle of delight.

Desperate for his last sight to be something other than the thing's filthy visage, Tir squeezed his eyes shut and thought of Liadan. Her fire dance lit up his memories, filled his mind and his heart with searing heat and wonder.

The demon screamed, released him, rearing away as though burned.

Tir sucked in a harsh breath, his body a twisted mass of agony. Before he could recover, the demon snatched him up again, so high, Tir's feet left the ground. It roared, the bones of its face contorting into a furious snarl before it unhinged its jaw to bite off his head.

Something slammed into its back, and a fiery, golden aura flared around it, bright enough to make Tir squint.

The demon swiveled around to seek its attacker and, with a shrill call, dropped Tir to streak off in pursuit.

Tir groped for his sword as volleys of fireballs assaulted the demon swarm. All around him, his people dropped from the sky like flies, some alive; some broken and contorted, their bodies crushed beyond recognition. Those still alive huddled around the flames, took up swords and raised them high to catch a fireball.

Tir struggled to stand, shaken, unsteady, and weak, and braced to fight against the demons murdering his tribe.

But none of them faced him; the mass of swirling darkness thinned as its venomous shadows streaked across the sky toward the greater source of fire. The sky brightened with countless stars, and its sudden vastness sent Tir back down to his knees. He dared not look behind him, couldn't bring himself to face what he knew he'd see.

Farraj helped him to his feet, held him steady, spoke urgent words Tir couldn't hear past the ringing in his ears. Heart thrashing, head pounding, Tir stared at the older *kharesh* and waited for him to say the only thing he could: that Liadan was dead, and they were doomed.

"…working! The fire…"

Tir frowned, shook his head, and focused on Farraj's mouth to read his words.

"…fire alone did not harm them, blades passed right through. But when the blade burns, the fire gets *inside*! It kills them from within!"

Tir looked down at the Northern sword imbued with magic that thrummed into his hand, and forced his grip to tighten.

"She is winning, Tir," Farraj said. "Your *shensari* is winning, and she is magnificent!"

Tir whirled around to see for himself, and nearly fell to his knees once more.

On the other side of what used to be their camp, the night was bright with Liadan's fire dance. Demons flared, one after the other, exploding in spectacular showers of sparks as she cut through them with her flaming scimitar, and with each one dead, the oppressive darkness lessened, the chill eased, and the survivors cheered louder. Even at such a distance, Tir felt the heat of that dance, knew it was brighter, hotter, and bigger than she'd ever conjured before.

She cut them down in a glorious display of beauty and grace, her face pinched in concentration. Just as she always did in his dreams.

And just as it always did in his nightmares, it would kill her.

32

Tir saw it happening. Her flames ebbed as her strength waned. The demons saw it, too, attacked harder, scored her with their claws and retreated before the fire could hurt them. Liadan's body glowed, her hair escaped from the confines of its braid to halo her head in a mane of living flames.

He'd seen her like this in Dai, but there'd been no smoke then, only fire and light. He'd seen her smoke, too—in the desert, when her flames had consumed her like dry wood.

"Magnificent," Farraj repeated in awe. He didn't know any better. Tir did. "Fall back…"

"What?"

"Get everyone away. Fall back, as far as you can—"

Another flare, and the following ebb extinguished her almost completely. "Liadan!" Tir took off running, even as the demons swooped down on her, so many, so thick, that her light disappeared in the center of their dark mass. He ran straight at the demons, turning a deaf ear to the cries of alarm sounding his reckless advance. Blade cold, with no light to protect him from their wrath, Tir roared, desperate to draw their attention away from Liadan, to give her just a moment more to recover her strength.

He was close enough to swing his blade at the outer circle, when a swirl of fire blazed out, cutting through the swarm in an arc so wide, Tir had no hope of avoiding it. He felt the fire pass through him. Its searing heat sank into his skin, flared across his heart, and came out the other side. But where demons squealed, and burst, and scattered before him, Tir remained unharmed. Shock stopped him in his tracks. Liadan was not fifteen paces away, slumped, gasping for air, but she was still alive. For just a moment, their gazes met, and her eyes widened in surprise to mirror his.

A moment too long. The demons regrouped and attacked once more. Though their ranks had been thinned, their fervor had grown. Liadan threw a fireball Tir's way, then she was engulfed again, fighting for her life. The sand burst into waist-high flames at his feet. Tir felt their warmth, but nothing more; just like in his dreams, he passed through the burning veil as if it were made of the softest gossamer. Ah, but now he had light.

In the middle of the swarm, Liadan cried out in pain, and rage lit his blood. Clutching his sword tighter, its blade holding fire as if made for that purpose, Tir smiled and picked out his first target.

~

Liadan's fire was running out; she didn't have the strength to keep up a steady attack. A burn like that required both concentration and fuel, both of which she had in short supply after the ordeal. Sooner or later, she'd weaken enough for the demons to take her. She couldn't let that happen.

Her retreat tactic had worked. Feigning weakness had brought the Dark bastards to her in droves, and she'd culled a good number of them in one shot, but it wouldn't work a second time. They were too smart; they sent in decoys to draw her fire, while others snuck up on her blind side. While Liadan was shrouded in flames, they couldn't kill her, but they could and did reach through her fire's weakest points to strike at her. Liadan's back stung where they'd clawed her. Blood seeped from her wounds, adding the wrong kind of fuel to her flames. When it burned, it smoked, hazing her vision, and with each drop she lost, Liadan's strength waned even more.

Slash, twist, duck, turn, slash. Decoys to the right. Throw a flame, pirouette to cut off the main attack at its knees—or where knees ought to have been. Didn't matter where she cut them; their human-like shape seemed to be only an illusion. As long as the burning blade slashed through the outer layer, the fire burned them alive from the inside out.

But two or three had burst from the heat alone earlier. At least she thought they had. Liadan could almost hear the dragon's voice in her mind: *Hunches and guesses will kill you faster than an arrow through the heart.*

Two demons swooped down from opposite directions, and Liadan rolled out of the way, using her escape to gather a fireball in her free hand, feed it heat until it turned blue. When she pushed to her feet, she let it fly, striking one of the pair in the face.

Others charged her shroud of fire to keep her off balance and disoriented, but even as she fought them off, Liadan kept an eye on the one she'd struck. It screamed, flying backwards into its brethren, but it was too late for them to help. Its face disintegrated, and the rest of its body followed, raining down onto the sand in a shower of sparks.

It worked!

You got lucky, a memory of the dragon retorted, and it was right. She'd hit the demon by accident, not by design. Blue fire required more energy to build, and it was erratic, shooting off without warning in any way it pleased. She might hit a demon, she might not, but she would waste precious energy in the process. She might also hit one of the tribe by accident.

Duck, swing, slash, flare. Three more demons down. Too many left, and she was tiring. No, individual shots wouldn't work, but if Liadan could build enough strength for one massive burst, as hot as she could handle, she might be able to take them out all at once.

Demonic shades parted, and for just a moment Liadan saw Tir not fifteen paces away. Her fire didn't burn him; he stood in a pool of it, the flames licking at his waist and higher, and instead of running, he used it to fight. He kicked up burning sand, infuriating demons into attack, and any who flew too close died beneath his flaming sword. But it wasn't the weapon Tir was used to; it was longer, heavier, and he wielded it too slowly. He wouldn't last much longer than Liadan.

That's that, then.

She spun, scoring the sand with her swordpoint, and a circle of fire shot up, high enough to camouflage her for a few moments. Drawing her fiery shroud back into her core, she banked the flame until it barely shone, then she fed it every last bit of power she possessed, drawing on her soul, her life essence. The fire turned blue, threatening to escape. She held it steady, fed it more, more, until the pressure almost shattered her. Her skin stretched to its limits, her bones ached with the strain of holding on to far too much. With all of her focus on her last weapon, the circle of fire began to die down. Liadan didn't need it anymore.

When she opened her eyes, everything looked blue, and the night had turned to day, the air wavering with Liadan's heat. Demons drew back, confused. She glowed, flickering like a star; not as bright as before, but much, much hotter. Liadan held out her hand, watched veins pulse with heat beneath her skin. Her every breath fanned the flames inside her, and each time it flared the slightest bit, her hand turned transparent, as if her body itself was becoming fire.

It frightened her. Too much power, too much fire could destroy the wielder as easily as his opponents. A true dragon might have withstood the heat longer, but Liadan's blood was diluted, too human, and already her core was burning as it never had before.

Twelve paces away, Tir cut through a demon and braced for more, but none attacked him, all of them intent on Liadan. He met her gaze, shook his head in a wordless message. He feared for her. He should.

A demon screamed, and the rest echoed it, launching another attack.

"Burn," Liadan ordered venomously, not recognizing her own voice. She threw her arms out to the sides, let the fire out. Its full force ripped out of her, exploding so fast, Liadan had no hope of containing it, and she prayed the tribe was far enough to escape the inferno. It lasted no longer than three frenetic heartbeats, during which Liadan was unaware of anything but the blue fire tearing through her.

When it ended, darkness reclaimed the night, and Liadan sagged, dizzy, naked, shaking from head to toe. She had nothing left in her, not even a spark to call up to defend herself. Her scimitar dropped from her numb hand, and she was relieved to be rid of the extra weight. Blinking hard against the gloom, she searched for any hint of movement, human or otherwise. As her eyes adjusted to the darkness, she saw the sand had turned black as far as she could see. Hard lumps marked charred remnants of whatever hadn't blown away in the demon storm, but she saw no sign of people, save Tir, lying still in the sand a fair distance away, tendrils of smoke rising from the last shreds of his clothing.

"Tir?" she called, anxious and hoarse. Her legs were too weak to carry her to him; she was barely keeping upright. "Tir, answer me!"

He moved, then stilled again.

Were her eyes playing tricks on her? She took a step, stumbled, and cursed. "Tir!"

He groaned, sitting up with a wince. "Calm yourself, woman, you haven't killed me yet!"

Liadan would have laughed if she'd had the strength. Instead, she looked up, basking in the glory of millions upon millions of stars and the bright, waxing moon. Cold seeped into her tired, aching bones, and she shivered in her nakedness, wincing at the twinges of pain in her back. In all of her young life, Liadan had never felt cold like this; always, her soul's fire had warmed her, even in the deepest winter, when tears froze on the cheek before they could fall. Now that it was depleted, Liadan felt hollow, yet heavy at the same time. She was tired.

"Are you all right?" Tir asked, getting to his feet with all the grace of an old man. He scowled down at himself, shaking his head.

Far behind him, shadows moved as the tribe began to emerge from hiding. Off to the side, a lone, hunched figure shuffled closer, rattling a string of bones. The Magi. He droned a chant of some sort, moving rhythmically around Liadan, tracing a large circle in the sand. She didn't know what he was trying to do, had no strength left to wonder, save to think it'd have been more helpful for the man to bring them some clothes instead.

Oh, who bloody cares, anyway? Breathing deeply of the chill night air, Liadan tasted nothing but ash and cold on the back of her tongue. The demons were gone, their taint burned away for all time. *We've done it. Inaras, you are free... And I am still standing.* "It's over," she said, allowing herself a smile.

33

She smiled. Shivering, moments away from collapse, Liadan smiled at him, and a terrible dread gripped Tir's heart. "It's over," she said, as she always did in his nightmares just before she turned to ash.

"No…" He made his feet move, rushing forward to stop what he knew was coming.

"We've won—"

The tip of a scimitar suddenly punched out of her chest.

"*No!*"

Liadan looked down, blood gurgling past her lips as her murderer yanked the weapon back out, let her crumple to the ground.

"Liadan!" Tir fell to his knees and gathered her limp form into his arms. Her eyes were closed, her heart silent, and she was cold as ice. Tir shook her. "Liadan! Open your eyes!"

Her head lolled.

"By the oath you swore to me, I command you—wake!"

Her murderer cackled. Not a demon, not a warrior of Aesimar, but an old woman *aseti*, one of their own, had done this.

"You?"

The old woman tossed the bloodied scimitar to the ground. "A deal is a deal," she said.

"Tir!" Farraj shouted. "Get out! Get away from the witch!"

Tir snatched up Liadan's scimitar, still hot from the flames, and launched at the old woman. With a single cut, her head toppled. Her body swayed, held upright by some invisible force.

Fire flared in a perfect circle around them, and Tir stared down at Liadan's face, searching for signs of life. But it hadn't been her spark. The Magus had set the fire, and even now chanted loudly, moving out to light the second of the three concentric circles Tir had seen him trace earlier that day. They were in the center, he and Liadan, and the old hag.

"Tir, get out!"

The tribe had followed Farraj, *kharesh* circling the flaming perimeter, but none dared to breach it while the Magus worked his spells.

"Hurry! Before—"

The outermost ring burst into flame, pushing Farraj and the *kharesh* farther back.

The tribe fell silent, while the Magus chanted louder, his fire circles flaring so high, Tir lost sight of them all for a moment. But against that bright backdrop, the black mist was easier to see as it seeped out of the witch's neck and poured to the ground like blood. It congealed there, taking on its true shape—that of the demon who'd possessed her. As it escaped its mortal prison, the witch's body withered like a prune, clothes disintegrating into dust until nothing was left but rattling bones raining to the sands.

Before Tir now stood—*floated*—a sight more evil than even the child had been. The *daeva* was incredibly tall, but as thin as a waif, with long hair elegantly pulled back into a queue that coiled on the sand where his feet ought to have been. His face was pale, but more human than any of the others Tir had encountered thus far. Red eyes slanted beneath dark, winged eyebrows; a narrow, regal nose slashed down between sharp cheekbones; and a thin, cruel mouth smirked at him with an arrogance borne of immortality.

The demon emanated evil so deep, Tir felt it down to his soul. It made him feel weak, frightened. His grip on the scimitar slackened until he felt it begin to slip from his hand as the demon circled around the very edge of their fiery enclosure, growling, "Clever little Magi.

Fire will not save you. It'll die down eventually, and I will be free once more."

Tir drew back.

Attracted by movement, the demon turned, tipped his head. "Is something the matter, *shansher* Tirasdunh? Have you lost your fighting spirit?"

Tir forced his hand to curl tighter. He raised the blade sideways into the flames, then brought it burning before him.

The demon laughed. "You think to defeat me with that? A burning blade might have sufficed for my court, but I am their prince; I draw on the strength of Darkness itself. Go ahead. Swing your sword." He spread his arms wide.

Tir dug his heel deeper into the sand, refusing to fall for the trick.

The demon rolled his red eyes, hissed a sigh. "I suppose you require incentive. Very well." He streaked forward, claws outstretched for Liadan.

Tir slashed through the black mist of the demon's incorporeal form, severing it mid-stream. The two halves veered off in different directions, circling the prison's perimeter before colliding together across from Tir to mend whole again.

The demon prince smiled. "Do you believe me now? You cannot win against one as powerful as me. Nothing so trite as a little fire can destroy me."

Again the demon circled, regarding Tir with what might have been amusement. "I must admit, I am intrigued. You guard that dead body as if it means more to you than your own life." He tipped his head the other way. "Tell me, *shansher* Tirasdunh, Tir the Demonslayer, did you love your Northern wench?" He sucked in a sharp breath, and his smile stretched wider in delight, revealing rows of pointed teeth. "You did. I can smell it in you. Poor little Dragonblood. She tried so hard to keep the oath from consuming you both. How selfless of her. How brave, and utterly futile." Circling left, the Dark prince hissed at the Magus beyond reach. "For your bravery, *shansher*, I will give you a gift."

"I want nothing from you!"

The demon speared him with a venomous glare. "This, you will want very much. Do you not want to know why your tribe has suffered so? What had brought so many torments down upon your people? Yes, I think you do. Listen well, Tirasdunh the Demonslayer. Listen and suffer! Do you see that pile of bones? It was she who summoned me into your midst, she who traded her soul in exchange for revenge.

"Your father sent the innocent Mari to her death in the North, and when her ashes were brought back, the proud Imarah did *nothing*. Like beaten dogs, Dhakir's defeat had broken all of you. Fabled warriors— *ha!* Even the *kharesh* tucked tail and retreated into mourning. No one thought to raise arms to avenge her. So the witch did it herself. And for their cowardice, she doomed Imarah to a long, miserable, painful death so they would all be swallowed by the desert sands, forever forgotten by man and god alike. One of your own tribe destroyed you, little king, and in your blind hatred, you brought an innocent from the North here to die for it. The young Dragonblood was not your executioner, *shansher* Tirasdunh; you were hers."

"No!" Tir slashed the laughing demon from shoulder to hip, severed the head from its body, speared his blade through the demon's black heart. He raged and cut, and all the while the demon remained unaffected, screeching with laughter at Tir's feeble efforts.

With one solid strike to Tir's chest, the demon sent him flying backwards against the fiery barrier. Tir struck it and bounced off as if it were solid. He fell to his hands and knees in front of Liadan's body. Her lips were pale, her sun-kissed skin turning gray. No heat to her, no telltale sign of even a spark of life.

His fault. "Liadan…" *Forgive me… Come back.*

"What happens to a Northman when his woman dies?" the demon mocked by his ear.

A cold breeze wavered the wall of flames, ruffling Tir's hair with a silent command: *Fight!* He didn't recognize the voice, but somehow it ignited a memory inside him. Demons feared light; they only came out in the dark of night, retreating into their lairs at the first hint of dawn.

The demon prince's long, forked tongue snaked out to lick across Tir's cheek. "Mmm… But you are not a Northman, are you? Your soul smells of the desert, not of snow. Your heart burns for battle, not for the heat of a woman's love."

Another cold breeze. *Stand and fight!*

Tir glanced to the east. He'd lost track of time through the night, but it had to be nearing sunrise.

"You've lost, Demonslayer. And oh, how I savor the taste of defeat." The demon inhaled deeply, his form wavering like a mirage as if he felt true pleasure at Tir's anguish. His smile was drunken, his eyes deepening to almost black as he asked, "What happens to an Aegiran when he loses his reason for living?"

"He prays to the gods for the strength to fight on," Tir replied, and stuck his arm into the flames. As fire licked along his skin, he clenched his jaw against the pain.

Only there was none. Even in death, the bond of Liadan's dragon-blood protected him from its heat.

The demon drew back warily as Tir pushed to his feet and raised his hand to the sky. Instead of burning upwards, the flames licked down to his chest and across his body, enshrouding him in protective heat. Another gust of wind turned it blue, and his skin pulled taut. He stooped to pick up the scimitar, then faced his enemy, head-on. "You want my soul, demon? Then come and take it!"

The demon screamed, streaked at him, but veered off at the last moment, circling around from the other side. He tried to get around Tir, to attack from his blind side, but with a bracing cold breeze, Tir's flaming shroud flared brighter, and he caught his second wind. Striking faster than he ever had, Tir followed the flames—moving where they swayed, spinning where they swirled, slashing where sparks jumped. Drunken on his premature victory celebration, the demon was too slow to react. Tir's dance was not as intricate as Liadan's, but it was fueled by a rage that set his blood boiling.

He couldn't defeat the demon prince.

He didn't need to.

All Tir had to do was stay alive, distract him long enough for the sun to do the rest. The Magus had forged a prison strong enough to contain the Dark prince, and his own minions had razed the camp so not a single tent remained to cast a shadow. When dawn came, the sun's rays would destroy the demon, and with him, the curse he'd wrought upon Imarah. Tir only needed to stay alive long enough to see it through, and that meant keeping the demon at arm's length.

The Magus' voice chanted louder, echoed by many from the tribe. The fiery circles flared with different colors as they tossed magic dust into them, agitating the demon into a frenzied, reckless attack. He knocked Tir down, clawed through the flaming shroud to score Tir's chest. A green flare made the demon flinch and rear back. Abandoning the sword, Tir rolled away. Sand stuck to his open wounds, the fiery shroud banked to nothing, and he was left exposed, disarmed, bleeding, crouching once again between the enraged demon and Liadan's lifeless body.

The circles flared blue and red, green and white; faster, brighter, until the demon suddenly raised his head to the sky. His shape wavered, dissolving almost completely before it reformed. Instead of attacking Tir again, the Dark prince threw himself against the fiery prison walls, seeking to escape. They repelled him as they had Tir, and each time he tried to rise higher to escape over the top, they flared up to keep him in place.

The demon screamed, and through his madness, Tir heard something he'd never thought demons could feel much less convey: fear. Again and again, the demon streaked upward to fly over the barrier, but with each attempt, the height of his jump decreased, as if his strength was fading. He squealed, shrank to pathetic proportions as the sky lightened, and with the demon the size of a child, Tir dared to take his eyes off him to look to the east. The sun peeked out from behind Temple Mountain, still weak, but already Tir had to squint against its brightness.

"You'll never be rid of me!" the demon growled, shrunken to all fours like a dog. His red eyes blazed at Tir, then shifted behind him to Liadan with dark intent. Desperate to escape his own doom, the demon hissed, streaking across the sand toward her, faster than a snake.

Tir leapt to intercept, forcing the demon up and over him. As the Dark prince rose waist-high, the first rays of sunlight speared through his shadowy, raven-sized form like dozens of flaming arrows. The demon screamed, fire bursting from him in sickening explosions of black slime and burning sludge. Tir fell over Liadan's body to shield her, to take the searing pain against his own back, when a flash brighter than day lit up the sky, accompanied by an intense burst of power that nearly extinguished the fire around them. Tir never felt a single drop of burning demon touch his skin.

When the glare had finally eased, he looked up. From a single point of light, a myriad of white flashes streaked to every corner of the desert lands, and with each one, the oppressive weight of misery he'd lived with for two decades lifted a little more.

In years to come, Imarah would recount the event to their children and their grandchildren, and consider themselves blessed to have been gifted with such a vision. For by the time the last streak of light had dispersed, the central glow had dimmed and reformed into a shape they all recognized: the welcoming, benevolent form of their patron goddess, Inaras. She reached down over the tribe, and Tir felt the warmth of her restorative touch deep in his soul.

Her divine power shivered through him, returning the strength he'd lost. His injuries mended, his heart beat stronger, breaths became easier to draw, and he knew all of his tribe would feel the same.

At once, his gaze shot down to Liadan again. Inaras had healed his tribe; surely, she could bring their savior back to life.

But the pale, Other female lying in his arms didn't stir; her eyes remained closed, her face serene in death, her heart still and silent in her chest. And Tir felt as if he'd lost her all over again.

Outside of the circles, the surviving Imarah cheered their victory. The demons were defeated, the curse was lifted, and at last, they felt hope again for their salvation. Many raised their hands to the sky, thanking the gods, while others bowed to the rising sun and kissed the sand at their feet.

Only the Magi, Farraj, and his *kharesh* looked deep enough into the circle to see the cost of their victory. Only they saw their *shansher* mourning over the lifeless body of his brave, fallen queen.

~

In the middle of the night, the sleepless, cavernous great hall of Castle Frastmir echoed with an unearthly scream of agony. The dragon raced out of the chamber, the royal couple following close behind. Terrified, led by that awful sound through the bowels of the castle and up the tower stairs, they burst into the library to find it engulfed in flames.

Queen Nialei cried out, fell to her knees, as the dragon boldly stepped into the illusion to kneel by the writhing body of Prince Fal. The boy screamed as if his soul were being torn in two. His skin smoked, his eyes burned bright gold, a living flame caged within his watery soul.

"Fal!" the dragon shouted.

In answer, the crown prince of Wilderheim fell silent and arched up off the floor, tensing so hard, bones cracked beneath the strain. When he collapsed, the illusion broke, and his parents rushed to his side. For the first time in too many years, they beheld the young man in his true form as if all of his illusions had been burned out of him. His mother caressed his cheek, and yelped in pain. Fal was a living ember, burning to the touch with far more heat than a water creature could hold.

Laying a hand against the center of the prince's chest, the dragon called to those flames, pulled them out of the boy to ease his fever. Fal gasped, roused a little to mumble incoherently. He tried to open his eyes, but they kept rolling back, and his heart thrashed too hard, too fast. He was in terrible pain, too weak to heal himself.

Queen Nialei did it for him, channeling her own magic into her son, mending bones, healing tears, soothing aches. But even when the prince was whole again, he would not wake.

King Saeran laid a hand on his son's forehead, adding his own strength to the two already fighting for his son's life. He soothed the fire burning in the boy's mind, searching for the cause of this firestorm, already knowing, and fearing, what he would find.

Tears streamed down the prince's cheeks, and his body jerked in quiet sobs. "She's dead," he said. "Liadan's dead."

PART THREE

IMARAH

34

For the third time in as many days, Dar knelt before his *shansher* with tidings both good and bad. For the third time, his hands grew cold, his mouth dry, and his spine weak. Acting as the *shansher*'s eyes and ears, a task in which he'd foolishly taken great pleasure, had now become a dangerous gamble the new High Magus dreaded most with each new sunrise. Ever since Itamar had disappeared into the desert with Kaliban's chest, Khiron had been plagued by terrible dreams that deprived him of sleep every night and haunted him during the day. Many times during their conference, the *shansher* stared off into the distance as though lost in memory. Sweat broke out on his brow, his hands quivered, and for long moments he neither saw nor heard anyone inside his tent. When the spell finally passed, the *shansher* was always shaken and unsteady. Dar suspected it was Kaliban himself tormenting Khiron from his desert grave, but Khiron would hear none of it, and so the Magi could do nothing to help.

Now, Khiron stroked his beard, deep in thought. "You are certain she is dead?"

"Our scouts have said it is so, your Highness. They have watched the survivors for two days. The camp has been moved to the northern oasis at the base of Temple Mountain, and the woman's body is laid out in the open. It has not moved a single time."

"Why have they not burned it? There is plenty of dry wood there."

Indeed, the oasis had plenty of wood. The grove of palm trees so old, their trunks were thicker than two men put together, had once provided shelter and solace there for journeymen visiting the temple of Inaras. It had all dried up, along with the underground river that used to feed it, many seasons ago, and was now as dead as the rest of the First Valley. "The young *shansher* will not permit it, your Highness. He keeps vigil by her body day and night, and will not allow it to be touched."

Khiron al-Bashir grunted his disgust. "The boy must be possessed."

"Perhaps not, your Highness," Dar ventured, uncertain how the tidings should be conveyed; whether he should speak them at all. Had Itamar been there, he would doubtless have conjured up the appropriate words. But for all of his dedication and study, Dar was still young—an apprentice, rather than a Magus in his own right—and with his master tutor gone, he floundered, wholly unprepared for such grave duties. Rafi and Pirro were younger still, untried in the ways of magic and politics, and though only three seasons older, Dar had, by necessity, become their master. *May the gods lead us true,* he prayed, for if ever the tribe needed divine intervention, it was now.

"Well? Go on. Do not keep me waiting."

Dar licked his dry lips, risked a glance at his *shansher*'s countenance. The thunderous expression he'd expected to see was not there. Instead, Khiron al-Bashir looked haunted. "The scouts say the body does not change. For two days, she has lain in the heat of the sun, and has neither dried, nor burned, nor withered in any way. They say she looks as if she only sleeps."

"Hmm…" Khiron fell silent, staring at the tapestry of his once proud Imarah lineage. "How did she die?"

Dar shivered. Though the query seemed a casual curiosity, this was the part he'd most dreaded relaying. The moment the scouts had returned with news of the woman's demise, the Magi had conjured a vision of that night. Horrified, they'd watched as the massive swarm of demons descended upon Imarah, a black stain on the desert. They'd borne witness to the tribe's bravery when facing their death head-on, and they'd stared in awe at the woman's majesty and courage in battle with the swarm. She'd reduced them to ash, one after the other, burning so hot, the sand at her feet had melted into glass.

And having defeated them so masterfully, for her end to have come in such a cowardly fashion had outraged all of them, even knowing she was the enemy.

"She was stabbed through, your Highness."

But that did not concern Dar. Death was death, whether dealt instantly at the point of a blade or transpiring after long years of disease and torment. What concerned him was that even in death, her body didn't yield to the natural process of decay. He'd not forgotten Kaliban's malicious jeer when he'd last been summoned; those words had tormented him every night since. *She is Vengeance. She Who Walks Through Fire will not be stopped by magic, or by sword. She will cut darkness with a blade of fire, and tear hearts out of the bodies of her enemies.*

Will not be stopped by magic, or by sword.

Did the *shansher* remember?

"Do you believe she is truly dead?" Khiron asked.

Dar hesitated. "No, your Highness, I do not."

"Neither do I. *Vengeance* does not perish so easily. Hmm… Yes. Perhaps Kaliban was right. She Who Walks Through Fire. Yes… You will bring her to me. In chains."

Dar blanched. "Your Highness?"

The *shansher*'s ire boiled up, flooding color into his sunken cheeks. "Was I not clear? Bring me the Northwoman! Dead or alive. Bound in chains."

Dar touched his forehead to the ground in supplication. "As your Highness commands. But we will need time to spell the chains. A creature like that is different from a demon. We will need to pray for guidance and power, to ensure she does not escape."

"The moon peaks full tomorrow night. I want the chains ready by then. We will attack after sunset and put an end to this, once and for all."

"Tomorrow night… but your Highness—"

"I weary of living like a gods-damned pauper, Magi! I want my birthright back, and she is the one who will win it for me! If the last dregs of Imarah aren't dead by the time the sun rises in two days, I will cut out your heart myself and burn it before your eyes as an offering to Aesma. Now leave!"

Dar scurried from the tent, cursing the traitor Itamar for abandoning their tribe to a madman.

35

The northern oasis at the base of Temple Mountain, once an inviolable place of worship, had become Imarah's refuge. Perhaps the final one. The tribe was defeated, and though no one had seen a single shadow of a demon threat since the battle, people were still terrified of closing their eyes at night unless fires burned high all around. Luckily, the oasis, once so lush and green, had plenty of fallen, dry wood to burn. Needlessly, perhaps, but it was worth their peace of mind.

Since they'd made camp, Tir had spent every waking moment sitting vigil over Liadan's lifeless body. The tribe had built a great funeral platform for her, an honor befitting the bravest of warriors, but Tir wouldn't allow them to lay her upon it. For three days, she'd lain in the desert as one dead, only to awaken again as if from a long sleep. Tir knew in his mind this time was different, but his heart refused to believe it. With each day Liadan persevered, untouched by the ravages of death, his hope grew that she'd eventually awaken. In a day. In a week. In a month, perhaps. One day, her heart would beat again; her chest would rise and fall, and her eyes would open.

And because the alternative was unthinkable, Tir kept his vigil, turned a blind eye to the pile of wood awaiting the *shensari*, and a deaf ear to Farraj telling him it was unseemly, that Tir dishonored her by keeping her on display and that his people were beginning to think him mad.

Perhaps he was. It hadn't escaped him that he was behaving in exactly the same way Dhakir had years ago, after losing his beloved first wife. The demon prince had mocked Tir for his Aegiran love of battle, but the men of his line seemed to carry in their hearts a passion just as powerful for their women.

She is not yours, an insidious whisper in his mind insisted. *Liadan was never* shensari. *It was a ruse. Your blood oath only bound you until your tribe was saved, and now she is free of you, and your ignorance, and your scorn.*

A hand on his shoulder broke him out of his dark musings. It was time for Farraj's daily visit. "Any change?" he queried softly. Since they'd made camp, he was the only one brave enough to speak to his *shansher.*

Tir shook his head.

Farraj sighed. "How long can this last?"

Tir pried his lips apart to answer, "As long as it takes."

"We must send word to her father."

Tir ignored this. If Liadan and her twin brother were truly as close as she'd said, then he already knew.

"The tribe is restless; they fear another raid. I had the *kharesh* gather weapons and prepare a path of retreat, but the only safety left to us here is up the mountain, and even Inaras' temple will not save us if Aesimar does attack again. They will not honor her sanctuary. We lined the cliff with scimitars, bows, and as many arrows as we could make, and instructed the men to do what needs to be done. Our women will not become slaves to that horde of savages." He paused, then huffed, adding in a softer tone, "Tir, we cannot stay here. We *must* move on."

"Sleipnir."

"What?"

"Her horse. Sleipnir. Where is he?"

"Run away, probably. No one has seen him since he broke free that night. Zara and Tarabas are gone, too. Just as well. We have nothing to feed them anymore."

Never had Tir seen that mount abandon his mistress. Even through the fury of her firestorm, he'd stood a distant watch over her until it had passed. Why would he leave her now?

"It's been three days, Tir. Even if this was the same sleep she'd slept before, you said yourself she would have awakened by now. You must allow us to burn her body. If we do not, her soul might become trapped here and haunt us forever, as surely as the demons did."

Better a vengeful Liadan, than no Liadan at all.

As if he'd heard Tir's thoughts, Farraj crouched down beside him. "Would you truly keep her from her ancestors? She has saved us, Tir. Even the Magus confirmed the darkness of our curse is lifted. She has done what no other could. She rescued us from the brink of death! And this is to be her reward?"

"What would you have me do?"

"Let us honor her. We have waited as long as you asked: three days, to allow her time to rise again, and still she lies lifeless. She is gone, Tir. Let us send her off the way she deserves."

Tir shook his head. "Our ways. Not hers."

"Perhaps," Farraj allowed. "But more than a Northerner, she is a creature of fire. What better way to pay our respects than to acknowledge her nature, return her to the element of her soul?"

He spoke wisely, and the longer Tir listened, the less he had to say in argument. Farraj suggested they give her the honors and respects of a *shansher*, something a mere woman would never have garnered before in Imarah, or any other tribe. The entire tribe would be summoned, dressed in their finest clothes, which now amounted to the golden armor and white robes pilfered from Aesimar corpses. To honor her Northern ways, men and women alike would strap scimitars to their sides, and draw them in salute. The *kharesh* would stand her guard as they would one of their own, armed against any who'd interfere with the rites. The Magus would speak his spells, bless Liadan's soul on its journey into the afterlife, and Tir himself would light the pyre.

With her death, the Northern princess, once scorned and hated by the entire tribe, had won more respect and adoration than she ever could have in life. Imarah no longer cared about her origin; they worshipped her bravery as if she'd always been one of the tribe—the best of them. The flame of their goddess, Inaras, shining their way to victory.

"Allow us to do this for her," Farraj pleaded. "It is the only way we have to thank her for her sacrifice."

"One more day."

Farraj paused. "What difference makes a day?"

For the first time in three days, Tir looked him in the eye. "I ask you the same. Tomorrow night the moon peaks full. We will light her pyre at sunset so all the stars will see it and welcome her among them."

Farraj's throat moved with a swallow, and he bowed his head in assent. "So shall it be," he said with difficulty, then left to relay Tir's instructions to the waiting tribe.

In no time, the preparations were under way. Gold gleamed in the corner of Tir's eye as his tribe scurried about, dressed in Aesimar colors, to do his bidding. He ignored them, his attention fully focused on Liadan as he watched her closed eyes for any hint of movement that might betray her awakening; held her cold, limp hand in his to feel her skin begin to warm with signs of life. But there was nothing.

Yet even when his mind insisted that Farraj was right, that she was gone, he still couldn't leave her side. Her skin, though pale, was as soft as it always had been. Her lips, though bloodless, just as plump. Hope, even as false as he knew it to be, was a fierce, stubborn beast inside him, insisting Liadan was still alive, somehow.

The next morning, the sun rose bright white over the desert. At Farraj's urging, Tir relinquished his vigil to prepare himself for the ceremony, and allow the women to do the same for Liadan. She'd be washed and dressed in clothes as befitted a queen; her hands and face would be painted with henna, her hair adorned with gold, her feet covered with silk slippers—the same way she'd have been attired for a wedding.

Tir, for his part, was ushered into the Magus' tent, where he submitted to a modest bath, then bowed his head for the cleansing ceremony that set his teeth on edge. The words were not ones of honor, but of protection—a plea to the gods to sever any remaining connection between him and the deceased, to guide the spirit into the afterlife, to banish it from the world of the living and to protect the tribe from its vengeance and wrath.

Tir refused to speak his part of the ritual.

Rather than insist on it, the Magus continued, concluding with a prayer to Inaras for Liadan's loved ones. When all was said and done, the Magus left Tir to his meditation and went to oversee the pyre preparations.

The imposed solitude did nothing to soothe Tir's mind, or his heart. Again and again, he remembered the heartbroken man in Frastmir, the terrible agony with which he'd wailed his grief over his mate. Not for the first time since Liadan's death, Tir wondered whether Geir had embraced the pain as readily as he. Liadan was gone; his grief was the only remaining proof that she'd ever touched his life. He'd rather remember her and ache, than dishonor her by forgetting.

At sunset, Farraj summoned him out of the tent. The *kharesh* lined a path directly to the pyre, each holding a scimitar in one hand and a burning torch in the other, creating a lighted passage, at the end of which a small bowl of oil had been set aflame—Tir's tool for lighting Liadan's pyre. They'd piled it up with even more wood, raising the platform so high, he couldn't see Liadan on top of it. What he did see were three horses standing solemnly in front of it, facing Tir in anticipation. Tarabas, Sleipnir, and Zara.

Tir frowned at Farraj.

"I was as surprised as you are," the older *kharesh* said. "They walked into camp to that very spot, side by side as you see them now, and refused to be led away. I think... I think they are waiting for you."

Tir nodded. What could he say? Tarabas was trained to return to Imarah whenever he wandered into the desert. So was Zara. But to see Sleipnir between them, head held high like a king in his own right, staring at him steadily... Tir didn't know what to make of that. He walked down the path, gaze focused just above the top of Sleipnir's head, but below Liadan's platform.

His people had gathered around at a safe distance in a silent congregation, faces solemn and hands clasped together. No one uttered a word as Tir took up the small torch and dipped it into the oil. Once it caught the flame, he moved forward again, meeting the final obstacle: the horses. Tears had tracked dark lines down Sleipnir's dust-covered face. The mount rested his forehead on Tir's shoulder with a bone-weary sigh, holding still as Tir stroked his neck and clenched his jaw against tears of his own. Sleipnir wouldn't act this way unless he knew his mistress was well and truly gone.

Once he'd realized this, the last of Tir's hope died silently inside him, and he whispered his condolences into Sleipnir's ear.

The proud stallion huffed, stomped a hoof, then shifted sideways to allow Tir to approach the pyre.

The wood was so dry, it flared up instantly, and within moments, the blaze roared to the sky so hot, it forced the tribe to retreat a few steps farther. Tir watched the dancing flames, imagined shapes taking form inside of them. For a moment, he thought he glimpsed Liadan's shadow twirling about. The next instant, he almost made out the shape of a dragon; a rearing horse; a warrior brandishing his sword—all fanciful illusions conjured by his grieving mind.

When the fire blazed at its hottest, Zara became restless, and finally allowed someone to lead her away to be brushed down. Tarabas and Sleipnir remained, standing guard to either side of Tir, and the three of them watched the massive pyre burn.

A log collapsed, sending an explosion of sparks flying outward. The women on that side cried out, pulled their children away, but the men remained steady.

Tir drew his dagger, and the rest of the *kharesh* followed suit. As one, they held up their arms and cut a long, shallow line across the backs of them—a sign of respect and affection. No less than they would have done for Dhakir, or Tir himself.

Farraj shouted a farewell, and his *kharesh* echoed him.

Then someone on the outskirts of the tribe screamed a warning.

36

From the south, a sea of torches spilled across the desert toward Imarah, with a roar worthy of a sandstorm. Aesimar in full strength: legions of foot soldiers, as well as mounted cavalry, polished blades flashing in the torchlight.

Farraj raised his sword high. "*Kharesh*, to arms!"

The tribe scattered in a burst of activity, men racing south to confront the legions, women herding children toward the mountain and the treacherous climb up to the temple, the only refuge left to them. Tarabas stomped. Sleipnir reared angrily.

"Tir!" Farraj called, mounted on Zara and ready for battle. "We need you!"

With Liadan's sword strapped to his back and his own at his side, Tir grasped Sleipnir's mane and mounted the warhorse, bareback. Tarabas was a faithful mount, but Tir had seen what Sleipnir could do in battle. He would need that fighting spirit today. "*Hyah!*"

Sleipnir took off at a breakneck pace that forced Tir to lean low over his neck as they raced straight into the fray, trampling foot soldiers, bowling over warhorses several hands smaller than the Northern stallion. Between Tir's knees, Sleipnir's girth all but vibrated with a furious energy that mirrored his own. Tir drew his scimitar and attacked, moving with the mount as a single being. He felt when Sleipnir tensed to rear, secured his seat, and leaned back to cut down the men attacking Sleipnir's flanks. When the mount kicked out with his rear hooves, Tir cut down the warriors to his right, then switched hands when Sleipnir twisted, and cut down those on the left.

He didn't echo his *kharesh* in their battle cries; instead, he left Farraj to bellow orders to keep Aesimar from cutting off their path of retreat. Tir was silent in his wrath, slicing through the Aesimar ranks like death itself. Under the cover of night, the farther he got from Liadan's pyre, the darker the battlefield became. Torches fell, banked as their bearers died, and men shouted for more light, but each time a new torch was lit, someone extinguished it. Lighted targets were easier to take out. Soon, the entire battlefield was shrouded in darkness with only the full moon left to illuminate the chaos reigning over the sands.

Tir looked to the southwest, where the Aesimar *shansher* presided over the carnage from a high sand dune, illuminated by the blaze of a brazier and two torches as tall as he was, protected by mounted riders to either side. Tir nudged Sleipnir to turn in their direction, then spurred him forward.

They didn't get far. Mounted Aesimar cut in front of him, pushed him back toward the main throng of Imarah, to crush them all at the same time. A lucky strike knocked his scimitar from his hand; a blade sliced across his arm. Sleipnir reared, throwing Tir as he attacked one of the other horses.

Lying in the dust, Tir saw nothing but massive, swirling shadows and hooves striking the sand too close to him. He was surrounded, vulnerable, and for a moment, he lay still, expecting a hoof to smash his skull to pulp. For a moment, he even prayed for it—a quick end, an honorable death, and peace at last; freedom to join Liadan in the afterlife. It would have been so easy to simply give in, to let go and fade away. Even with the curse lifted, Imarah still had nothing left and no strength to make it back to the First City. Less than fifteen hundred Imarah men, women, and children remained, and all of them would die.

He'd failed.

Sleipnir reared, screamed, and kicked out, intimidating the other horses into retreat. They collided, threw off their riders, toppled over in their haste to get away from the black stallion, and as the air cleared around Tir, the battle on the ground thickened.

A screaming Aesimar appeared above him, blade raised to strike him dead.

Tir rolled, instinct proving more powerful than his defeat. He pushed to his feet, then fell back again to avoid a flaming arrow. From Temple Mountain, arrow after fiery arrow launched into the warriors below. Such weapons were considered a coward's last resort; a true warrior faced his foe head-on, not from a distance. Aesimar, for all their cowardice in attacking them during the night, had never stooped to them in all the time they'd been raiding Imarah, but Tir's tribe no longer had anything left to lose. In the hands of their survivors—women, young boys, and old men who'd climbed up to Inaras' temple to escape the battle—the long-range bows proved to be an effective, deadly weapon.

Aesimar scum sprouted burning, wooden shafts from their chests and limbs, hungry flames quickly engulfing their oiled flesh. The fire spread from one to the next, culling the Aesimar ranks with swift efficiency. The archers aimed high and far, taking out the rearguard rather than the front advance. With so many pouring toward them, they had no need for practice or precision; their arrows found marks with ease.

Rather than cower and pray, the daughters and sons of Imarah stood their ground and fought. They wouldn't yield their own to the enemy. How could their king do any less? With renewed strength, Tir shoved to his feet and drew Liadan's Northern blade. It was longer than his scimitar, allowing a wider reach and more power behind each strike, and in the moonlight, the blade glowed an unearthly blue. The Aesimar were fast, but they were not *kharesh*. Sloppy technique, no discipline. He felled them one after the other, moving from memory rather than strategy. His feet knew where to step, his arm knew how to swing without Tir having to consciously command them.

And still, he uttered not a sound. In the face of enraged, shouting Aesimar, he cut his opponents down with silent precision, wasting no time on defense. He took injuries in stride, ignored the blood trickling from his many cuts, and never cowered, never retreated.

Soon, his stoic attack unnerved the Aesimar fighters into wary retreat, and they began to part before him when he advanced. With Sleipnir at his back, Tir stalked across the battlefield toward his true enemy: the Aesimar *shansher*.

He no longer stood atop the dune, yet his warriors weren't retreating.

Scanning the fray for any sign of him, Tir held out his glowing sword sideways, a silent summons for Sleipnir. As if he understood what Tir needed, Sleipnir pranced closer so Tir could mount, and from his high perch, Tir once again surveyed the battlefield. From the south, the mob parted to allow through a mounted contingent bearing torches, with the *shansher* himself wading into the battle, straight for Tir.

A battle horn sounded his approach, and the Aesimar rallied, swarming Tir once more. He fought back, losing sight of their *shansher* as Sleipnir turned in furious circles, battling as hard as any warrior Tir had ever fought. But against so many, they stood little chance. For the second time, Tir lost his seat astride the stallion, and gazed up from the sand as Aesimar fighters bore down on him. He cut them down at the ankles, then rose again to launch into a frenzied offensive, heedless of who fell beneath the arc of his sword. The handle warmed in his grip as if Liadan's fiery spirit still lived within the blade, and he clutched it tighter, embracing its heat, drawing strength from it when he began to wane.

An Aesimar fell. Then another. A third slashed his cheek open, and Tir ducked under his second swing, slicing him open just below the edge of his armor, then thrust upward, spearing him through the bottom of the chin. Kicking the dead weight off his blade, Tir swung around and connected with a scimitar.

Old, familiar eyes stared him down from a face he hadn't seen in too many seasons to count. Taken aback, Tir broke off, stepped away in retreat as the Aesimar *shansher* advanced.

For so long after the tribe had separated, Dhakir had consulted nightly with the Magi, always asking the same questions: *Where is my brother? Is he still alive? Has he found refuge?* For so long, he'd held on to the hope that some of his people at least might have found salvation, that one day his brother would find them again and lead them to fertile ground where the tribe could reunite and rebuild.

And here he was. Khiron al-Bashir, returned at last—to destroy them all. "You look as if you've seen a ghost, boy."

Khiron was the leader of Aesimar. Uncle Khiron, who'd taught Tir how to throw a dagger and saddle a horse, who'd regaled all of the children with wild tales of *djinn*, and beautiful princesses, and treasures hidden in secret caves that opened on command.

The tip of Tir's sword lowered to the sand. "Why?"

Khiron's mouth arched into an ugly snarl. "Dhakir was a spineless fool. Imarah should have been *mine!*"

"You destroyed our tribe out of greed?"

Khiron threw his head back and laughed. "Dhakir knew better than anyone: *might* is king in Aegiros. Look around you, boy. You have no more tribe to speak of. I have created a new Imarah, born from the blood of its enemies. With the Dark god's blessing, we've grown more powerful than Dhakir could ever have dreamed. The First Valley belongs to us now, and you will bend a knee to me, Tirasdunh, here and now, or I will give the order to slaughter the rest of your pathetic flock and mount your head on a spike!"

"*Never!*" Tir brought up the sword, guiding its heavy, blue blade with surprising ease. Khiron blocked, twisted aside and, using Tir's momentum against him, sent him sprawling into the sand with a kick to his back. Tir rolled, threw sand into the traitor's face, then launched up and forward, aiming for his heart. They locked blades, shoved apart, clashed together again. Khiron might have been old, but he was a trained *kharesh*, and his agility had not abandoned him. Assured of his victory, he toyed with Tir in a game of cat and mouse.

"Still the impassioned hothead." Khiron shook his head in disappointment, parried another blow and twisted, ramming his elbow into Tir's side. "What have I always taught you, boy? I, and Farraj, and your father, alike." Their blades sparked against each other, and with a palm to Tir's chest, Khiron shoved him back a few steps. "The fastest way to defeat your enemy is to make him angry."

One of Khiron's men attacked from the side, and Tir twisted to intercept, foolishly turning his back on Khiron. With a wide swing, he cut the warrior underneath his sword arm, but to his surprise,

Khiron followed through and severed the man's head from his body. Then he roared at the others locked in battle around them—he wanted Tir for himself.

Khiron met his gaze in silent challenge. "Where is your Northern whore? Surely, it is not her burning so brightly in your camp. Northerners bury their dead like dogs." Khiron feigned an attack, sneered when Tir twitched in readiness. They circled slowly. "Was she as good in bed as I've seen her on the battlefield? Tell me, what was it like bedding a woman who may as well have been a man? How many did she have before you?"

Tir bit his tongue, refusing to rise to the bait. When their blades clanged together again, he reined in his temper, took measure of his opponent, adjusted his strategy. Everyone had a weakness; Khiron would be no different. He'd already proven himself a formidable opponent, but the longer they circled, waiting each other out and seeking the best angle of attack, Tir noticed something odd.

"Shame I did not have a chance to try her out for myself. She might have proved entertaining. For a night or two." Khiron struck, pushed Tir back, herded him around the circle until their positions were reversed with Khiron facing the pyre and Tir's back to it. Every time they circled, Khiron forced them into this position. He wanted to keep the pyre in sight. "Well, perhaps I might get another chance."

Tir shuddered at the implications. He'd once warned Liadan that Aesimar had the means to imprison a demon, and probably even an Other, like her. If they could do that, what was to stop them from raising a soul back from the dead? Once Khiron had Liadan in chains, she'd be enslaved to him forever.

Tir snarled and struck out at Khiron's left. The Aesimar *shansher* deflected, shifting right, quickly launching a counterattack to reverse their positions once more, to keep his eye on the pyre. Tir wouldn't let him. He kept Khiron off balance, distracted enough to give up watching the flames, at least for the moment.

Khiron's temper rose to the fore and his strikes became sharper, more unfocused, his blocks and parries sloppy as time and again he tried to maneuver Tir around. They clashed and broke apart three more times before Khiron lost his patience and shouted for his guard.

Four came at Tir, faster than he could defend. He dropped one and knocked another back, but the remaining two overtook him, while the first recovered enough to slam his dagger's hilt into Tir's wrist. Pain pierced up his arm as bone shattered, and the sword fell from his grip. He braced against their hold, jumped up and, kicking out with both feet, sent the Aesimar scum stumbling backwards into Khiron.

The traitor of Imarah righted himself, ran his own guard through, then shoved him aside, coming for Tir with his blade raised to kill.

All at once, Sleipnir barreled through the press of bodies with a shrill whinny, heading back north, past Tir, toward the camp, where light flared brighter than midday. Khiron froze in his advance, eyes wide, mouth agape at the sight, and his guards loosened their hold enough for Tir to twist around.

In the sky above, a bright flash of light faded, then flared anew, as if the night was breathing. The pyre below mirrored it, throwing its flames high, then banking low to blue in an eerie cycle. With each burst of light, more heat drove back those closest to it, and the sounds of fighting and death stilled as, one after the other, the embattled warriors broke off to direct their gazes north.

Released from distracted holds, Tir faced the spectacle, breath locked in his chest as he witnessed the burgeoning flames dance and bend—higher, brighter, hotter. Sleipnir's shadow reared against the glare, hooves kicking out as if to add his strength, until a massive burst of fire exploded and spewed forth a cloud of thick, black smoke. The plumes swirled together and quickly condensed into a shape the likes of which none had ever seen.

Awestruck, the two tribes of Aegiros watched a creature unfurl its great, black wings, beat them in powerful thrusts to gain more altitude. Like an ember fanned to life, its body glowed and flickered, building from the smoke until a fully formed beast screamed to the sky, and the unnatural heavenly light faded.

"The chains..." Khiron muttered behind Tir, then found his voice and his resolve to shout, "Magi! The chains!"

The creature aloft turned its head south and speared the Aesimar *shansher* with a fiery glare. Its wings pulled tight to its body as it dove back through the flames, crashing into the pyre. Its wings unfurled once more with a snap, and scattered burning logs to catch the wind as it glided over the warriors toward Tir and Khiron.

"The chains! *The chains!*" Khiron screamed as his men dodged the fiery beast. He swirled his scimitar in the air, calling on his guard, his Magi—anyone! But in the face of such a monster, Aesimar held no allegiance to its *shansher*. The men scrambled for their lives, trampling over each other in their haste to escape.

Drawn by the commotion of fleeing prey, the creature flew right for them.

For a moment, as it passed overhead, Tir caught a glimpse of human arms and legs, the hint of curve around the breast and hip.

No, his eyes must be playing tricks on him in the darkness.

And yet…

Fire burst from the creature's hands in streams, instantly incinerating the fleeing Aesimar. It banked left, gained air once more, then swooped down for a second pass, and a hundred more Aesimar were reduced to ash in an instant. Those along the periphery screamed in agony, their bodies engulfed in flames they couldn't put out. A few brave souls launched an attack, scimitars raised high to slash at the creature. One must have struck true, because the creature twisted in midair with a scream, rose higher, and looked down at the culprit.

Close enough for Tir to see.

He couldn't believe his eyes.

Demons or raiders, Liadan had told him, *dark gods or magic men, I am not the one who should be afraid.*

She'd been right.

In the dark of night, Tir beheld what could only be Liadan's true form—a Halfling daughter of Halfling parents, a creature born of dragonblood, yet too tainted with humanity to completely take on one's true form. Her body, covered in shimmering black scales, was held aloft by massive black wings shaped almost like a bat's. Her hands were clawed, feet more dragon than human, a long, powerful tail snaking left and right behind her with a life of its own. Her eyes glowed red-gold; her hair was a mane of living flames that whipped around her. She had one pair of sleek, black horns that curled from her temples, over her head, and another, smaller pair that spiked up and back from her forehead, creating a bestial crown.

Her fangs gleamed pale white as she snarled at the men below, singling out the one who'd struck her. She snatched him up from the throng, flew him high overhead as he screamed. Holding him by the throat at arm's length, the Dragonblood princess brought her mouth to his and exhaled. The Aesimar warrior stopped struggling. His body lit up, briefly, then turned black like a piece of charcoal, disintegrating into ash that rained gently down onto his comrades below.

With a powerful beat of her wings, Liadan rose higher, twisted around, and let loose a spiral of flames in a grand display, then dove through them at the warriors.

"Now!" Khiron shouted, and from amidst the warriors, chains whipped upward as Liadan flew past.

"Liadan!" Tir shouted, but his warning came too late. One of the shackles clasped around her ankle, pulled her up short, and she tumbled to the ground. The troops descended on her like a pack of starving hyenas, falling onto her prone form to kill the beast before it could strike at them again.

Tir raced toward her, the pain in his wrist forgotten. With his good hand, he snatched up a scimitar and slashed through the thickening crowd, while Aesimar Magis chanted somewhere nearby. He had to slay them to break the power of those chains, but he spared them not a glance. The warriors would kill her faster than anything Khiron might conjure. He needed to free her first.

All at once, the mob exploded outward, bodies flying left and right as Liadan burst free and launched into the sky. But the chain again pulled her up short, and three men were dragged into the air in her wake before more took hold of the tether and yanked her back down. She screamed, extended her hand to throw her flames, but nothing came from her palm. The chains would weaken her ever more, until she was forced to bend to Khiron's will.

"Hold her!" Khiron ordered. "Get more chains! To me, men! Take hold! The beast will be ours!"

The mob had grown again, too thick for Tir to get through, all of them so intent on Liadan, they no longer fought him, hungry instead for her blood on their swords. Tir cut through them without mercy as they dragged Liadan down, little by little. Her tail whipped out, slammed a warrior into another, and she rose a little higher.

Then another chain was tossed, the shackle locking around her wrist. Liadan struggled to break free, but even with her added strength, she couldn't overpower an army of this size.

"Liadan!" The mob's roar swallowed Tir's voice. He cut down a warrior, then twisted and cut down two more, working his way toward the ones who held the chains.

Liadan's light and the mob's sway and rhythm were Tir's only indications he was moving in the right direction. When bodies did shift, what little they could, they pushed Tir forward and deeper into the center. He was close enough to hear blades scrape against a hard surface, men shouting taunts and dares, and Magi chanting their spells to keep the prisoner confined.

As he neared the center of the throng, the warriors parted enough for Tir to glimpse Liadan struggling on the ground. They'd dragged her flat, face-down, where she beat her wings against the sand like a trapped bird, limbs chained in place by the strongest of Aesimar's men. The weaker ones kicked her, stomped on her wings, and chopped down with their blades to break her skin, but her scales were impervious. Several blades lay broken on the sand, mocking Aesimar's bravest to test their might against her.

And Tir knew this stalemate wouldn't last. Already, Liadan's flaming hair was dimming; her eyes, when he glimpsed them in her struggles, darkening to the charcoal-gray he knew. As the chains weakened her, she seemed to be reverting back to her human form, and if it was really so, without the protection of her scales, the first blade cut might well kill her.

Tir fought harder, pushing and slicing through men disinclined to give up their view. So intent were they on the battle in the middle, they fought with each other to get closer, and Tir's advance went unnoticed.

Khiron shouted an order from the other side, but no one paid heed. He dragged one of his own men away from Liadan, shouted again, and this time, his loyal guard obeyed, corralling the impassioned warriors away from Liadan to make room for a Magus carrying a black, metal collar.

Liadan screamed when they dragged her up from the sand to kneel, and she fought against their hold, swiped out with her tail, flared her wings to beat them back. Several fell, broken by the powerful blows, but for each Aesimar who died, three more rushed in to replace him.

The Magus raised the collar high, chanting louder, and a chill seeped down from the dark sky, centering on the circle of black metal in his hands. Tir shuddered with dread, ran his blade through the warrior in his way, then burst into the center, sword drawn back to slash. The Magus' arm dropped to the sand, the collar still clutched in its hand, and Tir spun, putting his entire weight behind one more strike. The Magus' head dropped, followed by his body.

Khiron, drunk on his own power, had turned his back on the Magus to rile his warriors for more bloodshed, and didn't notice right away. Not until the groan and snap of a chain link freed one of Liadan's arms. The loose end whipped out, struck Khiron in the shoulder, and he twisted around in time to see Liadan regard her claws with a slight tilt to her head. When she looked up at him, her eyes flared brighter than ever, and Tir shuddered at what he knew would come next.

37

Sand. Blood. The reek of men.

Liadan smelled the desert on the air, felt the vast open sky above her, and yearned to soar up toward it. But they held her down. Cold metal locked around her ankles and wrists. It refused to obey her command, screamed in her mind with a voice dark enough to overshadow her glow and bank her fire. That darkness leeched strength from her core until she felt too weak to defend against the human onslaught. Their blades couldn't touch her; their soft human feet couldn't hope to cause her pain, even when they put all their strength behind the attack.

But that metal would kill her.

Dark chants echoed inside her head, throbbing down her spine and crawling into her wings until she couldn't raise them to protect herself. Her fiery blood cooled, her head swam. They raised her up, yanking on the chains, thrusting a blade against her back to arch her. She struck out with her tail, and felt the satisfying crack of bone; flared her wings and knocked a half-dozen warriors off their feet. Still not enough.

That gods-awful chant grew louder, reverberating through the metal of her chains like the gongs of a massive bell, rising to the sky, but leeching her strength down into the sand. Ice crawled across her forelegs, up into her thighs, and her eyes rolled back in her head, body quivering with a forced command: *Shift!*

And it began to obey…

Until that chanting voice suddenly fell silent.

Liadan breathed in, fresh air stoking her fire into a full blaze once more. She flexed her arm, strained against the pull of countless mortals. No need to overpower them; she only needed to snap one link.

And then she did. The deadened chain whipped across to the other side, and Liadan looked down at her free hand. Her fingers were tipped with thick, black claws, sharper than a well-tended blade, and she couldn't wait to make use of them. Another deep breath, and the weight of her hair lifted as it flared to life. Night illuminated into day in her dragonsight, and she looked up at the source of her misery, the one who commanded the magickers with their evil chains. Already the ones left alive were renewing their chants.

Liadan yanked her other hand free, then launched into the air, spinning to snap the chains that bound her ankles. The remains trailed from her like jewelry and she tore them off, hurled them down to the sand, and unleashed her flames.

The vermin below began to scatter.

Oh, but she had other plans for them. Liadan flew high, then swooped down in a wide arc, searing the outliers as they ran, cutting off all paths of retreat. Her fire was a living thing; it sang under her command, danced to the tune she set, leapt from man to man, raced across their skin and clothes to spread like a thick blanket over the lot of them. No mercy. No prisoners. The ground below lit up quickly with the blaze of hungry flames, but one man in the middle remained untouched.

She'd saved him for last.

With a thought, Liadan extinguished the fire in her hair and eyes, becoming a dark shadow against the sky. Then, with a shrill cry, she dropped straight for him, flaring her wings at the last moment to scoop him up from the inferno, high into the air. No quick death for this man; she wanted to feel his soul escape his mortal shell.

The Aesimar scum stared at her, wide-eyed, too terrified to scream his fear, too stunned to weep. Liadan allowed herself a feral grin, and his eyes widened even more, his mouth opening to shout for aid. She ran a single claw down the center of his chest, hard enough to scratch a thin, bloody line into his skin.

He did scream, then. "Kaliban! I summon you! Free me!"

Darkness pulsed in his core, a thin, cold link stretching deep into the desert night. At his cry, it throbbed, strengthened, drawing the chill around them both, and Liadan knew true evil lurked at the other end.

She snarled into his face. No one would rob her of this prey! As the black frost raced toward them, Liadan speared her hand into his chest, curled her claws around his heart, and ripped it out. His gaping chest rose and fell as blood bubbled out from his lips. He saw his heart beat in her palm, saw it compress and burst into flame as Liadan crushed it.

Then a black shadow swooped down between them and, tearing the human from her grasp, spun away with him. Liadan screamed, surged forward to reclaim her prize, but the demon didn't go far. With a skeletal hand to the human's chest, the Dark creature bared rows upon rows of sharp teeth, grinning at its dying captive. "I told you it would come to this," it hissed, its voice pulling Liadan up short to hover before it. "You wish to be freed, Khiron al-Bashir? Then I can do no other than oblige."

Liadan watched as Khiron's body convulsed under the demon's evil spell. A thin, pale mist of a soul seeped out from the hole in his chest, barely aglow. It carried too much darkness to rise to the sky as Liadan knew it should. Instead, it stretched like slime the demon swirled and looped around his finger until the last of it was in his grasp. "Your third wish is granted, *master*, and in return, I claim your soul as payment." Green saliva dribbled down his chin as he brought the wisp to his mouth and gobbled it down with a groan of pleasure.

He let the empty shell drop to the desert floor and with a curious sniff, turned his gaze on Liadan. "I smell dragon in you. You and your humans killed my brother." Liadan braced for an attack, but the demon merely grinned. "I thank you for it. With his death, his power passed to me." He inclined his head slightly. "We have no quarrel between us, Dragonblood. I certainly have no wish to follow my brother's path against the flame of Inaras. The valley is yours." Then he streaked away to the west, and disappeared.

Liadan scanned the ground for more enemies to tear apart, but found none. Above her, the sky glittered with countless stars, and a heavy moon crawled ever lower toward the horizon. Soon, the sun would rise to put an end to this wretched night.

Below her, the desert was ablaze with burning corpses. No one left alive, at least not to the south. To the north, where the remnants of a pyre still burned, the Imarah survivors huddled around their wounded, quietly weeping. Their fear was like an invisible mist hanging low in the air. Liadan could taste it at the back of her throat. Sweeping down over the enemy troops, she recalled her fire to restore herself, then caught a high wind to soar toward her tribe, basking in the freedom and beauty of flight.

For too long, her essence had languished, confined in her human shell. She'd never realized how small a prison it'd been, until the fire had set her free. Caught in the darkness of eternal sleep, she'd felt it calling to her, but she couldn't answer its summons until a bright light had shown her how. Spinning high toward the stars now, Liadan sent her quiet thanks to Inaras. Without the goddess' help, she never would have known this feeling of pure happiness.

As the patron goddess of Imarah had foretold, Liadan had, indeed, burned to ash in her service. But her dragon's blood had brought her back, reformed her in the way a dragon could, into something much more powerful. *I am free at last! A true Dragonblood!*

At the base of the mountain, she descended gracefully, stretching out her wings as she touched down on one knee, before she folded them against her back. The talons hooked together at her neck like the clasp of a cloak, the feathery soft membrane billowing around her. With a light step, she approached her tribe, taking stock of how many had survived, how many were injured, and how many wouldn't make it through the night. Imarah had been culled to almost nothing. She counted less than a thousand, their eyes haunted, terrified, but she didn't realize the true source of that fear until she drew close and people backed away from her, muttered prayers, and herded their children behind them.

Liadan stopped, tilted her head, and truly looked at them. Each soot-smudged, blood-stained face was turned toward her, eyes wide with fright and mouths set with the last of their courage. A lone child wailed pitifully nearby. Liadan started for it, to offer comfort, to help find its parents, if they were still alive.

Before she could reach the babe, a woman gave a shrill cry and raced over, snatching up the child and backing away from Liadan as if from a demon hungry for her soul.

Liadan frowned.

Where the woman retreated, several *kharesh* limped up to shield her, taking a stand between Liadan and the rest of the tribe. They could barely keep their feet under them, many bleeding from wounds that had yet to be dressed, yet each and every one had his scimitar drawn. Against Liadan—one of their own! She'd earned her rank, her sword, and her place among them!

But that had been when they'd still thought her human.

Liadan looked once more at her hands. Sharp, black claws; skin as soft as silk, yet as impenetrable as marble. Her body was covered in scales, and her hair was still a mane of long strings of fire. Her tail swished out and around her feet, which were more like a dragon's hind claws, balanced on the toes with sharp talons buried in the sand, the back spur on what should have been her heel, gleaming sharp.

No wonder they fear me. I am a monster.

"Stand down!" Tir called from a distance, racing across the sands on Sleipnir's back. "Liadan!"

Finally! He'd talk some sense into the tribe. They didn't know her; Tir did. He'd explain, and all would be well. Liadan had destroyed the demons, and Aesimar. Imarah was safe at last, the curse lifted. They could return to the First City, rebuild what they'd lost. And she could help. Flying ahead, she could chart the easiest route, spy out water to quench their thirst, hunt game to feed them on the journey.

She acknowledged Tir's approach with a glance, inwardly wincing at all the wounds he'd sustained, but when she noticed how quickly they were healing already, her attention returned to the *kharesh*. Why hadn't they dropped their guard? Their *shansher* had commanded them to do so.

King or no king, however, it seemed she'd been right after all. Their fear of her was stronger than their loyalty to him. They'd no longer obey Tir where she was concerned, and there would be no making them understand she was not a threat. Their king had brought her among them; bound himself to a monster, made her his queen—or so they thought. His judgment was impaired, and he couldn't be trusted. That they'd stayed their weapons this long was a sign of their respect for him. But it would only last so long. They needed someone they trusted to vouch for her.

Where was Farraj? Even with Tir's authority in question, surely they'd obey their commander.

But the old man was nowhere to be seen.

"*Kharesh*, stand down! Do not harm her!" Tir dismounted at full gallop, running up to the group locked in a standoff, but stopped ten paces away from Liadan, kicking up sand.

Liadan flinched. They stared at each other, and the longer the silence stretched, the heavier it became. He wouldn't approach. His gaze swept over her, from her flaming hair down to her clawed toes, pale eyes wide to take in all of her. And he wouldn't approach. "I thought you feared nothing," she said, not recognizing her own voice.

She wanted to shift back to her human body, but dared not make herself that vulnerable. Without her scales, she'd be defenseless against an attack, which seemed more and more imminent the longer Tir just stood there, staring. He schooled his features admirably to hide his true feelings, but Liadan could guess what they were, and for the first time in her life, she felt something utterly alien to her: shame. And hurt. And sorrow.

The torc at her neck felt cool against her hot skin, reminding her of home—water, snow, her brother's healing touch, and the dragon's ancient understanding. When the first rays of sunshine peeked out from the east, it threw Imarah's fear and mistrust into sharp relief. They didn't want her among them; they'd drive her off, or kill her, to restore their mortal balance.

"I do not," Tir replied to her question, yet he didn't move any closer. "I thought you were dead." How horrifying she must have looked in the growing light, for him keep so far. He was tense all over, stuck between a tribe who depended on him for their survival and the creature who could destroy them all with the ease of an afterthought.

Her fire banked. "That which is immortal cannot die." If only she *had* died. Then she'd never have known what true scorn felt like, from someone she'd come to regard so highly.

"I am… glad," he said, looking over his shoulder at his people.

Liadan's mouth twitched in a wry smile. "Yes, of course." She bowed formally at the waist, so he wouldn't see her blinking back tears. "Fear not, brave king of Imarah, our bargain is finally finished. Your people are safe. And by the oath we swore, this monster is free to return to her demonlands in the North."

"What? No, wait—"

"Farewell, Tirasdunh al-Dhakir. May your tribe flourish once more."

"Liadan—"

She crouched low, then launched herself into the sky, spreading her wings to soar. The warm air currents pushed her higher, and she rode them westward, away from the little tribe, and the little king who'd managed to destroy her so easily without ever drawing his sword.

38

"Wait! Liadan!" Tir ran after her, whistled to Sleipnir, and heard a sharp whinny in answer, but the stallion wouldn't come. He ran as far as his weary feet would go, strained to keep Liadan in sight, but she was too fast and disappeared over the horizon without the smallest trail for Tir to follow.

When he couldn't run anymore, he stumbled in defeat and fell to his knees, breathing hard. "I don't want you to leave," he said. Too late; she was gone, and he had no hope of tracking her.

Another whinny brought his attention back around to the east, where the rescued tribe of Imarah stared at their king in fear and disgust. Three *kharesh* held Sleipnir's reins, preventing him from going after his mistress. If they hadn't stopped him, could Tir have caught up to Liadan on horseback?

His tribe stared, waiting.

The war was won; Imarah was safe. Would their king abandon them for the fiery creature with dragon wings?

Might is king in Aegiros. In that, Khiron hadn't been mistaken. Imarah might be safe now, but they were still weak, vulnerable. They needed someone to lead them, to restore their strength.

They needed *shansher* Tirasdunh the Demonslayer, and though it broke his spirit, turned his heart cold and hard with resentment, Tir still had a duty to protect his tribe. He got up, turned his back on the west, and returned to his people.

His hands curled into fists at his sides before he remembered his shattered wrist. But the pain did little to distract him as he walked back among his tribe, trying to guess where Liadan might have gone. Home, no doubt. The crown princess of Wilderheim had had more than her fair share of the desert. She'd go home, back to her family, and a people who didn't fear her.

And Tir couldn't find it in his heart to begrudge her. As she'd said, their bargain was finished; she'd delivered his people from the jaws of death and, having done so, had moved on.

Liadan was gone.

How foolish he'd been to think, even for a moment, that she might have chosen to stay a while longer. How foolish to think Imarah might have let her.

Curling his injured hand tighter, he focused on the pain to keep from turning on his own *kharesh*. They'd not only dared to raise arms against Liadan, they'd disobeyed his direct order to stand down. He'd been too soft on them, too preoccupied with keeping them all alive to insist on obedience, when he himself had been ignorant.

No more.

"Tir."

He pulled himself out of his dark thoughts to focus on Farraj's second-in-command. "Report," he said hoarsely.

Sami bowed. "We have many wounded. Two score dead. The Magus has not yet returned from the temple." After a hesitant pause, he grudgingly asked, "What are your orders?"

Tir glared, but chose not to address the insult. "How many *kharesh* are still battle-ready?"

Sami looked around, counted nods, then replied, "Twelve."

"I want them to ride out south at once." Before Liadan had scorched the battlefield, a handful of Aesimar horses had managed to break free of the fight; he'd seen them wandering around as he'd ridden back on Sleipnir. They'd be there, still. "Find the Aesimar camp. If any are left alive, kill them. Whatever supplies they have, bring them to us, as much as the horses can carry."

"It will be done at once."

"Send someone up to the temple; make sure the Magus is safe. And find Farraj."

"*Shansher*," Sami said, "Farraj has been gravely injured. The women are tending to him, but he has not awakened since he was struck down."

Swelling fingers curled tighter still. "I will see him. Go do as I ordered."

"*Shansher...* The creature..."

Tir barely stopped himself from driving his fist into Sami's face. "The *creature* is the only reason any of us are still alive," he snarled. "The creature has a name, and if you value your life, you will speak it with reverence from this moment on." He raised his voice to address them all. "And if I see *anyone* draw a weapon against *that creature* again, they will taste the edge of my blade!"

"It's a monster!" someone objected.

Tir drew Sami's dagger out of its sheath and advanced on the old man whose head had been bound in bandages. Two *kharesh* intercepted him, moving slowly, worn out after the war. Tir struck one in the throat, ducked the other's swing, and drove his elbow into his side. Incensed beyond reason, Tir felt no pain as he grabbed the old man's shirt collar with his injured hand and pressed the dagger tip beneath his chin.

"Tir!" Farraj's hoarse voice cut through his haze of anger, just enough to stay Tir's hand. "We cannot afford for more of us to die," the *kharesh* commander said. His head dipped wearily as two men supported him between them.

The old man in Tir's grasp whimpered, wide-eyed, terrified. Tir shoved him down in disgust, then stood to his full height. Might was king in Aegiros. If Tir had any hope of keeping his tribe under control, there could be no doubt in their minds that he *was* in control. He looked closely at the faces surrounding him, met each challenging gaze and stared them down until each man bowed his head in submission. He turned on Sami last. "I gave you orders. *Move!*"

The man scrambled to obey.

Farraj sighed. "Sit me down." His handlers gently lowered him to the ground. He hadn't weathered the attack well—his arm was in a sling, his torso bandaged; he was covered in soot, and blood had dried on his face from a wound Tir couldn't see. The strongest, most fearless, most unwavering man Tir had ever known now looked exhausted, much older than his years.

Tir tossed Sami's dagger to the ground and sat down next to his mentor to watch his people go about the tasks he'd set them. One of the women, her veil torn from her face, approached timidly, keeping her head down. She carried splints and bandages and, after looking over his wounds with a cursory glance, gestured to Tir's hand, which he proffered without argument, though he kept his attention on Farraj to spare her modesty. "You look as if you just faced down an army of demons."

Farraj grunted a chuckle. "I am not so sure I didn't. Oh, stop fretting like an old woman. They have not killed me yet."

"And none have lived to attempt it again," Tir assured him.

Farraj groaned. "*Daeva* take them all. What am I supposed to die of now, old age?"

Tir allowed himself a smile. "If I'm lucky."

Farraj studied him for a moment in silence. "So, *shansher* of Imarah," he mused, wincing as he shifted to face Tir, "what do we do now?"

Tir rubbed his face, suddenly exhausted. "As soon as the *kharesh* return with supplies, we'll set out back west."

"After your dragon *shensari*?"

The woman binding his wrist paused, listening intently, while trying hard to pretend she wasn't.

"No," Tir replied after a heavy silence. "Liadan is gone. We will go back to the First City, reclaim what is ours, by right."

"You loved her," the woman said, surprising both men. Blushing fiercely, she ducked her head lower and tied off the bandage.

Tir caught her wrist before she could run off. "What is your name?"

She bowed low. "Nai'mah, *shansher*."

"Nai'mah, I would like you to do something for me. Gather the bows and any arrows we have left, and distribute them among the women."

Her gaze flicked up to his, before dropping away just as quickly. "S-*shansher*?"

"We don't have enough able-bodied men left to defend the tribe along the way, and we have no way of knowing what dangers lie between us and the First City. We'll need everyone who can carry a weapon to arm themselves and be prepared to fight for those who cannot. Do you think it can be done, or am I asking too much of our women?"

Farraj raised an eyebrow, but didn't say a word.

Nai'mah seemed to give the matter some serious thought before she answered, "It can be done."

Tir nodded. "I am grateful. And, to answer your curiosity, yes, I did love Liadan. I would have had her sit by my side as queen, had she accepted me. And, though it makes no rational sense to you—it most certainly does not to me—I will never stop wishing it could have been so."

The *kharesh* returned with news that the Aesimar camp had been dismantled, with not a soul left to fight, but in their haste to escape the burning scourge, they'd left everything behind: tents, livestock, barrels of water and oil. On the first trip, the *kharesh* brought back enough to feed all of Imarah, and for each to drink their fill, with still enough left over to properly clean and dress wounds.

Once they'd unloaded everything, the twelve took seven more men on a second trip. At sunset, they came back with horses, wagons, clothes, shoes, goats, weapons, skins filled with water for travel, and even musical instruments. As the tribe warily settled in for the night, someone struck up a mournful tune, and several women lent their voices to the melody, singing their soft lullaby.

Tir walked among his people, sat with each of them for a while, spoke with them, assuring them all would be well. His people were frightened, tired, hurt, and as many times as he repeated they were now safe, as many times as they nodded obediently, he knew they weren't convinced. They'd carry that fear and insecurity in their hearts for many seasons to come.

He also visited Sleipnir, who'd settled as soon as Liadan had disappeared. He'd allowed himself to be led away and brushed down, and now he stood silent among the herd, spurning even Tarabas' presence as he brooded alone in the roped enclosure. He turned away from

Tir's approach, refused to suffer his touch, snorted and tossed his head to hear him speak.

Tir couldn't tell whether Sleipnir blamed Liadan for abandoning him, or Imarah for keeping him from following. Either way, the result was the same: Sleipnir's heart was as broken as Tir's. He merely lacked the words to say so.

"I can't bring her back," he told the mount with a sigh. "I can't even follow, no matter how much I want to." And gods, how he wanted to. Tir gritted his teeth and untied the rope from the closest post, opening the enclosure right in front of the great stallion. "But you can."

For a moment, Sleipnir stood there, staring at Tir with one big, shiny eye, as if he couldn't comprehend what Tir had done. As if he waited for something.

"Go on," Tir urged. "Safe journey to you both."

Sleipnir turned his head to look at his own back, then stared at Tir again.

"Not this time. You must go alone."

The horse snorted with obvious disdain, then took off toward the west. Plumes of dust billowed in his wake, and Tir wished again he could have gone along. But when the dust settled, Sleipnir stood there, facing west, tail twitching. He raised a hoof, took two more slow steps, then looked behind him at Tir. Head bowed, he walked back into the enclosure, lipped Tir's shoulder, then dipped his head lower to nose the rope in Tir's hand.

Tir caressed his neck, touched his forehead to Sleipnir's. "No more binds. One of us, at least, should be free."

By morning, the Magus still hadn't returned, so Tir himself scaled the mountain to find him deep in a trance inside the temple, guarded by two *kharesh* who knew better than to interfere with religious rites. Tir nodded his thanks to them, and waved them out, back to the tribe to rest.

This was the first time he'd entered the temple of Inaras as a grown man. At her altar, Tir bowed his head in supplication, then gazed up at her statue, twice as tall as a man, pale marble arms outstretched in welcome. Her divine power seeped into every corner of the temple, from the largest boulder above to the smallest speck of dust at his feet, humming along his skin, soothing his mind, and Tir found himself relaxing enough for his eyelids to droop.

Soon, the ground melted away and warmth cushioned him on an invisible current that carried him outside to hover far above his tribe. He didn't linger there; the vision carried him west, across the desert to the First City, through its empty streets and abandoned houses, and on into the dry river basin, following the deep trench ever westward, faster, lower, until a bright light flashed and Tir found himself in a dark cave.

Narrow shafts of light speared down from a hole in the ceiling, illuminating rock as black as pitch, shaped by countless millennia into crevices and protrusions like a giant, tooth-filled maw. To the east, the cave narrowed into a black tunnel large enough for four men to pass through, side by side. To the west, the bubbling wall had been carved deep with symbols he didn't recognize. They looked ancient, but uniform, like magic spells embedded into the stone. And from the center of the floor, a small water well bulged up, spilling across the maze of rock formations toward the tunnel.

The Source.

Though he'd never seen it himself, Tir recognized the place from his father's impassioned ravings. Now, this strange vision showed Tir the truth of them. Before his eyes, time shifted, racing back through the ages. The cave changed, its rocky teeth receding into a smooth surface, the carved symbols fading from the western wall. Within moments, it was empty of everything, even sunlight.

But within its dark recesses, Tir heard the soft drip of water. It welled beneath him on a glow of divine magic, and out of the puddle emerged men and women made of clay. Light flared, searing their shape solid, giving them each a heartbeat. The First Tribe opened their new eyes, sucked in their first breath, and fell to their knees before the well of light, touching their foreheads to the ground in supplication. A spark floated up to caress the western wall, and a man traced its movements, carving spells into the rock. When he'd finished, the cave shuddered, the ceiling crumbled, and sunlight streamed inside to guide the First Tribe to the surface. As they emerged, the waters rose behind them, filling the cave, overflowing, forming the flood plains at the base of

Silver Mountain.

Where the sun sets, life begins, a soft voice whispered across the vision.

Water continued to well, pooling, then pouring east, carving out a basin for its path. Tir followed the small creek as, over time, it grew into a river; as the First Tribe grew in numbers; as the First City sprouted and grew in the now-lush valley. He saw the tribe flourish, spread, war, and fragment, and then the river itself carried him farther east on a mighty current. But even as it did, Tir sensed the selfsame current deep underground. Two sister rivers: one in the light, and one carving its way through darkness underground, both emerging from the same place in the west, both flowing to the same endpoint in the east.

Eventually, the rivers slowed. The surface one, having split a dozen times, trickled along the eastern edge of the valley, then quietly disappeared underground once more, dragging Tir with it back into darkness. This time, he saw light reflecting off diamonds as water pooled in a multitude of pits and caves, and dripped down the walls. This was the place Dhakir had sought for Imarah.

Where the sun rises, life begins anew, that soft voice whispered, and the vision wavered to show him the fleeing tribe of Imarah in the surface of a dark pool. Led by Inaras' visions, Dhakir took his people east instead of west, searching for this very place, for even had they found water at the Source, as long as the curse remained, Imarah would still have perished. Only here, in her temple where she still held some power, could the goddess of life have aided them. In her oasis, her light might have overpowered the *daeva*'s dark spell and freed Imarah. If only they'd reached her in time.

But war, famine, demons, and disease slowed their journey, and with every passing day, Inaras grew weaker, her call softer until she was banished behind the dark Veil and could no longer aid the First Tribe. And so they lost their way. Khiron fragmented the tribe, taking off to the south. Dhakir's beloved *shensari* died in his arms, and with her passing he lost his will to live and rule. Without his guiding voice, Imarah withered, while far to the south, Aesimar grew stronger, and as time once again moved forward, the diamond cave dried out, its countless pools shrinking down to puddles, then to nothing at all.

"Why show me this?" Tir demanded. "What meaning am I to take from it? That there's no hope left? That no matter where we go, Imarah is doomed to die?"

As if in answer, a nearby diamond glittered brightly, drawing his gaze. The spark detached, floated like a firefly around Tir, only to dash off down a dark tunnel, dragging him along. He saw nothing but what little the tiny spark illuminated. Miles passed him by in the dark, unchanged, until Tir noticed a second light beneath the first. A reflection. *Water!* The farther east he flew, the larger the puddles became, until they turned into a small but steady trickle, which spat him back out again into the first cave, with its maw of teeth, and spells carved into the western wall, now faded with time.

Where life once began, it can be restored, the voice whispered. *Seek salvation in the First Temple...*

With a gasp, Tir found himself back in the temple of Inaras, breathing hard, staring at her altar without seeing it at all. The Magus rose to his feet, touched Tir's shoulder, and nodded a bow when Tir finally focused on his face. "Inaras is weakened," the wise old man said. "She can guide us to salvation, but cannot restore us."

"Then what are we to do?"

"Find another way." The Magus bowed again and shuffled his ancient feet out of the temple, grumbling, "I am too old for magics like these. If only Imarah had someone younger to take over, someone who understood the ways of gods and men..."

Tir remained in front of Inaras' altar until the torches burned down to nothing, but no answer came to him. By the time he'd returned to camp, the sun was low and the tribe had settled in for the night. Tir sat with Farraj, needing someone to help him make sense of what he'd seen, but before he could utter a word, Sami approached to report the day's progress.

The Aesimar camp had been emptied of all supplies. They now had enough to last them a good week or two, if they rationed, but after that, they'd need to find another source of water. Having been informed of the plans to head out west, Sami assured them the day hadn't been wasted. Everything had been packed and prepared for travel, and at first light, they could break camp. Too many dead around this place; the tribe was eager to move on.

Tir thanked him, then ordered the preparations to be made.

"I have something for you," Farraj said, after Sami took his leave. "The women found it among the debris." He pulled cloth off a charred lump of a chest sitting beside him, motioning Tir closer. The chest had been burned beyond recognition on the outside, but had somehow retained enough of its shape to hold together. The iron clasp on the front caught Tir's eye and sparked a memory.

He pried it up, careful not to damage the seal of Imarah's *shansher*, then opened the chest he'd last seen on the morning of Liadan's *kharashan* and carefully withdrew the bundle within. He unwrapped its many layers, uncovering the treasure at its center, perfectly preserved and untouched.

"I'm no Magi," Farraj said, "but I don't think one would carry such a thing without reason, do you?"

"No, I don't," Tir replied, tying off the thong to hang the glass vial from his neck.

"Perhaps its owner will return for it."

Tir almost smiled. "Thank you, old friend."

He didn't speak to Farraj about his vision.

That night, he dreamed of the Source. He stood before the western wall, facing Liadan, their hands clasped together. A chalice appeared before him, a choice to be made, and as he reached for it, a deep, male voice warned, "There will be no going back after this, for either of you."

39

Liadan had learned a thing or two in her time alone in the desert lands of Aegiros. Her ordeal of *kharashan* had been nothing compared to the daunting task of surviving on her own in a land where only the heartiest did. While flying over the endless sands was faster than walking, her black dragon scales absorbed more sunlight, which intensified her thirst and her need for shelter during its strongest hours.

Out of necessity, Liadan returned to the only place she recognized: the First City. There, at least, the palace had tall ceilings to provide shelter from the sun and clothes to replace the ones that had burned away on her pyre. But it still had no water, forcing her to fly out daily, training her keen eyesight to distinguish real oases from mirages. Few and far between were places where water pooled on the surface enough for her to drink it. More often than not, only greenery marked where underground wells and streams existed. Her claws were ill-suited to the task of digging, so each time Liadan found a source, she had to revert to her human form to dig it out. With each try, the process became easier, but it still wearied her.

She ought to return to Frastmir. Her family had to be worried sick with no word from her for so long. But each time she peered into a pool of water, with Fal's name on the tip of her tongue, she drew back.

Each time she caught a current north, she veered off, back to the First City. As much as Liadan missed her family, she wasn't ready to return to them. She knew what awaited her in Wilderheim: a lifetime of imprisonment behind Other politics, duties to people on both sides of the Veil, and one day, if Fal's condition didn't improve, the weight of the crown. If she returned, she might never again leave the confines of Castle Frastmir. After two decades of living sequestered in a cave, she'd spend the rest of her life in one—better appointed, but still a cave.

No, Liadan wasn't ready for that.

Here, all of Aegiros was spread out for her to explore. From above, its landscape readily revealed its secrets, and lured her in with more mysteries yet to be solved. Despite appearances, life did thrive across the desert sands—small creatures scurried about, day and night; people roamed on horses and camels, built settlements, towns and cities, traded goods, sang, danced, loved, and warred. She could spend several lifetimes exploring these lands and never grow bored.

The life of a wanderer had its merits.

Until she remembered the looks of horror Imarah had gifted her for saving their lives.

At night, when the desert cooled and Liadan had time to think, the truth of who and what she was became inescapable. Perched on the palace roof, she gazed eastward, waited for sunrise, and remembered. They feared her, as anyone else would if they'd seen her true form. No matter how far and wide Liadan wandered, sooner or later, she'd be seen this way, with her wings spread wide, and her hair aflame, dark horns adorning her head like a demonic crown. She was well aware of how she'd look to the superstitious people of Aegiros. They'd hunt her, chase her off, or worse, try to imprison her again, as Aesimar had done.

For now, she was safe. But even now, Tir's tribe would be making its way back to reclaim the First City, and if they found her here…

I left Sleipnir behind.

It pained her to admit it. In her haste to escape Tir and his scorn, she'd left behind her every possession, as well as her companion and old friend. For days, she'd waited for Sleipnir to follow her, as he always did, but after so long, Liadan was forced to accept that this time, she was on her own.

I can go back for him.

But what good would that do? Even if she could sneak back into camp without being seen, she couldn't fly the stallion all the way back to Wilderheim. She'd have to ride the entire trek, however long it took, and how would Liadan feed him when she could barely feed herself? As much as she hated the thought of leaving Sleipnir with the Imarah, at least she knew he'd be safe and cared for among them. He'd be king of his herd, lavished with affection and the best of what little the tribe had to offer. He might hate Liadan for abandoning him, but at least he'd be safe, which was more than she could say for herself.

Forgive me, my friend. I'll see you again one day.

"Inaras, I call to you," she whispered. "I summon you. Appear to me."

A cold wind fanned her flames, but no godly light appeared.

"Vayu, god of Veils and in-betweens, ruler of the void between light and darkness, you spoke to me once, I beseech you to hear my call. Come to me again."

Silence answered her.

Liadan raked her claws across the roof. She should have known better than to expect gods to care about her problems; she, better than anyone, ought to understand their fickle nature. What use did deities have for humans and Others? None, save to alleviate an eternity of boredom.

Inaras had used her. She'd needed a powerful champion to free her and the other gods, and she'd found one. Now that the task was finished and she had her people and their prayers back, she would become powerful again and reclaim her world, and Liadan no longer had a place in it.

"I didn't ask for this," she grated. "I've fulfilled my oath; the tie is broken. Why does it keep calling me back?"

Back to Imarah. To Tir.

Gods, she hated this sick feeling in the pit of her stomach, twisting inside her, yanking her back eastward and at the same time shredding her like a knife in the gut with the knowledge that Tir wanted nothing to do with her anymore. He'd looked at her that night and had seen nothing but a monster. She'd known it would happen—in some part of her mind, she'd even expected it—but nothing could have prepared her for that look in his eyes, as if honor alone kept him from thrusting her own sword through her demon heart.

She could have left a thousand times, flown back to Wilderheim, or even Lyria—anywhere else, as long as it was far from here. She hadn't. Because some part of Liadan still hoped she'd see him again, look into his eyes and see something other than disgust. When she slept, Liadan dreamed of him holding her. She remembered the pressure of his kiss, the warmth in his eyes after their first night in the palace.

We are no longer bound, she reminded herself. Whatever he'd felt for her before had died the moment he saw the truth and realized she'd been right all along, that Others and humans did not mix.

Whatever she still felt would fade, too; in time, she'd close her eyes at night and no longer see him in her dreams. She'd remember her time in Aegiros as a battle she'd won, and she'd be proud of it. But none of that could happen here. If Liadan wanted to forget, she'd have to go where everything she saw and touched didn't remind her of the man who'd broken her heart.

It was time to leave Aegiros for good.

Standing tall, Liadan folded her wings, and burned herself back into her human shape. By some trick of magic she had yet to understand, the clothes she wore now became part of her when she shifted; they disappeared somehow in her half-dragon form, then reappeared when she was human. A useful thing, that.

As the sun peeked out and stretched long rays of light across the city, Liadan closed her eyes to bask in its caress. Her skin had darkened with her transformation, not into the brown shade of Aegirans, but no longer the pale cream of a Northerner, either. The sun's bright majesty, once a burning nuisance, was now a warm comfort.

Soon, night's chill had burned away, and the paved streets of the First City were awash in daylight. Liadan once again called to the dragonfire in her soul and dropped forward, shifting as she fell to catch the air before she hit the ground. She rose above the city, veering north. In no time, she crossed the parallel dunes and flew over the waterfall oasis. Not far off, she spotted a patch of charred ground where the firestorm had claimed her. Liadan kept going.

The market city of Sadirak appeared ahead, and she banked low, out of sight. Too many people there; too much danger of being seen. She circled in place a few times, debating what to do. Sooner or later, she'd have to touch down and continue on foot. Even in Wilderheim, winged creatures weren't a commonplace sight among the Others, and it wouldn't do to attract too much attention. She might have to rest by day and travel in the dark of night. A tricky proposition, but better than being mistaken for a malevolent beast and shot out of the sky.

The oasis would be a good place to rest. From there, she could fly straight north into Wilderheim; a much shorter path than the one she'd taken with Tir.

Yes, it was a good plan.

Liadan rose higher to catch a breeze back east, when a flash of color caught her eye. To the west, south of Sadirak, a caravan crawled across the desert—ten camels in the lead, four tent-carriages drawn by horses, and eight more camels to bring up the rear. All of the men were dressed in the same way, with the same striped scarves tied around their heads and faces and the same scimitars strapped to their sides.

Liadan remembered those colors only too well—they'd adorned the old woman's tent in Sadirak. She remembered, too, the taste of her sweet potion, the scent of smoke, and the hazy glitter of a golden collar.

With a furious beat of her wings, Liadan shot upward into the sky. Wilderheim could wait. First, she had a score to settle.

40

There were shadows, and within them a prison so dark, so powerful, even the Halfling god of trickery and deceit couldn't escape it. The walls of smoke have long ago stopped reverberating from his outbursts of maddened rage, the black corridors silent, allowing neither sight nor sound to intrude.

A once magnificent, fearsome creature, the Trickster was much altered by his imposed solitude. His bottomless eyes no longer carried their usual mischievous spark. Now, only madness and wrath swirled in their depths. His voice, once as melodious as the sharp twang of a breaking lute string, now growled ominously—if he chose to speak at all.

For two decades, the fabled Loki, lover of whimsy and practical jests, had wandered blindly through world after world, at first to flee the All Father's punishment, and later to seek a creature—any creature—powerful enough to restore him. But, to his utter frustration, this Shadowland was of his own making, flawlessly constructed to hide his presence from all beings—human, divine, or Other. Woden could not have devised a punishment more cruel than this, and with each passing day, Loki's hatred for him grew.

But the world of Northern magic was changing. The Veil, still weakened from Lady Nialei's fabled battle with the dark sorcerer, continued to grow thinner, leaking power—Woden's, and all the gods' with it. Loki sensed it first on a stray breeze flowing through the cavernous darkness of his prison, and as he inhaled the scent of sand and spices, he smiled, baring teeth too sharp to look human any longer.

Aegiros. He swirled the dark shadows with a wave of his hand and gazed out into more darkness. Unfolding his lanky body, Loki stretched and stepped forward. The Shadow moved with him, hazing his view once more, but he swept it aside again, forming the first window he'd managed in far too long, and he found himself strolling through the desert night.

The First City sprawled abandoned before him with its deep river basin bone-dry, and wind howling through empty clay houses. This was the result of a mortal's wish and, not unlike the one he'd fulfilled himself, it was beautiful. The night air was perfumed by decades of death, famine, and disease; destruction flowed in a clear path from the tall palace, through the heart of the city, down into the river, and eastward across the valley. An entire tribe brought to its knees, its legacy slowly devoured by the desert sands. And had the creature who'd wrought it been punished in any way? No! The divine laws were different in Aegiros. Humans bore responsibility for their own folly.

Snarling at nothing, Loki whirled around and streaked across the city to the palace. He sensed a trail of smoke, a familiar scent of homeland, and followed it up to the roof, where an odd creature perched. Lying low to avoid being seen, Loki watched the creature spread its wings as far as they would go to reveal a shapely, though odd, female body. Fiery hair, a horned crown, clawed hands and feet, and a restless tail…

Who was this? *What* was it?

She cocked her head toward him, and Loki shrank back, curious to see, but not to be seen. Scenting the air, the creature rose to her full height and faced east as the sky began to lighten. Her wings pulled in around her body and smoke rose from her skin, her form lighting from within like a live ember. The smoke crackled and hissed, billowing out briefly, before it settled back into her skin. Her pale, human skin.

Loki slithered closer across the roof, flattened the Shadow to blend in with its surface and, from a thumb's width in front of her toes, gazed far up at the Halfling's human face. Rage suffused him as recognition took hold. He knew that face! Its makers tormented his memory and stoked his fury every time he recalled them. This was the warped spawn of Nialei and her Dragonblood king—how dare she exist!

The sun emerged at last, its hot rays sliding across the Shadow, into it, and Loki shrank from its sharp glare. He clawed at the window he'd created, but though his hand passed through, on the outside, it became invisible, incorporeal. The Northern Veil had thinned, true, but it had yet to completely disappear. Its power was still potent enough to keep him prisoner, allowing only a glimpse outside its walls. As much as he ached to twist the Halfling's head from her body, he could not.

But he could bide his time, keep close, and wait for his opportunity. Yes, he could, indeed, wait. And scheme. And plot.

The Halfling closed her eyes, spread her arms wide, and smoke once again swirled as she leaned forward and dove off the roof. Loki leapt after her as her half-dragon body took shape mid-fall, wings flaring out to catch the air. She glided gracefully down the empty street, then beat those great wings to rise above it.

Following her path, Loki felt a sudden rush of freedom from the illusion of flight. So simple a thing, the smallest of pleasures, but one he hadn't felt in far too long. He was almost tempted to thank her for it.

Almost.

She banked left ahead, turning north, carried along on a strong air current that held her aloft over the vast expanse of golden sand. When she'd had enough of floating, she beat her wings, flying north so fast Loki's Shadow fell behind, hindered by too much light. Nevertheless, he kept her within sight, following her flight path over a lush oasis and toward a market city. She kept her distance, flew low to remain out of sight, circled in place several times as if unsure of where to go next.

Then something changed. She rose higher, and her fiery gaze locked on to something to the southwest. For long moments, she stared into the distance, clawed fingers curling and stretching at her sides, throwing off bright, golden sparks. Something had angered the Dragonblood.

I know the feeling.

With a sparking hiss, the female shot upward and, trailing her into the sky, Loki was momentarily blinded by light. Snarling, he swirled the Shadow thicker around himself and looked out again—

—at the furious visage of a bright, white goddess before him. Her eyes shone like stars; her face ageless, timelessly beautiful. "You do not belong here," she whispered, and Loki's Shadow squealed beneath the sheer magnitude of her power.

He shrank away, lowered into a respectful bow. This was Aegiros, wholly unaffected by the turmoil Wilderheim and its gods—Loki himself—currently faced. "I beg forgiveness of the great Mother." He shaped the foreign words with a voice he no longer recognized as his own. It was too dark, too deep and growling; more like the crack of thunder than the lilt of a sinister song. "I seek no trouble in her demesne, only what is mine."

A great, cold wind swirled his Shadow prison with an unseen presence that made Loki's insides quiver with unease. *And what is yours?* that presence hissed in question by his ear. It was inside the Shadow with him. How…?

Loki shuddered, feeling like a mouse in a lion's den. He greatly disliked it. "Revenge," he answered.

Seek it elsewhere, Trickster. There is nothing here for you. The wind god retreated, streaking out of the Shadow as if its walls were insubstantial.

Loki rushed after him, hoping to escape through whatever gateway the other god had created, and collided with the wall of his prison. "Oh, but there is!"

Inaras blazed, forcing him back into darkness. "You dare oppose our will!"

"The creature—"

"*She is not yours!*"

Her scream shoved the whole of his Shadow into a vortex of blinding light, threw him end over end to the edges of Aegiros and beyond, across realms and worlds so distant he'd only heard of them in stories.

By the time it had settled and darkened once more, Loki peered out at nothing. The glowing bitch had banished him to the very edge of the universe. It would take him months to get back. With a bellow of impotent rage, he struck out at the walls of his prison.

And felt them crack.

41

A journey that had taken Tir and Liadan two days would last twice as long in reverse for the whole of Imarah. Even with horses and carriages to ease the way, moving so many people at once was no easy task. With Tir in the lead, they walked for two days just to reach the river basin. Once there, the path was clear and Tir could fall back, check on the wounded, feel the pulse of his tribe. Everything seemed different now. A sense of hope had taken hold, keeping them on the move, even when they were too weak to continue.

During the day, conversation often turned to reminiscing, with the old ones telling the children about their once-beautiful city. They described its wonders, the carefree happiness and comfort they'd enjoyed before the curse.

In the evening, the tribe gathered around fires, told fables of brave heroes and beautiful maidens. Tir often found himself listening as raptly as the little ones, smiling and wishing Liadan was there to share in the wonder of it all.

He missed her.

Every time he glanced down at the vial of water hanging from his neck, every time he strapped on her sword in the morning or brushed down Sleipnir at night, she was there. She'd left them all behind when she'd flown off, and although Tir kept hoping she'd return for them, with each day that passed without any sight of her, his hope diminished. Even Sleipnir sensed it—he was surly, obstinate, and refused to let anyone but Tir come near him. He always pressed forward, ahead of the tribe, quivering with tension to run hard, but whether he wanted to chase down his mistress or simply get away from everyone else was impossible to tell.

The worst of it, however, came at night, when Tir finally succumbed to sleep. He no longer dreamed of fire, but water: the First Temple's underground well swelling, and the flood plains darkening with water that would eventually spill back into the eastern river basin. He dreamed of Liadan, too, sitting next to him on golden pillows, a diaphanous red veil covering her face and a spiked, golden crown adorning her head. Fanciful things. Impossible things. Things for which he'd have traded his sword arm.

As they neared the First City, talk among his tribe changed—men whispered to each other; women flocked together, clutching the weapons they'd been given for the journey. Tir doubted anyone would ever pry those bows out of their hands again.

"...the *shensari*?" one of the *kharesh* said, as Tir passed by on his way to the rear of the procession. His name was Matek, the man who'd taken Sleipnir into his care upon their arrival and, if memory served, one of the first to draw a blade against Liadan.

Unaware the *shansher* had heard, his friend, Ali answered, "Yes! With the hand of Inaras on her shoulder. I swear by my sword it was her."

"I dreamed the Magus was with her," Muhammad offered. His charred arm was covered in ointment and had to be tormenting him, but he betrayed not a hint of pain, guiding his new mount with one hand on the reins. "He was chanting as the goddess placed a crown on her head."

"Do you think...?"

Matek spotted Tir, and coughed, cutting off whatever Ali had been about to say.

Checking a scowl, Tir nodded to them and kept going.

"What happened then?" a woman asked breathlessly, a little farther back. Something in her voice gave him pause. He turned Sleipnir around, kept behind the group of women to listen in.

"She danced," came the answer, "in a way I've never seen before. I cannot describe it. You wouldn't believe me if I did—"

"I would!" another woman chimed in. "I saw it, too!"

"What did you see?"

"Fire! But it… it was alive. It obeyed her…"

"Tirasdunh."

Tir flinched, turning to Sami beside him. "What is it?"

"Farraj is asking for you. Something's happened."

Tir followed the *kharesh* toward the front, where the wounded warriors rode on horseback and on carts. Farraj, for all his insistence that he was fit enough to ride, still couldn't keep his seat on Zara. Having him sit next to the cart driver was as much to preserve his pride as to free up space for those more gravely wounded. Allowing him to keep his scimitar across his lap was purely for the sake of appearance; he couldn't lift it if he tried.

Having delivered Tir to the general, Sami bowed in his saddle, then veered off to give them what little privacy he could.

"Have you slept well, my king?" Farraj asked without preamble.

"As well as can be expected."

"No strange dreams to disturb your rest?"

Tir frowned. "No stranger than usual. What's this about, Farraj? Since when is my sleep any of your concern?"

"It is not your sleep that concerns me, *shansher*. There's been talk among the tribe about the mother goddess walking through our dreams—"

"So I've heard," Tir muttered.

"—showing favor to your *shensari*."

"What?"

Farraj bowed his head in a deep nod. "Ever since the princess Liadan rose from her ashes, it seems. At first, no one thought anything of it. But then a boy asked his mother whether the fiery one would be waiting for us in the First City, and word began to spread. We've all dreamed the same dream every night since Aesimar was defeated."

"And you think it's by the will of Inaras?"

Farraj rolled his bound shoulder and winced. "I am a warrior, not a mystic; I merely know what I see and hear."

"And what is it you see and hear?"

"I hear Imarah whispering about the *shensari*—their queen, not a beast. I see children dancing with veils and scarves and pretending they're flames. I hear men recall seeing her in battle, wielding a sword that sang when it slashed through the air, boasting about her intercepting a blow that would have killed them. I hear little girls talk of wearing armor one day and standing with the other *kharesh*."

"Easy enough to honor a hero without having to look at her true face. How quickly they've forgotten about that. But they'd remember just as quickly if they ever saw her again, of that I have no doubt."

"Perhaps," Farraj allowed. "But what if…?"

"What if, what?" Tir snorted. "What if Liadan came back and became my queen in truth? The only way she would, is if she sat beside me on a throne of her own. Do you truly believe Imarah's men would tolerate a woman giving them orders?"

"Not at first. Perhaps not for long years. She might go to her death many years from now, never having earned the respect she deserves. But what she has begun here, Tir, will outlive us all. Look around. Our tribe might be returning to the beginning, but it is a much different tribe than it used to be."

Tir scoffed. "I never knew you to be so sentimental. You grow soft in your old age, my friend."

"I've witnessed the misery love can wreak when denied," the commander replied gravely. "I would not wish it on anyone, least of all my *shansher*. There must be a reason why Inaras has chosen to appear nightly in our dreams, with her hand on Liadan's shoulder. Perhaps she wishes the same. We've all seen her above Liadan's pyre that night. She brought the princess back from the dead, and now she shows her to us, seated by your side, with a golden crown on her head and fire in her hand. One of us. Our queen."

"Indeed. It must be a sign, then."

Farraj ignored the retort. "If ever the chance lived for that dream to become real, it is now. *Now*, before we remember all the reasons why it shouldn't. When we reach the First City, we can go back to the way things used to be, or begin anew, find a different way."

"Rewrite the laws we've lived by for centuries to accommodate a Northern queen in our midst," Tir replied dryly. "Even if the goddess herself could appear in the palace and spell every man, woman, and child of Imarah to adore their new Northern queen, you forget one thing, Farraj."

"What?"

Sleipnir fidgeted, picking up on his rider's restlessness. "Liadan is gone. And she's never coming back." He kicked the horse into a gallop, pulling ahead of the front riders, then gave him free rein. The great stallion whinnied, raced like a shot to put as much distance as possible between himself and the rest of Imarah.

They reached the First City just as the sun set behind the horizon. Standing on the outskirts, Tir stared down the alley before him. Not a flicker of light to be seen anywhere, but the faint scent of smoke lingered in the air, teasing his senses to take a different path than the one leading directly to the palace.

Liadan is gone, he told himself again. The scent was nothing but his mind playing tricks on him. Nevertheless, his hand tightened on the reins, just enough to turn Sleipnir into the breeze and follow that scent to its source—if there was one.

The waning moon wasn't bright enough to illuminate the path, and if he lit a torch, he'd lose the scent trail, so Tir kept going in the dark. The shadow of the palace loomed to his left, but the smoke trail led farther west, more proof it couldn't have been Liadan. If it had been her, she'd have bedded down in the palace itself.

The farther he went, the stronger the scent became, and the more uneasy Tir felt. He pulled Sleipnir to a halt by the old marketplace, earning himself a grumbling snort. He held a finger to his mouth for silence when he dismounted. Drawing Liadan's sword from its scabbard, he waved Sleipnir back and continued on foot alone. Not far ahead, faint light flickered through a bare window. Tir approached silently, watchful for any movement in the shadows. Voices hummed inside that house, too deep to be women.

"What do we tell the sheikh?"

"A pox on the sheikh! A pox on all of them—*argh!* Watch it!"

"If I don't burn it, you'll bleed to death!"

Tir flattened himself against the wall, then leaned over to peer through the small window. Two men sat in front of a small fire inside, their clothes torn and covered with dust. One had removed his shirt, exposing four long, deep furrows across his chest, with the deepest still bleeding.

"Do it, then. But for all the gods' sake, be quick about it!"

His friend pulled a small dagger from the fire, then pressed the red-hot blade to the wound.

The injured man screamed, shoved his friend away, and curled in on himself, reaching out a shaking hand to rummage through a pile of cloth for a bottle. He spilled more out than into his mouth when he tipped it.

"Careful," the friend snapped, yanking the bottle away. "That's the last of the opium wine."

The injured man spat at him, belched, and leaned back against the wall.

With a sigh, his friend set the bottle aside, out of reach. "What do you think it was?" he asked after a while.

"Who bloody cares what it was?"

"You should. It killed…" The man shuddered. "*Everyone.*"

The opium drinker gave him a drowsy, lopsided grin. "Not everyone. It let the women go. Stupid. Kinder to kill 'em like the rest."

"Did you see what it did to the matron?"

"*Hmph!* A pox on the old hag. A pox on all of 'em. Soon as I heal up, you wait an' see. I'll hunt down the demon bitch myself. I'll—"

Tir's dagger struck him in the throat, cutting off the rest of his threat. Before the other *masar* had a chance to scream, Tir leapt in through the window, caught him by the throat, and slammed his back against the stone wall.

"W-wha—"

"Tell me what I want to know, and your death will be swift. Lie to me, and I'll make it last a week."

His eyes bulged in terror as he nodded, shaking from head to toe.

"Your *masiranah* was attacked?"

Another nod.

"When?"

"T-this morning. North of here—"

"By what?"

"I d-don't know. Never saw anything like it. Please—"

"What did it look like?"

His eyes darted to his dead companion, then back to Tir, and whatever he saw in Tir's eyes made him wail in fright. "Big, black demon thing! Wings… tail. It b-breathed fire—"

"Did you see where it went? What happened to the women?"

"No, please! I saw nothing, I swear!"

Tir squeezed his throat a little tighter, pulled a throwing knife out of his boot and pressed the tip to the man's cheek, just below his eye. "Think very hard."

"I don't know! On my soul, I don't. We ran away, fast as we could. It killed all the men—tore the matron limb from limb! Burned our caravan. Gods, please, I don't want to die!"

His fear was genuine. A kinder man would have taken pity on him, shown him mercy and let him go. But kindness wasn't a virtue Tir had in ready supply where the *masar* were concerned, especially the ones who'd have sold Liadan into slavery as an exotic treat. A man of his word, Tir gave the *masar* the quick death he'd promised in exchange for his cooperation. In truth, Tir ought to have thanked him. Without him, he never would have known Liadan was still in Aegiros.

Now, all he had to do was find her.

42

Wholly focused on her revenge, watching her flames consume the remains of the slavers' caravan, Liadan never saw the sandstorm coming. The powerful winds slammed into her back, knocking her to the ground and blowing her across the desert like a small sailing boat over a raging sea. She choked on sand, lost all sense of direction; no more fire, no sky, only sand—everywhere. She tried to shield her face with her wings, but the winds pushed even harder against the solid wall of their span. She could neither stand in place nor rise above. Against this desert force, Liadan had no protection, no path of escape; it carried her along, and all she could do was keep moving, keep the sand from burying her alive.

By the time it had finally ended, night had fallen, and Liadan was alone in the desert, far from familiar territory. Flying up for a better view helped little; as far as her dragonsight reached, the sands were dark, with not a single flickering light to betray any hint of a human settlement, and only a shadow in the distance to provide a focal point. With nowhere else to turn, Liadan flew toward it. She'd rest by that mountain range and find her way back north by daylight.

But the distance stretched longer than she'd expected and, exhausted by the flight, Liadan burned her wings the moment she landed at the base of the mountain. Her breath misted in the cold, and her skin began to glow to ward off the night's chill.

"Where am I?" This wasn't the red mountain she'd scaled for her scimitar. This rock face was a pale gray, almost shimmering in the moonlight. She took a step closer and gasped as the ground gave way beneath her, dropping her into an underground cave on a cloud of dust. Liadan landed hard. Her foot caught in a crevice, and she lost her balance, slamming into a rock protrusion.

"Ow!" Temper flaring, her skin glowed brighter, and fire sparked off her fingertips. She smacked the wall to level herself off the ground and nearly broke her own ankle to free her foot, stumbled again and fell onto her hands and knees in a puddle.

"Water…" Clean, cool water bubbled up from the ground and trickled between the rocks to disappear down a vast, black tunnel. She didn't wait for divine invitation, just stuck her face into the puddle and gulped down as much as her stomach could hold.

Her thirst finally quenched, Liadan sat back on her heels and looked around properly. The cave felt smaller than it ought to have been. Massive stalactites drooped from the ceiling, melting into stalagmites rising from the floor. It felt like being inside a giant maw filled with fangs, complete with a pitch-black tunnel of a throat stretching far to one side.

"Hellooooo!"

The echo of her voice bounced deep into the tunnel. No stranger to caves, Liadan was fairly certain this particular one stretched for endless miles far beneath the sands of Aegiros. It was definitely large enough for any number of creatures to live there, and with a steady supply of water, it'd make an excellent lair. With a small bed, a few tapestries and candlesticks, it might as well be home.

Liadan shook away the fanciful idea. What on earth was she thinking? She already had a home, and it was far away from here, where grass and trees painted the landscape green instead of gold, and water froze in the sky in winter, falling down in flakes of snow to cover the land like a fluffy, white blanket until spring.

Liadan gazed down at the bubbling surface of the ground well. "Fal. Brother, can you hear me?"

Nothing.

"Fal!"

The puddle glittered with firelight. "Liadan?"

Tears burned her eyes, even as she smiled at the image of her brother's baffled face.

"Liadan, is that you?"

She nodded, not trusting herself to speak. Her throat was too tight to form words anyway.

"I thought… Sweet gods, we all thought… Say something! Where are you? What's happened?"

Liadan wiped her nose, her wet eyes, and sucked in a deep breath. "I'm still in Aegiros. Alive and well, and free of my oath."

Fal gaped. He was pale, gaunt, and very much himself.

"What's the matter with you?" she demanded. "You look like death itself. Are you ill? Has someone died?"

Her brother rubbed his jaw. "You did."

"Oh… I suppose I did, at that."

Fal still hadn't blinked. "Is… are you real?"

Liadan looked down at herself. The blouse and pants she'd pilfered from the palace were covered with dust, the vest drenched from her earlier dive into the puddle. "I think so."

He reached out, mouth moving with a silent incantation. His hand broke the surface, and Liadan pressed her palm to his, felt him shudder. "All the gods above, you're alive!" Tangling his fingers with hers, he pulled her hand across the divide. "Bollocks. The surface is too small to bring you across. You have to find a bigger pool."

"I'd love to. Only I've no idea where I am. Have you got any food?"

Fal released her, and moments later a plate piled high with meats and cheeses appeared in the puddle's surface, pushing up and across. Liadan snatched it to her, dug in with her bare, dirty hands. The first proper meal she'd eaten in who knew how long and, gods, it tasted like heaven. Fal let her eat her fill before he began firing questions at her: Where had she gone? What happened to her? What was Tir's tribe like? How did she defeat the demons?

Belly full and heart content in her twin's distant company, Liadan recounted the whole of her journey, from the moment they'd crossed into Aegiros to the moment the last Aesimar had fallen. She skimmed over nothing, took heart in her brother's exclamations of outrage over the slavers and the Dark chains Aesimar's Magi had almost locked onto her.

She told him about Tir and his tribe, the *kharesh* and her ordeal to become one of them, then she listened to everything that had happened in Wilderheim since she'd left. The curse had kept all of them from Seeing into the First Valley; they'd had no news of Liadan, until the moment Fal had felt her die. He told her how the fire had seared across his mind, burning away the bond between them, and how he'd been bedridden for days after, refusing to speak a word to anyone.

"Mother and Da are inconsolable. They blame the dragon for…" His eyes suddenly went impossibly wide. "I have to tell them!"

"Wait, don't go yet!" If she let him, Fal would disappear and leave her alone again in this cave. "They've been mourning for days. One more night won't make any difference now. Stay with me a little longer. I've missed you so much."

He sighed. "What will you do?"

"Wait until sunrise, then climb out of this cave and look for north."

"Are you sure that's what you want?"

Liadan was proud of the way she was able to smile through the stabbing pain in her chest. "Of course I am. I want to go home."

"And you can, any time. I can teach you the incantations for passing through elements, and you can step through a pool of water, or even a tall flame, and be back in Frastmir in an instant. But…"

"But what?"

Fal huffed. "Will it make you happy?"

Home, family, a lifetime spent between stone walls; stuck in a land of green and white, far away from Imarah and its king. The stabbing pain turned into searing agony. "What should I do instead? Fly back to Imarah and hope they don't kill me before I can finish saying I mean them no harm?"

"You could speak to Tir."

Liadan shook her head. "It's better that I don't. Nothing good would come of it. Any of it."

"You can't know that. Look at Mother and Da. The entire kingdom was against their marriage in the beginning, and now… well, a good part of it is still angry, but we manage just fine. There hasn't been a rebellion in years."

"The dragon told me there would come a day when I'd have to choose."

"But this is not that day," Fal insisted. "Who says you can't have both? As long as we inhabit the same realm and the elements remain eternal, the passage between their aspects is only a spell away. You can fly across the whole of Aegiros during the day, and return to your own bed in Frastmir for the night."

How easy he made it all seem—simple, magical, and completely attainable. But it wasn't.

"What do you want, Liadan? What does your heart yearn for?"

"The impossible," she replied, tracing the grooves of her torc.

Fal kept her company until long after sunrise, until exhaustion dragged Liadan into deep sleep and strange dreams. She saw a powerful river pour out of a small bottle and a golden crown shaped into horns and flames, glittering in the hands of Imarah's Magi. She saw Tir holding a wooden chalice, heard the dragon's voice speaking words she didn't understand.

She awoke to a fresh plate of food, a bottle of mead, and a travel bundle on the ground by the bubbling pool, with Fal nowhere to be found. Likely he'd told the royal pair the good news, and they were even now scrying for her whereabouts.

Liadan yawned and stretched, working out the soreness from her muscles and joints. While she ate, she untied the bundle to see what her brother had gathered for her. A thick cloak, proper boots, a pair of knives, a pouch of coin, and two large waterskins—everything a Dragonblood princess could ever need on a long journey. Fal's thoughtfulness included the bundle itself, as well. It was small, with long straps that would easily tie around her shoulders and waist, with the bundle resting between her wings in flight.

"Thank you, brother."

Now all she had to do was find the waterfall oasis again. Fal had brought her back through it once. He could do it again.

Is that really what you want?

Yes. *It's all I can have.*

After packing up the treasures, Liadan sat on the ground to remove her silk slippers in favor of the sturdy leather boots. The oasis couldn't be far, but if she couldn't find it, she'd explore farther, look for another. She might even fly over the mountain range, try her luck on the other side. Aegiros didn't go on forever. Somewhere on its western edge lay the border with Synealee. Not a friendly place for Others, but it had water aplenty—

Sounds above. Hoofbeats galloping toward her, echoing along the tunnel in a familiar rhythm. Liadan moved everything into shadow, then crouched down by the rock wall, clutching her new blades.

Rubble rained down as the horse halted and stomped the ground a few paces from her. Liadan winced, pressing herself tighter against the solid wall. That ground was unstable. A little more weight and it would crumble, as it had where she'd fallen through last night.

A thump. Footsteps. A lone rider? No, that couldn't be. No one rode alone in Aegiros; the desert was too harsh and treacherous. Liadan hadn't seen groups of less than three anywhere, and they always had at least one extra beast of burden to carry supplies. A loner could only mean one thing: he was strong, and familiar enough with the desert to survive for long periods on his own, by any means necessary. He could be trouble.

Sand dusted down along the edge of the hole she'd made, and a shadow fell across the ray of sunshine spearing into the cave before a figure dropped silently inside with a much softer landing than hers had been. The man's back was to her, his head and neck covered with a scarf, a long, curved dagger sheathed at his waist. Definitely trouble.

But he only had one blade against her two, and one of his hands was bandaged. Liadan liked those odds. She shifted her weight to get a better look. He stared at the far wall, where something had captured his interest for the moment, but he'd move on soon enough. The trickle of water would distract him, and then he'd find her and try to rob her, or kill her and take over the watering hole before she could tell him he was welcome to it. Liadan was cornered where she crouched; no room to maneuver, and on the wrong side of the cave, with him standing between her and the way out. If he came at her, she'd be at a disadvantage. Better to take her chances in the open.

While his back was still turned, Liadan pushed away from the wall and rushed forward. He heard her, twisted around, blocked her thrust, knocked her blade away, then rammed his shoulder into her middle. Liadan fell back into the stream and took advantage of their momentum to keep rolling, throwing him over her head, deeper into the dark cave. They leapt to their feet at the same time, Liadan with one knife left and the man brandishing his own.

Their positions had reversed; Liadan now had a clear path to the surface, but the man didn't seem inclined to let her escape. He charged her head-on, so fast, she barely spun out of the way of his blade. She kicked out at the back of his knee hard enough to buckle it, but he caught himself against a stalagmite and stayed upright, pulling his injured hand away before she could grab it. Again, they clashed, and Liadan's back slammed against rock, knocking the breath out of her. She refused to go down. The man yanked her forward, bodily threw her back into the light and followed her down. But she was ready for him, clawed the scarf around his neck for a choke hold and pushed up, rolling them both until she ended up on top with her blade to his exposed neck.

"Liadan?"

She froze. "Tir?"

Metal clattered to the ground, and then his bandaged hand fisted in her hair so hard it hurt, yanking her down, and he cut off her cry with a hard, punishing kiss. She forgot to breathe beneath the pressure of his arms around her, lost all coherent thought in the taste of him, the desperate clutch of his hand in her hair, the curl of his leg around hers as if he feared she'd be ripped from him.

He rolled to trap her beneath him, but by then, her hands were entangled in his shirt, and she was kissing him back for all she was worth.

"Gods, I missed you, *shai'iss*," he said against her lips, and Liadan thrilled. She knew what it meant now. Her body warmed to his touch, her skin began to glow, and steam rose from her wet clothes.

All at once, she remembered herself, broke out of their kiss, pushed at him, and where her hands touched, his clothing charred.

But Tir wouldn't release her. "Calm, Liadan." He cupped her face, made her meet his gaze, and smiled. "You can't hurt me." To prove it, he kissed her again, slowly, then traced her jaw with his lips, caressed the side of her neck. His every touch stoked her fire hotter, yet he didn't withdraw. Where his clothing smoked, he pressed her hand directly to the center of his chest, looked into her eyes and made her see. "Your fire burns in my heart. It will never hurt me."

Uncertainty flickered in her eyes; Tir saw the memory of hurt in them and knew instinctively how much this frightened her. Imarah had turned on her once already, how could she trust one of them again?

But this wasn't a cowering mortal in his arms; this was the Dragonblood princess Liadan, and she feared nothing. "Kiss me," she whispered, and Tir could do no other than oblige. Her lips were life itself; her touch, the answer to questions he'd never thought to ask. Nothing would ever compare to the feel of her in his arms, and he had no intention of ever letting her go again.

Tir soothed her frantic breath by giving her his own, calmed her nervous quiver by letting her feel his steady heartbeat. They shed their clothes in a hurry, eager to touch, desperate to feel. Water hissed beneath them and filled the cave with a sensuous steam, a dreamy haze to soften every sight and sound.

Liadan's skin took on its familiar glow, bathing him in light and warmth, and he savored every inch of it, thrilled in the scrape of her nails against his back, the nip of her teeth at his shoulder as he sank into her welcoming embrace. Theirs was not a gentle joining—after everything they'd endured, neither of them had any patience left for feathery kisses and soft sighs. Too much death had shown them how short and how precious life was. Every moment apart was a moment wasted.

Liadan's impassioned cries echoed in the cave with each of Tir's thrusts; his pleasured groan rumbled from deep within him whenever she squeezed him closer, deeper. Alone in the desert, only the sky and sand could see them, and one man and one woman meant little enough to them. But for Tir and Liadan, even all of the desert and the sky, the entire world and the whole of creation became inconsequential for a few moments of the deepest happiness either of them had ever known.

They didn't move for a long time afterwards, content to simply lie together, to touch, to kiss, to pretend nothing existed outside of their little hideaway. Long after night had fallen, Tir finally made himself climb back out to check on Sleipnir. He removed the mount's saddle, gave him oats and water, then endured a lot of sniffing and stomping before Sleipnir allowed him to return to the cave and to Liadan.

She'd dressed and brought out a few small items from deeper inside the cave. With his hands full of blankets for the night, Tir stopped in his tracks, staring at the packed bundle by her feet. "What's going on?"

"Nothing," she said, though her smile faded much too quickly. "I just wanted to make sure I wouldn't leave anything important behind."

"Even if you did, the palace has everything aplenty. You can have your pick of whatever you need."

"Tir—"

"No, don't say it."

"I'm not going back to the First City."

Sharp pain shot up his arm from his injured wrist, and he forced himself to relax his hand. The blankets dropped quietly to the cavern floor. "Why?"

"Because nothing has changed."

He blanched. "What?"

"I'm still the same monster you couldn't come near of back there. Your people still fear me like a swarm of demons, and I still have no place here. Not among them, not anywhere in Aegiros. My family is waiting for me in Wilderheim; it's time I returned to them."

A thousand different arguments stuck in his throat. None of them would sway her. What could a mere man, even a king, offer an Other? What possible reason could he give to make her stay with him? "What if you're with child?"

She swallowed hard, touched a hand to her abdomen. "I'm not. I'd feel it if I was. But even if… More than likely, it'd… b-burn away with my next firestorm." Her voice quivered too much for him to believe the callousness behind her words. "Halflings are volatile and rarely breed. That my mother was able to birth me and Fal was nothing short of a miracle. I don't expect it to happen again."

"So you'll run back to your fortress of stone and ice, to live out your eternal life alone."

"What other choice do I have?"

"Stay here!"

"And do what? Hide in caves so humans won't try to kill me? Wait for you to sneak away from your kingly duties for a clandestine tryst every now and then?" Smoke curled around her, billowing out to hide her completely. When it retreated once more into her skin, Liadan stood before him in her true form. Black, shimmering scales covered her body, her wings pulled tight against her back, and her eyes shone red-gold from a familiar face turned alien with sharp cheekbones and pointed fangs. "Have you forgotten already? *This* is what I am. Look at me now and tell me I can walk into your palace and have my pick of whatever I might need."

In this form, she stood a hand's width taller than Tir, and with one flick of her tail, she could flatten him against the cave wall. But she was still his Liadan. Her eyes burned fiercely, but not with anger; her clawed hands clenched tightly, but not to attack. Tir had never seen a creature more magnificent. "*Shai'iss*, I did not offer you a single thing from the palace. I offered you the palace itself. And the First City, along with the entire valley. I do not want you to hide in caves. I need you to sit by my side, sleep in my bed, eat from my plate, and drink of my wine."

"And wait for your *kharesh* to cut off my head in the night?"

"The *kharesh* are even now singing of your bravery. They have their hands full with young men pestering them to be trained, insisting another *kharashan* be held so they can test themselves, now that you made it look so easy. The women have started plaiting their hair the same way you do, and little girls run around waving sticks in the air and pretending they're swords. How could nothing have changed? You saved us all, Liadan—*you* changed *everything*."

Her flaming hair banked down to red-brown tresses. "Centuries of laws and customs won't change overnight for one woman, even an Other."

He'd said the same thing to Farraj only two days before. The general's answer, before so naïve and shortsighted, suddenly seemed like the most sensible wisdom. "No, not overnight. But with time—"

"Do you remember what I told you before my firestorm? I'll only take a mate who is my equal in all things, and I will no more abide him taking another than he would me cuckolding him for sport. Do you expect me to sit in shadow of your reign, stand idly by while you take ten more wives to give you heirs when I can't?"

"Never." His simple answer seemed to startle her. "I remember what you told me, Liadan, and I remember what I said, as well. To share such passion with another, to look into her eyes and see a helpmate, would be a blessing beyond imagining. You are right, Imarah will not bow to a Northern queen right away—perhaps not ever—but they will show respect to the one who saved them, accept you among them. And when we breathe our last, *shai'iss*, you'll be in my arms, and you will know that I have loved you with all of my heart and soul, all the days since first we met."

She said nothing for so long, Tir began to lose hope. Then smoke and fire crackled around her and she emerged from them human again, her beautiful gray eyes flickering gold. "I'd never be a proper Aegiran wife. I never stop myself saying what needs to be said. I'd be brash, and do the wrong thing, and offend the wrong people. I wouldn't stop training or sparring, and I'd dance whenever the fire's song moved me, probably terrify your court with the flames. I'd disappear often, sometimes for days or weeks, to see my family, and if ever anyone threatened me or mine, Imarah would see my true form again."

Tir caught a lock of her hair, smoothed its silk between his fingers. "I've had a tribe's worth of proper Aegiran women to choose from and never once thought of taking a wife, until you. Say whatever needs saying. Do whatever needs doing. If the wrong people take offense, only remember you are *shensari*, and you'll always have me by your side, in court or in battle. I want you to train, and I'll happily spar with you day and night, if that's what you wish. Dance, fly, make a fortress of your flames, go to your family whenever you need them. I would never deny you any of these things, as long as you come back to me when all is said and done."

"You'd make enemies."

"You've already defeated more in one week than I could accumulate in another lifetime."

"You'd be scorned for taking an outsider to wife instead of one of your own."

"They already think we are wed, remember? And even if they didn't, how could I take another when your blood runs in my veins now? Fire cannot touch me. Who knows what other changes it had wrought?"

Liadan flushed. "About that…"

"What is it?"

"Our oath was fulfilled before…" She gestured to the ground, where rock had charred from their lovemaking. "The bond was already broken. Whatever changes it caused will eventually fade."

"Good."

She gaped. "*Good?*"

Tir smiled in the face of her outrage. "I do not want a wife bound to me by an unintended trick of magic; I want her to cleave to me of her own choice. If she so chooses."

Again, she fell silent, and Tir held his breath, waiting for her to make up her mind. Then her shoulders drooped, and she huffed. "You make it all sound so simple, and it isn't."

"Nothing worthwhile ever is."

Liadan rubbed the torc around her neck. "We should get you back to your tribe. They'll think you abandoned them again." She brushed past him, shouldered her pack, and climbed up to the surface.

Tir followed quickly, afraid she'd disappear again if he let her out of his sight. But when he finally clambered up to the desert sands, he found her standing frozen where she'd emerged. "Liadan?"

"You've been missed, child."

Tir turned on the stranger, dagger in hand, but couldn't move a single step. Not ten paces away stood a tall, pale man, dressed in nothing but billowing pants, with his hands clasped lightly behind his back, but his body so incongruously rigid, he may as well have been carved out of marble. His mouth smiled, but his ageless eyes were cold. Were it not for the horns adorning his head—the same ones Liadan wore in her dragon form—and the three floating fireballs illuminating the desert night, Tir would have gutted him on the spot.

Instead, he stared, baffled, as Liadan ran straight into the man's arms, with a happy cry of, "Grandfather!"

43

The dragon chuckled when she launched at him, caught her up in an embrace so tight it hurt. Liadan didn't care. Her heart sang and her eyes stung with tears to be with him again.

"Hello, little miss." He squeezed her a little harder, then set her back on her feet. "I am glad to find you alive and well."

"When did you get here? How?"

"Midday. I… didn't want to interrupt."

Liadan flushed. He must have heard… Gods, this would be bad. "Grandfather, this is Tirasdunh al-Dhakir."

"*Shansher* of the First Tribe," the dragon finished and inclined his head formally. "I've heard a great deal about you."

Liadan nudged the gaping Tir, who glanced at her, then touched a hand to his mouth, his forehead, and bowed deeply. "I humbly welcome the great dragon. I've heard much about you, as well."

"Well met, young man. You do your people proud. Most would flee at the sight of me."

"Are Mother and Father with you?" she asked to fill the silence. "And Fal? Did he bring you through water? How is everyone?"

"Easy, girl. All in good time. First, let's have a look at you."

Liadan grinned and stepped back to change. When her shape settled, she proudly flared her wings wide, swished her tail left and right.

The dragon smiled again, one those impossibly rare smiles that warmed his eyes for the briefest moment. "Well done," he said thickly. "Will your wings carry you?"

"Yes, but flying tires me."

"The muscles are the same as your human ones. They need practice. In time, flying will be as easy as riding a horse. I am proud of you, Liadan. We all are."

Tir, oddly subdued and silent during the exchange, sheathed his dagger. "You've come to take her home."

The dragon looked at him again. Liadan knew that piercing stare; the dragon could cow the bravest of the brave just by looking directly into their eyes. Most fell to their knees and swore to do anything the dragon commanded if he spared their lives. She quickly burned back into her human form and prepared to face off with the dragon, if need be. Tir had done nothing wrong, and she would not let the dragon shame him.

But Tir stood his ground, met that ancient gaze head-on. "I know I can't beat you. I know you could whisk Liadan away to the end of the world and keep her from me forever—"

"And I know you would never stop searching for her if I did," the dragon replied calmly. "I know your heart, young king; it burns as brightly for Liadan as hers does for you. I am not here to take her away; she's not mine to take. But neither is she yours to keep. Do you understand what that means?"

Tir drew himself up. "I do."

"Then, my girl, the choice is yours."

"I…" She looked to Tir, but he wouldn't meet her gaze. He'd already said all he needed to say down in the cave, offered his heart and his kingdom at her feet. The dragon, too, kept silent; he didn't need to tell her what she already knew: if she stayed, she'd forever give up her claim to Wilderheim's crown. Demons take it; she didn't care. But she needn't give up her family. If Fal could open a doorway through water, she could find a way to do the same with fire, and if not, she could always fly.

One thought, however, still kept her from speaking the words she so longed to voice: Tir was mortal; eventually, he'd die, and she'd have to go on, unchanged, for decades, perhaps even centuries, after his ashes had blown away across the desert sands. Everyone here would live out their lives before her eyes, and no matter how many friends she made, if she stayed here, among mortals, her existence would be a long procession of funeral pyres as, one after the other, everyone she cared about passed from this world. The same shadows that always swirled in the dragon's eyes would grow in hers, as well—ghosts of her loved ones, of Tir, until the pain of loving became too much and she retreated into solitude the same way he had.

Is it worth it?

Yes. She didn't need to read the answer in the dragon's eyes; it was already there, deep in her heart. If all she would ever have with Tir was a human lifetime, then she'd fill that lifetime to the brim with enough love and memories to sustain her for eternity.

Liadan touched a hand to Tir's shoulder, then drew his dagger from its sheath and pulled the sharp blade across her palm. "My choice is you."

"There'll be no going back from this," the dragon warned, "for either of you."

Before he'd finished speaking, Tir snatched the dagger from her, tore the bandages from his hand, and cut open his own palm, pressing the wound to hers as they clasped hands. His hand was swollen, bruised black, but he didn't feel any pain at all. He pulled her into him and kissed her right there in front of her grandfather.

The dragon cleared his throat and, with great reluctance, Tir pulled away enough to take a breath. "Blood binds all things, human and Other," the dragon said. "It'll forever join you, in this life and the next."

"We know," Tir replied.

"Then it is done."

"Thank the gods."

Liadan laughed, and the dragon's eyes twinkled. "Allow me to offer a gift."

Tir frowned at the wooden chalice the dragon held out to them. He accepted it, held it steady as the dragon produced a bottle of wine and filled the chalice, then raked a claw across his own palm and added three drops of his blood. The wine hissed, smoked, bubbled, swirling so hot, the cup itself warmed in Tir's hand.

"But he's human," Liadan protested.

"That's precisely why he must drink."

She took hold of the chalice. "It could kill him!"

The dragon remained unmoved. "You proved yourself willing to give up everything for the mortal you love, Liadan. You've passed your test. Now it's Tir's turn. Will you drink for her, human? Even if it kills you?"

Tir looked into Liadan's worried face. "My choice is you—always." And before she could stop him, he raised the chalice and downed the searing wine in three gulps. The heat blinded him. The world tilted, fell away as fire scorched him from within until he couldn't even draw breath enough to scream. His muscles clenched, his bones groaned. Tir gritted his teeth, stubbornly rode out the pain, felt it brand his very soul. But at the moment he was sure it would burn him to cinders, the fire banked into a soft glow at his core, and he breathed in, his lungs easily filling with air once again.

His head in Liadan's lap, he stared up into her eyes, brushed away her tears with a hand suddenly whole, as if it had never been broken. A thin, pale line cut across his palm, the wound mended with the dragon's magic blood. Liadan was now forever part of him.

"My blood will not protect you from injury or disease," the dragon said, "but it will help you heal much faster. Likewise, it will not make you immortal, but it'll prolong your natural life a great deal. And while it won't give you magical powers, it'll protect you from them for as long as you live."

Tir grinned and stood up, snatched Liadan around the waist and twirled her in circles until she squealed, clinging to him as hard as he held on to her. Then he set her back down to face the dragon once more with a deep bow. "Words will never be enough to express my gratitude."

The dragon nodded.

"We should get back," Liadan said. "Imarah is waiting for you."

"For *us*," he corrected.

"Aren't you forgetting something?" the dragon asked. "Your tribe is safe, but it still has no water."

Tir's heart sank. "He's right. If we can't bring the river back to life, we'll never revive the First City."

Liadan sighed. "Water is Fal's power, not mine."

"Your brother gave you the means before you left," the dragon said. "Don't tell me you lost it."

Tir caught her hand in his. "The vial. I left it in Sleipnir's saddle bag."

The dragon whistled a loud, shrill call, and within moments, the thunder of Sleipnir's hooves galloped toward them through the dark of night. He ran straight for Liadan, nearly bowled her over in his excitement, and she laughed while he lipped her hair, bumped his forehead against her. Tir couldn't help smiling at the sight as he crossed over to the pile of gear and supplies he'd removed from Sleipnir earlier. In the first light of morning, he withdrew the glass vial, held it up for the dragon's inspection. "I don't understand. How can a handful of water produce a river?"

"The vessel is only a conduit. All water is connected, eternal and unchanging. But it has no shape of its own. For a connection to the Eternal source to endure, it must be anchored, in shape and position."

Liadan grinned. "I think I can do that." She took the vial, and jumped back into the cave.

"Liadan, wait!" Tir dropped down after her, followed by her dragon grandfather.

"You saw this before I did," she told him, tracing the carvings in the western wall of the cave.

At first, the symbols seemed random, but from far enough away, their pattern became obvious: concentric circles, like endless ripples on the surface of a lake, and in the very middle, a small crevice. Yes, he'd seen it before. Inaras had been guiding him to this place from the moment she'd returned from her exile. *Where life once began, it can be restored.* This was the Source, the forgotten First Temple of Inaras.

"Fire burns," Liadan murmured, pressing her palm flat against the center point. Her hand began to glow, brighter, hotter, searing the rock beneath it.

"Slowly," the dragon said. "Too much too fast, and the rock will crack."

Steam rose from the stone, air wavering from the heat, and when Liadan pulled her hand away, her handprint remained, the rock bright yellow and *malleable.*

The dragon cocked his head. "You'll need to cool the rock quickly, or the glass will shatter."

Liadan stared at the vial in her hand. It had survived weeks of travel and elements, so it had to be stronger than it looked, but Tir still couldn't imagine it standing up to rock so hot it melted. Liadan seemed to have her doubts, as well. "I may need your help with this, Grandfather."

The dragon nodded, placed his hand on the stone beside her handprint. "Set the vial, and I'll cool the rock."

She touched the center crevice, manipulated it to open wider, and quickly placed the glass vial inside of it. In an instant, the heat's glow began to dim, and as the rock set around the glass, it darkened once more to natural gray. It happened silently, in the span of a few heartbeats, and everything seemed to be fine, until the faintest *chink* froze them all. The glass had cracked.

The dragon pulled his hand away, while Liadan leaned in close to check the damage. "I can't see anything."

Tir joined her to look for himself. "The glass might have cracked, but it looks like the rock sealed around it. I think it'll hold."

Liadan rubbed her brow with a shaky hand. "Now what?"

"Fal," the dragon called.

From somewhere behind and below Tir, Liadan's twin spoke up. "Remove the stopper, then I suggest you get back up top."

A hand pushed up from the surface of the bubbling pool, bathed in a pale blue glow. When Tir would have reached out to it, Liadan caught his arm and pulled him away, up and out of the cave after the dragon. The three of them stood well back from the opening, waiting for something to happen. When the ground rumbled beneath them, Sleipnir reared, removing himself even farther and, familiar with his superior senses by now, Tir pulled Liadan to follow him. But the sound of rushing water brought them all back to the edge of the precipice.

Tir gaped at the impossibly powerful geyser bursting out of the western cave wall. The current was so strong, water filled the cave within moments, spilling down the underground tunnels to the east. Soon, it bubbled up from the hole, flooded out into the surrounding area, turning the ground dark with more moisture than the Flood Plains had seen in decades.

So much misery, pain, and suffering, so many years of wandering, dying… all of it undone with one small glass bottle and a handful of water.

"We did it…"

Liadan whooped and jumped, splashing about in the pool growing around her stoic grandfather and speechless husband. She caught Tir's hands, pulled him into a dance, infecting him with her boundless enthusiasm. "We did it! We saved everyone!"

Someone laughed. "Liadan, the savior of Imarah. Is this any way for a queen to behave?"

Once again, Liadan pulled away from Tir and raced into the arms of another man—her brother this time, cloaked as before in layers of illusion. But this time, when Liadan stepped back, Tir caught the man up himself, heedless of custom and propriety. He'd have kissed Fal for this miracle, but he still had a smidgen of manly pride left, so he twirled Liadan around and kissed her instead.

When the pool began to spread into a small lake, the group set out back toward the First City. The water, Fal assured them, would flow and follow, filling the riverbed as it had long ago.

"Will you stay awhile?" Tir asked. "I'd be honored to have you both as my guests in the palace, as neglected as it is."

"I can't. Mother and Da will be looking for me. They still aren't allowed to leave Wilderheim." He turned a stern look at Liadan. "So they'll expect you to visit—*soon.*"

Liadan leaned against Tir, hugged herself to his side. "We will. As soon as Imarah is taken care of." If possible, her words made him love her more.

They spoke a little longer, shared a midday meal beneath a small tent, and then Liadan's kin took their leave, with promises to see each other in a few days. When they were gone, Liadan sighed and set about packing away their tent.

"Are you sorry to see them go?"

"Always," she replied. "But not as sorry as I would have been had I gone with them."

Tir took the bundled tent out of her hands and kissed her knuckles.

She smiled thoughtfully. "It's strange, I always knew in my heart my path would lead me far away from them. I just never imagined how happy I'd be to arrive at my journey's end."

"Ah, *shai'iss*, my love, but this is not the end. We have only just begun."

EPILOGUE

In the realm of the Divine, the wind god gathered everyone around a massive copper bowl. Swirling the sand therein, he summoned a vision of Aegiros. The First City took shape in the center, a mighty river flowing lazily from west to east. Inaras shone with pride at the sight of children playing on the banks, horses filling the stables, farmers tending the first harvest. After years of lying fallow, the earth once again bore fruit, more abundant than ever before, and the First Tribe flourished.

The great palace at the heart of the city bustled with activity, droves of merchants and traders arriving and leaving under the watchful eye of the *kharesh*. The king himself presided over court, alone, listening patiently while angry men told him how his queen had defied tradition yet again. He cared not a whit—smiled in the face of their rage, laughed at their threats, then sent them off without punishment. Old men considered it their duty to complain, but unless one took action against the order the *shansher* and his *shensari* had established, Tirasdunh the Demonslayer had far more important matters to think about.

Far in the back of the fig grove, the new queen's guard-in-training encircled a clearing where Liadan faced off with two *kharesh*. All women with muscled bodies and uncovered faces, they shared many of their *shensari's* traits: defiance, strength, courage. She hadn't called them; they'd come to her, seeking purpose, a way to carry on after losing their husbands, brothers, and sons. They came from all across Aegiros, and they'd each taken a knee to swear their fealty to Liadan, as any knight would to a Northern lord. As any *kharesh* did to his general. They cheered their queen as she sparred, listened intently when she explained to the *kharesh* how and why they wound up on their backs. Rare was the battle Liadan lost. Whenever she did, she smiled brightly, praised her opponent, and offered him reward.

"What is to come of this alliance of north and south?" Inaras asked. Although she rejoiced to have reclaimed her demesne, like the others, she fretted over the many changes her people had undergone since her exile. The minutiae of everyday life blinded her to the inevitability of their fate.

Vayu swept among the gods, seeking confirmation of what he already knew. It was there, in each of them, though they didn't know it yet. *A great storm is coming. It will sweep across the North and reshape it in the image of a lone god.*

The news was met with but a faint gasp. "Shall we help them?"

No, Vayu replied. *We are none of us yet strong enough to stand against such a force. We must gather our strength and look to our own, for once the storm is done with Wilderheim, it will come for us, as well.*

Inaras hugged herself, her beautiful glow dimming. "What of Aesma?" She would not look at the dark god standing next to her. Like a sheath to her blade, his darkness absorbed her light, his cold robbed her of warmth. Part god and part shadow, Aesma was everything men feared: war, death, pain, suffering. Merely looking at him could reduce a brave man to tears.

Vayu remained unaffected, impartial. *He is not responsible for our exile, only for using it to his own advantage.* Indeed, Aesma Daeva had had no hand in shaping the barrier Veil, but neither had he been imprisoned by it, and his influence over Aesimar, the violence it had caused, was simply a manifestation of what he was. No one could be held at fault for carrying out their purpose. Balance had to be maintained. Life could not thrive without death.

Still, Aesma's influence had unduly disturbed the delicate balance, endangering not only the First Valley, but all of its gods as well. Reparations would need to be made. *Inaras, you suffered the most among us. His judgment is yours to carry out.*

The goddess of life turned her gaze upon death, shuddered delicately when he smiled, revealing black, rotted teeth. His shape was as much blood as it was shadow, and it dripped from him in congealed chunks, only to reabsorb into his dark form in a sickening cycle. "If it is as you say," she answered at length, "then we may need him for the battle yet to come. But can he be trusted?"

Aesma bowed his head, poured rivulets of crimson tears over the sand bowl. "I would not dare oppose the will of Vayu," he grated in a voice as sharp as a thousand swords scraping together.

Vayu looked to Inaras and saw acceptance in her shining eyes. Fealty to Vayu, once given, was eternal. She calmed, her face once more settling into a mask of serenity, certain in Aesma Daeva's obedience.

She could not see what he saw. None of them could. The force rising to sweep over them would not come gently. It would flood the world with blood, and none of them would survive it any better than myths told to children around campfires. Aesma himself would become a facet of the new faith. The lone god would feed on his strength, use him to conquer the world, and then banish him into the darkness to reign over demons and corrupted souls.

All things must come to an end, Vayu thought.

Perhaps it was for the best.

Not Quite The End…

ALIANNE DONNELLY was a wordsmith long before she became a reader. Driven by an insatiable curiosity about everything from history and mythology to science and philosophy, she grew into a fiction writer who hates coloring inside the genre lines. Her books all have elements of romance, with different series sorted under paranormal, science fiction, fantasy, and erotic. And then there's *Wolfen…*

Alianne lives in California, doing hard time in a corporate 9-5, while secretly scribbling away any chance she gets. She loves pizza, hiking, and avoiding small talk, and hopes to one day win the lottery jackpot. To find out more about Alianne's books and works in progress, visit her website at AlianneDonnelly.com.

www.ingramcontent.com/pod-product-compliance
Lightning Source LLC
Chambersburg PA
CBHW030553170726

48283CB00002B/309